# LOVE'S SPIRIT

## ELIZABETH MEYETTE

AUTHOR OF *LOVE'S DESTINY*

*Madyson,*
*Wishing you*
*peace, love, and joy.*
*Elizabeth Meyette*

CRIMSON
ROMANCE
F+W Media, Inc.

This edition published by
Crimson Romance
an imprint of F+W Media, Inc.
10151 Carver Road, Suite 200
Blue Ash, Ohio 45242
*www.crimsonromance.com*

*To my beloved husband, Richard,*
*who has shown me the truth of love's spirit.*

# Acknowledgments

Sincere thanks to Kate Bode, Janet Martyn and H.J. Smith for reading *Love's Spirit* as a work in process and giving constructive feedback. A special thanks to H.J. for incredible editing. Thanks to Jennifer Lawler for believing in me again. Thanks for the love and support of my family and friends who encouraged me and listened to me "plot out loud." A very special thanks to my beloved husband Rich who endured burnt broccoli and overdone chicken when I was focused on writing instead of the stove, and who told me to listen to the waves.

# Chapter 1

*Virginia, March 1776*

Emily Brentwood slowly rose to consciousness steeling herself against the assault of anguish and sorrow that accosted her at every dawn. For the last four months the memory of her beloved husband Jonathon, shot and dragged into a British skiff, had been the image that lifted her from her sleep and carried her to waking. The terror she had felt as that scene had unfolded before her, leaving her to believe that he was dead, seeped through her as if it were all happening again.

But something was different this morning. What was it? She battled waking to delay the pain, but there was a whisper of awareness that eased her reluctance. The sun was not rising; it was slanting in the western sky, and the pungent aroma of cedar surrounded her. Slowly coming awake, she started at the sensation of strong arms holding her and warm breath tickling the back of her neck. Jonathon was beside her. She gasped as her eyes flew open.

"Jonathon," she breathed.

"Love," he answered sleepily.

She rolled toward him and buried her face in his chest. His scent was intoxicating and the thick mat of hair tickled her nose; she burrowed into him and he kissed the top of her head. Her arms encircled him and pulled him closer, but his gasp reminded her that his injuries were still fresh. She released him.

"No, do not let me go," he whispered.

"I fear I will hurt you. You are badly beaten, Jonathon."

Emily recalled the shock of first seeing her husband so bruised and battered when she had arrived at the cabin. His left eye was swollen almost shut, and his cheeks, chest and back bore the marks of a cat-o'-nine-tails. She had been reluctant to touch him at all for fear of inflicting more pain, but he had reached out his arms to her and she had melted into them. Gently, slowly, she had eased against his body tentatively testing each move until they lay together, lost in the bliss of the other's touch.

She saw him grimace and knew he was he remembering his treatment at the hands of the British. Then his warm brown eyes turned tender as he gazed at his wife. He brushed back a tawny tendril that had fallen in her eyes and leaned down to brush her lips. The fire within him burned, but they had discovered earlier that his injuries had sapped his strength too much for lovemaking yet, though his response to her touch indicated his desire.

Emily returned his kiss, lightly so as not to cause him more pain. Reaching up she ran her fingers through his thick brown hair and then traced his jawline, across his lips and down his throat. Her hands traveled across his broad shoulders, rubbing them, trying to heal them with her touch. Then her eyes held an impish gleam as she reached down to tease him, and she smiled as she felt his response.

"Love, if you continue to tantalize me thus, I shall have you arrested for torture," he laughed. But even the effort of laughing made him wince, and Emily removed her hand.

"Oh, Jonathon, forgive me. For so long I thought you were…," she stopped. "I cannot help myself, I want you so," she apologized.

"Em, I long to press you to me and take you now. Soon my love, for your presence has been the best elixir I could receive. Holding you in my arms, feeling your desire, hearing your voice has made me stronger." He smiled into her violet-blue eyes. "Soon, my love," he repeated.

Emily kissed him softly again and started to pull away. Jonathon held her closer.

"Stay, Love," he murmured against her throat.

Emily felt her passion inflaming, and for a moment considered yielding to his request, but common sense prevailed.

"Jonathon, Andrew will be returning soon, and my younger brother would be shocked to find us so," she glanced down at their nakedness.

"Ah, this is true, Love," he laughed and released her.

Emily slipped from under the quilt and walked to the chair that held her hastily shed clothing. The late afternoon sun streamed in through the west window and illuminated her skin to a golden glow. She smiled seeing that Jonathon's eyes never left her form.

"Come here, Love," he whispered.

Emily stepped back to the bed. Jonathon lifted his hand and traced the slight swelling of her abdomen. He leaned forward and whispered to it, "How are you, my child? Is all well in there?"

Emily laughed and pulled his head closer. He kissed her midsection and nuzzled his nose against her.

"Are you well, Em? Is our baby well?" he asked lying back on the pillow.

"Our baby is active and making his presence known more each day," she laughed.

Jonathon's eyes held hers and she could feel the love and passion they shared as if it were tangible. He closed his eyes and Emily saw his weariness in his drawn face. Dressing quickly, she then helped Jonathon back into his breeches and linen shirt.

"As I recall, sir, you were helping *me* into *my* clothing the last time we occupied this cabin," she said.

"Yes, that would be the night you seduced me as I recall," Jonathon said feigning distress. "I believe it was the result of over-imbibing strong brandy."

"Which you induced me to drink…" she countered lightly slapping his uninjured shoulder.

"…to ease the pain of your injured leg," he laughed. "I am glad you seduced me, Em, for I was on the verge of ravishing you, and that would not have been proper behavior for a guardian toward his ward. We both tried to honor your father's dying wish and maintain a respectable relationship. But, Em, the stories he told about you and Andrew led me to believe you were children! You can imagine my surprise when I first saw you at your home in London. Here was this beautiful young lady descending the stairs with fire in her eyes, I might add. I was captivated by you in that instant. I remember you were still wearing black, and your blue eyes were blazing at me. How could I resist your charm?"

"Andrew and I assumed that you would be Father's age or older," she smiled. "Instead I found a handsome man, tall and virile, standing at the foot of the stairs. I was so surprised I almost descended in a decidedly unladylike fashion, but I maintained my footing and my pride. You stole my heart in your first glance," she whispered kissing him softly.

Hearing the sound of a rider outside, Emily quickly tied the top of Jonathon's linen shirt and pulled the quilt to his chest. At the sound of a knock on the door, Emily bade him enter. Expecting Andrew to walk in, they were both surprised to see Randy O'Connor come through the door swinging two bulging saddlebags as if they were filled with feathers. Tall and red-headed, Jonathon's best friend grinned broadly he strode to the bed and pulled Emily into a bear hug, spinning her around. His green eyes gleamed contrasting sharply with his ruddy complexion.

"Well, I am glad to see you both decent this time! The last time I walked through the door to find you in here, I was scandalized," he boomed. Jonathon laughed at his lifelong friend and Emily blushed furiously.

"We were just discussing that day, Randy. I was reminding my wife of how she seduced me under the influence of strong brandy."

"Jonathon, please," Emily said.

"Just so, just so," Randy replied. "And I am sure you fought off her advances as any man of principle would, Jonathon. But she was too powerful for you and, unable to fend off her attack, you yielded and were overpowered," Randy laughed.

"Stop this, both of you. The truth is, I was influenced by Jonathon who led me astray and caused me to adopt evil ways," Emily laughed, joining the fun.

"But though Emily was injured that time, Jonathon, your injuries look far worse," Randy said as he approached the bed and took a long look at his friend. He scrutinized the welts and bruises that covered Jonathon's face. "Why, Jonathon, this is far more serious than I had expected."

"The British were bent on teaching me a lesson, Randy. They did not spare the rod," Jonathon grimaced.

"Well, you have been known to interfere with their plans of late, Jonathon," said Randy, winking. "You have been instrumental in supporting the Sons of Liberty and providing a means of communication for the Committees of Correspondence, and your ship the *Destiny* is famous along the Atlantic coast. Your involvement in the patriot cause is known far and wide, making you a prime target for the British."

Emily reflected on how Jonathon's patriot fervor also had caused a rift between them. Having grown up in London, she had little knowledge of the economic havoc being wrecked upon the colonies by the British Parliament. Eventually she began to understand the outcry of the colonists and their demand for fair representation, but prior to this understanding, she had demanded that Jonathon take her back to England. It was during that trip that Jonathon was shot and captured by the British as they attacked Norfolk. Believing Jonathon to be dead, Emily had insisted upon returning to Brentwood Manor so that their child could be born in Jonathon's home.

Emily felt her face afire with shame as the two men bandied about their jests, for she still felt guilty about Jonathon's injuries. If she had not demanded to be taken back to England, he would not have been captured. She stared at her hands, sadness clouding her eyes. Looking up, she saw Jonathon hold up a finger to his lips signaling Randy to be quiet. Confused, Randy looked at Emily and then understood.

"Harrumph…well, then…I shall go get the supplies I brought to take care of this errant sailor," Randy said, quickly exiting.

"Emily, my love, come here," Jonathon said softly.

She rose and moved toward the bed, her heart heavy. Sitting beside him, she took his hand.

"Jonathon, I will never forgive myself for what you have endured due to my selfishness," she said.

"I would have been there, in Norfolk, whether or not you were with me. It is not your fault, Emily." He placed his finger beneath her chin and gently moved her face toward him. "I had business to attend to for the committees, Em. I would have been there."

She nodded her assent. He pulled her down to lie beside him and cradled her in his arms.

"You need to release this, Emily. I am here with you now. If you allow this pall of guilt to envelope you, it will destroy us. I need you to help me heal, Em, and that requires your loving attention. Not distractions of the past."

Emily saw the sense in what he said. She did not know if it were possible to forgive herself, but no longer would Jonathon be aware of the anguish she felt. She smiled and kissed him blinking back tears.

"I will do whatever you ask of me, Jonathon," she said.

He kissed her forehead. "Then I will ask you this. Know that I am well and improving every day. Seeing you and knowing that you and our baby are well speeds my recovery, Em."

There was a commotion outside and the sound of laughter. Randy returned accompanied by Andrew who carried three brace of rabbits. Emily looked fondly at her brother who, at seventeen, had not yet finished growing in height and was dwarfed by Randy's six-foot, four-inch frame. His hair was chestnut, darker than her own, but his eyes shone as blue, more like a clear mountain lake than her blue-violet shade. His smile was quick, and his laugh infectious and it ushered them into the cabin.

Randy pumped Andrew on the back and exclaimed, "See, I told you they would be dressed by now!"

Andrew avoided his sister's eyes, blushing furiously, and set the rabbits by the hearth. Emily rose from the bed and hugged her brother.

"Andrew, you have given me a most precious gift. Jonathon told me of how you saved his life in Williamsburg," she said.

"He was near death the night he stole into my room at William and Mary College. Jonathon, you frightened me nearly to death when you collapsed beside my bed. Fortunately, Mrs. Beresford had plenty of household items that facilitated my clumsy attempts at medical treatment. Your body was ice cold, and you had lost so much blood that I did not know if any care I administered would succeed."

"Whatever you did worked, Andrew, for here I am. And I am beholden to you for saving my life," Jonathon replied.

"I would say we are even now, since you saved my life aboard the *Destiny* when we traveled here from England," Andrew said, smiling.

"You will both be the cause of my prematurely gray hair!" Emily exclaimed. They all laughed. Then Andrew's face turned serious.

"Em, we had best leave for Brentwood Manor in order to return before sunset," Andrew said picking up two brace of rabbits and leaving one. "Jonathon, I shall leave these for your dinner, but I must show some reward for our long afternoon outing. We must avoid any suspicion of where and why we were gone the entire afternoon."

"I agree," Randy said pensively. "Your whereabouts must be kept secret lest the British find you, Jonathon. Thanks to Michael

Dennings's false lead, the troops are currently searching the coast to the southeast. But the fewer people who know you are here, the better. An innocent comment or a careless word could lead the redcoats right back here. In fact, I am convinced they will revisit Brentwood Manor believing that you, too, will eventually return there. Even those most loyal could slip and reveal your whereabouts. Let us keep this only among ourselves. Oh, and Gates knows, too. He should arrive in the next day or two to see to your wounds, Jonathon."

Jonathon sighed in relief at that news.

Emily smiled thinking of Robert Gates, Jonathon's first-mate aboard the *Destiny*, who was very knowledgeable about medicinal treatments. He had tended Jonathon and Andrew when both were seriously injured during a storm at sea, and both credited him with saving their lives. Mr. Gates had been commanding the ship during Jonathon's recent imprisonment and, with her blessing, continued to support the patriot cause.

"I long for news of the *Destiny* as well as for news of the increasing conflict between colonial and British troops," Jonathon said.

Emily sat beside him on the bed and took his hand. Their eyes met and she saw the unspoken longing and love there. She looked up at Randy who nodded his head and led Andrew toward the door and the two left the cabin.

"Jonathon, I do not want to leave you," Emily said, her eyes stinging with unshed tears. "I shall return as soon as possible for each day without you, knowing you are nearby, is torture. I shall find any conceivable excuse to ride out here to be with you if only for a moment."

"My love, my greatest wish is to have you here beside me, but we must be cautious. If you visit too often, it will arouse suspicion. And you must take care of yourself and our baby. I will send for you again when it is safe."

"But, Jonathon, I have lived these past months believing you to be dead; I fear if I leave I will never see you again. I long to be here to help nurse you back to health, to comfort you, to hold you."

"And I long for the same, Em. But I will heal faster if I know you are safe and in good health. Please understand how much I need this of you," Jonathon said.

"I will do anything for you, my love. My deepest wish, my fondest dream has been answered today. I thought I had lost you forever, yet here I am beside you." Emily leaned down and kissed his lips tenderly. "My love," she whispered against them.

Jonathon reached up and ran his fingers through her tawny locks gently pulling her closer. She felt his tongue trace her lips and slip between them and she responded eagerly, kissing him deeply, moving against him. Desire rekindled, their kiss lingered until Andrew's subtle cough brought them back to the moment.

"Em, we must leave now to ensure our arrival before dusk."

Emily slowly rose, reluctantly releasing Jonathon's hand, their eyes locked in the intensity of their love.

"Good-bye, Jonathon," she whispered over the tightness in her throat.

"Not good-bye, Love, but until we meet again" he answered, attempting a half-smile.

Emily turned and left the cabin.

• • •

Lighted lanterns and candles greeted Emily and Andrew upon their arrival in the gathering dusk. Rich aromas from the cook-house announced a hearty supper of stew and biscuits causing Emily to realize how very hungry she was since she had not eaten since morning.

"I have missed Dora's cooking!" Andrew exclaimed causing Emily to laugh at his enthusiasm. "While Mrs. Beresford runs a comfortable establishment, her cooking leaves one wanting. Dora could boil old stockings and make it a feast!"

"Oh, Andrew, how you make me laugh!" Emily smiled. "How you cheer me."

"Emily, I know how difficult it has been for you of late. I was beside myself not revealing Jonathon's hiding place until today, but I honestly did not know if he would survive. I could not bring you to him until I was certain. To lose him once must have been dreadful, but to lose him twice, unbearable."

Emily gazed at her brother once again struck by his maturity and good sense. Although two years younger than she, at seventeen Andrew was often her counselor and advisor.

They arrived at the carriage house and released the horse and carriage to a stable hand. Walking arm-in-arm into Brentwood Manor, they encountered Joanna Sutton, Jonathon's sister, carrying William who would turn one-year-old the next month. Seeing Emily, William broke into a smile and reached out his arms to her.

"Will, are you pleased to see me? Come here, my fine fellow, for Aunt Emily has missed you today," Emily laughed as she relieved Joanna of the child.

"You two had quite an outing today," Joanna said.

"And a successful day it was," said Andrew holding up his two brace of rabbits. "I shall take these out to Dora and see what magic she can conjure with them." Emily heard a note of relief in his voice as he left her to attempt to explain their long absence, and he hurried toward the back of the manor.

"So you were hunting all day?" Joanna asked. "I did not know your penchant for the sport, Emily." Emily noticed that Joanna's brown eyes, so like her brother's held a hint of amusement.

"Oh, I relaxed while Andrew hunted. It was a delightful day," Emily replied burying her face in Will's neck tickling him with her kisses. She could feel the color suffusing her face both as a result of her white lie and her memory of lying in Jonathon's arms. Charming both of the women with his laughter, Will quickly became the focus of their attention.

"Emily, I believe he will take his first steps soon," said Joanna, beaming. "He has discovered if he balances while holding onto the furniture, he can let go with one hand. Of course, he is so pleased with himself that he bounces with glee and then drops to the floor."

Emily laughed with her sister-in-law and commenced another round of kisses against Will's neck causing him to squeal with delight. Like his mother, Will had soft brown eyes and his golden curls were already darkening, hinting at the chestnut brown color his mother and uncle shared.

"Are you going to walk, little man, and make our lives even more hectic as we chase you?"

"The outing must have been very good for you, Emily, for you seem almost giddy," Joanna remarked.

• • •

Andrew's presence at supper was a delightful surprise for David, Joanna's husband. With the exception of Will, he had been the lone male at the table, and while the conversation was always lively, it often centered on more domestic arts with which he was unfamiliar.

"Andrew!" David boomed as he entered the candlelit dining room. He was tall and solidly built with blond hair that tumbled over his brow beneath which blue eyes smiled a welcome. His long strides took him across the room in just a few steps and he shook Andrew's hand heartily. "At last, an ally to join me in verbal jousting with the women of the household."

Andrew laughed and patted David on the back. "It looks to me as though you have been holding your own quite well, David."

"I am barely holding on, Drew. They wear me down day after day. Soon I will be taking up embroidery and joining them for the evening gossip!"

"How you exaggerate, my husband!" Joanna countered. "Andrew, he enjoys the attention a single male always elicits from a group of women. And our conversation has been far more interesting than neighborhood gossip with all that is going on with the House of Burgesses."

"What news from Williamsburg, Andrew?" David asked.

"George Mason continues to work on the Virginia Declaration of Rights calling for individual freedom, power vested in and derived from the people, elimination of the slave trade, and rejection of cruel and unusual punishment—ideas foreign to the suppression of Parliament."

"I have read Thomas Paine's *Common Sense* calling for independence from Great Britain. These ideas are both exciting and dangerous. Is it true that the British have evacuated Boston?" David asked.

"Indeed, and the British navy has relocated in Halifax, Canada," Andrew replied.

Emily listened as the men continued to discuss the rebellion rampant in the colonies. Initially, it was difficult for her to hear others speak with such hatred of Great Britain for it had been her home until two years ago. After her father's death, Jonathon Brentwood had been appointed guardian to her and Andrew as provided for in George Wentworth's will. She had attempted to foil Jonathon's plan to relocate them to Virginia, but found all of her resistance fading as she fell in love with him. Until she saw for herself the financial ruin the pronouncements of Parliament were causing in the colonies, she had been a loyal Tory. As she gradually recognized the dire conditions of many friends and neighbors, as well as the toll Parliament's pronouncements were taking on Brentwood Plantation, she came to understand the patriot cause for which Jonathon worked so passionately.

She looked across the table at Deidre Manning whose blond hair blazed in the candlelight, her hazel eyes moving from Andrew to David, enrapt in their conversation. *As well she should be,* thought Emily, *for she lost everything to the British.* Deidre's family had been lifelong friends of the Brentwoods, and she had grown up with Jonathon and Randy. Two weeks earlier she had arrived at Brentwood Manor looking disheveled and thin. She had mortgaged all she owned to the British and could not repay the debt. Her slaves had flown, some because of the invitation of the British to join their side and earn their freedom, others because there was no food and they were starving, as was Deidre. Having nowhere else to turn, she arrived at Brentwood Manor despite the trouble she had caused Emily.

Remembering her shock at Deidre's appearance that night, Emily noted that she looked far healthier since her arrival, for due to David's careful stewardship, Brentwood Plantation was still viable and had ample foodstores. But Deidre had not yet regained the voluptuous sensuality that she displayed wantonly many times in attempts to draw Jonathon from Emily. Aware that at some point Jonathon and Deidre had been lovers, Emily had been quite threatened by Deidre's obvious charms, which she exhibited in dresses with breathtakingly low décolletage. One such example was the scarlet dress she had worn to Emily and Jonathon's wedding when she kissed Jonathon so passionately in front of the guests that people were frozen in shocked silence. Deidre had vowed to win him back, but she seemed to have none of this fire within her now. She seemed defeated and grateful to Emily for having invited her to stay at Brentwood Manor. Joanna had been stunned at Emily's largesse, but as mistress of the manor, Emily's say was final. She was brought back to the conversation at Andrew's words.

"Mason has included freedom of the press as well," Andrew said.

"The Virginia Convention of Delegates is convening to determine the structure of our government. Who would have believed it?" David remarked as if to himself.

"Well, I had best set off if I am to return to Williamsburg tonight," Andrew said.

"Andrew, when will I…when will you…will you be coming for a visit again soon?" Emily stammered.

"With this beautiful spring weather, I have no doubt that I shall return soon to escort you on another outing, Em," he replied, winking at her.

Emily saw Joanna look from brother to sister, but no one else seemed to notice anything unusual about the exchange. Andrew rose, and bidding all a farewell, took his leave.

• • •

Emily sat at her dressing table brushing her thick honey-colored hair, taking in the beautiful furnishings in their bedroom. A mahogany bed nestled between two tall windows, its four posts topped with carved pineapples—a symbol of home and welcome. The tester and counterpane were rich silk, ivory in an alternating stripe, and pale blue brocade curtains framed the windows. Thick rugs covered areas of the highly polished floor, their rose patterns mirroring the hues of the other fabrics. This was their sanctuary when Jonathon was home, and the possibility that he would return shifted her focus.

Her thoughts traveled miles away to the hunting cabin where Jonathon lay suffering from wounds inflicted by British troops. Recalling how wan and drained he had looked today despite his brave smile caused her heart to ache, and she longed to be beside him at this moment tending to his wounds, caring for his pain. His words had eased the guilt she felt about his capture, guilt that was increased by words Deidre had flung at her when she returned to Brentwood Manor after Jonathon's apparent death. *Do you know why he is dead? Because of his blasted Tory wife!* Emily shivered as she remembered that confrontation just two months ago. Now Deidre was living beneath their roof with no idea that Jonathon was just miles away, and Emily knew it was best to preserve that secret. Silence was of the utmost importance to ensure Jonathon's safety. He was a major prize to the British as he would serve as an example to all patriots who fought for the cause of independence.

But Emily's heart was full to bursting with joy at seeing him. How she longed to confide in someone, to relive each moment she had spent with him today, to share the news of his safety. But for Jonathon's sake, she would hold the secret in her heart and anticipate the next opportunity to visit him.

She stepped to the bed and pulled back the covers. Climbing in, she reached beneath the pillow and retrieved Jonathon's shirt. Each night since her return to Brentwood Manor, she had tucked his shirt against her cheek as she waited to fall asleep. Dressing for their trip months ago, he had put it on briefly, and then changed it for another. It still held his scent, and had comforted Emily during long nights of grief. She smiled as she smoothed the linen thinking back to the afternoon spent lying beside him. She nestled the shirt against her face and inhaled his scent once more. He was alive; her beloved Jonathon was alive. She lay against the pillow and cradled the shirt; soon she would have no need of it for Jonathon would be beside her.

• • •

Brentwood Manor was known far and wide for its beauty. Stately catalpa trees stood sentinel along the circular drive that led up to the manor. The emerald green lawn swept up from the drive to the carefully groomed shrubs that surrounded the home. In contrast with the verdant lawns, the Flemish-bond, red brick manor rose two stories high in classical symmetry, and large double-hung windows flanked either side of the central entrance. Two enormous chimneys were stationed at either end of the hipped roof, and five double-hung windows ran along the second story on the front of the house.

The gardens were also symmetrical with paths running throughout the sculptured shrubbery. On this spring morning, manicured flowerbeds contained multi-colored tulips bobbing in the breeze creating a wild kaleidoscope of color sweeping along the garden's edge. Tucked in among the shrubs, irises, azaleas and Virginia bluebells turned their faces toward the sun. Dogwoods and cherry blossoms burst against the azure sky, the air redolent with the aroma of spring blossoms.

The morning sun streamed across the veranda infusing everything with springtime radiance, and Emily basked in its warmth and her memories of Jonathon. She and Joanna were enjoying their customary morning tea, and as was often the case, a comfortable silence had fallen between them. Again Joanna found herself studying her sister-in-law, for the Emily who had left for a carriage ride with Andrew yesterday was not the Emily who had returned last evening. Her complexion was rosier, the crease between her eyebrows, erased. The curtain of anxiety that had enveloped her since their discovery that Jonathon lived had given way to a lightness of movement. At this moment, Emily was quietly humming a song, and her fingers tapped the arm of her chair. Sensing Joanna's eyes upon her, Emily fell silent and looked up at her.

"Emily, I am pleased to see you so full of spring fever this morning," Joanna said, smiling.

"It is a glorious day, is it not, Joanna?"

"Indeed, and it certainly has brightened your mood. How wonderful to see your face looking so peaceful and to hear you softly humming a tune. Spring will bring out the best humor in people; do you not think so, Emily?" Joanna could not help encouraging Emily to share whatever she had discovered the day before. She was convinced it was news about her brother because of the transformation in Emily. And as difficult as Jonathon's presumed death, and then the discovery that he was alive and had escaped, was for Emily, it was also very difficult for Joanna. She and Jonathon had always been very close even as children. Her grief had been deep and terrible as well, but she at least had David and little Will to comfort her. Yes, Emily's grief was a dark abyss from which Joanna thought she might not return. She looked fondly at her sister-in-law and smiled.

"I am content to see your happiness return," she said giving up the attempt to pry.

"Joanna—I," Emily began. She longed to confide in her, to share her joy at seeing Jonathon, touching him, kissing him. Joanna had been her confidant many times, with Emily eventually even acknowledging that she and Jonathon were lovers after their first stay in the cabin. Joanna, so level-headed and compassionate, had always been supportive and never judged harshly. It was Joanna who had helped Emily when a British captain had attempted to rape her while his troops camped on Brentwood Plantation. Yes, she longed to share her secret, and Emily knew that Joanna would guard it as sacred. Joanna waited patiently for Emily to continue, for her inner struggle was evident on her face.

"Joanna—I want to..." Emily began but stopped speaking abruptly as Deidre stepped out onto the veranda.

"What do you want to do, Emily, dear?" Deidre asked.

"Uh...I want to take a stroll through the garden," Emily replied, color rising to her cheeks. Deidre tilted her head watching her closely.

"You seem to be encountering trouble making that decision. It is really not that difficult, Emily, just rise and walk," Deidre laughed. "Or perhaps I interrupted a more meaningful conversation."

"Not at all, Deidre. We were just remarking on the beauty of the day and the lure of the gardens," Joanna replied.

"Of course. I am curious about Andrew's visit, Emily. Did he bring any news of Jonathon? What are they saying in Williamsburg?" Deidre asked.

Joanna looked quickly at Emily, and it did not escape Deidre's notice.

"Andrew did not tell me anything about Jonathon, nor did he mention what the news is from Williamsburg," Emily replied rationalizing the truthfulness of her statement with the fact that, indeed, Andrew had not *said* anything to her about Jonathon. He had simply delivered her into his arms.

"How odd that you spend the whole day with your brother and the topic of Jonathon never arises. It seems to me that all you would wish to talk about is your husband." Deidre's attempt to sound innocent was not lost on Emily. Beneath her words hovered a subtle sarcasm.

"Oh, certainly we talked about Jonathon. We…we discussed what many are conjecturing about him; we discussed where the British are likely searching for him. Yes, yes of course we discussed him," Emily stammered.

Joanna broke in and rose, reaching for Emily's hand.

"The garden awaits us, Emily. Let us take our stroll now," she said gently pulling Emily to her feet. "Deidre, would you like to join us?" Joanna added as an afterthought.

Deidre looked slowly from one woman to the other, and then shook her head.

"No, you two seem very anxious to be among the flowers. I shall rest here in the sun for a while."

Nodding slightly, Joanna led Emily out to one of the paths. With a voice louder than was necessary, Joanna related Will's antics upon waking that morning, her laughter floating on the breeze behind her where Deidre scowled at the backs of the two women.

When they were safely out of earshot, Joanna fell quiet and they walked along in companionable silence. Emily's turmoil was almost tangible, and Joanna sympathized with her. It was obvious Emily had learned something of Jonathon's whereabouts from Andrew, but she no longer desired to pry. That would make her just like Deidre. She knew Emily would confide in her when she felt comfortable doing so.

"I thought that Deidre's difficulties would have transformed her, but I believe I was too optimistic," Emily said.

"I wondered at your generosity in offering her a place here. I am not surprised because that is what your heart is like, Emily, but she has caused you nothing but trouble since you arrived in Virginia."

"I feel sorry for her, in a way, Joanna. I believe she is still in love with Jonathon. I know they were lovers at one time, and I do not think she ever stopped loving him. My coming to Brentwood Manor complicated the situation for her, because I suspect she believed she would eventually win Jonathon back. In her way, she fought for him, even on our wedding day. When she lost everything to the British, I felt so sorry for her—I have everything and she had nothing."

"Well, not everything, Emily. We still do not know where Jonathon is."

Emily stopped in the path and looked at her sister-in-law. How difficult it was not to blurt out her story and share the weight of her secret. She searched Joanna's eyes finding love and compassion, but she could not bring herself to reveal her knowledge. Joanna took her hand, turned and continued walking, bringing Emily along.

"You need to be very cautious with Deidre. Do not trust her with any information that might put Jonathon in danger," Joanna said. She looked back at the veranda where Deidre sat watching them. "In fact, Emily, just be very cautious around her in all circumstances."

"I will be, Joanna, do not worry. I—I trust you implicitly, Joanna, but…"

Joanna gently shook her head and smiled.

"In time, Emily, in time."

• • •

Deidre watched the two women speaking earnestly as they strolled the path. She, too, had noted a tremendous change in Emily upon her return yesterday. The silly girl was as transparent as glass, and she was certain that Emily had been with Jonathon. Fiery hatred kindled in her belly and crept up to her throat at that thought. The fact that Emily carried Jonathon's child only increased her hatred, for Emily had everything that Deidre felt should have been hers—Jonathon, his heir, and Brentwood Manor.

# Chapter 2

Emily fidgeted over the next days, her mind filled with the thought that Jonathon was just a carriage ride away. She flitted from reading a book to strolling in the garden to playing with Will, but her thoughts were always elsewhere, at a cabin with her Jonathon. Noticing her restlessness, Joanna tried all kinds of diversions: games of whist, sewing clothes for the baby, redesigning frocks to suit Emily's changing figure. But none of these were successful, and Emily was growing impatient and short-tempered. One morning while playing with Will, Emily scolded him stridently for throwing a toy drum across the parlor.

"William, we do not throw toys!" Emily shouted at the child. Startled by the volume of her voice, he began to wail.

"Emily, what is wrong?" Joanna asked, for she had never spoken thus to William.

Emily felt her eyes brim with tears as she looked from Will to Joanna. She knelt down beside the child and reached out to comfort him. He twisted away from her and held out his arms to his mother. Joanna scooped him up and took a seat on the nearby settee. Unable to hold her emotions in check any longer, Emily released her pent up tears, her shoulders shaking. Sobbing, she looked at Will and Joanna.

"Forgive me, Will, Aunt Emily is not...not herself today," she managed to get out between sobs. She reached out to stroke the child's leg, but he turned from her and buried his face in Joanna's neck, his wailing intensifying.

"There, there," Joanna murmured against Will's forehead. "It is all right, William, it is all right." But he would not be consoled. She gently bounced and rocked him, softly singing a lullaby, and after a while his cries settled into whimpers, tears streaming down his face.

"Oh, Will, I am so sorry that I frightened you," Emily said. "Aunt Emily is so sorry." She rose, wiping her own tears from her face, and gently approached him. "Do you forgive your aunt who loves you so, Will?"

Will eyed her suspiciously as she neared him. He turned his face away from her and then looked back. When she stood before him, he laid his head against Joanna's shoulder and peeked up at Emily who reached out and brushed a curl that had fallen against his eye. She smiled tenderly at him, and the trace of a smile lit his eyes. Leaning forward she kissed his cheek tenderly.

"Aunt Emily loves Will," she said softly tickling him and was rewarded with a smile. Emily's eyes shifted to Joanna's.

"Forgive me, Joanna," she said softly.

"Of course, Emily, but I am worried about what initiated such an uncharacteristic outburst,"

Emily's eyes drifted away from her sister-in-law's and fixed on the view from the terrace window. She watched a robin swoop down and tug a piece of straw caught in a flower pot on the veranda. The bird wrangled the straw until it came loose from the soil, twisting its beak this way and that until freeing its prize. Finally victorious, it flew off to improve its nest. Nothing in life came easily, it seemed. Struggling within, she weighed revealing her secret to Joanna with her promise to keep silent about Jonathon's whereabouts. Surely she could reveal that she had seen Jonathon, yet still keep his location a secret; Joanna would understand the need for discretion. The thought struck her: what if something had happened to her own brother, Andrew? It would be agonizing not to know if he was all right. Yes, Joanna must be told at least that much; she must be told that Jonathon is alive and safe—for now. Making up her mind, she turned to her sister-in-law who held a now-sleeping Will in her arms.

"Joanna, I have been so unsettled of late," she began.

"Yes, I have observed that," Joanna laughed softly. "What bothers you, Em? How can I help?"

Emily stepped to the parlor door and peered into the hallway. Closing the door behind her, she approached Joanna and sat beside her on the settee, taking her hand.

"Joanna, I have seen Jonathon!" Emily whispered excitedly. "Andrew brought him to safety...Andrew saved his life...he is very weak...I want to be with him so...Andrew is taking care of him...I cannot tell you where he is..." Words tumbled over words in a hodgepodge as Emily attempted to organize her jumbled thoughts. Joanna laughed and hugged her causing Will to stir and whimper.

"Emily, I suspected as much when you returned with Andrew. Oh, I am so grateful to Andrew and so glad that Jonathon is alive and safe," Joanna whispered, tears shimmering in her eyes.

"I am sworn to secrecy as to his whereabouts for fear it could get back to the British. Even the most loyal in our household could inadvertently slip and reveal his location. For his safety, I must keep this secret. But I was able to see him, Joanna! We spent the afternoon just lying together, and it was wonderful. But his injuries are severe, so Andrew has sent for Mr. Gates," Emily explained.

"Emily, I am so pleased for you—for myself, as well," she laughed, giddy with gratitude for her brother's safety.

"I am beside myself waiting for Andrew to return and take me to Jonathon again. Every horse or carriage I hear on the grounds sends me fleeing to a window in hopes it will be my brother. But the longer I wait, the more I am on edge. I am not able to concentrate on any task, or even carry on a civilized conversation."

Joanna smiled at this, for indeed, conversing with Emily had been rather confusing of late. While beginning on one topic, she would suddenly introduce another or make some unrelated comment. Or she would begin speaking as if picking up the strands of a conversation only she had been hearing. All of this had convinced Joanna that something was troubling Emily, and she had suspected it involved Jonathon.

"Now I will be more sympathetic when your rambling thoughts digress for no apparent reason," Joanna said, smiling.

Emily laughed. "I suppose I have been rambling when speaking, for God knows my mind has been rambling like a babe lost in the woods! Oh, Joanna, it is a relief to confide in you, for I thought I would burst."

"I am honored that you trust me so, Emily," Joanna said sincerely, hugging her.

The parlor door opened and Deidre stepped in noticing the tearful women embracing.

"What causes such a display of emotion?" she asked as she took a seat across from the women.

Releasing Emily, Joanna said as casually as possible, "We are celebrating Emily's relief of morning sickness." She blushed at her white lie.

"Oh," said Deidre noticing Joanna's discomfort. "Of course." She rearranged her skirts, hiding a smirk.

Silence fell between them as Joanna and Emily searched for a segue to a safe topic of conversation. Outside the window birds chirped merrily and voices floated in from the garden. The sun streamed through the windows casting a warm rosy glow on the scene. All seemed so normal, yet underlying it a man's fate hung in the balance.

"Such a beautiful morning," Joanna finally said. "We should enjoy it with a carriage ride...or rather..." she stumbled casting an apologetic look at Emily.

Deidre carefully observed the silent communication appearing to pass between the two women. Both seemed uncomfortable and unable to carry on a conversation. Emily had been particularly inarticulate of late, and Deidre had noticed how she often went to the windows to stare down the drive as if expecting someone. Deidre's suspicions were growing that Emily had been with Jonathon. Noting Deidre's silence, Emily spoke.

"A stroll would be lovely. Who will join me?" Emily asked.

"I must put Will in his crib," Joanna replied.

"I would love to join you, Emily, dear," Deidre said, smiling.

The women rose, Joanna carrying William upstairs, Emily and Deidre proceeding to the door to the gardens. The women paused to don sunbonnets, tying the ribbons beneath their chins, and then stepped out into the morning sunshine. Emily felt lighthearted having unburdened her secret, or at least part of it, to Joanna. Her step was lighter and the crease between her brows that often shadowed her face had vanished. Deidre noticed all of this and her suspicion deepened. Emily breathed deeply inhaling the heady scent of lilac that wafted through the air.

"I love springtime," she said.

"The season certainly agrees with you, Emily, for you seem downright carefree today. Spring has certainly lifted your spirits, despite the weighty concerns you carry," Deidre said.

"Yes, the warmth and flowers are an elixir for me," Emily replied.

Deidre glanced at her and tried again.

"How do you bear it, day after day, with no word of Jonathon, no idea of his whereabouts or even if he is still alive?" she asked gently, her face a mask of compassion. "Has there been no word sent to you of any hope for his safe return? Why, Emily, how strong you are, how brave to carry on with the ordinary details of life when inside you must carry such worry, such heartbreak. To be separated from your husband, to hope he lives, but not know anything more. I so admire your courage and strength," Deidre cried.

Emily walked beside her, keeping her head down, feigning interest in the flower beds they passed. Expecting difficulty in keeping this secret, she felt the full effects of dissembling at this moment. Of all the people who must be kept in the dark, Deidre was the person she most mistrusted. Though she had invited the woman to live with them after losing everything to the British, Emily harbored wariness in matters that concerned Deidre. Their relationship had been antagonistic until the moment Deidre arrived at Brentwood Manor seemingly a broken woman.

As if reading her mind, Deidre stopped, reached for Emily's arm and turned toward her.

"Emily, thank you for your generosity in allowing me to stay at Brentwood Manor. After the way I had behaved toward you since your arrival, it would have been completely understandable for you to turn me away. It is obvious why Jonathon fell in love with you, your kindness, your gentleness—what man could resist such delicate qualities? But I had nowhere else to go, you understand. The Brentwoods are my lifelong friends, and I had nothing left," Deidre's voice caught. She wiped at her eyes, and then smiled at Emily. "You are so good, Emily."

Caught off guard, Emily looked closely at Deidre. Her eyes shone through her tears, and her smile was contagious.

"Deidre, you are most welcome. No one should suffer as you had; why you lost everything. Hopefully this conflict will be resolved soon—and peacefully—and your property restored," Emily said.

Deidre hugged her warmly and kissed her cheek.

"Yes, hopefully everything will be resolved and we will all have what rightfully belongs to us," Deidre replied.

• • •

Overcast skies kept Emily inside on an early April morning. Sitting by the front window of the parlor, she was embroidering tiny flowers along the hem of a linen baby dress, when, hearing a carriage approaching, she jumped up to peer through the window. Her pulse raced, for Andrew was the driver and this knowledge sent her heart soaring. Could it be that today she would again see Jonathon? Hear his voice? Kiss his lips? She dropped the dress into the sewing basket and ran to the front entrance of the manor. As the carriage drew up to the door, she dashed down the steps to meet her brother. Noticing a difference in her balance as she hurried, she smiled as the baby moved within her.

"Andrew!" she called in greeting. "How wonderful to see you!"

Grinning, Andrew hopped from the carriage while his eyes swept the windows and grounds. He pulled his sister into an embrace and called loudly, "Em, I have missed you so!" and hugged her tightly.

"Are you feeling up to a carriage ride today?" he whispered in her ear.

"Oh, yes!" she replied happily.

Releasing her, he again took in the scene. Gardeners were trimming hedges and tending flower beds, but no one else seemed within earshot. Just to be safe, he maintained the ruse.

"Emily, I need your sisterly advice and a break from my law books. Come for a ride with me today. I believe another hunting expedition is just what I need," he laughed.

"I would love to accompany you and dispense my pearls of sisterly wisdom," she said, smiling back at him. "Let me get my wrap and bonnet."

Linking arms, they ascended the steps to the front entrance. Emily left in search of Joanna to inform her of their plans while Andrew went in search of Dora in the kitchen house. Finding Joanna in Will's nursery, Emily went to her and grasped her hands.

"Joanna, Andrew is here to take me to Jonathon!" she whispered excitedly.

Her sister-in-law hugged her.

"Wonderful, Emily. Please give him my love," Joanna said.

"I cannot do that, Joanna, for no one must know that I have told you anything about this," Emily replied. "But I shall tell him that you pray for his safety every day, as I know you do, and that we speculate together where he might be. Oh dear, I believe I am becoming entangled in deceit," Emily sighed. She hugged Joanna, and proceeded to her room to get her wrap and bonnet.

• • •

Andrew was returning from the kitchen house, his arms loaded with a picnic lunch from Dora when Deidre appeared and stood before him halting his progress to the front of the manor.

"Well, Andrew, what a pleasant surprise. I do hope you will be spending a few days with us," she said sweetly. She walked toward him and stood close enough that he caught the musky scent of her perfume. Looking deeply into his eyes, she placed her hand on his forearm. "I do so miss your company, Andrew," she lowered her eyes, and then peered at him from beneath thick lashes.

Taken off guard, Andrew blushed furiously and stammered a few unintelligible syllables. Finally, able to speak he began, but his voice cracked and caught in his throat.

"I am here to take Emily for an outing, but we will be back in time for dinner," he finally managed.

"What a considerate brother you are, Andrew," she purred. "Emily is in desperate need of distraction what with Jonathon missing and she not knowing if he has even survived."

The mention of Jonathon's name brought Andrew back to his senses. He moved away from Deidre and cleared his voice.

"Yes, indeed. Well, I had best load up the carriage so we can be on our way," he said.

"My, you have quite a bit of food there, enough for several people," Deidre said taking in the large rucksack he carried.

"Dora fears we will die of starvation if she does not provide a feast," he laughed.

"True," Deidre said. "I hope to see you at supper tonight, Andrew." She smiled invitingly and turned to walk back down the hall. For a moment, Andrew was riveted by the swaying of her hips. Shaking his head, he continued to the front foyer.

Emily was anxiously awaiting him when he arrived, and she laughed when she realized what he carried.

"You visited Dora, I see," she smiled.

"Of all the things I miss about Brentwood Manor, Dora's cooking is the main thing," he said.

"I shall try not to be offended," she laughed.

"Oh, I meant after you, of course," he teased, helping her into the carriage.

Laughing and teasing, they rode down the drive unaware of hazel eyes that followed them, noting the direction they turned at the end of the drive.

Shortly after they left the manor, Deidre entered the stables. Choosing Shadow, Emily's horse known for his swiftness, she urged the horse into a gallop and followed the path of the carriage.

• • •

Emily could barely contain herself as they rode toward the cabin. Andrew kept up a continual monologue of his experiences at William and Mary College in an attempt to distract her, but Emily's focus was unyielding. He smiled indulgently as he glanced at his sister. Her face glowed with anticipation, and her eyes, bright with happiness, mirrored the deep blue ribbons on her bonnet. She glanced back at him and laughed realizing that she had not been attending to his stories.

"Andrew, forgive me for my inattention, but I have waited so long to see Jonathon again. My mind is full only of him right now," she apologized.

"No need to apologize, Em, for I know how you love him. I hope that someday I will be blessed with a wife who loves me so," he said gently. She smiled at him gratefully.

The ride seemed interminable for Emily, though Andrew urged the horse along at its full pace. Finally, when the sun, hidden by the overcast clouds, reached its peak in the sky, they arrived at the cabin. Emily could hardly bear to wait for Andrew to alight and circle the carriage to help her down. She raced to the door and flung it open, then flew to the bed and into Jonathon's arms.

His arms encircled her, and he kissed her forehead, her cheeks, her eyes, and finally his mouth found hers and he kissed her long and full.

Laughing and crying simultaneously, Emily murmured, "Jonathon, oh Jonathon, my love." Tears streamed down her face as she traced her fingers along his jawline, across his lips and eyebrows. They embraced again unable to remain apart.

Eyes averted and blushing with embarrassment at the passion he was witnessing, Andrew finally spoke.

"I shall take some of Dora's delicious feast and be on my way," he said.

Emily went over to her brother and hugged him.

"Thank you, Andrew," she said through tears of joy. "Thank you." Andrew kissed her forehead and left the cabin.

Emily turned back to her husband and returned to the bed. He was sitting propped on the pillows, but still appeared weak. Studying him, she saw that the bruises on his face, though still shades of yellow and purple, were fading. His eyes were clearer and his face not as drawn. He was still gaunt, and the muscles in his shoulders and chest had weakened considerably, but his vitality was returning and the glint of humor sparked in his eyes.

"Will you peruse me all day and deny me your comforting embrace?" he asked.

"I want to be sure I am not going to add to your discomfort," Emily teased, just out of arm's reach.

"Have mercy, woman, I am in need of your ministrations!" he laughed, and she was in his arms.

Jonathon kissed her, deep and full, and then drew his head back to look at her. Her eyes held his in unspoken joy, awareness that they might never have been reunited flooding her mind. Slowly, Jonathon lowered his face to hers, his lips moving against hers, tasting, exploring. Emily moved against him, enkindling a fiery passion both had been denied. Their bodies strained toward each other, their lips pressed, hands searching. Emily finally pulled away as Jonathon protested. Slipping out of bed, Emily stood before him, eyes smoldering. Smiling seductively she reached along the side of her gown and began to loosen the stays that accommodated her growing abdomen. She allowed the dress to slip forward revealing the swell of her breasts, round and full with her pregnancy. As the dress slipped to the floor, she teased, bending forward to free herself from it.

"You torture me more severely than the British," he groaned.

"But there is a reward with this torture, my love," Emily whispered.

Pulling the shift off of her shoulders, she let it slip to her waist, her breasts now unbound, bobbing with her movements. She slid it to the floor, bending again to step out of it. Slowly she walked to the bed and stood before him; Jonathon reached up and cupped her breasts, full and ripe. She leaned forward so he could kiss them, taste them, tease them. Emily gasped, and she held her breath surrendering to the utter pleasure of his lips. Alive with yearning, she felt her desire mount unbearably, her legs shaking. In order to keep her balance, she straightened and then sat beside him on the bed.

Reaching down, she untied his linen shirt and slipped it over his head. Her breath caught again, but this time in response to the evidence of the violent beatings he had endured at the hands of the British. Ugly scars were forming where the cat-o'-nine-tails had scourged his chest; raised welts were still tender. She looked back at his eyes, soft and loving. Leaning forward, she gently kissed each scar, running her lips along the length of them, her tears falling on his skin. He brought her face to his, smiling gently, and their lips met. Passion reignited, replacing her sadness. They strained toward each other, as Emily ran her hand along his shoulder, his chest, his thigh. His response made it obvious that his wounds would not deter his desire, and she helped him remove his breeches, tossed them on the floor, and climbed into the bed and into his arms.

"I see that even torture at the hands of the British cannot daunt your passion," she said, stroking him gently.

"Their cruelty is no match for your love," he said against her lips.

Thirsty for the feel of her skin, Jonathon pulled Emily close, stroking her, burying his face in her neck. Still weak from his maltreatment, he allowed her to move against him. She rose above him enticingly dangling her breasts in front of him. He buried his face in them kissing them, tracing their curves. Emily could bear it no more, and she guided him, gasping as he thrust against her. They moved together, clinging to one another, reeling in lovers' rhythm to the peak of their passion.

Emily fell against Jonathon, both spent in their lovemaking, breathing against each other, clinging to the moment of ecstasy. Jonathon's arms held her close; her head nestled on his shoulder. They lay in the afterglow, content, fulfilled, silent in the awe of their union. Gradually they fell asleep.

As Emily stirred, the sun still battled the overcast sky as it sloped toward the west. Jonathon's regular breathing signaled that he still slept soundly, so she gently slipped from his embrace and slid off the bed. Quickly donning her clothing lest her brother return and find her naked, she raked her fingers through her tawny hair to tame it and conceal its evidence of their passion.

Rummaging through the rucksack, she found that Dora did not disappoint. Spreading a cloth on the nearby table, she laid out cold ham, cheeses, biscuits and candied fruit. She opened a bottle of wine and poured two glasses, sipping from one of them. She pondered the predicament they were in, and wondered what solution could possibly free Jonathon and allow him to return to Brentwood Manor. Living without him, knowing he was so close, was becoming impossible, as was the ability to keep this arrangement secret. Andrew, Randy and Mr. Gates had obviously been tending to him, but Jonathon would soon be more mobile and would be chafing at his seclusion. If he must move, it might be to a location farther away from her, and Emily knew she would be unable to bear that. Also, their child would be born in a few months, and he must be present for that!

Sensing eyes upon her, Emily looked over at the bed. Jonathon lay on his side, arm tucked beneath his head, his eyes glowing with love for her.

"You were concentrating very hard on something, Love. Would you care to share these musings with your husband?" he asked.

Emily looked at him, still weak, still recovering. He did not need to worry about anything but healing right now, certainly not her fears. Not wanting to share her thoughts with him for fear of adding to his distress, she searched for some other topic to discuss.

"Em, you know you can be honest with me. Whatever you are thinking, please trust me with it."

She looked at him; he had been her rock, had protected her in dangerous times, but he needed to regain that strength before she could burden him. But had they not always been honest with each other? This was not the time to be less than honest. This was the time for trust.

"Jonathon, is it safe for you to be here for this length of time? What if someone discovers you? Will you have to move farther away from me? What about the birth of our child?" she asked, her fear and confusion evident on her face.

Jonathon held out his arms to her and she went to him. Lying in his arms again, she felt anything was possible. She felt his strength as if it were passing from him to her, his determination, his courage, his spirit.

"This place will be safe for a while longer. Gates has scouts tracking the British, and they have not yet finished scouring the southeastern coast for me. When they turn back this way, I will probably have to move, and it may be a farther distance. But I swear to you, I will be present at our child's birth," he finished resolutely. He kissed the top of her head.

"I believe you, Jonathon. I love you so," Emily whispered.

"Now, love, you have sapped me of all strength, and I believe I spy Dora's hand at work on the table yonder. Please be merciful and provide some sustenance to this weakened lover."

Emily laughed and rose from the bed. She prepared a plate for him and brought it with a glass of wine to where he lay propped against the pillows.

"What, no brandy?" he teased.

"I didn't think you could tolerate it in your weakened condition," Emily laughed as she joined him on the bed.

Sitting side by side, they enjoyed Dora's feast, talking softly, shoulders touching.

• • •

Deidre had followed the carriage as it wound its way along the road until it turned off into a denser part of the woods. She sensed that Shadow knew this route, for he seemed to know where to turn before she guided him. On into the woods she rode, following at a distance to remain undetected. Even from this distance, she could see that Andrew did all of the talking, and Emily appeared anxious. As they drew into a clearing, she slowed her pace to increase the gap between them. Dismounting, she tethered Shadow to a sturdy oak tree and continued on foot through the woods. Thick trees and underbrush allowed easy concealment as she inched forward. Ahead she spotted a small cabin in the clearing; stacked split logs, a water barrel and fresh tracks were evidence that someone was living there. It was not difficult to guess who it was.

Deidre had found Jonathon.

# Chapter 3

The breeze blew from the south bringing warm moist air, fore-shadowing a humid summer. The gardens were a medley of color, tulips, geraniums, and daffodils vying for attention. Today they bobbed their heads in rhythm with the gentle wind and welcomed the attention of bees as they pollinated. Cotton clouds scudded across the azure sky, and sparrows soared and dipped on the draughts.

Joanna hurried out to the veranda where Emily relaxed with a cool glass of apple cider. Putting down her book, Emily turned at her sister-in-law's greeting.

"You are absolutely glowing! Why, your eyes are the color of the sky today, and your cheeks are absolutely rosy!" Joanna cried, and then lowered her voice. "Could it be that an outing in the country should lend such a glow to your countenance?"

A blush appeared above the neckline of Emily's dress and spread up her throat to her face.

"Hush, Joanna, you make me feel flushed!" Emily scolded, fighting a smile.

Joanna squeezed her hand in camaraderie, and placed a kiss on her forehead.

"I have news, Emily! David's brother Edward has inquired about the possibility of sending his daughter Jennifer to stay with us at Brentwood Manor for a while. His brother is concerned for her safety in Boston with the rebellion at such high intensity there. Of course, we ask your permission as mistress of Brentwood Manor—"

"Joanna, you do not need *my* permission; Brentwood Manor is your home!"

"Yes, Emily, however—"

"Joanna, of course David's niece can stay here, for as long as is necessary. Have I met her?" Emily recalled the galas that had been held in her honor since arriving at Brentwood Manor, one for her birthday and the other when she and Jonathon married. Meeting so many people at once had made it virtually impossible for her to recall who was in attendance.

"No, they have been unable to travel to Virginia because of the increasing danger. In fact, we have not seen Jenny since she was quite young. I will tell David that the plan has met your approval. Thank you, Emily." Joanna smiled and squeezed her hand. Turning to leave, she paused, and then knelt beside Emily's chair. "How is Jonathon?" she whispered looking into Emily's eyes. Emily glanced away remembering the scars that covered his body. She returned her gaze to Joanna.

"He continues to improve, but he was beaten severely, Joanna." Emily's eyes burned with tears. "The scars are extensive and he was without nourishment for a long time, so he is still quite weak." She quickly smiled, then blushed and looked down at her hands. "Well, he is regaining his strength I am happy to report." The women laughed together. "But it will be some time before he builds up his strength enough to be left on his own. Randy, Mr. Gates and Andrew are tending to him, and he is past any serious health concern. Their effort now is bringing him back to full health."

"Thank you, Em, for being so honest with me."

Joanna left the veranda in search of David leaving Emily to her musings.

. . .

Deidre entered the parlor dressed in her riding habit and stood before the women. Emily noted how the sage green outfit intensified her hazel eyes, framed by thick, dark lashes. The fitted waistcoat outlined her curvaceous figure and the skirt accented her tiny waist. Her golden hair was swept up beneath the felt cap angled jauntily on her head. Emily was struck by her beauty and instinctively ran a hand over her enlarging abdomen. Emily knew that when she entered a room, Deidre's beauty intimidated many women, but Emily felt no apprehension.

"Emily, may I ride Shadow today?" Deidre asked.

Surprise flickered across Emily's face. Shadow was her horse, and though she had not been riding him as often lately, her fondness brought her to the stables with apples for him quite often. A bond had grown between them as so often happens with rider and horse. But Shadow needed exercise, and this selfish feeling on her part was foolish. Shrugging away the feeling, she smiled at Deidre.

"Of course, Deidre. I am sure Shadow would love a ride on such a beautiful day," Emily said.

Joanna peered at Deidre as she turned to leave. She had noticed her riding Shadow before but did not recall that Deidre had ever asked permission, nor had she explained where her long absences were spent.

"Where does adventure take you today, Deidre?" Joanna asked.

Deidre stopped, and then turned back to look at the women. For a moment, she didn't speak. Clearing her voice, she looked down at her gloved hands and clasped them together.

"I plan to ride over to my home," she said, wiping at her eyes. "I know Manning Estate is no longer mine, but I miss it so; I just want to see it and ride on the property. Even though the British seized it from me, I believe it is abandoned, so they will not be aware of my visit. Somehow the need to be on that land is so intense that I cannot resist."

Emily rose from her chair and went to the woman, wrapping her arms around her. Recalling the grief she had felt on leaving her home in London, her heart went out to Deidre.

"Oh, Deidre, dear, yes take Shadow. I understand your sadness at losing your home, for I felt the same when I left my home in London. I felt my heart was wrenched from my breast." She looked at Joanna and smiled. "Of course, all ended well as I found my home here with Jonathon."

Unobserved, Deidre blanched at that. Her eyes hardened, but she resumed her tearful expression and wiped her eyes as Emily released her. Smiling with gratitude, she squeezed Emily's hand.

"You are kindness itself, Emily. Thank you," Deidre said, and then turning, she swiftly left the room.

• • •

Jonathon stirred in his sleep, disturbed by a noise. He slowly rose to consciousness noticing the sun high in the sky. Randy was not due back until evening, but he heard the unmistakable sound of hoof beats slowly approaching. Every muscle tensed in his body, for he knew the British would eventually discover they had been combing the southeast coast in vain. Surely they would return to Brentwood land and thoroughly search for him. Jonathon knew the precarious position he was in as well as the danger his friends were in as a result of concealing him. From the sound of it, the rider was alone, but if he were a scout, one shot from a pistol would bring the whole company here. Reaching beneath his mattress, he grabbed his revolver and pointed it at the door. Footsteps grew closer and he watched as the latch slowly lifted; he cocked the gun. The door swung open and in stepped Deidre.

Jonathon gaped at the woman and slowly lowered his pistol. His mind grasped for logic in this scene, for Deidre standing at the door of the cabin made no sense.

"Well, are you going to shoot me or welcome me, Jonathon, dear?" she purred.

"I damn near did shoot you!" he shouted. "What are you doing here, Deidre? How did you find this place?"

She slowly walked around the room examining each item carefully, as if interested. She paused at the window and peered out at the landscape. Turning back to Jonathon, she tugged off her gloves one finger at a time and placed them on the nearby table.

"I followed your wife and Andrew the last time they visited. It was obvious from Emily's *glow* after her first visit that you had enjoyed a rendezvous. Poor girl could not keep a secret if her life depended on it." She walked over to the bed and sat beside Jonathon. "But your life does depend on it, does it not, Jonathon?" she smiled.

The sugar-sweetness of her voice caused Jonathon's stomach to twist. Uncocking the pistol, he replaced it beneath the mattress. He looked at Deidre, uncomfortably aware of her beauty. The familiar scent of musk she wore brought vivid memories of nights he would rather not recall. She sat gazing at him, her hazel eyes afire in the sun's glow from the window. Slowly reaching up, she removed her hat and loosened the pins in her hair. Waves of gold descended around her face and shoulders. Shaking her hair loose, she tossed her head and the scent of musk enveloped them.

"What do you want, Deidre? I am certain you did not ride all the way out here to provide moral support in my time of need," Jonathon said shifting away from the heady scent.

"Jonathon, you think so badly of me. Of course I wanted to see you for myself and know that you are well. Emily most assuredly would not confide in me, although I do believe she sees me in a more sympathetic light than she did. Why she was almost in tears today when I told her I was riding back to my home because I missed it so," she sniggered.

Jonathon knew that Emily would respond in sympathy to Deidre's story, for it had taken much courage and grief for her to leave her home in London. One thing was certain, Deidre was a genius at discovering people's weaknesses and assaulting any vulnerability.

"Deidre, why are you here?"

"Why, to see you, Darling. To see for myself that you are alive and well, although you do not look well, Jonathon," she said.

"Deidre, if you care for me at all, you must keep my whereabouts secret. If the British find me, they will shoot me on sight. It would be best if you leave immediately. The fewer people who travel here, the safer I will be," Jonathon reasoned with her.

"But I only just arrived, Jonathon. I want to help you, to make you feel better. And you know I can do that, darling," she purred.

"Deidre, the best thing you can do for me is leave right now. Truly, you put me in danger by coming here at all. British scouts can be anywhere, and if you are a part of my household, they will follow you. Please, Deidre, I thank you for your concern for me, but I ask that you leave," Jonathon insisted.

"I think I will stay and see to your needs, Darling. You see, I believe that you need a real woman. Your infatuation with that girl drove you away from me, but she is a child and does not know what satisfies a man." Staring into Jonathon's eyes, Deidre began to unfasten her waistcoat slowly, a small smile playing at her lips.

"No, Deidre! What are you thinking?" Jonathon exclaimed.

"Based on the smile on Emily's face when she returned, I believe your injuries are not all that severe, Jonathon. Shall we discover what you are capable of today?" she crooned. She removed her waistcoat revealing a thin silk shift pulled taut across her breasts.

"Are you insane, woman? I have no intention of lying with you, so put your clothes back on!" he shouted. He leaned back against the pillows, his rage costing him strength.

"Jonathon, I want you to consider something. I am at Brentwood Manor with your wife every day, so I am aware of her well-being and health. It would be terrible if something were to happen to her, I mean the staircase in the manor is steep, and there are many sharp implements in the out buildings. How horrible it would be if she should stumble or cut herself…unwittingly, of course," Deidre stated.

"What are you suggesting, Deidre? Surely you do not mean to…" Jonathon's face went pale.

"I am merely suggesting that we both have the good health and the safety of your wife and child in mind." Rising from the bed, Deidre unfastened her skirt and let it slip to the floor. Sunlight flooded in from the window behind her, sharply silhouetting her shape, and she turned slightly to afford Jonathon a view of her ample breasts. He sucked in his breath and averted his eyes, but he could not deny the stirring that signaled his arousal. And he hated himself for it.

Deidre stepped to the bed and began to unfasten his linen shirt, but he pushed her hands away.

"Stop it, Deidre. Put your clothes back on and ride away, and we will both forget this ever happened," he snapped.

"It will happen, Jonathon, if you value the life of your wife and child," she countered.

"You cannot mean this! Deidre, what are you thinking?"

"You are married to the wrong woman, darling. We were always meant to be together; you know that. Do you not remember—"

"That is in the past, Deidre, when we were young. You married Robert, and all of that ended," Jonathon said.

"I was forced to marry Robert. Merging our lands meant a great deal to my father, even at the cost of my happiness with you. But I took care of that, did I not, Jonathon? I made it possible for us to be together again. Of course, we waited and were discrete so no one would suspect."

"What are you talking about, Deidre? Suspect what?" Jonathon asked.

"Oh, do not be coy with me, Jonathon. You cannot deny that you suspected there was something amiss with Robert's death."

Cold seeped into Jonathon's gut. Ringing in his ears shut out her words, but deep within he recognized a seed of truth in what she was saying. Many questions had been raised in the death of Robert Manning for he was a seasoned sailor and knew the river that ran through his property from a lifetime of navigating it. But no evidence of foul play emerged; it appeared he simply fell overboard and drowned. Of course, it was a mystery why he would take his boat out at such an hour when he had no trip planned. The truth crept into Jonathon's consciousness like an icy mist. He looked into Deidre's eyes, and the truth was confirmed. He felt sick.

"I did it for us, Darling. So that we could finally be together as we ought. It was quite simple, really. I suggested a moonlight boat ride, so romantic. And Robert actually believed that he pleased me, but no one ever pleased me except you, Darling. We strolled down to the river, I with my glass of wine, Robert with his ale. Oh, how he loved his ale. It is amazing how quickly a sleeping draught works in ale. Robert was not a big man, not like you, Jonathon; it was very easy to slip him over the side of the boat."

Silence filled the cabin; shock filled Jonathon. Deidre leaned into him, her breasts pressing against his chest. Feeling as though he were in a dream, Jonathon pushed her away. She opened his shirt and viewed the scars, still raw. Running her hands along the scars, she traced each one, gently scratching them with her nails. Awakened to his senses, Jonathon pulled her hands away and held them in his.

"Deidre, you must leave now," he whispered.

"Jonathon, I do not think I have made myself clear. We are meant to be together. I want you to make love to me, hold me and please me as you once did."

"Deidre, that was long ago; it is over now. I am married to Emily, and she is going to have my child."

Fire flashed in Deidre's eyes.

"I was waiting for you to return to me, Jonathon. Instead you came home with that British wench! Well, you will be mine, Jonathon, if you value her life," she cried. Yanking the ribbon at the neckline of her shift, Deidre opened it and let if fall. She ran her hand along Jonathon's chest, past his stomach, along his thigh. Jonathon was dismayed at his response, and Deidre's eyes were triumphant.

"Yes, Jonathon, see how you love me? See how you want me?" she cooed. She climbed above, straddling him, knees on either side of his hips. Reaching down, she tugged his breeches past his thighs then ran her fingers along their length. Smiling mischievously, she reached down and grabbed him, stroking him, smiling at his response.

"No, Deidre, please, no," he whispered.

The blood pounded in his head and instinct took over as he felt her lower herself until he entered her. He moaned, not in passion, but in self-loathing. Deidre began a rhythmic rocking motion that his body matched, intensity increasing. She leaned into him, her breasts pressing as she undulated above him, her breath hot against his face. Unable to control himself, Jonathon moved with her, aching for relief, hating himself with every thrust. Finally, he felt himself explode within her, grateful for the release, repulsed at what he had done. Moaning, Deidre began to sob.

"Oh, God. Oh, God," she cried, shuddering. She dug her fingernails into his shoulders as she reached her climax, pressing her face into his neck. With a final shudder, she fell against him.

Gasping with the exertion, they lay together for a moment, and then Jonathon pushed her off him.

"Hold me, Jonathon," she said.

He turned away from her. She snuggled against him, putting her arm around him. He shrugged her off.

"Jonathon, lovers lie together after making love, Please hold me," she asked again.

"We did not make love, Deidre. We did what dogs and horses do; there was no love involved here," he snapped.

"Jonathon, you forget that Emily's safety is in a precarious position, as is that of your unborn child," Deidre warned in a steely voice. Just as quickly, it softened again. "Please hold me, Jonathon," she wheedled. He looked into her eyes. As tender as her voice sounded, her eyes were like ice, and he knew Emily's life was in his hands. Resigned, he put his arm around her and she snuggled against him. He stared at the ceiling, his jaw clenched, his fists balled. He had been trapped as an animal hunted, and he loathed her—and himself. Gall roiled in his stomach, rose in his throat and left a bitter aftertaste in his mouth. He fought down nausea, and he fought back tears of bitter hatred and remorse. After a time, he spoke.

"Randy is due to arrive soon. It would be best if you were gone."

"Are you ashamed of me, Jonathon? Goodness, Randy has known of our love for all of these years. I doubt that he would be shocked to find us together," she answered.

Jonathon recalled a warning Randy had given him before he left for the voyage that eventually took him to London and Emily. Oh, Emily. He squeezed his eyes shut trying not to think of the pain she would feel knowing about this encounter. She must never know. But Randy knew that Deidre still had feelings for Jonathon, and had warned him to be careful when he returned. Neither of them had known at that point that he would return with Emily and ignite the fury that Deidre had just avenged.

"No, he would not be shocked, but he would be enraged. You see, he is very protective of Emily, and could harm us for this indiscretion," Jonathon answered.

"So you are trying to protect me? See, you do love me," she laughed.

"You had best dress and be on your way," Jonathon urged.

Deidre sat up and looked at him.

"Do not forget this, Jonathon, our time together. I will return so we can make love again."

"Deidre, we did not—"

She pressed her fingers against his lips.

"Be careful what you say, Jonathon. We want your baby to be safe, do we not?" The sweetness of her voice did not match the hardness of her eyes.

"Just to be sure you remember our time together, I will give you a souvenir," she chuckled. Jonathon looked at her quizzically, then his eyes widened in pain as she raked her nails down his chest across the recent wounds inflicted by the British. Droplets of blood beaded on the still-healing scars. Jonathon looked at his chest and then at Deidre in disbelief.

"I do not suppose you would want dear Emily to see those lover's wounds, now would you, Jonathon?" She laughed as she rose from the bed.

• • •

Emily lay back and let the sun warm her face, slip down to her throat and along the rise of her breasts like a lover caressing a beloved. She lounged in a chaise on the veranda sometimes looking out at the gardens, sometimes closing her eyes and reliving the feel of Jonathon's embrace. A smile played on her lips, and memories caused her to flush with warmth. Seeing Jonathon had been wonderful, but her desire to be with him again was not sated. She longed for Andrew to arrive in his carriage and take her once again to the arms of her husband.

"Your dreams must be very pleasant if your smile is any indication."

Emily jumped, startled at Deidre's words. She opened her eyes shading them against the sun that set Deidre in a dark silhouette.

Drowsy with daydreaming and slower with the weight of her baby, Emily gently sat up. Deidre moved to a nearby chair inching it closer to Emily.

"Tell me what you were thinking about, Emily. You looked positively enraptured," Deidre said.

Emily flushed again at her memories as well as at the need to dissemble.

"I was simply enjoying the sun, Deidre," she answered.

"Oh, I do not think it was solely the sun that warmed you, my dear," Deidre chuckled.

Emily looked down at her hands searching for another topic of conversation. This one was entirely too dangerous. Of all the people she wished to hide her knowledge from, Deidre was second only to the British. While Deidre seemed to be genuinely grateful for being allowed to remain at Brentwood Manor, something deep inside Emily prevented her from trusting the woman entirely.

"Did you hear that David's niece will be arriving at Brentwood Manor soon? David's brother Edward is quite concerned for her safety in Boston," Emily said.

Deidre stared at Emily for a long moment before she replied.

"Yes, Joanna informed me of this yesterday. How very thoughtful of you to be so concerned for this young woman when the life of your husband is in such danger. I imagine my thoughts would lie with him day and night if I were you. How terrible to sit here day after day not knowing his fate or even if he still lives. I am impressed by your courage and ability to put him out of your thoughts," Deidre said.

Emily's eyes sparked and she bolted upright.

"How dare you question my love for Jonathon! He is never out of my thoughts or prayers and it is abhorrent of you to suggest otherwise. Be careful what you say, Deidre. You are in no position to anger me," Emily snapped.

"Oh, dear, Emily, you misunderstand me. I never intended to question your love of Jonathon; I was merely complimenting your abundance of compassion. That you could even consider the safety of David's niece while you daily live with the anguish of ignorance about Jonathon's health and safety is admirable. You misinterpreted my compliment." Deidre rose and straightened her skirt, dusting it off lightly. "I apologize if I offended you in any way," she said, patting Emily's hand.

Emily watched as Deidre walked away, unconsciously wiping the spot where the woman's hand had touched hers.

• • •

Randy approached the cabin as the sun was sinking below the tree line. The peacefulness of the woods was a balm after the upheaval of port cities. Breathing in the pine scent, cool and crisp, he reviewed the day's events. Emotions were running high in Williamsburg as talk of independence from England became more and more heated. As the largest of the colonies, Virginia possessed enormous influence, and its actions could sway other colonies to favor independence, too. Britain's demands on the colonies to fund the army and navy and recoup economic stability after the war with the French had become untenable, and rebellion had been simmering for years. Now it had come to a head, and the call for independence from England was mounting. The Raleigh Tavern in Williamsburg was a center for debate and planning, and it was from just such a lively session that Randy was returning. Approaching the cabin, he took the usual precautions, carefully scanning the woods for hidden spies. He had taken a circuitous route there, doubling back several times to ensure he was not being followed. They had planned carefully for Jonathon's safety as he was not only a good friend, but instrumental in the effort against the British. His work for the Committees of Correspondence using his ship, the *Destiny*, was well-known, and many patriot successes were due to his courageous leadership. He had rallied many to the cause, and there was much more he was needed for in order to continue the fight. No, it was not just friendship that called Randy to aide Jonathon; he was, in essence, a major part of the spirit of the revolution.

Riding up to the cabin, Randy secured his horse to a tree, removed two overstuffed saddlebags and stepped up to the door. It was quiet, as usual, but Randy sensed an added layer to the quiet. Opening the door, he stepped into the shadowy room. Jonathon lay against the pillow, his face pale, his arm thrown over his eyes. Randy hurried to the bedside.

"Are you well, Jonathon? What is it?" Randy asked. Concern gripped him as he dared to think that all of their ministrations had been for naught. "Jonathon, are you ill? What do you need?"

Jonathon lowered his arm and looked at the friend who had shared his life, a trusted friend. Self-loathing again surged through him, and he ripped open his shirt revealing scarlet strips angled across the wounds inflicted by the British. Jaw clenched, twitching with anger, he spat out his words.

"Nothing that the British did can compare to the consequence of these scars."

Randy looked at him in confusion, shifting his eyes from the fresh wounds to Jonathon's face.

"Whatever happened to you, Jonathon? Did the British find you? Who was here?" he asked, for indeed, if the British had discovered Jonathon, he would be dead. These were surface scratches, certainly not even life-threatening. The gravity of Jonathon's situation left no room for injuries such as this.

"Deidre," Jonathon whispered, his voice strangled with emotion.

Randy looked at him, uncomprehending. Nothing was making sense. He pieced together what he was seeing with Jonathon's words, and slowly comprehension dawned.

"Good God," he breathed.

"She was here and…" Jonathon could not continue. He closed his eyes and brushed his hands across his eyes as if blocking out the scene. "I had to—she threatened Emily and our child. I tried to talk sense into her, but I think she is crazed. Randy, I had to, do you understand?"

"You lay with her?" Randy demanded.

"She threatened to harm, no to kill, Emily and the baby, Randy. I talked to her, tried to reason with her, but she was like one possessed. One minute laughing and gay, the next menacing. She was like someone I did not know. No, she was like the darkest side of Deidre that one could imagine. Yes, I did lie with her. I am ashamed—ashamed that I could not fight her. Ashamed that I cannot be with my wife to protect her! And the worst thing is, even though I succumbed to her, there is no guarantee that Emily is safe. Emily must never know, Randy. I must leave this place and be far away where she can never see these marks that shame me."

Randy's mind raced with the consequences of this news. How could all of the precautions they took to hide Jonathon from the British be undone by one scheming woman? Anger rose like bile within him and he stood and paced the room. Kicking one of the saddlebags, he swore an oath and continued back and forth across the room.

"We must move you immediately. Gates is not far behind me, and he is in a carriage. Are you strong enough to be moved?" Randy asked.

"I am far stronger now than when you first brought me here. Yes, I can be moved, but Randy no one else can know what happened," Jonathon said.

"Gates has been tending your wounds, man. He will certainly see that witch's marks," Randy said.

"Of course, you are right, and Gates is my trusted friend. But please, we must keep any knowledge of this from Andrew."

Randy nodded. Andrew adored his sister, and learning what Deidre had done, and was threatening to do, could lead him to murder. No, they would find another reason to justify Jonathon's move. He looked over at his friend who stared off in the distance, anger simmering just below the surface. He would heal, and this anger might even spur that on. Randy did not envy Deidre when Jonathon fully recovered.

"We must get a message to David. I worry about Emily's safety in the manor with that woman. We will send Andrew with two messages, one explaining my relocation to Emily, and one warning David of the peril she is in now," Jonathon said. "But how do we explain this danger to him without revealing what occurred?"

Randy thought about that for a while, but neither man could construct an excuse for Deidre's threat to Emily.

"We will have to inform him as to what occurred here," Jonathon admitted. He slumped against the pillow, exhausted and overwhelmed.

# Chapter 4

Spring brought the war ever closer to Virginia, and the *Destiny* was busy sailing up and down the coast delivering messages, personnel and munitions. Loaded down with cannon, she looked vastly different from her days as a merchant ship and conveyer of Emily from London to Virginia two years earlier. Under the competent leadership of Robert Gates, the *Destiny* continued fighting for the patriot cause that was Jonathon's vision.

John Murray, Lord Dunmore, governor of Virginia had fled to a navy ship off the coast of Virginia several months earlier, but from there Dunmore continued raids against plantations and forays into towns. Most of the Loyalists had followed his example, fleeing to British ships as violence on land escalated. British troops continued marching through Virginia, but it was becoming more difficult for them with most of their support at sea. The squadron searching for Jonathon realized they were on a wild goose chase and returned to the area around Brentwood Plantation.

• • •

Joanna was walking in the garden with William, who was just beginning to teeter with unsteady steps. An early morning rain had freshened the plants and left shallow puddles that she deftly navigated. The toddler lurched along, gripping his mother's fingers and beaming with glee, his giggles merging with her laughter as it wafted on the afternoon breeze. Stumbling and recovering, Will made his way between the neat hedgerows delighted with his own progress. Joanna's heart swelled with joy as she beheld her miracle child, born healthy and happy after several miscarriages and the loss of an infant. As she guided him back in the direction of the manor, she heard the pounding of horses' hooves approaching. Stopping to look, she automatically picked up a protesting and wiggling Will holding him closer at the sight of scarlet uniforms. She hastened toward the manor noting that Emily was rising from her seat on the veranda. Gripped by fear for Jonathon's safety, Joanna's legs wobbled beneath her as unsteady as Will's had just been.

The riders slowed their pace to a trot as they neared the manor, and Joanna joined Emily to meet them. Relief rushed over both women as they recognized Captain Michael Dennings in the lead. Although an officer in the British army, Michael had proven to be an ally a few months earlier when Emily, fending off an attempted rape, had seriously injured another British officer, Captain Arthur Walters, almost killing him. In danger of being arrested and possibly hanged, Emily was saved when Michael stepped in and forced Walters to drop the charges. Michael and Emily had grown up together in London, and eventually Michael had proposed allowing Emily an opportunity to remain in London rather than sail to Virginia with Jonathon. Already falling in love with Jonathon, Emily had refused Michael's proposal not knowing she had broken his heart. His miraculous appearance when Emily was in desperate need, gave the women hope that again he would help their cause. They found each other's hand and gave a squeeze in mutual support and optimism. The troops halted in front of them.

"Good morning, Mrs. Brentwood," Michael said formally. Emily knew that she must not reveal the friendship they shared at the risk of endangering both Jonathon and Michael.

"Captain Dennings," she nodded. "Do you have news of my husband?"

"We have been unable to locate him, and have once again returned to advise you to surrender him for your own safety," he said curtly.

Emily remained silent for she knew she would be unconvincing if she attempted to lie about her knowledge of his whereabouts. Sensing her reluctance, Joanna replied.

"We have no knowledge of my brother's whereabouts," she said honestly, for indeed, she herself had no knowledge of his location.

Michael dismounted, handing his horse's reins to a soldier. With his back to his men, he stood before Emily looking into her eyes, cautiously choosing his words.

"Mrs. Brentwood, I assure you we will be scouring Brentwood land in search of your husband. When we find him, and we will find him, he will be returned to Norfolk to hang as a traitor to the king." His words were callous and cold; his eyes held a contradictory kindness and warning. Emily understood and silently thanked him for his caveat. Gratitude flashed for an instant in her eyes, and he understood, and then she spat her words loud enough for all of his men to hear.

"Captain Dennings, you will never find my husband. He is not foolish enough to remain in this area, or perhaps even in Virginia. You may search all you wish, but it will be in vain."

Snapping a smart salute, Michael turned and mounted his horse. He looked down at Emily, sneering.

"We shall see just how foolish a man in love with his wife can be," he said. Turning his horse, he shouted a command and the troops rode off.

"Joanna, we must get word to Jonathon to move immediately," Emily cried.

"They will have scouts watching our every move, Emily. If anyone in the household should leave, he most certainly will be followed. We would lead the British right to him," Joanna answered.

"Oh, good heavens, what are we to do? I feel trapped like an animal, and Jonathon will surely be captured," Emily said, pacing along the drive. "What if we send one of the grooms?

"They will be watching for any activity now. We must bide our time and hope they do not stumble across his hiding place before we can warn him," Joanna answered.

Deidre appeared at the front door of the manor and rushed down the steps to join the women.

"What were British troops doing here? Have they captured Jonathon?" she asked, a note of panic in her voice.

Emily looked at Joanna, then at Deidre trying to determine what to tell her. Dissembling was not natural for Emily, but something within urged caution, and she tried to remain as ambiguous as possible.

"They have been searching for Jonathon along the southeastern coast based on a tip Captain Dennings had received. Not finding any trace of him there, they have returned to search Brentwood land thoroughly," Emily said, watching Deidre's face go ashen.

"My God," Deidre whispered, tears in her eyes.

Both women noticed the intensity of her reaction, each drawing a different conclusion.

"Deidre, I told Captain Dennings that Jonathon had probably fled the colony by now; he could be in Boston or Philadelphia, or—do not fear, Deidre, I am sure Jonathon is far away by now," Emily said, trying to console the obviously upset woman while trying to stem her own panic within. In a way, she was touched by Deidre's concern for Jonathon.

Joanna narrowed her eyes as she observed Deidre's reaction and suspicion grew within her. She had no doubt that there was more to the force of the woman's emotions.

The women climbed the steps and entered the manor. The marble floor and shuttered windows of the foyer provided a cool respite from the growing warmth outside. Before them the marble staircase gracefully curved arcing up to the second floor. A breeze blew from the opened door at the end of the hall moving the air across the entrance. Suddenly drained of energy and needing quiet to think, Emily headed for the staircase. Deidre watched her slow ascent, an eerie glint in her eyes.

•••

The carriage rumbled along the road jostling Randy, who drove, and Gates and Jonathon, who rode in the back. Jonathon gritted his teeth against the pain caused by the movement, and tried shifting positions to accommodate the bouncing of the wagon. The half-moon rose above the treetops signaling midnight, and the surrounding woods were alive with nocturnal sounds. All three men were tense with eyes and ears alert for any sound that was unusual for a forest at night. Constantly scanning the woods along the side of the rutted road, they held pistols and muskets at the ready.

When Gates had arrived at the cabin the night before, Jonathon was sick with shame as the man examined his chest. Never one to judge, Gates listened sympathetically as Jonathon related the encounter with Deidre. Gates applied a balm to the scratches she had left and wound a bandage around Jonathon's chest, not because it was needed, but to allow him a reprieve from the reminder of her vengeance and his self-imposed shame.

It had taken both Gates and Randy to assist Jonathon to the wagon. They put as many blankets as possible in the back to ease his journey, and loaded all the supplies and guns that had been stored in the cabin. Randy scouted the area surrounding the cabin as a double check that it was safe to transport Jonathon. Satisfied that all was clear, they started a slow journey toward Williamsburg. Jonathon had slept at first, the result of a sleeping draught Gates added to his ale. As they rode along, the men discussed different plans.

"I believe the safest place for him now is aboard the *Destiny*," Gates said. "We are armed with enough cannon to repel the British now, and our function seems more and more to be defense rather than communications."

Randy grimaced, for he knew Gates was right, but he was reluctant to yield responsibility for his friend. Although he knew of a few places where Jonathon could be concealed, none of them would provide long-term safety. Virginia was becoming more and more violent as the war intensified. For now, they would bring Jonathon to a planter's barn that had been transformed into a munitions supply site. He would be safe there for a couple of days, but the British troops marching through the colony were increasingly finding just such sites.

"Yes, you are correct, Gates. Jonathon will be safer with you aboard the *Destiny* than on Virginia's soil," he admitted.

As they rode along this second night of the journey, the sky was clear, though high clouds scudded in from the west. Jonathon dozed and awoke intermittently, allowing Gates to provide nourishment as they traveled along. Despite the jouncing of the carriage, eating on a regular basis seemed to increase Jonathon's strength, and he insisted on propping to a sitting position to help with the watch.

The stillness of the night was interrupted with distant thunder, and Randy urged the horses to speed their pace. A light rain was falling as rose streaked the eastern sky, but the mild temperature deterred too much discomfort. Golden rays of the rising sun greeted their arrival at the munitions site. Hearing their approach, the planter came to check on the disturbance and greeted Randy heartily.

"Randy! Good to see you, my friend. Who do we have here—my God, is that you, Jonathon?" the man exclaimed peering into the back of the wagon.

"Stephen, this is Robert Gates, Jonathon's first mate aboard the *Destiny*," Randy said. "Gates, this is Stephen Alcott."

The two men shook hands then turned to the carriage.

"What I ask of you is dangerous, Stephen, for Jonathon must be concealed as he is wanted by the British," Randy quickly explained.

"Are we not all, we Sons of Liberty, wanted by the British?" Stephen laughed, clapping Randy on the back. "It would be an honor to aid you, Jonathon," Stephen continued.

The men lifted Jonathon from the back of the wagon and carefully carried him into the barn. They propped him against a grain sack as they unloaded the rest of the supplies, then created a mattress with hay and blankets and helped him to lie down. Exhausted from the trip and the pain it had caused, Jonathon gratefully lay back and closed his eyes. Before him he saw Emily, his love. He fought the tightness that gripped his throat and the desire that burned in his gut, for his longing for her was physical pain. Then her image transformed to Deidre, snarling, laughing, scratching his chest, and he opened his eyes. Gates had remained with him, and stood watching him now.

"Emily must never know what happened," Jonathon said through clenched teeth.

"She will never know, Jonathon. But you must remember that her life was at stake. What transpired between you and Deidre was blackmail, and she forced you into it. You were trying to ensure Emily's safety and that of your child," Gates reminded him.

Jonathon looked at his friend and tried to find comfort in his words, but a deep, guilty sorrow possessed him and he did not know how to be rid of it. He did know, however, that somehow Deidre would pay for what she had done. He swore to the stars she would pay.

• • •

Emily lived in constant fear and guilt wondering how she could get a message to Jonathon. Occasionally someone spotted the scarlet of a British uniform along the road or on the edge of the woods surrounding Brentwood Manor. Each day she seemed a little more frantic, unable to concentrate, unable to eat, unable to think of anything but Jonathon's safety. A week after Michael had provided his veiled warning, a carriage rolled up the drive. Emily's heart raced; it was Andrew. She rose from her seat on the terrace, and went to meet him.

"Andrew, how wonderful to see you!" she cried as he wrapped his sister in his arms.

"We must talk somewhere completely safe," he whispered as he hugged her. Releasing her he said in a loud voice, "I have missed my sister, and had to forsake all other duties and visit." His eyes surreptitiously roamed the property as he spoke.

Arm in arm they returned to the terrace. Emily went inside, carefully checking the parlor as she passed through to ensure no one was occupying it. She rang for Dulcie. The woman who had been nursemaid to both Jonathon and Joanna, and who now supervised the household slaves, hurried in from the back of the manor.

"Yes, Miss Emily?"

"Dulcie, Andrew has arrived. Would you please bring us some cider?" she asked. Returning to the veranda, she checked the parlor again to ensure their privacy.

"Andrew, the British are searching Brentwood land for Jonathon. Surely they will find him in the cabin—it is just a matter of time before he is captured." With each whispered word her voice rose in notes of panic, but Andrew patted her hand in an attempt to calm her.

"He is not there, Emily," he said quietly noting that his words did not register. He took her face into his hands and silenced her. "Emily, Jonathon is no longer at the cabin. Randy and Gates moved him last week."

She stopped and looked intently into his eyes trying to understand his words. When comprehension struck, she slumped back in her chair and began to tremble. She wiped away the tears of relief that streamed down her cheeks.

"Where is he, Andrew?" she asked quietly.

He reached into his pocket and produced a note. Emily recognized Jonathon's handwriting, although it appeared shaky and as though written in haste. She held the note in her hand afraid to open it, afraid of what it might say. Would this be his farewell to her? Would he be unable to ever step foot on his beloved Brentwood Plantation again? Her hands shook, and she carefully turned the note over, broke the seal and opened the folded page.

*My dearest Emily, love of my life,*

*I must relocate for my own safety, and I do not know at this time where I shall be. Your visits meant everything to me; I shall cherish the memories of our brief times together. As soon as it is safe to do so, I shall return to you. I made a promise that I shall be there when our child is born and I shall move heaven and earth to keep that promise to you. I carry you in my heart and live for the day when I can again hold you in my arms.*

*Your Beloved,*

*Jonathon*

Tears spilled onto the paper blurring some of the words, and Emily quickly dried them saving the script. She looked at Andrew, smiling in gratitude.

"When did you last see him?"

"I did not. Randy gave me the letters to deliver," he answered.

"Letters?" she asked.

"Yes, I have another for David. Jonathon had some instructions for him about the plantation as well as some news about the upcoming vote in the Virginia Convention," he explained. "I had best go find him as Jonathon said it is imperative for him to read this immediately." With that he rose, hugged his sister and went in pursuit of David.

Left to herself, Emily reread the note and kissed his signature. She traced each letter that he had written knowing that her fingers touched the paper where his had rested. Knowing this made him feel closer somehow and she repeated the motion until the ink began to smudge from the oils on her fingers. Gently she folded the note and tucked it into the bodice of her gown.

• • •

Andrew found David in the stables just returning from one of the fields. His shirt clung to his back and sweat trickled down his face. Brushing his hair off his forehead, David turned and spotted Andrew.

"Good day, Andrew! What brings you to Brentwood Manor?" David greeted him.

Andrew waved and approached the man, glancing about the stables and noting two grooms tending the horses.

"Good day, David. A need to visit my sister and see how she fares brought me here today," he replied. As the two walked out of the stables, Andrew again looked around, and seeing no one, he handed the note to David.

"I have news for you from Jonathon," he said in a low voice.

"Jonathon! Good God, man, where is he?" David said in a hoarse whisper.

"I do not know where he is now; Randy gave me this note and said it was imperative that you read it at once," Andrew said.

"Well, then I shall read it immediately," David laughed and broke the seal. His smile faded as he read the missive, eyes darting to Andrew then back to the note. A frown, then a scowl crossed his face before he was able to disguise them and look back at the young man.

"What is it, David?" Andrew asked sensing the man's anger. David's face was dark and serious, but he avoided Andrew's eyes and stared at the manor house. Lost in thought for a few moments, he finally turned back to Andrew.

"There is news from the Sons of Liberty," he lied. "Jonathon said it is best if I remain at Brentwood Plantation rather than attend the planning session for the convention in Williamsburg later this week." He glanced at the manor again, and the sight of Deidre appearing on the veranda brought storm clouds to his face.

Andrew followed his gaze but with a decidedly different reaction. Ever since his encounter with her earlier in the month, Deidre's effect on him was one of bemusement and desire. She had enkindled a fire that he did not know how to satisfy. Both men stared at her for a moment, and then David turned and spoke to Andrew brusquely.

"Is it possible for you to remain at Brentwood Manor for a while?" he asked. Andrew started since his innocuous question seemed more like a challenge.

"Yes, I can. The term at William and Mary has ended for the summer, and I could easily stay here rather than in Williamsburg," he answered.

David's tone softened and he placed a hand on Andrew's shoulder, noticing for the first time how much Andrew had grown since his arrival two years ago. He was a man now, tall and strapping and handsome. David realized why Jonathon would not want Andrew to know of Deidre's threats to Emily, for Andrew would probably do her great harm.

"I could use another man around here with the British sniffing about. Thank you, Drew," he said, smiling. He clapped the young man on the back realizing that he would soon reach him in height. No, Andrew was no longer a boy.

They walked toward the manor house in silence as David wrestled with the news in Jonathon's letter. His initial reaction was to immediately dismiss Deidre from the house, but that was not his decision to make. Jonathon was the owner of Brentwood Manor, and in his absence, Emily must be consulted on all decisions. How could he justify Deidre's dismissal without revealing Jonathon's secret? It was Emily who had invited Deidre to stay after the British seized her property, therefore, he would be opposing her decision. As much as he wanted to banish Deidre from Brentwood Manor, his hands were tied.

# Chapter 5

A fierce May thunderstorm ushered in David's niece, Jennifer Sutton.

Andrew watched from a front window as her coach fought its way along the drive, battling winds that threatened to topple the covered carriage. Gusts pushed against the coach causing it to lean precariously to one side, and the horses lowered their heads and dug in their hooves in an effort to keep it upright. Slanting rain pelted the driver whose hat was shoved down to his nose in an attempt to protect his eyes. Slowing as it reached the front of the manor, the coach stopped and the driver scrambled down, opened the door and lowered the steps. A young woman emerged and gingerly stepped down from the carriage, hopping over a puddle in the drive. Andrew hurried out with a large umbrella that he quickly held above the young woman. She raised her head and looked at him with gratitude, and he felt struck by her as surely as if a British soldier had run him through with a sword. Laughing gray eyes that tilted at the corners were ensconced in thick, black lashes. Looking up at him, their owner's voice floated lightly on the sodden air, and Andrew was sure he was sheltering an angel.

"I do love a storm, but this one seems a bit vicious," she laughed.

Andrew stood stock still, captured by this vision who looked at him with a half-smile.

"Shall we go inside?" she encouraged him.

"Oh, of course," he said, regaining his senses. Offering her his arm, he led her up the steps to the front entrance of Brentwood Manor. Their shoes echoed on the marble floor of the front hall and left puddles where they stood. Andrew lowered the umbrella, unable to take his eyes off the girl. A wayward drop of rain slipped from the brim of her hat to rest on her full, soft lower lip. Andrew's knees went weak. Laughing, she brushed a gloved hand across her lips to capture the errant drop, and Andrew felt a stirring deep within that left him dizzy. Slipping off her bonnet, she shook raindrops from jet black hair curly with the humidity. Tendrils framed her face and danced across her forehead softening her heart-shaped face. She took in the foyer with its curving staircase, tall windows and stately furnishings.

"My goodness, Brentwood Manor is lovely!" she said. She turned back to him and offered her hand. "I am Jennifer Sutton, David's niece."

Andrew took her hand and began to shake it, then half-bowed awkwardly over it refraining from kissing her hand lest he lose all control. He straightened, recovering his composure, and smiled at her.

"I am Andrew Wentworth, and I do not know of a simple way to explain how I am related to David," he laughed. Their eyes held for a moment, and then each looked away and moved apart. Glancing back at her, Andrew noticed how her cinnamon-colored silk waistcoat followed the shape of her figure, the stripes in the fabric gently curving around her bosom and narrowing at her waist. The ivory lace that trimmed the bodice delicately revealed the swelling of her breasts, though not buxom, shapely. He again felt that stirring that unsettled him throughout his entire being.

Joanna entered the hall, arms outstretched.

"Jenny! You are safely arrived," she said as she wrapped the soaking girl in an embrace.

"Aunt Joanna, you will get drenched," the girl protested, laughing and trying to save her aunt.

"No matter, dear, it is worth seeing for myself that you are here and safely arrived," Joanna said. She stood back and took in the girl from head to toe.

"My goodness, Jenny, you have grown since I last saw you! Why, you are a young woman now," Joanna exclaimed.

"It has been five years since we last saw each other, Aunt Joanna, and much has happened since then," her niece replied. "Where is William? I am so excited to meet my new cousin. And where are Uncle Jonathon and his new wife?" Jenny glanced at Andrew, her eyes alight with humor. "I have met Andrew," she said.

Andrew felt a flush rise to his face unbidden as he stammered, "Yes...yes, we have met."

Emily entered, taking in the scene and subduing a smile. "You must be Jenny," she said taking the girl's hand. "I am Emily. How wonderful to have you here at Brentwood Manor."

"Thank you for allowing me to visit, Mrs. Brentwood," Jenny replied.

"Please call me Emily, for we are close in age and though not related by blood, certainly by our love for Joanna and David," Emily replied.

"When is your baby expected to arrive?" Jenny asked having noticed Emily's condition.

"In August," Emily said, smiling and unconsciously smoothing the fabric across her abdomen.

"Let me show you to your room so that you can change into some dry clothes," Joanna said. "Your trunk should be up there by now."

The three women began to climb the winding staircase as Andrew stood captivated, watching them ascend. As they disappeared along the second story corridor, he shook his head slightly as if awaking from a trance. Somehow he knew his life would never be the same.

• • •

Jenny's presence brought a sense of joy to Brentwood Manor that helped assuage the sadness of Jonathon's absence and ever-present peril. Her gentle humor and quick wit provided lively discussions

70

at supper, and her comprehension of politics surprised all. Andrew looked forward to these gatherings and his seat across the table from her provided the perfect vantage point for studying her innocuously. Captivated by her beauty, he could scarcely endure it when her face became animated as she talked. When she smiled, a dimple graced one cheek, and not having a twin on the other cheek made it maddeningly appealing. Her eyes, at first judged as gray, actually transformed to green, gray or palest blue depending on the color of her gown or riding habit. And when he was close enough to her, and able to maintain such closeness, he noticed flecks of gold that accentuated her eye color, adding depth that threatened to engulf him and that left him feeling as if his soul had been laid open.

As they sat at table on this mild May evening, Jenny informed David of recent events in the North.

"In March, Brigadier General John Thomas, under orders from General Washington, secretly led troops that moved more than a dozen cannons from Fort Ticonderoga into the fortification at Dorchester Heights. General Howe hoped to destroy them from the British fleet, but storms prevented the attack. He fled to British ships in Boston Harbor and British ships fled to Halifax. Many Loyalists followed, and patriots celebrated the victory," Jenny explained.

"I know the people of Boston have chafed at the occupation of the British for many years," David replied. "It was an outstanding victory for which I hear General Washington was awarded a medal by the Continental Congress."

"Indeed, he was," Jenny answered. "But there is still much to do. Washington hurried to New York fearing a British attack there; Loyalists are being disarmed across the colonies." Her eyes flicked to Emily who was speaking to Joanna. Deidre noticed the glance. "North Carolina has empowered its delegates to vote for independence."

"It is coming, Jenny; it is but a matter of time. We are awaiting news from France for financial support," David said.

David enjoyed supper conversations with Jenny. His brother Edward had obviously kept her informed about the political climate in Boston. In addition to her knowledge, her perceptions of the political ramifications were astute.

Andrew had been unable to contribute to the conversation due to his complete absorption in Jenny. He had mumbled a reply or affirmation now and again, but seldom followed the thread of discussion. Jenny turned her eyes, pale blue this evening to reflect her lavender gown, toward Andrew and bestowed the charming half-smile he was becoming familiar with.

"Andrew, what do you think Virginia will do?" she asked.

Andrew frantically tried to recall the most recent topic of conversation. He thought "independence" had been mentioned and summoned his courage to respond hoping he would not appear foolish. Or besotted—which he was.

"I believe Virginia will vote for independence," he stated, hoping that a firm response would conceal his confusion.

"Well said," Jenny laughed. "And, Emily, what do you think?"

Emily and Joanna had rejoined the conversation earlier, and were current on the discussion.

"Virginia will vote for independence; I have no doubt," she replied.

Jenny studied her face and believed she was being truthful. She smiled at Emily and returned her gaze to Andrew.

"I believe you promised me a game of whist this evening, Andrew. Who will join us?" she asked.

Andrew's heart skipped when she said his name. It did not help that her gaze was so direct. He smiled at her, disguising his discomposure and rose to help her with her chair.

...

Jonathon awoke to the swaying rhythm of the *Destiny*. He was aboard his ship, lying in his cabin, reclaiming his life. Each day aboard the *Destiny* was a tonic for him. Breathing deeply the sea air, he filled his lungs and felt the energy that the saltwater mist infused into his limbs. Gates had said he was astounded at his recovery knowing it was a tincture of sea air, passion for Emily and odium of Deidre that accelerated his healing. Jonathon concurred, for all three possessed him.

Rising from his bed, he smoothed the covers and donned tan breeches and a linen shirt. He shoved his feet into his boots and strode to the door tying his shirt as he went. Pain in his left thigh reminded him that the healing was not complete, but he kneaded the muscle and continued to the deck.

Men scrambled about readying the ship for departure, murmuring, "G'morning, Captain," as he passed. Looking eastward to gauge the sunrise, he spotted Gates talking to crew members across the deck. As he approached, the men smiled, tipped their caps at him and returned to their duties.

"When do we sail, Captain?" Gates asked.

"Within the hour, Gates. I want to reach New York as swiftly as possible, take care of business there and return to Virginia immediately." Jonathon leaned against the rail looking out to sea. He knew the peril of this trip, for British ships had been threatening all along the coast, and New York in particular, since they fled Boston. He stretched his shoulders and arms attempting to strengthen the muscles and flout the pain that persisted there as a result of hanging by his wrists for hours at the flogging post. He grimaced remembering his torture at the hands of the British. This revolution was as personal as patriotic for him now. With the additional revelation of Emily's treatment at the hands of Captain Walters, personal reasons had surpassed patriotic.

The thought of Emily brought the familiar anguish and desire that caught him in the gut and spread throughout his being. Remembering her body against his, the silkiness of her skin and the scent of jasmine that wafted to him when they embraced brought heat that started at his belly and threatened to embarrass if this line of thought continued. He had promised to be there when their baby was born, and he would move heaven and earth to make it so. It was early May, and their child was expected in August. He most certainly could make this trip to New York and return in adequate time to arrive at Brentwood Manor for the birth. The difficulty would be avoiding the British in the Virginia countryside.

Preparations accelerated as they readied to set sail. Jonathon was eager to be at sea again, his first voyage since the fateful one to Norfolk that almost cost his life. He loved the rolling motion beneath his feet that caused him to adjust his gait to match the *Destiny's* movements, almost like lovers moving together, coupling and undulating. At one time in his life his ship had been enough, but Emily changed all that, for nothing in his life made his heart swell to bursting as she did.

There was risk in this trip, for many British leaders such as Lord Dunmore and General Howe had fled to ships, and the British were launching attacks from their fleet. The Continental Congress had authorized privateer raids on British ships, so encountering a single ship would allow for confrontation and delay their voyage; Jonathon wanted no delays. Caution and alacrity were imperative to the safety of the *Destiny*. Clear skies promised a good sailing day, and Jonathon knew he could reach New York swiftly barring any unforeseen encounters.

• • •

Andrew brushed Neptune until he glowed, black satin in the sunlight. Jonathon's stallion stood sixteen hands and was broad across the shoulders. Andrew loved riding him, feeling the power of the horse beneath him as they galloped across the fields. In Jonathon's absence, few had been riding Neptune as he was a challenge to command, but Andrew had a way with him, and Neptune was most compliant under his rein.

They had just returned from a vigorous run, and both felt exhilarated. As Andrew groomed him, Neptune snorted in gratitude and nuzzled his cheek. Andrew whispered softly as he tended to the horse. As often happened, the image of Jenny floated into his consciousness. He thought about her waking and sleeping, and his dreams were embarrassingly vivid. He warmed at memories of her laughing across the table at supper, teasing him at a game of whist. Often his insides seemed to turn to liquid when she was near. He wondered what it would feel like to take her hand into his, or even more, to press his lips to hers.

"Whatever you are pondering, Andrew, I believe Neptune would prefer it be about his care," Deidre spoke from behind him.

Startled, he turned to face her. She stood against the sun, so he squinted and shaded his eyes with his hand. She stood arms akimbo, her eyes hooded. Lace fell low against her breasts, revealing deep décolletage, and her green silk gown was laced tightly to enhance her small waist. Still recovering from the warmth that thoughts of Jenny brought, Deidre's voluptuous form threw Andrew off balance. He stumbled back a couple of steps and then recovered.

"Forgive me, Andrew, for I did not mean to frighten you. You were so engrossed in your thoughts that I was compelled to speak," she said, her voice low and husky.

"I was just startled, Deidre; no harm done," Andrew said and resumed brushing Neptune.

Deidre approached the horse and ran her hand along its muzzle. The horse nickered and drew back.

"Such a spectacular horse," Deidre murmured stroking its flank, keeping her eyes on Andrew. "So powerful, so strong, so masculine."

"Yes, he is all of that," Andrew said, smiling at the horse and feeding it oats.

Andrew took the reins and led Neptune into the stables.

"Neptune seems to have taken a liking to you. There are few who dare to ride him, but I imagine you let him know who the master is," she said following him. Dust and bits of hay danced in the shaft of sunlight that slanted across the center walkway of the stables. They passed through it and continued to Neptune's stall at the back of the stables. Andrew led the stallion in and added fresh hay to the floor. Closing the gate to the stall, he turned, surprised to find Deidre immediately behind him. She looked up into his eyes and held him with her gaze.

"You have grown into a very handsome man since you arrived at Brentwood Manor," she purred. "I imagine Jennifer is quite attracted to you, Andrew."

At the sound of Jenny's name, Andrew felt warmth spread through him, infusing his face with scarlet. Deidre chuckled.

"Just as I thought. You are quite taken with David's niece," she said.

Andrew looked past her trying to focus on anything but the increasing arousal he felt thinking of Jenny and being so near Deidre. His jaw twitched.

"Oh, I see you do not wish to discuss it. I understand completely, Andrew. You are too much a gentleman to reveal such personal emotions," she said, her voice low and enticing. She placed her hands on his chest surprised at the muscles she felt beneath his lawn shirt. Moving closer, she rose up on tiptoe, pressed her breasts against him and whispered her next words against his ear.

"When you are ready to take her, you will want to be experienced in the art of love. I can help you with that, Andrew. You are a man, but you lack the knowledge that a man must possess. When you are ready, come to me." Sighing against his ear, her breath was hot against his skin.

A jumble of emotions took hold of him, but Andrew stood rigid and still. As Deidre backed away from him, Andrew stared straight ahead, not meeting her eyes. She patted his face, turned and walked away swaying her hips provocatively.

Andrew began to tremble and sank to his knees. His body was raging with intense emotions. Desire threatened to overcome him and he felt carried away by savage hungers. Never when he thought of Jenny were such fierce feelings involved. Passion, yes, for he longed to make love to her. But the feelings Deidre elicited in him were feral and urgent. He was aghast at her proposal, but at some animal level, he wondered if he could resist her.

# Chapter 6

Jonathon was relieved that they had encountered no British ships en route to New York. He completed the delivery of munitions and supplies to the Sons of Liberty, and met with them to coordinate information among the colonies. More and more, the call for independence from England was raised, for patriots were no longer content to allow the British to rule from afar.

Arriving at the wharf, Jonathon looked out at the *Destiny*, anchored just off shore. No matter how many times he returned to her, her beauty stuck him and pride surged within him. A three-masted merchant ship, she now sat low in the water due to heavy cannon, munitions and supplies she carried to be delivered to Virginia, but the position did not detract from her magnificence. Windows lined the raised quarterdeck and the sun sparkled off the leaded panes and glistened off the brass fittings. The bowsprit sloped gracefully up from the forecastle and the mahogany gleamed as crewmen oiled and polished the rails.

Jonathon bounded up the plank observing the neatly coiled ropes and watched his men scramble up and down the sturdy rigging. His ship ran smoothly, each man knowing his responsibility and following through, not only out of obedience to Jonathon, but out of an intrinsic sense of ownership and pride born of loyalty to Jonathon. They tipped their caps or greeted him as he strode along the deck. He felt invigorated and strong imbued with the spirit of the sea and of a just cause. Fighting and danger would increase, of that he was certain, but the patriot cause was noble and the dream of independence was becoming more a reality each day. What would that mean for them? For the future of his family?

Again his thoughts turned to Emily. How he longed to be with her and share the excitement of the life that grew within her, a result of their love. He wanted to feel the baby moving and kicking and see the joy on her face at each sensation. He wanted to hold and comfort her through the discomfort and fatigue. He wanted to lie with her at night, touching and caressing in the sleepy stillness, aware of each other's presence in their drowsiness. He wanted to look at her body in the candlelight and see how her eyes deepened to violet with her passion. How he longed for her, an aching, physical yearning. He shook his head to banish such thoughts. Right now he needed his wits about him. The trip back to Yorktown would be rife with peril.

He sought out Gates and ordered the anchor raised. The *Destiny* slipped out to sea leaving the port behind.

• • •

Evening crept across the gardens and gathered the group on the veranda into the shadows. The mild breeze brought with it the scent of the old blush roses, and the setting sun lent a rosy hue to their faces in the dusk. Relaxing after Dora's feast of shepherd's pie, freshly baked bread, and strawberry meringues, conversation was light.

Andrew had traveled to Williamsburg on business for David who had explained that the fields demanded his full attention at this time of year. Andrew had been gone for most of the week, but was now galloping up the drive at breakneck speed. David dashed to the front steps to meet him as the others followed.

"David, I have news!" he shouted.

Emily hastened out to him.

"Is it news of Jonathon?" she cried out to him.

He reined in Neptune and looked at his sister apologetically.

"I am sorry, Emily. I should have restrained my excitement in anticipation of your hope. No, it is not news of Jonathon," he said seeing her crushed look. He dismounted and turned to David.

"King Louis of France has committed one million dollars in financial support and munitions, and Spain says they will follow suit."

"My God, this could change everything," David shouted with glee, clapping Andrew on the back.

"There is more," Andrew continued. "The Continental Congress has authorized each colony to form a provincial government."

"Good God, good news," David cried. "It is becoming reality. We are indeed breaking away from England."

Emily listened, torn. In the two years since she had arrived in Virginia, she had become acutely aware of Parliament's stranglehold on the colonies, but she had been raised in England and she still loved her homeland. Her chest felt heavy at this news.

They retreated again to the veranda where Dulcie had laid out wine and brandy. A lively discussion of possibilities ensued as each tried to imagine what freedom from British rule would mean. Throughout the discussion, David studied Deidre as he had been wont to do since receiving Jonathon's letter. He had seen no indication of her ill intent toward Emily; in fact, if anything, she seemed quite solicitous toward her. He had made vague references to Joanna about the relationship between the two women, and she agreed that Deidre appeared concerned for Emily's well-being. But she had added a comment that made his neck hairs stand on end.

"But I would not trust her as far as I could toss her," his wife had added.

This evening Deidre appeared quiet, almost disconnected from the conversation flowing around her. He did notice her watching Emily often, perhaps more often than was usual. He also noticed an unusual interplay between her and Andrew. If their eyes met, she would smile but he would turn away. If she was not looking at him, he would stare at her appearing perplexed. David decided to heed his wife's counsel for all did not seem as it appeared.

• • •

Andrew's hasty return to Brentwood Manor was not solely due to the exciting news he had to impart. During his stay in Williamsburg his thoughts had continually turned to Jenny, and the image of her laughing eyes and crooked smile haunted him day and night. He had ridden Neptune hard along the roads, but the horse seemed eager to take the challenge and their flight home had been swift. Now Andrew sat across from Jenny, entranced by her every gesture. He watched the candlelight reflect golden off her face, the flame mirrored in her eyes. When she was speaking, the lilt of her voice was soft in the evening air; when she was listening, she leaned in toward the speaker, rapt and engaged. Occasionally, her glance would find Andrew, and their eyes would lock and he believed she, too, felt the expectant, hopeful recognition, understanding subconsciously that their lives were meant to intertwine, but not yet consciously aware of how this would progress. A simmering, nascent understanding of their shared destiny, pregnant with promise and nurtured by untapped passion held him. But the moment was fleeting, and their eyes would search for grounding in the ordinariness of the moment.

Something primordial happened when Andrew's eyes met Deidre's, too, but the deep emotion it evoked held neither the innocence nor the purity of the other. Deidre's eyes slid to meet his, and a small seductive smile played on her lips. She shifted her position to allow him full view of the swell of her ample breasts as she ran her hand along her thigh. Heat spread through Andrew as he recalled her offer, but the desire he felt was antithetical to the tenderness he felt for Jenny. Looking away, he strained to concentrate on the conversation.

"May I go riding tomorrow, Uncle David? I have not had an opportunity since my arrival, and the days have been so beautiful. I would love to explore Brentwood Plantation," Jenny said.

"The British still scout Brentwood property. I am not sure it would be safe for you to ride alone. I am unable to stray far from the plantation at this time," he said stealing a look at Deidre, then Andrew. "Andrew, would you escort Jenny?"

Startled, Andrew felt the heat rising from his neck to his face. He was grateful that others would not notice in the darkening evening.

"Yes, I would be happy to accompany you," he said turning to the girl. The single dimple showed in the candlelight when she smiled at him causing the already simmering heat to intensify in his gut. He swallowed.

"Thank you, Andrew. I look forward to our outing," she said.

"Mmmph," he replied unable to connect any words.

• • •

As she watched the interaction between Andrew and Jenny, Emily hid a smile at her brother's discomfort remembering the effect Jonathon's words had on her early in their relationship. Thinking of Jonathon brought a pang of loneliness that grabbed at her heart. How she missed him. She remembered the ride they took to view Brentwood lands, and how it resulted in the consummation of the love they had tried to deny for so long. Those first moments in his arms were as vivid to her now as they had been at the time. How she longed to be in his arms at this moment, skin to skin, his touch, his lips covering her body. Desire mingled with sadness as she realized that more than physical distance separated them; the future of the colonies depended on the spirit of patriots like Jonathon to leave home and families to fight against an unjust rule. While Emily understood this in her mind, her heart felt no relief from its longing for him.

• • •

Andrew strode to the stables to prepare the horses for their ride. Neptune greeted him with a nicker and nuzzled his shoulder as Andrew presented the horse a handful of oats. He helped the groom saddle Neptune and Shadow, and was just running a final check when Jenny approached.

"Good day, Andrew. Thank you for offering to escort me on our ride today," she said smiling, the single dimple launching darts through his heart.

"Good day, Jenny. We have a perfect May morning in which to ride," he replied pulling his gaze from her to study the cloudless sky. Every one of his nerves was taut with awareness of her, every sense alive with longing.

She rewarded him with a full smile, her eyes gray against her burgundy riding suit. She patted Shadow's neck and, removing her leather riding gloves, offered the horse some oats from her hand.

"You are a beauty, Shadow. Thank you for allowing me to ride you today," she murmured against the horse's muzzle.

Andrew helped her mount and was greeted with the soft scent of lilac. Unconsciously, he breathed deeper urging the scent into his being. When Jenny was settled into the saddle, he mounted Neptune and urged the horse into the drive. They cantered along the road, and Jenny's expert horsemanship was evident immediately. Smiling a challenge at her, he broke into a gallop and she laughed and followed suit.

They flew through the countryside relishing the feel of the wind, savoring the beauty of a verdant May morning. Jenny kept pace with no trouble, and Andrew was impressed with her riding acumen. After a while Andrew slowed Neptune to a walk, and Jenny reigned in Shadow.

"Well, I do not know how much of the scenery I have observed, but I did enjoy that ride," Jenny laughed. "I believe that was a test of skill, Andrew. How did I fare?"

Andrew laughed with her. "Quite well, Jenny. I sensed that you would have no problem even keeping up with Neptune."

"Will there be other tests that I must prepare for, Andrew? What else do you wish to know about me?" she teased.

Andrew blushed scarlet, and Jenny pretended to be enrapt in viewing the field of daisies that lay ahead of them. She urged Shadow to a trot and Neptune pursued her. They crossed fields and meandered through forests until the sun had reached its peak. They rode toward the shade of a copse of trees to enjoy the meal Dora had prepared. Usually anxious to savor Dora's cooking, Andrew noted a distinct lack of appetite, replaced instead with a swarm of butterflies in his stomach. Dismounting, he then stepped to Shadow to assist Jenny. As she bent to his reaching arms, he again caught the scent of lilac and breathed it in as he helped her from the horse. With his arms still at her waist, he set her on the ground and looked into her eyes. All sensations halted as they looked at each other. Jenny's eyes held none of the teasing humor he usually detected, but rather a simmering longing that echoed in his own. Suddenly Deidre's words drifted through his mind, *you lack the knowledge that a man must possess.* And he released her.

Birdsong resumed as they backed away from each other in the embarrassment that comes when hidden feelings have been exposed. Andrew coughed and Jenny brushed her skirts and turned away.

"I'll get the saddlebags if you would like to spread out the blanket," he said.

Shaking out the blanket, Jenny allowed it to drift, open, to the ground. Andrew brought the saddlebags and laid out sausages, cheeses, wine and fruit. As usual, Dora had outdone herself and there was an abundance of food. They piled food on plates, poured the wine and settled in for a feast. Propped up on one elbow, Andrew lay across one edge of the blanket and began to eat. Something about the sight and smell of Dora's cooking dispelled any lack of appetite he had experienced earlier. Jenny sat across from him with her feet tucked beneath her.

"Tell me about Boston," Andrew said.

"Boston is an exciting city, Andrew. Shops of every description line busy streets, and at one time they were filled with goods from England and Europe. The *Boston Gazette* informs everyone about events in these troubled times, and we have seen our share of fighting. Ever since the massacre, we have had British soldiers walking our streets, and tensions are higher than ever. But I love Boston, and I shall return when Father believes it is safe," she said.

"I imagine it is difficult to be away from your family and friends," Andrew said.

"Yes," Jenny replied spreading honey across a biscuit. Andrew watched her intently, captivated by how small and slender her hands were and how gracefully she performed even such an ordinary task as that. He looked up and met her eyes.

"Do you have any *special* friends?" he asked feigning innocence.

Jenny cocked her head and looked at him for a moment as if trying to come to a decision. Finally, she gave him her half-smile and said, "Oh yes."

Andrew's face fell. "I see."

"Let me see, there is my dearest friend Amy, my cousin Charlotte, whom I count as a bosom friend, and then my lifelong neighbor, Mary." She hid a smile.

Andrew looked at her closely and sensed her mirth.

"I am not very practiced at subtlety, Jenny," he confessed. She smiled and patted his hand.

"If you mean do I have a beau, no, Andrew, no one has captured my heart…" she paused.

Andrew blushed and hated himself for it. Looking up, he saw tender humor in her eyes, not mockery.

"I am so glad you have come to Brentwood Manor, Jenny," he said.

"I am very glad, too, Andrew," she whispered.

He reached across and took her hand, glancing at her for acquiescence. She smiled and squeezed his hand.

"You are a mystery to me, Jenny. You bring about sensations I have never experienced before. When you enter a room, it is as if the sun entered with you. When you laugh, it is as though angels sing. I am befuddled by the feelings that somersault through me when we touch like this." He stopped. "But I confess too much. I am not learned in the ways of wooing, but, Jenny, I seem unable to stop these words from tumbling out." He dropped her hand and rose. "I suspect David would frown on my frankness, especially since we are unchaperoned."

Jenny rose and stood before him, the breeze catching errant strands of ebony hair and tossing them around her face. Her eyes shone with happiness and her lilac scent made Andrew dizzy. She reached out and again took his hand.

"Andrew, I am honored that you trust me enough to bare your feelings. You have a similar effect on me, and I am often at a loss when you are near."

"You never seem wanting for conversation, and you listen to others with such focus and intensity," Andrew replied.

"Yes, often I pretend quite well when all the while, I am conscious only of where you sit or how you move. Gracious, this is unseemly of me, but I have never felt so free with anyone before," Jenny said looking at the ground.

They stood together, hands clasped. Slowly, Jenny raised her eyes to his, and unable to resist any longer, Andrew bent and slowly brushed his lips across hers. Fire spread through him at the taste of her, and desire spread through his body. His arms went around her tiny waist and he drew her toward him. Jenny's arms encircled his neck as her lips moved against his. Feeling her soft curves against his body inflamed him even more. Moving instinctively, he parted his lips and gently passed his tongue along her lips, which parted as she answered with hers. Deidre's voice shot through his head again, and he abruptly backed away. Jenny, caught off balance, swayed and stepped back.

"What is it, Andrew?" she asked.

"I do not...I do not..." he stammered suddenly feeling unsure of himself. "I think we had best start back to the manor," he said in a hoarse voice. He felt confused. No, he did not have the experience of which Deidre spoke, but never had he felt as confident as when he was holding Jenny in his arms a moment ago. He had felt as though he could conquer the world. So why did Deidre's voice haunt him, stripping him of all self-assurance?

"Jenny—I," he started.

"Dismiss it from your mind, Andrew," Jenny snapped. "Perhaps I am not as desirable as your Williamsburg women."

"No, Jenny, that is not it. I mean, there are no—Jenny I just need time," Andrew said.

"Time for what, Andrew? Time to decide whether I am good enough for you? Time to decide whether you might have a more alluring alternative?" Jenny slammed the remnants of their meal into the saddlebags.

"No, Jenny. None of those things. Time to—never mind," he shot back. Grabbing the blanket he wadded it up and flung it over his saddle. How could he explain to her the doubts that Deidre had raised in him?

Jenny mounted Shadow without his assistance and galloped off the way they had come. Swearing, Andrew launched himself onto Neptune and pursued her, barely catching up. They flew across the landscape, each fighting voices that railed in their heads, fears that railed in their hearts.

• • •

Deidre sat on the terrace watching the two riders approach the stables. Judging by their speed, they were anxious to return to Brentwood Manor for it was not the leisurely pace of lovers reluctantly returning from a tryst. She observed that Jenny did not wait for Andrew to assist her dismount, as a smitten girl would do, yearning for any chance of touch. Instead, she led Shadow to the stables without even a glance in Andrew's direction. He, in turn, dismounted quickly and followed her several paces behind.

Smiling to herself, Deidre was sure that the seeds she had planted in Andrew's mind had taken root and were sprouting. It would be quite simple to take that boy, she imagined, for he had lost all self-confidence in his abilities as a lover. But she would train him, coach him, have him and then crush him. And then she would gloat in watching Emily's horror when all of it was revealed. And was that not her goal? To hurt Emily in any way possible?

But she must take care, for her ultimate plan must be in place before she seduced Andrew.

• • •

Jenny flung herself across her bed at last releasing the tears that had been threatening all the way back to the manor. She would not let Andrew see her cry! Gracious! What magic had this man wrought upon her? Used to being self-assured, skilled in conversation, gifted with intelligence, and aware of her effect on the opposite sex, all of this confidence had flown out the window around Andrew. In his presence, she had to focus all of her concentration on the conversation at hand lest she stare at him, a gaping fool.

Oh, how she warmed at his touch. She brushed her fingers across her lips, still burning with his kiss. Closing her eyes she pictured him bending toward her, every nerve in her being crying out for his touch. She remembered how it felt to be against his body, strong and muscled, and yes, obviously desiring her.

But what had happened? Why did he pull away? Did her kiss displease him so? Was there another who had already captured his heart? It was obvious he did not want her. Never one to suffer from insecurity, Jenny found herself wondering if she were desirable enough. She rose from the bed and sat before her mirror. Eyes brightened by tears gazed back at her, gray and cloudy in their sadness. Her mouth turned down with her despondency, hiding the dimple that usually signaled her mirth. Pallid and wan, her skin lacked its usual rosy glow. This was no encouragement for her, neither was her lack of vibrancy.

She returned to the bed, crawling under the counterpane. Yielding again to her tears, she cried herself into a deep, but restless sleep.

• • •

Andrew stirred from the chair in his room when he heard the supper bell. How he dreaded facing Jenny across the table tonight. Perhaps he should visit her room and talk to her there. Oh, he had really muddled things today, all because of his damned insecurity. But what if Deidre were right; what if he should bumble his way along and make a fool of himself? Beautiful and intelligent, Jenny deserved a man of equal measure. Andrew did not feel he measured up, especially in the art of love, having had no experience there.

Pacing, he recalled the sensation of her body pressed to his, her lips against his and responding with desire. She seemed to want him as he wanted her. Damn! It was he who complicated the moment. Perhaps Deidre was right. She could coach him in the art of loving a woman. No! What was he thinking? He wanted no woman but Jenny. If it meant he appeared a bumbling fool, so be it. Resolved that he would be hers alone, he pulled a brush through his hair, straightened his cravat, smoothed his jacket and went downstairs to the dining room. But disappointment followed disappointment for Jenny was not there.

Andrew greeted Emily, Joanna and David as he took his seat. He glanced at Jenny's empty place.

"How was your ride this afternoon, Drew?" David asked.

"Fine," Andrew answered as Deidre entered the room. Looking up, he saw her watching him as she made her way to her chair; he looked away.

"The weather was perfect for a ride," Emily said.

"Yes," Andrew answered noncommittally. Emily and Joanna exchanged a look. Andrew glanced at Jenny's empty chair.

"Jenny was not feeling well enough to come down for supper. She has a headache," Joanna explained.

"Oh," Andrew replied staring at his plate. Deidre hid a smile as she took a sip of water.

"Well, uh, shall we say grace?" David suggested.

All bowed their heads as David led the brief prayer. Throughout the meal, conversation centered on plantation business and speculation about Jonathon's whereabouts. Andrew played with the food on his plate and excused himself early.

Silence followed him as he left the room, but he did not notice. His thoughts were full of Jenny.

# Chapter 7

Jonathon felt the yearning to return to Virginia as profoundly he felt the surge of the sea beneath the *Destiny*. Somehow he would discover a way to return to Brentwood Manor, for he could no longer bear to be parted from Emily. Calling for full sails, he sent men scrambling up the riggings to ensure their fastest speed. Gates watched him with amusement tinged with caution for he knew how deep Jonathon's passion for Emily was, and he knew the many obstacles they had overcome thus far.

"The wind is teasing us, Gates. One minute a gale from the west, the next a zephyr from the south," Jonathon groused. He was in ill temper today as the early June winds seemed to play tricks.

"We are ahead of schedule, Captain. We should arrive in Yorktown within the week," Gates replied grinning. "If the winds had the power of your lust, perhaps we would be there this evening," he teased since no crewmen were within earshot. "In any event, Captain, what can you do once we reach port? It is far too dangerous for you to return to Brentwood Manor, and Mrs. Brentwood should not travel all that way to see you."

"I will find a way, Gates. I must return to her. Besides, I promised I would be there for the birth of our child, and I hold that as a sacred vow."

"Your child is not due to arrive for two months, Captain. We will probably be called upon to sail again before that. It would be impossible for you to make such a dangerous journey and return to—,"

"I will find a way," Jonathon avowed, his eyes flashing.

"Aye, Captain," Gates replied, tipping his cap. Jonathon watched his friend stroll away and regretted the harshness that he had used with him. He turned and looked out to sea. The churning water mirrored his emotions. Gripping the rail, he cast his mind back to the last time he held Emily, watched her tease him, felt the silkiness of her skin. He burned to know that she was safe and that their baby was well. Despite Deidre's promise, he didn't trust her for a minute; the look in her eye was unlike any he had seen before. The memory of their encounter caused his stomach to turn over and the blood to run cold in his veins. Squeezing his eyes shut he rubbed them and shook his head to rid his mind of that memory, but he knew it was useless. It came to him in the darkness of the night bringing shame and regret. But what could he have done? He was convinced that had he refused Deidre, she would have harmed Emily and their child.

"Blasted witch!" he cursed into the wind. He had to see for himself that they were safe and in no danger from Deidre's jealous scheming.

• • •

As the morning sun streamed in, Emily sat beside the window embroidering the edge of her baby's gown. The crisp linen felt cool against her fingers, and the needle slid smoothly through the fabric. Soon she would put this very garment on her child, hold him in her arms and kiss his sweet face. Would she have a boy or a girl? She vacillated from day to day believing the child to be one sex one day and the opposite the next. While she dreamed of a son who would resemble Jonathon with warm brown eyes and thick brown hair, she also dreamed of a petite girl, perhaps with blue eyes and tawny hair like her own. She loved playing with Will and laughed at his boyish rough-housing, delighting in his imagination that turned every object into a toy drum. But a girl would be gentle and long for poppets. While Will allowed cuddling as he drifted off to sleep, usually he wished to be exploring and running. Perhaps a girl would allow more cossetting, which Emily would love as much. Sighing, she gazed out the window knowing that it mattered not the sex of the child; she would love the baby utterly. This child was a part of Jonathon and a product of their loving. Glancing down at her rounded middle, she smiled and ran her hand along the curve of her belly.

The parlor door opened and Andrew entered. Seeing that Emily was alone, he crossed over to her, bent to kiss her forehead and sat beside her.

"Emily, may I ask you something?" he said softly.

"Of course, Andrew."

"Emily, when you and Jonathon discovered your feelings for one another—that is when you knew you were special to each other—what I mean to say is…" he paused.

Emily waited and took his hand in hers.

"Andrew, I love you, and I long to help you in any way I can. You can trust me to keep a confidence and to withhold judgment of any kind," she said, smiling at her younger brother.

"Em, Jonathon was quite a bit older than you, and he had experienced many…um…experiences in his life before he met you. He knew things that…uh, you perhaps did not know yet…" his voice trailed off.

His meaning began to dawn on Emily. Of course, Andrew did not have the benefit of his father's advice about matters of the heart, for he had been only fifteen when George Wentworth died at sea. Jonathon was not here to mentor him in the art of wooing at a time when the attraction between Andrew and Jenny was obvious to all, and since David was Jenny's uncle, it would be unseemly to ask his counsel. Emily smiled and patted his hand.

"Is this about Jenny?" she asked.

Andrew blushed furiously and nodded.

"How can I help?" Emily asked.

"Em, I do not have any…well, experience in courting a woman. I do not know even where to begin. How do I—that is, where do I—I mean to say…" his voice trailed off.

"Andrew, when two people care for each other, they often travel this journey of discovery together," Emily said.

"Is that how it was for you and Jonathon?" he asked.

It was Emily's turn to blush as she recalled how skillful a lover Jonathon was from the beginning of their relationship. Andrew dropped her hand.

"I see," he said.

"But, Drew, had I married Michael Dennings, it would have been so!"

"But you did not marry Michael. You chose Jonathon over him," Andrew said looking at the floor.

"Because I did not love Michael, not because he lacked experience," she countered.

"But you hated Jonathon when you refused Michael's proposal," he exclaimed.

Emily smiled wryly. "Well, I was trying to convince myself of that, Drew, but I think I fell in love with Jonathon the first night I met him." She took his hand again and turned his face to hers. "And I knew nothing about his experience or lack thereof at the time." She smiled at him. "Do not risk love because of self-doubts, Andrew. Finding love is worth any humbling incident that may occur. Believe me, I know!"

Andrew's face brightened. "Thank you, Em. Your counsel is sound and I shall take it to heart."

As he kissed her cheek, the door opened and Deidre entered. Her turquoise gown heightened the golden shades of her hair. Her skin seemed translucent against the lace trim that followed her neckline plunging deeply to reveal the swell of her breasts.

"Good day," she said brightly.

"Good day, Deidre," Emily answered.

Andrew mumbled a reply and stood to leave.

"Stay, Andrew, I do not mean to shorten your visit with your sister," Deidre said walking to him and taking his hand. Her touch sent a charge up his arm and into his gut and her breathing affected the rise and fall of her breasts. Wanting to retain her touch, yet despising it, he stood transfixed, dizzy from her scent of musk.

"Andrew, I believe David is looking for you; he is in the back of the manor right now," Emily said returning him to reality, wondering at his discomfort. "He wants you to run an errand for him today. Perhaps you should go talk with him."

"Thank you, Emily," he said. "Good day, Deidre," he said bowing slightly.

Emily looked at Deidre curious at her slight smile as she watched Andrew leave the parlor. Joanna's warnings about Deidre came to mind.

"I see you are making progress on the gown's trim," Deidre said.

"Yes, it is coming along nicely," Emily replied, smiling as she held it up for inspection.

Deidre smiled sweetly and then looked out the window. She sat beside Emily on the settee.

"Have you heard any news of Jonathon?" she asked.

"No," Emily said trying to concentrate on the garment to keep her mind off her longing for Jonathon.

"Do you not wonder every day, every minute about him?" Deidre cried.

"Of course I do, Deidre," Emily said turning to the woman.

Deidre looked at the garment in Emily's hand then at her eyes.

"Should you not be doing something to help your husband? Should you not send someone to find him and bring him to safety? What are you doing to help him, Emily?" she demanded as she clasped Emily's hands.

"I—ow!" Emily cried out. "Oh my goodness, I have stuck my finger. I must not get any blood on the baby's gown!"

Deidre sneered at the distraught woman, her sneer quickly transforming to a look of concern when Emily looked up.

"Oh, let me help you, Emily," she said taking the gown from her. Reaching into her bodice, she brought out a handkerchief and bound Emily's bleeding finger. She pressed the cloth against the wound.

"That will staunch the bleeding and keep it from staining the gown," Deidre explained.

"Thank you Deidre," Emily said.

"Let me get you a glass of wine, Emily. You look pale," Deidre said. She walked over to the side table and, with her back to Emily, poured the wine. Bringing the glass to Emily, she watched her drink it. "Oh look, you did get blood on your own gown, Emily. You must go and change."

"Yes, yes, of course," Emily replied. The room seemed suddenly very warm, and dizziness overtook her making her swoon. Deidre rushed to her side, grabbing her arm to support her.

"What is it, Emily?" she cried out.

"I—I feel so faint," Emily quivered.

"Let me help you to your room," Deidre offered leading her to the door of the parlor.

Emily stumbled through the door and into the hallway. The staircase was swimming before her, undulating and swaying. They reached the staircase and began to climb.

"There, Emily, I have you; lean on me," Deidre reassured her.

Emily's head felt heavy and though she tried to respond, she was unable to speak. Losing her balance, she lunged and grabbed for the step ahead of her. She felt Deidre's grip tighten and the woman pulled her forward up the stairs.

Emily's mind kept echoing, *I feel so dizzy,* but she could not say a word. She leaned against Deidre, grateful for the woman's support.

"Just a bit further, Emily. We have almost reached the top. We need to get to the top," Deidre said. She hefted Emily up, feeling her weight become heavier as she began to lose consciousness. "A few more steps…"

At that moment Andrew and David appeared in the hall below them. Looking up, David halted.

"What is this?" he shouted as he took the steps two at a time. Andrew stood below staring up at the women, trying to make sense of the scene.

David reached the women and gently took Emily from Deidre lifting her in his arms. He glared at Deidre and demanded again.

"What is this?"

Deidre stepped back as if slapped, her eyes bright and wide. Looking at David and then at Emily, she began to cry.

"Emily pricked her finger as she was embroidering the baby's gown. Some blood fell on her dress, and she was coming upstairs to change. I believe the sight of the blood made her faint. I was helping her to her room," Deidre said.

Andrew had reached the top of the staircase by now and was softly talking to his sister who was unable to respond.

David moved Emily away from Deidre and looked at Andrew.

"We will take her to her room. Thank you, Deidre," David said, dismissing the woman.

Deidre pulled herself up, raising her chin, her eyes glittering. She looked at Andrew who appeared confused at this confrontation. With a swirl of skirts, she turned and retired to her own room.

"Andrew, let us get her to bed quickly. Then we must send for Dr. Anderson," David said.

"But, David, why? Deidre said she fainted at the sight of her own blood. Surely she will revive momentarily…" Andrew replied.

"Look at her, Andrew! Does she look as if she is going to revive?" David demanded. He carried Emily to her bedroom and gently laid her on the bed.

Just then, Joanna entered. Seeing Emily's ashen face and limp form, she rushed to her bed.

"David, what happened? What is wrong with Emily?" she cried out. She looked from Emily to her husband whose mouth was set in a grim line. He stared at Emily for a moment and then glanced at Andrew's serious face. Emily stirred and opened her eyes.

"What happened?" she whispered. Joanna sat beside her on the bed and Andrew stepped over to stand beside her. Joanna brushed her hair off of her forehead and smiled.

"You had a bit of a fainting spell, Emily," she said.

"I was in the parlor..." Emily said.

"What happened in the parlor, Emily?" David asked quietly.

She looked over at him and frowned, trying to remember.

"Oh, I was embroidering the border on the baby's gown, and I pricked my finger. Oh dear, some blood fell on my dress," she said trying to sit up and find the stain. Joanna gently pushed her back down.

"Just rest, Em," she said.

"Deidre was with me, yes, she got me a handkerchief to stem the blood so it did not soil the gown. Then she poured me some wine because I felt dizzy..." her voice trailed off.

David's eyes met Joanna's, but Andrew was focused only on his sister. He took her hand and smiled at her.

"You need to rest, Emily. We shall send for Dr. Anderson to check you over and make sure everything is all right," David said.

"I shall stay with Emily, dear," Joanna said smiling at her husband. "Perhaps you and Andrew can send someone for the doctor."

"Yes, that would be fine," he replied.

The two men left the room, and Joanna covered Emily with a light shawl. Emily's eyes were heavy, and soon she was dozing. Joanna stared at her sister-in-law whose lashes lay dark against her ashen face. Her breathing was even, and she seemed to be sleeping peacefully. Joanna lifted her hand and turned it over. There on her finger was a mark where she had stuck herself. Emily's embroidery skills were far above her own; how strange that this mishap had occurred. Joanna's suspicion grew, and she thought of the look on David's face. She knew her husband well enough to recognize he had been holding in some strong emotion. Initially, she believed it was concern for Emily, but that assumption was beginning to change. She thought about Deidre who had been a part of their lives since childhood. Their families had been close, socializing and supporting each other over the years. At one time, Deidre was Joanna's dearest friend, but as they grew older, they drifted apart. Yet, Deidre had always seemed like a family member, and Joanna assumed, as did most, that Jonathon would marry her one day. Something changed in Deidre after her father forced her to marry Robert Manning—a hardness, sharp-edged and cutting came over her. Joanna remembered a sense of foreboding the night Deidre arrived at Brentwood Manor asking for help, and she wished that Emily had never allowed the woman to move in. A chill went through her and she pulled the shawl up around Emily's shoulders.

. . .

Deidre's slippers beat a hard rhythm against the floor of her room as she paced. She dug her nails into her palms in an effort to contain a scream of frustration. How close she had been to eliminating what was standing in her way of happiness with Jonathon. If only David and Andrew had not appeared at that moment. It would have appeared as if Emily had simply fainted at the top of the stairs and tumbled to her death…and the death of her child. Deidre pounded her fists into her thighs as she walked. So close, so close.

Next time she would not fail.

. . .

Jonathon kicked the horse's flanks urging it to accelerate. The mount was no match for Neptune, and Jonathon fought the desire to whip it into compliance. In the distance, he heard horses behind him closing fast, and his heart sank as he heard the baying of hounds. Heart racing, he zigzagged through the woods trying to throw the dogs off his scent. Dusk was falling, and trees became shadowy forms reaching out to claw him from the horse, but he was on Brentwood Plantation now, familiar with the lay of the land. He continued calling commands to the horse, galloping through the wooded property he had known all his life.

The hoof beats were drawing closer and he cursed and reined in his horse. Jumping down, he wrapped his jacket around the saddle horn and slapped the horse's flanks. As the horse took off in a northerly direction, he slipped into the shadows heading south. Running through the woods, he was rewarded when he smelled the fecund swamp. Branches slapped at him as he broke through the underbrush and heard his feet hit the water. His pursuers were growing closer, and sweat broke out on his upper lip as he searched for what he needed. Darkness had fallen, and the moon was still low in the sky. Using his hands he reached out feeling his way until he felt a stand of reeds. He took out his knife and slashed one of the sturdier reeds and waded farther out in the water. Closer and closer he heard the yelping of the dogs, intent on finding their quarry. Sticking the reed in his mouth he sank into the water completely submersing himself and breathing through the stalk. He forced himself to remain calm and breathe through the stem, not stirring the water, not making a sound.

Racing up to the pond, the dogs started to whine, trotting back and forth along the water's edge. The riders reached the water and dismounted. Cursing, they walked along the perimeter stabbing into the water with their bayonets. They stepped into the water just yards from where Jonathon lay hidden. *Steady* he thought to himself. *Just breathe.* The soldiers' feet were coming closer, their bayonets getting more forceful with their frustration. Jonathon winced as one blade rippled the water around his head. Suddenly, they turned and waded to dry ground. Through the water he heard the muffled voice of one soldier call out.

Feet tromped out of the pond and in a few moments, the sound of hoof beats started up and faded away. Jonathon waited a full ten minutes to ensure it was not a trap, and then slowly began to rise out of the water. Still he waited, sitting in the fetid water, listening for any incongruity in the night sounds. Finally, satisfied, he rose to his feet and sloshed to dry land.

He shivered despite the mild June night, more from relief of escaping certain capture than from cold. He turned toward the manor and began his trek through the Brentwood forests.

• • •

Emily slowly woke and gazed, bewildered, around the room. How did she get here, and why was she napping in the middle of the day? Lids heavy, she succumbed to the tug of drowsing, aware that her limbs felt thick and cumbersome. Confusion held her and she struggled to open her eyes again, struggled to make sense of her lethargy.

"Mrs. Brentwood, are you awake?"

Emily turned toward the voice of Dr. Anderson, her confusion deepening. She gasped and dropped her hands to her abdomen, fear overtaking her.

"Your baby is fine, Mrs. Brentwood," the doctor said patting her hand. As if to confirm this diagnosis, the baby gave a hearty kick. Emily smiled in relief.

"What happened; why are you here, Dr. Anderson?" Emily asked.

Joanna approached the bed and sat beside her sister-in-law. Emily tried to assess the look that passed between the two. Joanna took her hand and held it lightly.

"You had a fainting spell, Emily. We were concerned and sent for Dr. Anderson," Joanna said.

Emily fought the fogginess that trapped her mind trying to recall what happened.

"I was in the parlor, with Deidre…" she mumbled. She felt Joanna's grip tighten at her words. "I think I pricked my finger, and Deidre wrapped it for me so I would not stain the baby's garment." She held up her hand and examined her finger as if to substantiate it for herself. "I cannot remember anything after that."

Dr. Anderson felt her forehead and checked her pulse.

"You just need to rest for a while, Mrs. Brentwood," he said gently. "It would also be beneficial for you to eat a hearty meal," he winked at Joanna.

Emily's bewilderment grew at the apparent relief they communicated to one another, but her muddled mind prevented her from concentrating enough to make sense of their behavior. She closed her eyes, sighing. As if from a distance, she heard their conversation.

"Will she be all right, Dr. Anderson?"

"Yes, she and the baby were not in serious harm from what appears to have been a sleeping draught. How did this happen, Mrs. Sutton?"

"We are exploring that question, Doctor." Joanna's voice sounded harsher than Emily had ever heard before.

"The effects of the sleeping draught should be wearing off, but it will be gradual. Encourage Mrs. Brentwood to eat and, when she is steady on her feet, to walk a bit. That may help dissipate the drowsiness more rapidly."

Their voices drifted away as Emily sank into sleep once more.

• • •

Quiet sounds that usher in summer evenings surrounded Brentwood Manor. Cicadas rhythmically predicted a warm tomorrow, workers returned to the outbuildings to replace implements and have supper, and leaves rustled in the soft breeze. The peacefulness that enveloped the exterior of Brentwood Manor belied the tension within. Like a rope held taut to fraying, the group gathered in the parlor barely contained the brittle anger beneath their civility and effort to protect Emily.

Still groggy and bewildered, Emily sat propped on the settee with her feet resting on a footstool. She watched David pace the length of the parlor, hands behind his back, scowling. Joanna watched him, a crease between her brows. Her hands were idle, leaving the embroidery in her lap untouched.

"David, I think we should…" Joanna began.

"No, Joanna, not yet," he cut her off, looking at Emily. He went to her and knelt beside the settee. "How are you feeling, Emily? How is the child?" he asked gently.

"I still feel a bit tired, and my brain is full of cotton. My baby has been quiet, but as is often the case, seems livelier as the day winds down," Emily replied with a smile.

David squeezed her hand and rose. Resuming his pacing, he seemed lost in thought.

Emily looked at Joanna. As muddled as her thoughts were, her mind was clearing enough to realize that something was amiss. And the time it was taking to recover convinced her that this had been no ordinary fainting spell. With the supper she had eaten, and the short stroll, leaning heavily on David's arm, her senses were returning and with them, suspicion. Sitting up and pushing the footstool aside, she spoke convincingly.

"I believe it is time for you to be truthful with me."

David looked at Emily, then Joanna, who nodded. He again approached the settee and knelt beside Emily taking her hands.

"Emily, we are not certain of what transpired today. Dr. Anderson believes you ingested a sleeping draught. We are trying to sort out why and how you were given it." Trying not to alarm her, he looked to Joanna for help.

"Emily, do you remember what occurred when you and Deidre were talking this morning?" she asked.

Emily cast her mind back to the ordinary encounter with Deidre. Vague images emerged, but nothing extraordinary had happened.

"I was embroidering a gown, Deidre came in and we were talking. Oh! I pricked my finger, and she kindly wrapped it in her handkerchief so I would not soil the gown. And wine, she gave me a glass of wine…" her voice trailed off as the images disappeared.

"I was attempting to help Emily, David. Just what are you implying?"

Golden hair loose and flowing, eyes flaming with indignation, Deidre stood at the door of the parlor.

• • •

Perched above the trees, the waxing moon lent a silvery glow to the forest. With the aid of this light and his own cherished memories of the land, Jonathon navigated smoothly through the trees. Animals scrambled through the undergrowth, and the mournful call of an owl eerily echoed on the night breeze. Jonathon was oblivious to all of this, his heart beating a tattoo of home and Emily.

In the weeks of sailing to New York and back his physical health had improved rapidly, but the gnawing guilt of his encounter with Deidre incessantly ate at his gut. Long conversations with Gates had helped assuage the shame he felt, but imagining Emily seeing the proof of his infidelity scratched across his chest thrust him back into despair. Despite his trepidation, the unremitting longing to be with his wife drove him on. He would face the consequences of his actions and beg her forgiveness. If it meant spending the remainder of his life somehow atoning for this, he would do it. He would do anything for his beloved.

Spurred on by thoughts of seeing Emily, Jonathon persisted on his journey. He had scrabbled together meals from berries, roots and fruit he found along the way. Fleeing from the British guard that had pursued him the previous night had sapped his strength, and the little food he had scavenged barely sated his hunger; it was his determination to see Emily and know that she and their baby were well that drove him on.

His clothes were still damp from his swim that afternoon. After hiding in the swamp, he could barely stand his own reeking smell, and he had deliberately taken the route past the Manning Manor so he could wash in the river. Standing at the bank, he had felt loath to dive in knowing that nearby Robert Manning had been murdered by Deidre. The odor he emitted had overcome his reluctance, and he had surrendered to the cool waters, emerging refreshed.

His heart pounded as he climbed a knoll and caught his first view of Brentwood Manor. Candlelight softly glowed from many of the windows, and the familiar sounds of days-end floated up to him on the evening air. Soon he would see Emily; soon he would beg her forgiveness.

• • •

As if frozen in time, the scene in the parlor hung suspended. Each person grappled with emotions that threatened to explode. Deidre stood with her hands on her hips, chin lifted, eyes defiant.

David rose and stood in front of Emily as if to protect her.

"You have not even bothered to listen to my account, David. You have not even bothered to ask it," Deidre said.

"I think I know your explanation, Deidre," he snarled.

Deidre sauntered into the room looking at each in turn.

"So quick to judge, so misguided," she said over her shoulder as she poured a glass of brandy.

David clenched and unclenched his fists. His knowledge of what had transpired between Deidre and Jonathon gave him a very clear picture of Deidre's intentions, but to reveal that would betray Jonathon. Jonathon's deepest wish was that Emily never discover that he had lain with Deidre.

Deidre half-turned and slid her eyes over David, then turned to them all.

"I was trying to help Emily," she stated.

David snorted and Joanna looked at him, brow furrowed.

"She has not been sleeping and I feared her health and the health of her baby would suffer. I thought if she had something to relax her, she would finally get some much needed rest." She crossed the room toward the settee, but David would not move away from Emily.

"Deidre, you must leave Brentwood Manor," David said flatly.

Deidre stepped back as if struck. Emily's head was spinning; none of this made any sense to her.

The silence in the room was broken when the terrace door opened and Jonathon stepped in.

"Jonathon!" Emily cried struggling to get up from the settee.

He rushed to his wife, kneeling beside her and gathering her into his arms. Burying his head into her hair he fought back sobs that pushed to the surface.

"My love, my love," he repeated against her cheek.

"You are trembling, Jonathon! David, pour him some brandy, please!"

David had already poured a glass and was bringing it to him. Joanna knelt beside her brother, crying and laughing at the same time. Only Deidre stood off to the side taking in the scene.

Jonathon covered Emily's face with kisses, and she returned them, tears of joy streaming down her face. Emily's hands swept over his back, his shoulders, pulling him closer, unable to satisfy her need to hold him. Jonathon wept into her neck, embarrassed by his tears yet unable to stop them.

Finally, releasing their embrace, they drank each other in with their eyes, laughing and crying and touching. Jonathon sat back on his heels and took in Emily's form. His hands stroked her abdomen and the baby gave a hearty kick. His eyes held hers in a gaze of pure joy. He threw his head back and laughed.

"Our baby!" he chortled. "Our baby just greeted his father."

Emily's eyes shone with happiness and tears. She could not believe her beloved was right before her. She leaned forward and pulled him into an embrace. Jonathon held her, but when she turned to kiss him full on the mouth, he pulled back and looked away feeling unworthy of the boundless love she offered. Shame stabbed at his heart as he realized that, finally, he must confess to her. She looked at him quizzically, and he stood.

"Jonathon, it is too dangerous for you to be here," David said. "British troops have been patrolling Brentwood land for weeks looking for you."

"I had to come back. Emily, I had to see you, to know you were all right…" his voice trailed off as he noticed Deidre standing nearby.

"Jonathon, your return is perfectly timed. Something has occurred that has been terribly misconstrued," Deidre said, her eyes soft and pleading.

"Nothing has been misconstrued, Deidre, and you know it," David countered.

Emily listened to this exchange trying to comprehend it, her mind still muddled. Why was David so angry at Deidre? Awareness dawned on Emily, and her bewildered expression turned to anger as she looked at Deidre.

"What is going on?" Jonathon asked stepping toward Deidre.

David recounted the events of that morning, and as he listened, a knot tightened in Jonathon's stomach. He knew full well what Deidre was capable of, and had no doubt that David's version was the truth.

"I just explained that I was trying to help Emily..." Deidre began, but David cut her off.

"Save it, Deidre. Jonathon, I just told her that she had to leave Brentwood Manor. I defer that decision to you, however, since you are here."

Jonathon trembled with rage. Even though she had promised, her intent had been to harm, no kill, Emily and their child all along. He fought the urge to strike her, clenching his fists at his side.

"David is correct, Deidre. Gather your things; you will leave Brentwood Manor in the morning," Jonathon said.

Emily rose and stood beside him.

"I do not think I shall leave Brentwood Manor, Jonathon," Deidre smirked.

"Yes, Deidre, you will," he replied.

"I believe not, Jonathon, for I carry your child."

# Chapter 8

Once Dr. Anderson had announced that Emily and the baby would be fine, Andrew had been sent to Stephen Alcott's on another errand for David. He wondered about this since David had been so active in the political discussions in the House of Burgesses until recently. Now he seemed determined to remain at Brentwood Manor, in fact, as close to Brentwood Manor as possible. Perhaps Joanna was with child again; how wonderful that would be. Their love and devotion was so evident that having another child would only enhance their life together. Cheered by this thought, Andrew urged Neptune to a faster pace anxious to return to the peace of Brentwood Manor after learning about the churning events in Williamsburg from Stephen.

Filled with these thoughts and anxious to relay the news to David, Andrew spurred the horse even faster. But it wasn't just the excitement of the political upheaval that ran through his blood; he wanted to see Jenny. Their encounters had been awkward since the day of their ride. There had been no opportunity for them to speak alone, and Andrew was convinced that Jenny enabled that. He so desperately wanted to explain his pulling away from her that day—but how could he explain his fear of looking the fool to her? Just that explanation would make it so.

His thoughts turned to Deidre. What power did she hold over him to both repel and attract? He avoided her, and when they were in the same gathering, he avoided making eye contact. But he often felt her staring at him, as though somehow her gaze bore a hole right through him. And when she was not watching him, he stole glances at her and—he admitted to himself—wondered what it would be like to lie with her. She was beautiful with her golden hair and her shapely body. Perhaps he should accept her offer and learn the ways of love so that he could be the kind of lover that Jenny deserved. Suddenly he was filled with disgust at the thought of lying with Deidre, and even the thought of her repulsed him.

He shook his head. He wanted no woman but Jenny. He recalled how her dark hair shimmered as auburn highlights danced in the sun. When she laughed that single dimple caused heat to rise from his gut and spread throughout his limbs making him long to reach out and pull her into his embrace. Her skin, so fair and smooth, was golden in the evening candlelight, and he wondered what she would look like totally revealed in the glow of firelight. With these thoughts, he called to Neptune and dug in his heels. Consenting with a powerful neigh, Neptune leapt forward and took the road at a gallop.

• • •

Restless, Jenny paced her room. It had been a strange day at Brentwood Manor. Emily apparently had a fainting spell and the doctor was summoned, but somehow there seemed to be an underlying tension about the whole occurrence. She had been out riding when it happened, but Aunt Joanna had informed her of the incident upon her return. It was Uncle David who surprised her with his pent up emotion. Although she saw him only briefly at supper, his obvious anger was seething just below the surface. She had thought it best to remain in her room and allow events to sort themselves out.

Stopping at the window, she gazed out at the stars. Silvery against the night sky, the rising moon etched shadows across the lawns of the manor. She stared down the road wondering if Andrew would return this night. The strain between them had lasted since their outing, and she was unsure how to resolve it. She knew that he was attracted to her, the truth of that resonated in her heart. Yet, he had pulled away, and she felt rejected and humiliated. Was she not pretty enough? Was she too vocal in her political views? Her father had warned her that men were often intimidated by intelligent women whose interests ranged beyond the domestic arts. She sighed. Well, if that was the case, despite her feelings for him, Andrew was not the man for her, for she craved information and knowledge about the world. The events occurring across the colonies engrossed her, and she was accustomed to discussing them with her father at supper each evening. While David initially had been very involved with Virginia's rebellion, he seemed to be distracted of late. But their discussions were always lively and she craved more involvement herself.

She had been staring down the road for several minutes and thought she saw movement in the garden. She closed her eyes, rubbed them and peered out again. It must have been an animal moving across the yard. She moved to her dressing table and pulled the pins out of her hair letting it drop down her back to her waist. Taking the brush, she performed her nightly ritual, brushing until her hair shone in the candlelight.

Images of the outing with Andrew flooded her memory. She remembered the feel of his lips on hers, his tongue gently probing, seeking, almost asking. She smiled recalling his gentleness, his gallantry. These were the traits that had instantly attracted her to him, and she knew he would carry them into his lovemaking. She wondered what it would be like to be loved by such a caring man, and warmth seeped through her as her imagination wandered. Andrew did not reject her because of her looks or her political views, of that she was certain. He was too kind, and his love for her was evident every time their eyes met. Whatever was blocking his approaching her again needed to be faced, and she would probably have to initiate that discussion.

• • •

Silence filled the room as each grappled with Deidre's revelation. Suddenly clear-headed, Emily strode to her and slapped her soundly across the face.

"How dare you say such a horrid thing," she cried, her eyes stormy, her fists balled and ready to strike again. Jonathon reached out and gently pulled her back.

"Let me go, Jonathon, she has no right to accuse you of such infidelity!" She glanced up and saw David's horrified look, and turned to Jonathon in rage.

"Jonathon, how dare you allow her to slander you like that! She surely must leave Brentwood Manor now!" Emily trembled with fury.

Jonathon's insides curdled as he faced this dreaded moment. It was not the way he had intended to tell Emily, but there was no use in attempting to lie now. Looking at Deidre, anger flowed through him like a tempest, and a red heat seared his brain as he fought to control his emotions. Seething, he drew Emily behind him and stood directly in front of Deidre.

"You whore," he spat. "You intend to destroy all that I love, all that is good in my life."

Stung by his words at first, Deidre recovered and straightened, raising her chin in defiance. Triumph gleamed in her eyes.

"I bear your child, Jonathon. Did you not tell your wife about making love to me in your secret cabin?"

The British cat-o'-nine-tails that had ripped his flesh did not cause him as much pain as Deidre's words. He felt cut through, sliced with the blade of the truth. Emily pushed him aside ready to do battle with her, but Jonathon caught her, restraining her.

"Jonathon, make her stop saying such horrid things! Make her stop!" Emily cried out.

Jonathon turned to her and watched her eyes change from stormy anger to shocked realization and finally to profound sadness.

"Emily," he said.

"No," she screamed. "No, no, no!" She held her hands over her ears, squeezing her eyes shut.

The color had washed from her face and he caught her as she slumped toward the floor. Gently lifting her, he buried his face in her hair whispering, "I am so sorry, my love." He laid her on the settee and turned back to Deidre.

"Are you satisfied, you bitch?" he growled at her.

"Careful, Darling, you are speaking to the mother of your child," she smiled.

Anger roiled within Jonathon's gut, and he felt the blood coursing throughout his body, throbbing at his temple. Never in his life had he felt like striking a woman as he did at that moment, but Deidre would not drag him into her world of evil; she had done that to him once. He clenched and unclenched his fists feeling a need to move, to shout, to release the fury that surged within him. Pacing the length of the room, he scrubbed his fingers through his hair.

"One thing you need to consider, Jonathon, is that if Emily bears a girl and I bear a son, my child will be heir to Brentwood Manor, so not only do I carry your child, I may carry your heir." Deidre's voice was soft and low as if she were speaking to a young child. She smiled and moved toward him. "This is how it was always meant to be, Jonathon."

She reached out to him and he recoiled from her touch. Sorrow and shame etched his face in deep lines and dulled his eyes. Wiping his hand across his face, he looked from David to Joanna. His sister looked at him with confusion, slightly shaking her head in disbelief. He turned back to Deidre.

"Is this what you wanted, Deidre? To destroy my life? To destroy Emily?" he asked.

"I wanted us to be together as we were meant to be, Darling," she purred.

Fear gripped Jonathon at the incongruous sound of her voice. Surely she realized the utter havoc she had wreaked tonight, yet she seemed to live in a dream world. He looked again at David and saw concern creasing his brow as well.

David stepped towards Deidre.

"You must leave Brentwood Manor, especially now, Deidre. I will travel to Williamsburg tomorrow to make arrangements for you," David said.

"Oh, but no, David, dear. Now more than ever I must remain at Brentwood Manor for I may carry the heir. Surely Jonathon would want the mother of his child to be taken care of properly. Is that not correct, Jonathon, darling?" Smiling, she looked at him.

Jonathon slumped into a chair. He leaned forward and held his head in his hands, his voice barely audible.

"She is right, David. My God, she is right."

Joanna ran to her brother, kneeling beside him.

"No, Jonathon! She can be taken care of very well in Williamsburg. It would horrible if Emily were forced to see her every day. Please, Jonathon, let David make other arrangements for her," his sister pleaded. She took his hands from his face and forced him to look at her, but he simply shook his head.

"Like it or not, Deidre is correct. She may carry the heir to Brentwood Manor. She must remain here." He turned and looked at the woman. "But I warn you, Deidre, if you harm Emily, you will pay with your life." His eyes bored into hers.

Joanna stood and approached the woman, still haughty, still defiant.

"God help you, Deidre, for those who play with fire often get burned."

Emily moaned and stirred. Jonathon went to her, but Joanna pushed him aside.

"I think it is best if she does not see you at present. Allow her some time to consider all that has occurred," she said.

Jonathon strode to Deidre, thrusting his face close to hers.

"Listen to me, you whore. I never made love to you. You know what happened in that cabin, and love had no part in it. Even your promise is obscene. You sicken me."

Deidre shrank back, her eyes pleading, shoulders hunched forward.

"Please do not be angry with me, Jonathon. I only acted out of love for you." Her voice was childlike, high-pitched and sing-song. Jonathon scowled at her, but unease shifted in his gut. There was a nightmarish feeling to her reaction which mingled fear with his anger.

As he turned, his eyes found Emily's. She was now alert and sitting up. His heart melted with regret and despair as he saw the overwhelming misery in her eyes. She looked away.

"Deidre, you are to stay in the east wing of the manor. Your meals will be brought up to you, and when you venture outside, you are to avoid the terrace," he said, his face strained. He turned and looked at her squarely in the eye. "And do not ever, *ever* go near my wife. Do you understand what I am saying?"

"Yes, Jonathon," she replied, looking to the floor.

David approached her taking her by the elbow. "Come with me, Deidre," he said leading her toward the parlor door. No one moved as the sound of their footsteps echoed across the marble hall and faded as they climbed the staircase.

Turning, Jonathon looked at Emily.

"Emily—," he began.

"No, Jonathon. Please do not speak to me. Please do not come near me, not now, not ever! How could you do this? You have destroyed our love! You bastard!" Shakily she tried to stand, teetered for a moment, and then stood erect. Nodding to Joanna, she took her arm, leaned on her, and keeping her eyes downcast, moved past him and headed toward the parlor door.

Standing helplessly alone, Jonathon became aware of the evening sounds through the open terrace door. How could nature continue as if nothing had happened when his whole life had just crumbled before him? How could crickets sing when his wife would not look at him? Why did the stars cast light on a world gone dead? Despair filled him. How had it come to this? In his attempt to protect and save her, he had lost the love of his life. No battle he had fought, no storm he had conquered, no sorrow he had felt had ever carved him out inside as losing his beloved Emily had.

• • •

Emily lay on her back looking at the canopy above her. Her eyes traced the silken stripes that shimmered in the flickering candle-light. Shock had prevented tears from falling; she felt lifeless and empty. Her ears still rang with Deidre's words: *I carry your child, Jonathon.* As if it were smoke that she could not grasp and keep, the meaning of those words eluded her one minute and attacked her the next. She draped an arm across her eyes attempting to block the images that swirled in her mind, but the confirmation of Deidre's accusation in Jonathon's eyes could not be denied. She saw his anguish, his guilt and his shame and it gripped her and tore at her heart.

How long she had waited to see her husband, to hear his voice and feel his embrace. Upon seeing him, her joy made her heart leap, and the subsequent events dashed it to the depths of despair. A moan escaped her lips, deep and feral. How could this be? How could he have made love to Deidre?

She rolled over and gripped her pillow as, at last, the tears began to flow. Sobs racked her body and she shuddered as she gasped for breath between each. The baby, who had been quiet through the evening, stirred and stretched which normally would bring a smile to Emily's face. He began kicking and moving in protest to her quivering body, as if to announce his distress at her despair. She massaged her belly drawing strength from the life within, demanding to be noticed. But she was not the only one who felt life created by Jonathon. He had betrayed her, had given himself to another, to his former lover. Yes, Deidre had won.

She dug her fists into her eyes trying to black out the image of them lying together. Did he whisper tenderly in her ear while he embraced her? Did he have a special name reserved only for her? Did he hold Deidre after their lovemaking as he had her?

"Aaaahhhh!" she cried out unable to contain her misery any longer. "Oh, please, dear God, make this just a dream. Please take away this pain! Oh, God help me!" she cried into the pillow. Her hand touched something; she pulled it out from beneath her pillow—Jonathon's shirt. All the nights it had brought her comfort...was he lying with Deidre while she clutched only his shirt? She hurled it across the room and broke down sobbing once more.

There was a tap at her door. She braced herself for Jonathon's entrance.

• • •

Jonathon stared blankly into the fire. The evening could not have gone worse; his moment to tell Emily could not have been couched in crueler circumstances. How she must hate him, and he did not blame her. He had felt like striking Deidre this evening, a rage such as he had never felt before. What had become of him? What had she turned him into? A violent monster? But she had robbed him of every good and sacred thing in his life; everything she touched turned foul.

He recalled her revelation about Robert Manning's death and how repulsed he had been. Surely he should have realized that no matter what he had done that afternoon, her intention was to harm—no, to kill Emily and their child. Recalling her strange behavior this evening, he was convinced she was going mad.

David entered the parlor and sat across from him. Leaning forward, he patted Jonathon's shoulder and then stood.

"You need a good, stiff drink, Jonathon," he said. "I do not think things could have been any worse than what transpired here this evening."

Jonathon snorted. "You have read my mind, David."

Returning with two crystal glasses, David handed one to Jonathon and held his up for a toast.

"To you, my friend, for attempting to protect your wife and child." He clinked his glass against Jonathon's.

Ruefully, Jonathon looked at his brother-in-law then into the brandy that he sloshed around the glass. He took a long pull of the liquid, and released breath fiery with the drink.

"I thought she would be safe, David," he said softly.

"Who knew what Deidre was capable of, Jonathon?"

"When she came to the cabin that day, I was still weak, unable to leave the bed for any length of time. She surprised me when she arrived—I almost shot her thinking she was a British scout. Now, I wish I had." He paused and took another drink. "She had seduction on her mind; she knew exactly what she would do…"

"Jonathon, you do not have to tell me this. You do not have to relive it," David said.

"No, please, David, let me explain it. Perhaps in the telling, I will find a way to forgive myself. She teased, she stripped, I could not control my reaction, my response. That made her even more intent on completing the mission she had set out for that afternoon. She climbed over me, and, my God, David, I could not control myself. I was like a damn rutting stag and once she began to ride me, I responded in kind…" Jonathon's voice broke and he began to sob. "I was unfaithful to Emily and I will never forgive myself let alone expect her to forgive me."

David stood and put his hand on Jonathon's shoulder. The ticking of the parlor clock was all that broke the silence. Finally, David sat across from Jonathon again.

"David, she killed Robert. She drugged him and pushed him over the side of his boat," Jonathon's eyes were intense, burning with rage. "As I related in the letter I sent to you, she threatened Emily's life and the life of our child if I did not lie with her. I thought they would be safe, but fear gripped me throughout my time away. I had to return, to see for myself that Emily was safe, and when I heard what happened today—I hate that I cannot be here to protect her." He dropped his head in his hands and wept again.

"Tell her, Jonathon. Explain to her as you have to me," David said.

"She does not want to be near me. How can I get her to listen? And if I told her, would she live in fear, a prisoner in her own home? And, David, what if our child is a girl? And what if Deidre bears a son? Oh, this is a disaster!"

Outside, the sound of hoof beats signaled an approaching rider. Jonathon looked around wildly.

"That is probably Andrew returning from Stephen Alcott's," David said.

Jonathon spoke quickly. "David, I will contact you as soon as I am able. I must leave and travel through the night." Jonathon leaned alongside the window and peeked out. "David, I promised Emily that I would be here when our child was born, and I vow I will keep that promise. Please, protect her. Keep Deidre away from her. Oh, God, I do not want to leave her."

"Jonathon, you must get away quickly. If you are captured, you will be no good to Emily. I will talk to her, try to make her understand what happened. She loves you, Jonathon, you must trust her."

Jonathon looked at his brother-in-law, his eyes clearer, hope a small flame within his heart.

"Thank you, David."

The men stood and clasped each other, patting each other on the back.

"Godspeed, Jonathon," David whispered as Jonathon slipped out the terrace doors and disappeared into the night.

• • •

"Come in," Emily called softly and sat up in her bed. Bracing herself for an encounter with Jonathon, she was both relieved and disappointed when Joanna entered her bedroom. She carried a tray of tea to the nightstand and set it down.

"I suspected you might still be awake, Emily," she smiled tenderly noting her sister-in-law's red, puffy eyes.

"Joanna, I—," Emily began.

"Hush, Em. You have had a very traumatic day. You need to rest and stay well for your baby," Joanna said as she poured tea into the delicate porcelain cups. She handed one to Emily and then sat beside her on the bed. Emily sipped hers and a brief smile crossed her face.

"Is this your special blend of tea, Joanna?" she asked.

"Let us just say it will help you sleep," she chuckled.

Emily's fleeting smile was replaced with a somber look as she gazed at the liquid in her cup.

"Joanna, what am I to do? How can this be true? How could Jonathon…I do not even know what to think right now; my world has been turned upside down." Tears burned her eyes, brimming then streaming down her face unchecked. "How can this be possible? Jonathon and…and…she? How could he betray me like this?"

Joanna stood and crossed to the window watching Andrew arrive at the stables. She pressed her forehead against the glass pane and shrugged her shoulders.

"I have no answer for you, Emily, for I do not know what transpired. My brother is not this kind of man; I cannot believe he intentionally hurt you like this," she said.

"Well, I do not know how it could be unintentional," Emily sniffed.

"You will need to talk to him, Emily, to hear him out."

"I do not want to be near him," Emily said curtly.

"Then you will never learn his side of the story, Em," Joanna said gently.

Turning to place her empty cup on the nightstand, Emily looked at Joanna.

"Perhaps learning his side of the story would only bring more pain, Joanna. What if he loves her? What if she predicted the truth? That Jonathon got tired of a 'child' and needed a real woman? What if he loved her all along and merely felt sorry for taking me from my home? What if—." Her voice had risen in pitch at each question, and now the tears flowed freely. Joanna hurried to her bedside and took the trembling girl into her arms. Emily laid her head on Joanna's shoulder and yielded to sobs that shook her whole being. Joanna rubbed her back and stroked her hair.

"I am so sorry this ever happened, Emily. But I know one thing for certain: Jonathon loves only you. He risked his life tonight to come to you. I do not know what occurred between them, but I suspect it had nothing to do with love," Joanna said.

Emily's sobs subsided, but her trembling continued. Joanna helped her lie back on the pillows and tucked the counterpane around her despite the warmth of the night. She brushed a stray curl from her eyes and kissed her forehead. Seeing the heaviness of Emily's eyelids, she lowered the wick on the oil lamp and placed her cup and saucer on the tray. When she looked back at her, Emily was asleep. She sat beside her for a while, then feeling the effects of the brandy-laced tea, she rose and headed for her own bed.

• • •

Andrew dismounted and led Neptune into his stall. Sweat gleamed off the ebony horse, evidence of their ambitious ride, and Andrew patted his flank in gratitude.

"Nicely, done, Neptune. You are truly the finest horse in the colonies," he murmured, feeding the horse some oats. Neptune nickered and tossed his head trying to move out of his stall.

"Yes, he is," a voice answered from the shadows. Startled, Andrew reached for his pistol as he turned and peered toward the sound. Neptune neighed and trotted toward the voice. As Jonathon emerged, Andrew replaced his pistol and smiling broadly, hugged him.

"Jonathon, how good to see you so well." He stood back and looked closer. "However, I see a heavy weight bears you down this night."

"Andrew, much has transpired, but I must let David inform you of it. British troops have been pursuing me since I left Yorktown, and I must be away quickly. If they suspect I was here, it will put all of you in grave danger."

"Then be off, Jonathon. Neptune has brought me swiftly from the Alcott Plantation where there is great news of movement toward independence from Britain, but your horse has many more miles left in him before he rests." He laughed observing Neptune's obvious pleasure at being with Jonathon. "I believe you have given him his second wind."

Jonathon mounted and turned to Andrew, his eyes dark with sadness.

"Andrew, you must see to your sister's safety. She is in great peril, and I entrust her to you and to Joanna and David's care. He will explain." With that, Jonathon nudged Neptune and horse and rider rode seamlessly into the night.

• • •

Noticing a light burning in the parlor, Andrew peeked around the door to see David staring out at the night. Andrew saw how fatigued he looked as he entered and sat across from him.

"I have just seen Jonathon," Andrew said quietly.

Pulled back from his reverie, David looked at him and sat up.

"He said that Emily is in danger and that you would explain everything to me."

"It has been a long and difficult day, Andrew. We discovered the cause of Emily's illness today and it seems there were other... uh...difficulties..."

Andrew caught his breath.

"No, not complications with Emily or the baby, rather, other problems.

"Emily is all right, then?" Andrew asked looking toward the staircase.

"Emily and the baby are healthy and safe..." David said weighing his words. "I believe she is asleep now."

Andrew nodded, satisfied that he could wait to check on his sister until the morning.

David brushed his hand over his face. Looking at Andrew, he realized that he was no longer a child, but a man who deserved to know the facts, all of the facts, that surrounded his sister's close brush with death.

"Andrew, pour us each a brandy and have a seat."

David explained the events of the day and what had occurred between Jonathon and Deidre to cause such misery. A cold lump settled in Andrew's gut as he listened carefully and recognized clearly what Deidre was about. And he had almost participated in her devious plans. He winced as he realized what effect this news must have had on Emily, and what effect it would have had on Jenny had he complied with Deidre's offer. He shuddered as he comprehended how fortunate he had been to avoid Deidre, and rage burned within him at the thought of his sister's close call.

"She will not come near my sister," he vowed.

"She has been banished to the east wing of the manor, and to grounds away from the terrace so to prevent any encounter with Emily," David explained.

"Is that enough? We cannot trust her," Andrew argued. Rising he snatched the poker and stabbed at the cold logs in the hearth sending one rolling impotently onto the floor. "She must leave Brentwood Manor!"

"Yes, we believed that, too, but if she carries a son and Emily a daughter, she will bear the heir to Brentwood Manor. Jonathon insisted she stay here, as would be expected," David said quietly. The parlor clock ticked loudly in the still night as Andrew digested this information. Letting out a deep breath, he returned to his seat. This night had not evolved as he had anticipated as he urged Neptune along the roads. This would require much contemplation. Expecting to find serenity at home, Andrew instead had found personal danger to rival what the patriots faced in Williamsburg. And while his family was of utmost importance, he realized that the larger cause of freedom and the spirit that inspired people to risk their lives to attain it demanded their attention as well. Finally, he leaned forward.

"David, I have news from Williamsburg," Andrew whispered excitedly.

"What news, Drew?" he asked.

"The Virginia Convention has adopted the Declaration of Rights, David. Jefferson is drafting an explanation of our quest for independence to be sent to Great Britain. Williamsburg is abuzz with talk of war, of being free from the constraints—no the chains—of Parliament," Andrew's words tumbled out. He had ridden so far and waited so long to share such exciting news, and yet David seemed a bit reticent. "They want you to go to Williamsburg to join the debates and discussions, David."

David looked down at his empty brandy glass. "I am not sure I can leave Brentwood Manor at present, Andrew," he murmured. Despondency filled his eyes as he looked up at the younger man.

"You must go, David. They are depending on your guidance and your leadership. I will remain at Brentwood Manor to ensure

Emily's safety. Believe me, the hounds of hell could not get to her if I can help it." Andrew's jaw clenched and his hand tightened around his glass.

David reached out and clapped his shoulder. "You are a good man, Andrew," he smiled.

Andrew warmed at his compliment, especially since he used the word, "man." *Yes,* Andrew thought *I am a man. Fully capable of protecting my sister, and fully capable of presenting myself to Jenny and proclaiming my love to her.*

David rose and wiped a hand across his eyes. "It will all need to be sorted out, but that must be left for another day for I am weary and in need of my bed," he said. "Thank you for taking on the responsibility of communications with Williamsburg. You have done exceptionally well, Andrew," David said, smiling at him. "Let us retire, for tomorrow may hold some interesting possibilities."

They climbed the stairs, and as he turned toward his room, Andrew glanced down the hallway toward Jenny's room. No light shone beneath the doorframe. He shrugged and entered his bedroom.

# Chapter 9

Emily awoke aware of a heaviness that had nothing to do with her pregnancy, for it was a heaviness of heart. Opening her eyes, she spotted Jonathon's shirt flung across the room, lying in a heap near the hearth. Like a stab, it brought back the painful reminder of the previous evening. Tightness gripped Emily's throat as she fought back sobs. She closed her eyes as if willing the truth of Jonathon's infidelity away, but she knew it was not possible. If what Deidre had proclaimed last night were true, her life would never be the same.

How fate had frowned on her life with Jonathon, tossing obstacles in their path of happiness at every turn. First, the awkwardness of their situation as guardian and ward, then Emily's accusation of Jonathon as a traitor, the attack on the Cosgrove house in Williamsburg, the death of James and Martha Cosgrove, Jonathon's dear friends. He had brought her to them because they shared her Tory loyalty, and he thought she would be safe in their home. But the rebellion had reached fever pitch and after the attack on their home, they, too, planned to return to England with Emily. James was killed by the British who captured Jonathon, and Martha died of a broken heart.

Jonathon's capture. She rolled over and clutched her pillow, tears dampening it as she cried. She had thought he was dead... because of her. For months she had grieved for him thinking her life was over, too; only their child kept her alive. Then news of his escape, proof he was alive. Oh, it was all too much.

Lying on her back, Emily stared at the canopy. Images ran through her mind of all the hardship that had befallen them. She had much to consider, but she knew wallowing in self-pity was not going to improve her health, her state of mind, or the circumstances. As if a fog were clearing, she began to see more lucidly. She would need to confront Jonathon and hear him out, no matter the cost in anguish. Then she would decide a direction to move in, once she had all the information. For she would not live beneath the same roof as Deidre. She was not sure that she was incapable of doing her harm.

Sitting up, she felt stronger, determined to face what life had presented and to ascertain the best path for herself and her baby. Unyielding resolve filled her, and she knew that lying here feeling sorry for herself was ill-advised. And she certainly would not be held captive in her room in order to avoid Jonathon or Deidre. She had once made the mistake of believing Brentwood Manor was not her home, and that had brought about disastrous results. Brentwood Manor *was* her home and she was its mistress. No one would take that from her.

She rose and stood before her dressing table shocked at how severely her red, swollen her eyes contrasted with her pale skin. She dampened a cloth with water from the ewer and held it over her eyes, its coolness revitalizing her. She freshened up and brushed her hair, each stroke of the brush strengthening her resolve. The baby stretched and kicked and, despite her misery, she smiled inwardly at this child to whom she had already lost her heart.

Donning a plum colored frock, she noted how it brightened her lavender-blue eyes. She fluffed the lace that cascaded out of the sleeves and lay across her bodice. All of her frocks strained across her bosom and mid-section as her pregnancy added voluptuous curves to her body. She pinched her cheeks to heighten their color and dabbed jasmine scent at her throat and wrists. She would not cower in terror, afraid to leave her room. No, Deidre would not prevail. Sweeping her hair up into combs studded with pearls, she straightened her shoulders and opened her bedroom door. If she was to confront Jonathon this morning, she would look her best.

On entering the dining room, she saw that some had already partaken of their breakfast. As she approached the sideboard, the sight of ham, eggs, biscuits and fruit made her stomach lurch, and she knew the despair that possessed her was thinly disguised by her bravado. Taking a biscuit and some honey, she poured a cup of tea and sat down. She needed a plan for facing both Jonathon and Deidre for the first time after last night's revelations. Staring out at the gardens, she pondered her options. Despite her sorrow at his infidelity, deep within she knew her love for Jonathon conquered any trial they encountered, and, if she were honest with herself, she wanted desperately to see him this morning.

David and Joanna entered the dining room interrupting her musings. Joanna took in Emily's appearance and knew that her spirit had overcome her despair. She walked over to her chair and embraced her sister-in-law.

"How are you feeling this morning, Emily?" she asked.

"A bit drained, but I am well, Joanna," she replied. The question she wanted to ask burned within her *Was Jonathon still here?* As if he had heard it, David sat in the chair beside her and took her hand.

"Emily, Jonathon left last night. British patrols have been pursuing him; he risked his life to come here and ensure that you and your baby were safe and well," David said, his smile gentle.

Disappointment caused Emily's heart to plunge. Swallowing the lump in her throat, she nodded through her tears.

"Emily, Jonathon wants me to explain everything to you, but I will wait until you are ready to hear his story, all right?" he asked searching her eyes.

Emily nodded again unsure if she wanted to hear about Jonathon and Deidre's affair, but burning to know it.

"I must leave for Williamsburg at once, but I will remain to relate this to you now if you wish. Otherwise, on my return, when the shock of these events has eased, we can discuss it. Would you prefer that?"

"Yes, David, thank you. I believe I need some time to digest the recent occurrences." Emily said wiping the tears from her eyes. Joanna handed her a napkin, and a fresh cup of tea. Emily smiled at her. "You have both been so kind to me ever since I arrived at Brentwood Manor. It seems I continue to depend on your kindheartedness."

"Emily, dear, we love you. You are my sister, and we care about your well-being, and now your baby's too." Joanna smiled at her and brushed a lock of hair from her eyes.

David rose.

"I must depart for Williamsburg. The Virginia Convention is finalizing plans for a separation from Great Britain. I will return as soon as I am able, but Andrew will be here with Joanna to watch over you, Emily. Please take care. Deidre has been instructed to stay away from you, but I do not trust her. You need to be aware of the danger you are in and take every precaution," David said, a crease between his brows.

"I will be careful, David. And I have Andrew and Joanna," she said smiling at her sister-in-law.

David pulled Joanna to him in a warm embrace and kissed her long and full. Emily's heart ached at the sight of such devotion and wondered how her life with Jonathon had come to this. Releasing Joanna, David placed his tricorn on his head, nodded to both women and left the room.

• • •

The golden summer sun warmed Jenny as she walked among the deep purple, lavender and pale periwinkle hues of the echinacea and hydrangeas in the Brentwood garden. The humidity that caused her hair to dance in small spiral curls around her face felt heavy, but being in the garden was soothing, so she opted for the mugginess rather than her room where no breeze stirred. She had chosen her lightest linen frock of mauve not realizing how she harmonized with the flowers that held her attention. Removing her sunbonnet, she dangled it by the yellow ribbons as she strolled along the paths brushing her hands along the petals and leaves, contemplating her relationship with Andrew. Since his return from Williamsburg, she sensed an awakening within him, a maturity hinted at in the set of his jaw and steady gaze, and a command in his demeanor carried in his self-assured posture. Of course, this only enhanced his attractiveness, and she often found herself staring at him trying to discern the source of his change. Hearing footsteps approaching, she turned and found herself face to face with the person of her musings.

"Good day, Jenny," Andrew said. She noted a strength and confidence previously missing.

"Good day, Andrew," she replied.

"May I join you on your stroll?" he asked.

"Of course."

They walked along in silence for a while, occasionally noting a particularly beautiful blossom or the song of a bird. Strangely, the silence did not feel awkward; it was as if, on some deeper level, they had already begun this necessary conversation. Coming upon a wrought iron bench, they sat down.

"Jenny, I need to discuss something with you," Andrew began, looking down at the path.

"Andrew, you do not need to explain—," she started.

"No, please, Jenny, just listen to me for a moment. When we were…that is, when I…" his youthfulness seemed to return as he searched for words. Jenny waited for him to continue. Then, as if drawing from some inner reserve, his mien changed and he turned to her and took her hands. Looking into her eyes, he began again.

"Jenny, I love you. I have loved you since you first arrived in that teeming thunderstorm months ago. I think of you day and night, and I want to be with you every moment. Each time I enter a room, each time I open a door, I hope that you will be there. When you speak, my heart strains to catch every word. When you laugh, it is like the angels are singing. I apologize for my response to you on our ride. I was—well, I was unsure I would measure up to your vision of what a man should be."

Jenny started to interrupt, but he placed a finger against her lips.

"I realize that if you return my love, I will become the man that is that vision, for your love would give me the strength, the courage, the integrity to be that man."

He looked into her eyes and saw tears welling up in them, softness saying what words need not.

"Andrew," she breathed as his lips found hers.

His arms encircled her and brought her close, and heat poured through him as he felt her body pressed against his. She answered his kiss ardently, leaning into him, her arms reaching up around his shoulders. At first tender, their kiss intensified as passion flamed. His mouth searched hers hungrily. Andrew's mind reeled, but he did not feel insecure; in Jenny's arms he felt bold and worthy.

Finally they parted, each breathless with their desire. Andrew gently brushed the curls from Jenny's face and smiled into her eyes. She smiled in return, revealing the single dimple that caused him to melt. He took her hands into his and kissed them.

"Jenny, we must be careful, for I do not want to do anything improper. But I can barely keep from coming to your room at night and holding you in my arms. Now it will be even more difficult to restrain myself."

Jenny laughed, her voice floating lightly on the summer breeze.

"Andrew, my father will have Uncle David's hide if something unseemly were to occur right under his roof. We must temper our emotions as best we can."

"I am not sure I am able, Jenny, but I will never do anything to hurt you. I love you so," he said.

"And I love you, Andrew."

He bent his head to kiss her again when the thunderous sound of hoof beats intruded.

"Oh no, the British," he said, rising from the bench to look over the gardens toward the drive. "Jenny, we must return to the manor. When we get there, go into the house, find my sister and Joanna. All of you need to stay together inside. We must hurry." He took her hand and they ran together toward the manor.

• • •

Emily and Joanna heard hoof beats and the baying of hounds reverberating up the drive as they played with Will on the shaded terrace. Will had lined up tiny tin soldiers along a paving stone when the sound of approaching horses reached them. He pointed toward the drive in excitement.

"Oook, oook, Mama," he cried.

Joanna snatched him up and clutched him to her. Heart sinking, she turned to Emily whose face was ashen.

"Oh my God—Jonathon," Emily whispered, shaking as she rose from her chair.

Holding hands, the women approached the drive as the soldiers halted before the manor. Out of the corner of her eye, Emily saw Andrew and Jenny returning from the garden.

Chaos filled the front yard as horses cantered up. Clustering around the legs of the horses, several hounds were sniffing the ground and pulling at their tethers. The soldiers reined in their horses and the officer in front dismounted as the dogs continued their frantic howling. Ordering the soldiers to quiet the dogs, he approached the women.

*Captain Arthur Walters.*

Emily felt as if she would swoon when she recognized the British soldier who had attempted to rape her while encamped at

Brentwood Manor the previous year, searching for Jonathon. Her stomach lurched as she saw a scar along his face—the scar she had inflicted. Her legs trembled, and she looked at the contingent of soldiers hoping to find the face of her childhood friend Captain Michael Dennings. His face was not among the troops, however.

Surprise flickered across his face when Captain Walters noticed that Emily was pregnant. He sauntered over and stood before her. His eyes blazed into hers as he greeted her.

"Well, Mrs. Jonathon Brentwood. How I have anticipated this encounter and the opportunity to repay your hospitality." His voice was slick and low. "And now I see you carry Brentwood's brat; how delicious. I may enjoy this visit more than I had thought."

Emily recoiled at his unctuous tone and insinuations. She leaned back, away from him as his words, coated in false pleasantries, slid over her senses. Sensing her abhorrence, he leaned in closer. "Now there is even more at stake, is there not, Mrs. Brentwood?"

Emily turned and looked at him.

"I believe your last visit did not end well for you, Captain Walters. I will do my best to ensure this visit provides equal distress," she said, her eyes boring into his. She saw him flinch for one instant, and then recover, sneering at her.

"Is that a threat to a soldier of the king, Mrs. Brentwood?"

"That is a promise to a villain, Captain Walters," she spat back at him.

Like a shot his hand snapped up and he slapped her forcing her to lose her balance. Stumbling, she recovered and stood scowling at him.

"I see you are still a gentleman."

He shifted under her gaze, discomfited at her courage and his inability to intimidate her. Turning toward his men, he ordered them to dismount.

"We know Captain Brentwood is here," he said indicating the hounds. "It would be best for all if he simply surrendered to us now."

"My husband is not here."

"Mrs. Brentwood, tell your husband not to be a coward but to come out. It will save us searching, and that could involve damaging your beautiful home, even possibly injuring some of your household." He looked at Will.

Joanna clutched her child closer, and he began to cry.

"Take Will inside, Joanna. I see in addition to being a gentleman, Captain Walters also chooses to harm those weaker than he," Emily said.

"Emily, I will not leave you alone out here," Joanna said.

"I will be fine, Joanna; Will is frightened by Captain Walters," Emily said.

"As should you be, Mrs. Brentwood," Walters smirked.

Andrew appeared and stood beside Emily.

"Jonathon is not here," he stated firmly. "Your hounds have indeed picked up his scent since he was here last night, but he is long gone, Captain."

Emily started at her brother's words wondering why he would reveal Jonathon's visit. Then, realizing his ploy, she understood why he gave a deceptive answer for the timing of the visit, for Jonathon had been there two nights previously. Andrew's fabrication would influence where they searched for Jonathon based on the timing of his visit.

Captain Walters turned his attention to Andrew.

"So, Brentwood's apprentice is left in charge. This could be rather amusing," he said stepping toward Andrew, scowling. His words hissed through his teeth. "You are in danger yourself, Wentworth, for rumor has it that you are involved in many of Brentwood's traitorous plots."

Andrew stood fast, not flinching. "Remove your men from our property, Walters," he said.

With a quick move, Captain Walters raised the butt of his musket and slammed it into Andrew's gut. Doubling over,

Andrew let out a loud gasp, and then coming up, pointed his pistol at Captain Walters's face. Several soldiers drew pistols and aimed them at Andrew and time seemed to stop. Suddenly in a commotion behind the manor, a horse and rider shot out of the stables. Flying along the path, they leapt over shrubs and tore down the road.

"Jenny!" Andrew gasped as he watched Shadow carry away the woman he loved.

Confusion reigned as Captain Walters shouted orders for his men to mount and chase her, but the dogs began their baying again and in their excitement, wound their tethers around the legs of several horses. Men kicked at the dogs trying to get them out of the way and disentangle the leashes, but it took a few minutes before any were able to mount and pursue Jenny.

Walters turned and caught the look of fear on Andrew's face.

"So, perhaps we have yet another bargaining chip in this game," he smiled. "You seem quite distraught over the lady's escape, Wentworth. Do not worry; when we catch her, I shall take special care of her, as Mrs. Brentwood knows I can," he said running a finger along Emily's jawline.

Brushing his hand away, Emily stepped toward him her face in his.

"Be careful whom you play with, Captain Walters. She has a better aim than I."

"We shall see, Mrs. Brentwood. Now I am afraid I must leave you for a brief time, but do not fear. Several of my men will remain with you to ensure Brentwood's capture should he return. I promise you that when we capture your husband, I will bring him to you so you can enjoy some of the consequences of his treason."

Emily's stomach reeled at his words, but her face never betrayed her. Steely-eyed, she stared at Captain Walters before spitting out her words.

"What I will enjoy watching, Captain Walters, is your death at my husband's hands."

Grinning, he replied. "I am afraid you will be disappointed if that is your goal." Turning to his men, he gave instructions to the four of them who would remain and ordered the others to mount their horses. Sensing the continuation of the chase, the dogs took up their howling, pulling at their tethers, anxious to be off. Over the din, Captain Walters turned back to Emily.

"Until we meet again, Mrs. Brentwood." Saluting, he turned his horse and rode down the drive.

The remaining soldiers moved toward Emily, but she stopped them with a look.

"Stay where you are, gentlemen, for you are not invited guests. Make yourselves comfortable in the stables with your horses."

Startled at her resolve, they looked at each other in confusion. Finally, they took their horses' reins and led them to the stables.

Once they had moved away, Emily grabbed Andrew's arm as her knees gave out. Reaching around her back, he supported his sister as he led her into the manor.

• • •

The sun beat down as Shadow's hooves pounded the road. As the scenery flew by, Jenny tried to think. Unsure which direction to head, she knew her path was east toward Williamsburg. The rain had been a torrent the day she had arrived at Brentwood Manor, so the road was not familiar, but she held steady toward the east and trusted she would find her way. Praying that Shadow would be swift enough to outrun the British, she patted the horse's flank and called out encouragement as they sped along the road.

The image of Andrew facing the British officer was burned in her brain. Watching out the front window, she had seen the cruelty etched in the captain's face, the brutish pleasure in his eyes.

No, she could not remain safely in the house while others faced the enemy. She had witnessed the ruthlessness of the British in Boston, and she felt compelled to act. Heart racing and ears filled with the incessant beat of Shadow's hooves, she dug in her heels pressing the mount to go faster. As if sensing the urgency, Shadow complied and they shot ahead.

Fear gripped her as she wondered about Andrew's safety. Aside from the plantation slaves, Andrew stood virtually alone, for David was not expected back for at least a week. She knew of Emily's earlier encounter with Captain Walters, and she marveled at the woman's mettle to stand up to him as she had today. Indeed, the Wentworth siblings were courageous.

Jenny rode for what seemed like hours before she sensed Shadow's strength waning. Knowing that the horse needed rest, she slowed their pace and began to look for signs of shelter. Passing several possible paths into the forest, she dismissed them as too difficult to distance them enough from the road. Surely if Shadow was tiring, any British troops who might have followed her would find their own mounts tiring as well. She risked her lead and slowed Shadow to a trot. Up ahead she saw a road diverting off to the north. Pressing her lips together, she pondered the consequences of following it and pulled Shadow up to a halt and listened. Cicadas sang in the trees and small animals scurried through the underbrush, but no hoof beats sounded in the distance. Engulfing them like a shroud, the humid air was stifling and Jenny's frock was sodden with sweat. She could feel that Shadow's coat was drenched as well, and she patted the horse for offering its best efforts. Realizing the horse needed water and rest, Jenny pulled the reins and guided Shadow to the tree-lined side road. The shade was a welcome relief and they continued along at a slower pace. Jenny scrutinized the woods on either side of the road looking for some hint of the sympathies of the property's owner. If he were a Tory, she was as good as captured; if a patriot, perhaps she could enlist some assistance. Gradually the trees thinned and a purposeful row of elms lined either side of the drive. Pulling up the reins, Jenny led Shadow into the woods to survey the residence.

A manor house soon came into view, but there was no sign of any inhabitants on the front lawn. Staying hidden in the trees, Jenny circled the manor to the back of the house where she saw several people in the gardens and a man walking toward the barn. Still unable to determine the leanings of the owners, she decided to dismount and observe for a while, though time was of the essence if she were to be of any help to Andrew.

She heard the crack of a twig at the same time she heard the click of a pistol near her ear. Frozen, she instinctively raised her hands in surrender as her captor whispered, "Who are you?"

Remembering Emily's courage, she breathed deeply and turning said, "I am Jennifer Sutton. Who are you?" As she faced the man, she was startled to note his smile beginning.

"Good day, Jenny. I am Uncle Jonathon."

# Chapter 10

They sat in Stephen Alcott's study, candlelight flickering off somber faces. Jonathon rose and paced the room flicking the ash of his cigar in the fireplace as he passed it. The ticking of the parlor clock seemed to mock his need for action, but caution reined him in as they discussed optional plans of action.

"Jonathon, I say we gather neighbors and show those British who is in charge in Virginia," Stephen Alcott said, slapping his hand on the rosewood desk.

"Stephen, while I admire your devotion, they outnumber us at present," Jonathon replied returning to his place on the settee. He sat beside Jenny looking at her earnestly. "Now tell me again, Jenny, how many soldiers did you see?"

"There were about twenty-five in all, Jonathon."

"And their arms?"

Jenny thought for a moment, her eyes transfixed as she cast her memory to the scene on the Brentwood Manor lawn.

"They all had muskets with bayonets. I believe the captain had a pistol as well."

Jonathan rubbed his hand across his chin, thinking. He shifted in his seat and tapped his fingers lightly on the arm of the settee. Finally, he looked at Stephen and spoke.

"I need to return to the *Destiny* and rally my men. If I leave immediately, I can have them back here by tomorrow night."

"Jenny will need to leave here as well, and Shadow needs rest after their ride today. Do you have a mount for her?"

"Yes, and I will have saddlebags packed with supplies for you both," Stephen said standing to ring for a servant.

"No, wait, Stephen. The fewer people who know of our presence here, the better. Pack whatever you can gather yourself, for we must be away soon."

Stephen dropped the bell rope and returned to his chair.

"Jenny, you must go to Williamsburg and find Randy O'Connor. Ask for him at the Raleigh Tavern; if he is not there, someone will know where he is. Tell him what has happened—he will know what to do. We will share the road part of the way, but if British troops accost us, you are to ride away as fast as you can, do you understand?"

"Jonathon, my uncle is in Williamsburg as well," Jenny said.

"I do not know where he stays, Jenny. Randy will know. You must find Randy first, do you understand?"

Jenny nodded, and he was assured by her gray eyes intent in the candlelight.

The three of them rose as one, each focused on what must be done. Jonathon shook Stephen's hand.

"You have been a loyal friend and a faithful patriot, Stephen. Thank you."

"Do not dismiss me yet, Jonathon," he chuckled. "Send word on your return and I shall help you rout those bastards."

Jonathon clapped him on the arm. "I shall appreciate having you beside me, friend."

Jonathon and Jenny slipped out the back door of the manor and stole to the stables to saddle the horses. When they were preparing to mount, Stephen returned with a saddlebag of supplies for each.

"Godspeed," he said to them.

"Thank you again, Stephen," Jonathon replied, then gently kicking Neptune, he rode out into the moonlit night, Jenny following close behind.

• • •

Andrew paced the length and breadth of the parlor as Emily and Joanna watched, each ignoring her sewing. His mind raced with possibilities of what might happen should Jenny be caught, each image bringing a surge of apprehension, and he was gripped by a compelling urgency to race to her aid. But where was she? Unfamiliar with the territory, she would not know where to flee to for help.

"Damn!" He slapped his hands down on the table behind the settee causing both women to jump. "Damn," he repeated brushing his hands through his hair. "There is nothing I can do to help her. The soldiers forbid anyone from leaving the property, and they guard the stables as if they were made of gold. I must get to Jenny, but how?"

Emily went to her brother placing a hand on his shoulder. He turned to look at his sister, noting a wan smile on her face.

"Andrew, we must believe that Jenny made it safely away," she said, rubbing his shoulder.

"I know, Em. She is an excellent rider, and Shadow is swift."

"And she is not loaded down with muskets, bayonets and a heavy uniform," she smiled. "I believe she will be all right; you must believe it, too."

"How have you done it all these months, Em? How have you lived not knowing whether Jonathon was alive or dead?" His eyes burned with unshed tears, and he saw the answering tears glisten in his sister's.

"You must be strong for her, Drew. You must pray and trust and believe that she will evade the British and find help somewhere. You must do all of this for her."

Feeling drained, Andrew walked to the window and leaned his forearm against the frame. He stared out at the grounds as if willing Jenny to appear. Resting his head against his arm, he closed his eyes and prayed. It was as if a fist clutched his heart, sharp and unrelenting. Inaction was unbearable; how could he help her? He thought of her slender body, her gentle smile, and then the sneer of Captain Walters invaded his imaginings. Anger coursed through him at the thought of Jenny in that brute's captivity. He pounded a fist against the frame, impotence engulfing him.

"I must do something," he uttered. "How can I sit here in the comfort of our home and remain idle while she is out there..." his voice trailed off unable to voice his darkest fears.

Again, Emily approached her brother and laid a comforting hand on his shoulder.

"Because you have no other choice," she said softly. Her words burned into him.

• • •

Jenny had left Jonathon at a fork in the road over an hour earlier. Riding beside him had been comforting, and now that she was alone again, the fears that she had not allowed into her mind seemed to possess her. The night brought little relief from the heat and humidity of the day, and the mount she was on now was considerably slower than Shadow had been. Her heart beat in rhythm to their pace as they made steady progress toward Williamsburg. Jonathon had given her clear directions, so she at least felt as though she were no longer flying along the road with no course. Nevertheless, she knew danger was still possible if she encountered any British troops along the way.

Cottages seemed to appear more frequently along the roadside, and pasture fences ran together signaling the proximity of a town. Soon, lights flickered a welcome from residences and taverns ahead, and she knew she had reached Williamsburg. The streets were quiet since the hour was so late, but as she turned up Duke of Gloucester Street, she heard sounds of activity ahead. Reining in her horse, she dismounted and entered the Raleigh Tavern. Her eyes, used to the inky night, took a moment to focus on the scene before her. Men gathered around tables engaged in lively debate or laughed at a shared joke as serving girls brought tankards of ale. Her entrance caused a gradual lull in the raucous interactions, as one by one each table became aware of her presence. It was unusual for a lady to stay at the taverns, and unheard of for one to appear out of nowhere, unaccompanied, after dark.

Glancing down at herself, Jenny noted how disheveled she looked in a dress which that morning had mirrored the color of the flower garden. Her long ride in the humidity made the dress cling to her form in a most unladylike manner. She tugged at it trying to compel it to fall loosely about her, but to no avail. Reaching up she brushed the hair from her face in an attempt to tame the tousled curls. Finally, giving up, she simply looked at the crowd and focused on her mission.

"Where is Randy O'Connor?" she asked. Exhausted from her ride, her voice was soft and her limbs tingled from being held taut.

Men looked at each other in bewilderment leaning forward and remarking on her appearance.

"Where is Randy O'Connor?" she said again, raising herself to her full height and using the voice she had commanded the horses with throughout the day. "I need to speak to him immediately."

"Randy, it appears one of your bawdy adventures has caught up with you," shouted a voice near the stairs. Laughter erupted and several rude remarks rose over the din.

"The Brentwood Plantation—," she did not even finish the sentence before a red-haired man rose, his six-foot-four inch frame dwarfing the men around him.

"What about the Brentwood Plantation?" he demanded. Jenny was amazed that a man of that size could close the distance between them so quickly. Now she looked up into green eyes fierce with urgency, fists doubled as if ready to join a fist-to-cuffs.

"The British are there. They are searching for Jonathon who visited the manor the other night. They have tracking dogs; they are on horseback, but Jonathon is safe and headed to the *Destiny* to get his crew." Her sentences shot out in quick bursts, partly from lack of breath, partly because she was trembling.

She grabbed the door frame for support, but her legs buckled beneath her. She felt herself lifted into strong arms and carried to a chair where Randy settled her in and ordered some cider. When the tankard arrived, she drank deeply, dry from riding the dusty road. Feeling a little stronger, she turned to him urgently.

"We must be off quickly, Mr. O'Connor, for Jonathon hopes to meet up with you en route to Brentwood Plantation. We are not sure where Captain Walters—"

"Captain Walters? Has that scoundrel returned? Oh yes, Jonathon would enjoy finding him and repaying his treatment of Emily," he laughed. "But you need rest, Miss—what is your name? And how do you come from Brentwood Manor?" Randy asked, a frown creasing his brow.

"I am Jennifer Sutton; David Sutton is my uncle and I must find him as well."

At the mention of David's name, Randy signaled to another man to go in search of him. Then he turned his full attention to the young woman.

Jenny explained her arrival just a few months earlier, finishing with the events of the day. She watched his brow furrow in concentration as she spoke about the arrival of British troops that morning. When she had finished, he shouted orders to several of the men nearby who sprang into action. One of the men threw a longcoat and tricorn hat to him which he deftly caught.

"Please, Mr. O'Connor, I must find my uncle, and we must be off at once," she said grabbing the sleeve of his linen shirt.

"Lass, call me Randy. My dear father was Mr. O'Connor," he said good-humoredly. "We will be off very soon, as soon as the men are ready to ride. But you, lass, need some sleep and I know just the place for you."

"No, please, Mr.—uh, Randy. I must return and see that Andrew is all right," she clapped her hand to her mouth and felt the heat rise to her face in embarrassment. "That is to see that everyone is safe," she amended.

Randy's eyes crinkled at the corners and Jenny felt flushed.

"So we are to rescue young Andrew, Lass?" he teased. "Aye, we will see that all at Brentwood Manor are safe and well, but having a half-asleep lass will slow us down, do you not see? Rest here for a few hours and I will leave a couple of lads behind to escort you and your uncle back to the plantation. It is for the best—for both you and us."

Jenny saw the logic of his argument and suddenly felt leaden. Her eyes were heavy and the relief of completing her task washed over her. The bedlam in the tavern became a dull, low, indistinct din that inundated her ears her making no sense at all. Suddenly a shout brought her to her senses.

"Jenny!" David rushed to her pulling her into his arms. "Are you all right? What are you doing here?" He released her looking her up and down for any sign of injury, and then gently set her back in her chair kneeling beside it and holding her hand.

Randy summarized Jenny's information for David, whose eyes darkened as he listened. Jenny noticed the twitch in his jaw at the mention of Captain Walters.

"I must return with you, Randy!" He looked at Jenny. "Will you be all right if I leave you here to rest, Jenny? Randy has assigned some good men who will escort you back to Brentwood Manor safely—after we have routed the British out of there."

Nodding, she rose and followed David to a room upstairs where a servant girl waited with a pitcher of fresh water and a clean frock. Kissing her forehead, David bid her goodnight and left. Jenny allowed the girl to assist her out of her damp clothes, and then she washed up and donned the fresh dress. Lying on the bed, she succumbed to sleep.

• • •

As the cry for independence increased, so did animosity between Loyalists and patriots. Many cities and towns were witness to brutal treatment of one side against another. After the discovery of an assassination plot against General Washington, New York city erupted into a frenzy of skirmishes between the opposing sides. Loyalists were attacked, beaten, and sometimes tarred and feathered. Anger mounted on both sides, and the British bore down on the patriots with renewed fervor. Fighting raged from the ports and cities and seeped into towns and the countryside.

Jonathon and his men rode through the darkness, ears sharp, guns at the ready. The early morning breeze brushed against his face as he rode in the lead reflecting on the night's events. He had left Jenny at the crossroads to Williamsburg and assumed she had found Randy who would be well on his way by now. Upon arriving at the *Destiny*, he had roused Gates and together they had selected crew members to accompany Jonathon. Knowing that Walters was on a single-minded mission to find and kill him, Jonathon believed that Emily and the others would be safe; after all, Emily was Walters's bait, so it would be foolish for him to harm her. If Walters killed Jonathon, he could not imagine what her fate would be. He shook his head; he could not allow thoughts like that to cloud his thinking. Taking a deep breath, he blew it out in a gust.

Splashes of red stretched across the eastern horizon signaling the break of day, but grey clouds hung leaden above them with the threat of a storm. Birdsong began intermittently in the trees, and shadows waned as a subdued dawn began to lighten the sky. Cantering at a steady pace, the group had made good time along the road, and Jonathon sensed before he saw the nearness of Brentwood property.

Holding up his left hand, he reined his mount to a halt and the others clustered around him. He looked at the faces surrounding him, stern in their determination, respect in the manner they returned his gaze, and he was grateful for these men. They had faced many dangers together at sea, and he was confident of their skill and loyalty as they faced this threat on land. He knew that he must be honest with them for that had been their covenant for all the years they had sailed together, and that was what had earned him their allegiance.

"I am not certain what to prepare for at present. The troops may still be at the manor, or they may be combing the woods for me. Be on guard to fight on horseback as well as ready to dismount and take up a position in the woods. You know our signal if you see British troops."

The men murmured or nodded consent, and they continued on at a slower pace scouring the woods on either side of the road. Jonathon had several plans depending on the situation they encountered, and each had been laid out carefully before the men. Of one thing he was certain: he must kill Captain Arthur Walters.

• • •

The crystal vase of flowers was reflected in the huge cherry dining table, which was polished to a high gloss. Candles, lit against the morning gloom, held flames that flickered and danced in the soft breeze wafting in through the tall windows. All of it felt ludicrous to Emily as she surveyed the room. Here she was surrounded by rich tapestries, lush damask drapes, glistening crystal and somewhere out there Jonathon trudged through the woods or sloshed through swamps evading capture. She picked at the food before her, sliding the pieces of ham into the sliced fruit. A half-eaten biscuit rested on the side of her plate, the sweet syrup pooling at the center.

Where was he? Was he safe? Would he return to Brentwood Manor? To her? Why should he after her treatment of him in the parlor. And the major question of all: could she forgive him? Looking out the window, she spied Deidre in the distance walking in the garden. Gall rose in her throat, and her hatred of the woman burned within her. The image of her lying beside Jonathon came unbidden into Emily's consciousness and she rubbed her fists against her eyes as if to banish it. How would she ever overcome this searing jealousy? How would she stop the image of them together from invading her mind? But underlying all the hatred, the jealousy, the fear, Emily knew that the flame of her love for Jonathon, however faintly it flickered today, had not been extinguished.

Emily looked up as Joanna entered and saw the sympathy in her eyes, unlocking a flood of tears. Falling into her sister-in-law's embrace, Emily released the pent-up sorrow that had been her constant companion since the revelation of Deidre's pregnancy.

"Emily, I am so sorry that you have to endure this," Joanna said as she looked out the window.

Emily's body racked with sobs as Joanna rubbed her back.

"Oh no," Joanna whispered.

Emily followed her gaze out the window and her heart sank as she watched Captain Walters and his men ride up the drive. All the life drained out of her as she searched the group for any sign of Jonathon. As much as Walters wanted him dead, he would ensure that Jonathon would first suffer at the hands of British prison guards. Trembling, she rose and stepped to the window; relief swept over her as she realized they held no prisoner. Looking at Joanna who was white with fear, she took her hand and started toward the front foyer. Stopping in Jonathon's study, she opened the gun cabinet, took out a pistol and tucked it between the folds of her skirt.

Together Emily and Joanna opened the front door to face the British soldiers. Walters had already dismounted and was about to climb the steps, but the women had come out on the porch and descended to him instead. Emily noted the grim line etched around Captain Walters's mouth and ascribed it to his frustration in not finding Jonathon. She observed that the dogs were held at bay at the rear of the group this time should a quick departure be in order, and inwardly she smiled and sent up a prayer for Jenny's well-being. Hearing a sound behind her, she glanced back and saw Andrew approaching from the out buildings, his musket held loosely in his hand. She returned her gaze to Captain Walters seeing the twitch of vexation in his jaw.

"I see you continue to search in vain," she said.

"Your husband is elusive, but all is not lost, Mrs. Brentwood. We have picked up his trail and should overtake him soon."

"And yet, you are here, Captain." Her voice was even and low.

"I believe I shall leave a few more men behind to…let us say… protect you," he sneered.

As he said this, the four soldiers who had remained behind approached from the stables and saluted their captain. Leaving the women and Andrew at the porch steps, the men gathered by the horses and conversed. Walters was clearly giving instructions as the others listened bending in to catch his every word.

Turning, he walked back and stood before Emily.

"Some of my men will remain here, and they will *not* be lodged in the stables. We are taking over the house, and my men will supervise the movements of everyone here."

Emily gasped. "How dare you—"

"I am a soldier of His Majesty, King George III and you are all his subjects. Certainly you, above all, understand that, Mrs. Brentwood." He smiled into her eyes stepping closer to her. "My troops are prepared to enjoy your famous hospitality, and you are to treat them as you would an honored guest." He pressed his face inches from hers. "Do I make myself clear, Mrs. Brentwood?" His lip curled up in a sneer as his eyes bored into hers.

"Move away from my sister," Andrew said gripping his musket.

Walters turned his face toward Andrew but did not move away from Emily.

"Careful, Wentworth," he warned.

Emily brought the pistol up and placed it against the captain's chest.

"Move away," she said.

Walters stepped back and smirked. "I see you siblings are much alike—both reckless in the guise of bravado. We'll see how brave you are."

He revealed his own pistol that had been tucked in his breeches. Still looking into Emily's eyes, he raised his arm and fired. Andrew spun around and dropped to the ground.

# Chapter 11

Realizing his men and their horses had to rest, Jonathon led them into a copse of trees near a stream. While resting and watering their horses, Jonathon searched the nearby woods for any sign of the British. He paced the area where the men and animals rested circling out farther on each round. Over a rise, he spotted a wisp of smoke and crept in to investigate. Clearly, the troops had stopped there for the night, for there was evidence of a campfire and the surrounding ground had been trampled by many horses. Staying low, he surveyed the area for signs of any scouts left behind, and then he made his way back to his men.

"Gates, they were here just last night." He kept his voice low, but excitement quickened his words. Pointing to the area he had just returned from, he indicated where the troops had stayed. He roused his men informing them of his find, and they gathered their supplies and headed over to the campsite. They entered the area in single file in an effort to preserve any traces of the direction the British had traveled when they left. Carefully searching the ground, Jonathon discovered their direction and his heart sank. They had ridden in the direction of Brentwood Manor. He dashed to his horse and mounted.

• • •

Emily screamed as she saw her brother fall. She hastened to him and knelt beside him as he writhed on the ground moaning.

"Oh, my God," she cried. "Andrew, Andrew! Oh my God!"

She cradled him in her arms as Joanna knelt beside them. His eyes were closed, his mouth open gasping for breath and his right hand gripped his left shoulder.

"We need to stop the bleeding," Joanna said, ripping the hem of her dress into a long strip and wrapping it around Andrew's shoulder, pressing it against the wound.

"Let that be a warning to you, Mrs. Brentwood. I am weary of your silly games. I do promise you this, however; before I release your husband to the British prison, I will return here with him so each of you can enjoy the other's suffering." Laughing, he turned his horse and sped down the drive, his soldiers following.

"We must get Andrew inside," Joanna said as drops of rain began to spatter on the ground beside him. "You must not lift him, Emily." She turned to look at the eight remaining soldiers. "Please, help us get him inside."

They looked at each other, hesitating and a voice from behind them commanded, "Help them. Now!"

Looking up, Emily saw Deidre standing there with a pistol pointed at the head of one of the soldiers.

• • •

Jonathon was itching to break into a gallop and speed to Brentwood Manor. He kept telling himself that Emily would be fine as long as he was alive—and after Walters was dead. But doubt crept into his mind because he knew that the man was brutal and uncaring. Wiping his hand across his eyes he forced himself to concentrate on the immediate mission. They were close on the heels of Walters and his men, and today, God willing, they would meet face to face.

Hoof beats sounded fast and heavy ahead. A scout Jonathon had sent out came pounding up to him.

"Sir, British troops are approaching. They are about a mile down the road. They should be here within a quarter-hour." He gasped for breath and his horse snorted and reared.

"Did they see you?" Jonathon asked.

"No sir. I did just as you told me; I stayed in the trees, and I stayed low."

"Excellent." Jonathon patted the crewman's arm.

"Men, lead your mounts deep into the woods. We will ambush them from both sides of the road." He motioned for half of the men to go on one side of the road and the rest to the other. At once, they disappeared into the trees and the road looked as undisturbed as if they had never been there.

Jonathon tethered his horse to a tree deep within the woods, unseen from the road. He crept back scanning the woods to see where his men were. Through the trees he saw them moving cautiously to avoid snapping twigs beneath their feet, bent over as they walked to remain concealed. Nearing the road, Jonathon took cover behind a shortleaf pine. He checked his rifle and pistol, and unclasped the top leather strap of his knife sheath. Rubbing his hand along the barrel of his Brown Bess, he knew his shot must be accurate...and deadly. Gates signaled him from across the road that all of the men were in place, and the ordinary forest sounds echoed around them.

Finally, hoof beats sounded in the distance, and Jonathon gripped his weapons. If there were twenty-five British soldiers, they were outnumbered by ten; Jonathon liked these odds, for they had the element of surprise on their side, and his men were intrepid. The beating of hooves grew closer, but the forest around him projected a sense of innocence as none of his men stirred. They knew the signal: Jonathon would fire first.

The initial British troops appeared on the road; the men held their place. In the lead, Jonathon saw Captain Walters, and his finger tightened on the trigger. His shot had to be clean and precise. The riders came closer, and Jonathon waited until the distance was best for the range of his rifle. Just as he pulled the trigger, the soldier to Walters's left pulled in front of him catching Jonathon's shot in the chest. The man's mouth formed an O of surprise as he jerked back, and then death took him and slid from his horse. Chaos ensued, and while the horses shied and bucked and the British troops tried reining them in, Jonathon's crew leapt from the surrounding woods, weapons firing.

Jonathon cursed his bad luck and scrambled between the horses and men looking for Walters. Shots rang out around him and men cried out in pain or in victory. The mounted men were at an advantage for taking aim at the crewmen, but at a disadvantage in ability to maneuver in the limited space afforded by the narrow road. The horses also pushed the men on foot, sometimes knocking them to the ground. Bayonets jutted out of the soldiers' muskets, and after firing, they stabbed at the attacking crewmen. Outnumbered, Jonathon's men realized their disadvantage, but continued fighting valiantly. Out of the corner of his eye, Jonathon saw his men firing at the mounted soldiers, or dragging them from their horses and using their knives, but it was clear the British had the upper hand.

The sound of approaching riders was concealed by the surrounding din, so Jonathon did not hear Randy, David, and the men from the Raleigh Tavern arrive, but as they grew closer, he caught sight of them. Relief flooded him as he watched the insurgence of support riding into the melee and leveling the advantage.

Gaining the upper hand, his men were driven by their success, but the one man Jonathon sought seemed to have disappeared. Frantically, he searched for Walters and finally spotted him through a group of mounted soldiers. The captain's eyes roamed the patriots intently, and Jonathon knew he was looking for him. Moving with catlike precision, Jonathon wove his way through the horses until he stood in front of the horse bearing Walters.

"Brentwood," he said, his eyes glinting, a sneer crossing his face.

"Walters, are you prepared to die for what you did to my wife?" Jonathon asked raising his arm and pointing his pistol at him.

"I thought our fight was about loyalty to the king," Walters sneered, his eyes glinting with anticipation.

"There is no loyalty to the king here, Walters," Jonathon said, cocking his gun.

Walters raised his arm revealing his own pistol. Both men fired, but the jostling of the fighting men around them caused their bullets to miss their marks. Startled by the close shots, one horse leapt between them, knocking Jonathon to the ground. He quickly rolled to his left to avoid being trampled by the rearing horse, and as he sprang back up, he saw that his men were winning the skirmish; most of the British were dead or wounded. Walters, quickly surveying the scene, reached the same conclusion. He turned his horse to flee back down the road, but before he sped off, he spat his threat back to Jonathon over his shoulder.

"This is not finished, Brentwood. I will come back for you, and I will kill you!"

Jonathon took in the scene around him. His men had been victorious, but at the cost of some of their lives. Going to each of the wounded men, he assessed their conditions and acknowledged their efforts. He had lost five men, and he knelt beside each of them and offered a prayer.

Reaching Randy and David, he clapped each man on the arm.

"Excellent timing, my friends," Jonathon said, a rush of affection for his lifelong friend and brother-in-law running through him.

"You did not afford us much notice, Jonathon." Randy's eyes crinkled at the corners. "And sending a sweet lass to pass along your message caused me a moment of confusion, for she is a lovely young thing."

"*Young* is the word to which you should attend, Randy! And my brother-in-law David here would have you strung up should you dally with his niece!" Jonathan replied, his attempt at lightness overshadowed by his sorrow at the loss of his men.

"Jonathon is correct, Randy!' David laughed.

Jonathon knelt beside more of the wounded offering comforting words. Rising, he grabbed a mount and vaulted into the saddle.

"Gates, bury our lost men, and care for the wounded. Randy, form a contingent to take the soldiers who are able to travel to Williamsburg to be jailed, and then join David at Brentwood Manor to ensure my family is safe. I will contact you as soon as I am able."

Turning his mount in the direction Walters fled, Jonathon spurred the horse into a gallop.

• • •

Andrew's face was ashen against the crisp, white linen pillowcase. Dulcie's son, Jedadiah, accompanied by a British soldier, had been sent to fetch Dr. Anderson over an hour before, but Emily knew that he often attended the Virginia Convention in Williamsburg these days. She prayed that he would be at home and able to tend to Andrew soon. Brushing a lock of hair from his forehead, she pressed a damp cloth against it. Her eyes took in the amount of blood that seeped into the cloth Joanna had bound around his upper arm and chest where the bullet was lodged. She knew it was imperative to remove the bullet and clean the wound, but she was frightened to try to accomplish that herself. Surely Dr. Anderson would arrive soon. She tried to calculate the time it would take them to return with the doctor, and even if they rode swiftly, it could be too late.

The remaining soldiers had taken over the manor, and were presently lounging in the dining room drinking brandy and ale having commanded Dora to prepare a meal for them. Their raucous laughter floated up the stairs, and they harassed the house slaves. At Deidre's command, they had hefted Andrew up and carried him to his room, laying him on his bed roughly.

"You will likely lose this one," one of the soldiers said to Emily, smirking. Anger rose within her, and she slapped his face. He reached for her, but Joanna stepped between them.

"It would be best if you go downstairs now," she said, setting her mouth in a firm line.

He looked from one woman to the other, shrugged his shoulders and left the room.

Deidre looked at Emily. "I did not do this for you, Emily. I did it for Jonathon because I know he is so fond of Andrew. And because I hate the British for all they have taken from me."

Emily saw the defiance in the woman's eyes.

"Nonetheless, I thank you, Deidre," she said. The smirk on Deidre's face told her that she could never trust the woman. They stared at each other for a moment, and then Deidre turned and left the room.

Emily ran to Andrew's bedside, tears falling freely now. She untied his shirt, and carefully spread it open to reveal his wound. Joanna tore strips of cloth from the extra pillowcase, poured water from the porcelain ewer into the bowl and wet the strips. Sitting beside Andrew, she cleaned the wound and gently wrapped it. These were the strips Emily stared at now watching crimson seep further into the linen.

She heard the door open and Joanna's soft footfall.

"Joanna, even if they ride as swiftly as the wind, it might be too late," Emily whispered. Fear gripped her and she recalled the first time she almost lost her brother when they sailed on the *Destiny*. Jonathon had saved his life; oh, how she wished he were beside her to help save Andrew's life again. And to hold her and give her strength because at this moment, she felt helpless and afraid.

"The British sit with their feet propped on the dining table," Joanna said, her voice low and her eyes flickering toward the door lest they be heard. "They are uncivilized oafs!"

"And we are to house them and feed them?" Emily asked.

"It is the law. We are required to house and feed any British troops who demand it," Joanna said. "That is a major cause of contention against the crown."

Raucous laughter rose through the floor. The women looked at each other. Emily felt helpless to stop the cruelty of the soldiers, and she could see concern etched on Joanna's face. How long would this go on? But Emily knew it would continue as long as Jonathon was free—or until Captain Walters was dead.

Andrew moaned softly, and Emily turned to scan his face. His eyes were open, and he looked at his sister. Leaning down, she kissed his cheek and smiled softly. His eyes were glazed and unfocused, and he reached for her hand. She grasped his and was alarmed at how sweaty and hot it felt. He closed his eyes and his grip slackened. Emily looked anxiously at Joanna.

"Dr. Anderson will be here soon, Em," she whispered.

Emily nodded, feeling tears spill down her face. She looked at her little brother, his face so pale, his life so precious.

They sat together in silence, praying for Andrew's recovery, each lost in her own thoughts. The afternoon heat hung in the room, and Emily shifted uncomfortably in her chair beside the bed. She noticed that Joanna had dozed, and wished she could do the same, but worry for Andrew and discomfort from her increasing size kept her awake.

Dulcie entered the room, and her eyes conveyed the news Emily dreaded.

"Miss Emily, the doctor is away in Williamsburg," she said, hands folded in front of her, eyes downcast. "I am most sorry, ma'am."

Emily felt hope disappear in the closing of the door as Dulcie left. There was only one thing to do, then. She must remove the bullet from her brother's shoulder as best she could. Rousing Joanna, she mentally listed what she would need. Joanna started up at Emily's gentle nudging.

"What is it, Emily?" she asked.

"Dr. Anderson is not coming, Joanna. We must tend to Andrew ourselves."

Joanna looked at the young man lying on the bed, and Emily followed her gaze, aghast that he seemed to shrink into the bedclothes. She pulled herself up and gathered her wits. She crossed to the bell and rang for Dulcie.

Returning to the bed, she gently unwound the cloth around her brother's shoulder. Removing the last of it, she forced herself to look closely at the wound. An ugly gash surrounded a hole that dug deep into his shoulder. Blood continued to ooze out, but not at the alarming rate it had been. Cautiously, she probed the area, feeling his muscle, bones and finally, a hard, unyielding lump lodged just below his collarbone.

Dulcie entered the room. "Yes, ma'am?"

"We need sheets, thread, needles, and water, boiling water and fresh water in the pitcher, Dulcie. And we need a knife, but first clean it well."

Emily saw Dulcie's eyes widen and she looked frozen in place.

"Hurry, Dulcie. We must remove this bullet from Andrew's shoulder." She instructed her on what herbs to bring as well.

After the maid left the room, Joanna sat beside Emily taking her hands.

"Emily, are you sure...?"

"What choice do we have, Joanna? Andrew will die if the bullet remains there." She searched her sister-in-law's eyes seeing the fear and doubt. "I will need your help." Joanna nodded, straightening her shoulders.

When Dulcie returned with the items, Emily instructed her to rip the sheets into strips as Joanna had done with the pillowcase. Each of her senses was magnified as she prepared the items for the impending procedure. The sound of the shredding sheet was rhythmic and steadied her nerves. She felt she could almost hear the heartbeat of each person in the room so acutely perceptive was her hearing. As Emily took the knife and dipped it into the pan letting it soak there, the boiling water scalded her hands making them sensitive to whatever they touched. She removed her hands cooling them as she poured fresh water from the pitcher into the basin, and then dried them on a clean strip of cloth. The brightness of the sun streaming through the windows on either side of the bed slanted across the floor, and she saw with sharp clarity the outline of each item in the room. Her mind seemed to have reached a different plane of awareness while it refused to acknowledge what she was about to do, holding her fear at bay.

Leaning over Andrew, she gently washed the area around the wound, cleaning the blood from his skin in order to see the open gash clearly. She hoped she could simply follow the path and retrieve the bullet from there. But she saw that would not be possible; she would have to cut into Andrew to successfully remove it. Her brother moaned and shifted in the bed as though aware of what was to happen.

"You will be well soon, Drew. I promise you," she whispered.

Taking the knife from the scalding water, she again probed his shoulder to find the exact spot where the bullet lay. As if watching someone else's hands, she saw the knife cut a slice in one direction and then across the first to mark a bloody X on Andrew's skin. He cried out, but Emily placed a folded up strip between his teeth and he bit down on it. She continued deepening each cut until she felt the metal of the bullet against the knife. Andrew squirmed and squeezed his eyes closed, but she could not allow herself to acknowledge his pain.

"Joanna, press a cloth here," she said indicating a place to the right of the incision. When Joanna did that, the bleeding slowed.

Emily nudged the bullet with the knife in an effort to move it toward the opening. At one point she had it balanced against the knife ready to roll it out, but Andrew moved and it fell back into the wound. She made the cut wider so she could place her index finger into the wound, and then wedged the bullet between her finger and the knife. Andrew moaned through the cloth and arched his back in pain. Emily waited for him to settle back, and with agonizingly slow movements, she balanced the bullet, gradually withdrawing it from Andrew's shoulder. She dropped it on a strip of cloth, and then probed the wound to check for any other metal shards that may have broken off. Finally, satisfied that she had removed the entire shot, Emily washed out the wound and pressed more clean strips against it. Andrew was soaked in sweat and was panting from the pain. Emily's forehead was also beaded with sweat and her frock was drenched.

Joanna had threaded a needle with a long, double strand and handed it to Emily.

"I am so sorry to cause you more pain, Drew, but this is necessary," she said softly.

Taking the threaded needle, Emily began to sew the ragged edges of the wound together. Andrew bit down on the cloth between his teeth, and tried to lie still. Emily's movements were quick and deft, and soon the gash was closed. Looking through the tray of remedies Dulcie had brought in, Emily was pleased to see the evening primrose she had requested, and she made a poultice and placed it against the wound. Gently she wound strips around it to hold it fast against Andrew's shoulder. She saw that Andrew was no longer losing blood; she reached up and removed the strip from his mouth. Seeing the wan smile he gave her, she caressed his face.

"You are going to be all right, Drew." She smiled at him.

"Thank you, Em," he whispered.

Dulcie entered with a tea tray and set it on the round table near the bed.

"This lavender tea is for Master Andrew," she said handing mug to Emily. "It will help him sleep."

"Thank you, Dulcie," Emily said.

"Miss Emily, you need to eat somethin', but I dunno what will be left from those soldiers," Dulcie said shaking her head. "I snuck some cheese and fruit for you." She lifted a napkin revealing the food.

"Thank you, Dulcie," Emily said taking the woman's hand. "You always know what I need." She smiled fondly her.

"Well, see if that lavender tea don' help Master Andrew," Dulcie said waving toward the tray.

Emily gently raised Andrew's head supporting it with her arm and held the cup to his lips. He sipped the tea and nodded, so she laid him back down. After a few moments, she helped him drink more of the tea. She checked his shoulder and saw that he was not losing blood as he had been. When she looked back at his face, his eyes were closed, no crease between his brows. Soon he was breathing evenly. She knew only time would tell if he would recover, but at least now he had a fighting chance.

• • •

Emily dozed in the chair beside Andrew's bed. He had been restless since that afternoon when she had removed the bullet, and to her dismay, he was now running a fever. Despite Joanna's urging, she would not leave her brother's side. Joanna was sleeping in Will's room because, as she had told Emily, she was reluctant to leave him alone while the British prowled the house. Emily had listened to their rowdiness throughout the evening, and was relieved when they finally settled down near midnight. Since then she had been sleeping intermittently between shifts of tending Andrew.

The windows were open to the summer night taking advantage of any available breeze. The moon slipped behind clouds that teased with the promise of a cooling rain, but none had fallen so far. Emily had just settled into the chair again, when she heard the soft tinkle of glass breaking; she started up. Were those soldiers now breaking the crystal having consumed all of the brandy? But no raucous noise ensued and she wondered if she had heard the sound at all. Then, she heard a rustling on the veranda below. Stealing to the window, she stood against the drapes and peered out. The night was still, the clouds scudding before the moon again. Nothing stirred in the heavy, dark heat. Then she saw movement at the edge of the veranda. The clouds cleared and she saw two figures: Randy and David.

Her first thought was that she must warn them of the soldiers inside the house, but then she realized they must know, or else they would have entered through the front door. The front door! It was locked—she must get to it!

She jumped up and hurried to the stairs, running down them as quietly as possible; she started to cross the foyer but froze. Before her stood a British soldier with his pistol pointed at her face.

"Stop!" his voice echoed off the marble floor. Scuffling feet sounded from the rooms above them.

"I need some air—it is stifling upstairs," Emily said.

He looked at her, his eyes narrowed, and the gun remained aimed at her head.

"Please, sir, just allow me to step out onto the porch," she asked.

Looking up, she saw several soldiers in various stages of undress appear on the balcony and move toward the staircase. Their eyes were bloodshot from the spirits consumed, and they teetered down the stairs. Joanna and Deidre appeared at the balcony as the soldiers descended.

Suddenly she heard the sound of breaking glass from behind the study door; the soldiers seemed to shake off their state of intoxication quickly. The guard with the pistol grabbed Emily and she gasped with pain as he twisted her arm behind her. His grip was fierce as she struggled against him, and she stumbled over his feet as he turned toward the study door. He placed her before him as a shield facing whoever would appear. Joanna gasped and ran down the stairs, halting at the base when the soldier pointed his pistol at her.

"Stop right there!" he ordered.

"Please, sir, let her go. Do you not see that she is with child?" Joanna begged.

"Yes, the child of a traitor," he said roughly shoving Emily toward the study door.

Frantically, Emily looked at Joanna and barely nodded toward the front door; Joanna looked at her quizzically, and then nodded in return. She watched the other soldiers form a semi-circle around the study, their eyes trained on the door. Out of the corner of her eye, Emily watched as Joanna slowly sidled to the front door and stood in front of it with her hands behind her back.

"You there! What are you doing?" shouted a soldier who had looked back at Joanna.

"Leave her alone, you bastard!" Deidre shouted from the balcony. The soldier looked up at her and pointed his weapon at her.

"Get down here," he commanded.

Emily smiled to herself as Deidre slowly descended the steps, her breasts swaying beneath the bodice of her nightgown which was pulled low, captivating the soldier. Emily watched as one by one the other soldiers lost their concentration on the study door and watched her descend. Almost at the bottom, she leaned against the rail of the sweeping staircase bending forward enough to provide ample inspection of her bosom by all of them, and affording Joanna enough distraction to unlock the front door. For once, Emily was grateful that Deidre knew how to use her charms.

"What has you so distraught, officers?" Deidre asked, holding her pose. Their mouths hung open as they viewed Deidre's half-hidden breasts propped so invitingly on the bannister.

Suddenly the front door burst open and David stood in the entrance, Randy close behind. Shots resonated as men poured into the foyer. Emily saw Joanna crouch on the floor behind the front door. Deidre fell against the steps, and Emily was not sure whether or not she had been shot. The soldier who held her pulled Emily in front of himself as a shield, and pointed his pistol into the middle of the melee.

Emily kicked at the soldier, but to no avail; his grip on her was like iron. Men fell all about her as she searched the group of patriots for Jonathon. She did not see him, and her heart sank. Had he been captured at last? She dreaded the thought of Jonathon at the hands of Captain Walters. Looking up, she saw Randy struggling with one of the soldiers who was as tall as he. They were evenly matched, and they twisted and grunted as each tried to overtake the other. A shot sounded and the two froze staring at each other as if they had just come face to face. Emily's heart stopped as she watched Randy drop his hand. *Oh my God,* she thought, searching Randy's face for evidence of the outcome of the struggle. The British soldier smiled at Randy, then his head dropped and he slid to the floor. She let out the breath she had been holding.

Randy turned toward Emily and the soldier who locked her in his grip.

"Let her go," he commanded pointing his pistol at the man.

In answer, the man raised his pistol and Emily felt the cold metal against the side of her head.

"Go ahead and shoot; she will die with me," he sneered.

Randy held his position, but did not fire. Like statues, the men stood frozen. The soldier cocked his pistol and a shot rang out. Emily jerked up as the soldier fell beside her, his eyes open in wonder at what had just befallen him. David ran to her from the side and caught her as she slumped to the floor.

"He is dead, Emily; you are safe," he said.

Trembling, Emily surveyed the area around her. As if in a dream, she watched the scene, each person seeming to move slowly. Joanna slowly stood up, holding the door jamb for support. Bodies carpeted the floor in front of her, crumpled and contorted in gruesome poses. One man stared up at her, dead blue eyes sending a chill along her spine. Deidre rose slowly from the steps, dazed, her nightgown still low and open in the front. Two wounded British soldiers were being hefted up by members of Jonathon's crew, while the dead British were being dragged out the front door leaving swaths of crimson ribbons behind. One of Jonathon's crewmen was seriously injured, blood pooling beneath him a stark contrast to the white marble floor. A man from the Raleigh Tavern lay dead beside a British soldier their arms eerily outstretched toward each other as if in friendship. As if at a signal, several house servants gathered to help the wounded and carry away the dead.

David helped Emily up and took her into the parlor, easing her down on the settee. Joanna followed and as he lifted Emily's feet to lay them across the settee, Joanna propped pillows behind her head. Then falling into David's arms, Joanna began to tremble and cry. Dulcie entered with tankards of ale.

"This is all we got left, Master David. Them British drank all your good brandy and wine," she said, shaking her head.

"Thank you, Dulcie." He took the tankards and gave one to Emily. Turning to Joanna, he put his arm around her to steady her as she drank. Emily watched the tender scene wishing that Jonathon were there to comfort her. Or, would he be comforting Deidre? Then another thought struck her.

"Andrew," Emily said attempting to rise from the settee.

"I will see to him," Joanna said.

"Where is Andrew?" David asked, looking around as if he would appear.

Joanna explained what had happened earlier that day.

"That must have been just before we engaged them on the road," he mused.

"David, did you fight all of those British soldiers?" Joanna cried looking back at the small number of men who had accompanied him.

"Well, there were many more of us. Jonathon brought crewmen, and Randy and I brought men from Williamsburg…"

"Jonathon was with you?" Emily gasped as she sat up. "Where is he? Is he all right? Why is he not with you now?" She fired questions at him.

David sat beside her.

"Captain Walters escaped our ambush; Jonathon chased after him. I do not know his whereabouts at present, but I do know he will chase Walters to the end of the earth for what he did to you."

Emily stared ahead wondering where Jonathon was at that moment. He was a skilled marksman and an excellent rider, so she had no doubt he would engage Walters. But Walters was ruthless and dishonest. There was no telling what he would do to entrap Jonathon.

"Emily, you have had an exceedingly difficult day, and you need to rest. When you are able, Jonathon charged me with explaining all that occurred between him and Deidre. I will await your permission to have that conversation with you. At present, we need to care for Andrew and the wounded. And for you. You were extremely courageous tonight." She saw the admiration in his eyes as he smiled at her.

Suddenly overcome with exhaustion, Emily nodded and closed her eyes. Sleep overtook her immediately, so David and Joanna left to attend to the others.

• • •

Slop, swish, slop, swish.

Emily awoke to this strange sound. A crick in her neck reminded her that she had spent the night curled up on the settee.

Slowly raising herself, she craned her neck in each direction until the muscles loosened, and then she stretched and rose.

Slop, swish, slop swish.

Curious, she opened the parlor door to see Jedadiah mopping the marble floor; the bucket of water was brownish red, and ribbons of red ran through the path left by his mop.

"Mornin' Miss Emily," he said, stopping to greet her. "You jus' go back inside the parlor; you don' need to see all of this blood. It be bad for your baby."

"Thank you, Jedadiah. I saw plenty of blood last night." She smiled at him as she sidestepped the area he was working on.

Climbing the stairs, she proceeded to Andrew's room and opened the door. Joanna was sitting beside him pressing water-soaked cloths to his forehead and neck. When she turned to her, Emily saw the lines of concern on her face and the circles under her eyes.

"Has his fever broken?" Emily asked.

Joanna shook her head and continued bathing him with cool water from the porcelain bowl. Her exhaustion was evident in every move, and Emily knew that Joanna had tended Andrew throughout the night allowing her to sleep. Emily walked over to the bed. Leaning down, she felt Andrew's forehead and gasped.

"He is burning up!" she exclaimed. "What else can we do, Joanna?"

Shaking her head, her sister-in-law looked at Emily with tear-filled eyes.

"I do not know what else to do, Em." One tear escaped and ran down her cheek.

"No," Emily cried. "No, he cannot die. There must be something more."

Joanna stood and eased Emily down on the bed. She took a fresh strip of cloth, wrung it out and gave it to Emily.

"We can pray," she said simply, and she walked out of the room.

Emily felt tears course down her face as the reality struck her. She looked at Andrew's white face and watched his shallow breathing. How could she lose her last family member? Her baby brother who had shared her life, her memories, her adventures? How could this happen? Feeling dreadfully alone, Emily sobbed. She prayed desperate prayers for her brother. She begged him to be strong, and she washed him with her tears.

Through the open window she heard the approach of several riders. Her heart raced as she ran to the window to discover who was arriving. It was a group of five including Jenny and Mr. Gates. But no Jonathon. She pressed her palms into her eyes and fought back the despair. How could she lose her brother and possibly her husband? Where was he? But hope ignited within her at the sight of Mr. Gates for both Andrew and Jonathon owed their lives to his medical knowledge. She hastened downstairs to greet the party.

As she descended the front steps of the manor, Jenny ran up to her eagerly.

"Is everyone all right? Is Andrew all right?" she asked.

Emily looked at the younger woman, her heart heavy. She watched as Jenny's smile faded to disbelief as she looked past Emily to the door, her eyes searching.

"Where is Andrew?" she asked, her voice small.

"Jenny, Andrew was shot; he is not doing well."

"No!" she cried looking at Emily for denial. "NO!"

"I will bring you to him," Emily said softly.

Robert Gates approached her, concern showing in his eyes.

"Mrs. Brentwood, you look exhausted."

"Oh, Mr. Gates, please come and examine Andrew. He has been shot; his fever is high, and I believe—," she could not continue.

Jenny's tears ran unchecked down her face as the three hurried into the manor. Leading them upstairs, Emily was surprised at two things: her sudden exhaustion and the realization that Jenny was experiencing what she had aboard the *Destiny* when she believed Jonathon was dying. Their love had been new then, too, but even then her desolation at the thought of losing him was overwhelming. How odd that someone would feel that way about her little brother. She saw Jenny as if for the first time. Yes, she was a woman in love, and her brother was a man now. Too drained to follow this train of thought any further, she entered Andrew's room. Jenny ran to Andrew's bedside followed by Mr. Gates. Emily stood where she was, unable to take another step. Feeling dizzy, she grabbed the arm of a nearby chair and sat down. The scene before her brought back memories of tending Jonathon aboard the *Destiny* and she watched Jenny leaning over Andrew, tears spilling on the sheets and Mr. Gates telling her what needed to be done. With an overwhelming sense of relief, Emily leaned back in the chair and knew that if Andrew were to live it would be because of the skill of Mr. Gates and the love of Jenny Sutton.

• • •

The subdued group crowded around the supper table. The day had been busy with burying the dead, caring for the wounded and assessing the food stores remaining after the British occupation of the estate. David planned to visit neighbors to barter with them for food, but he was reluctant to travel far from the plantation so long as Captain Walters was at large and Jonathon was in danger. Jenny had been caring for Andrew all day, and Emily had noticed the strain in her face, the lines around her mouth and eyes. David could not take his eyes from Joanna, and Emily could feel his love for her like a tangible entity in the room. She remembered when Jonathon would look at her like that, and it had been as if a shield of love protected her from any harm. But at this moment, she felt cold and empty. Mr. Gates was still at Andrew's bedside with Jenny, administering remedies that had proven effective after sea battles.

Emily felt rested after a long afternoon nap, and her appetite seemed to have returned. Upon waking, she visited Andrew, who was still running a fever and was becoming delirious. She watched Jenny apply cool compresses to his forehead and neck, following Mr. Gates's instructions, just as she had for Jonathon. Her heart went out to the girl, for if Jenny loved Andrew as she had Jonathon, her heart was breaking right now. Looking again at the girl, the sadness conveyed in her eyes confirmed Emily's thoughts.

Still no word from Jonathon, no sighting of him or Walters. Emily shifted in her chair, hungry to know how he was faring. Hungry for any knowledge of him at all. Gazing across the table, she caught David watching her. His eyes were soft and caring.

"David, may I have a word with you?" she asked.

"Of course, Emily," he bowed slightly.

The two excused themselves and rose from the table. Emily needed to know about Jonathon and Deidre; despite the havoc of the last days, she was ready. It was time.

# Chapter 12

Emily sat at her dressing table brushing her hair, pondering all that David had told her about Jonathon and Deidre's encounter. While relief washed through her like a soothing stream at the knowledge that Jonathon had been coerced, still a distressing image of them lying together nagged at her mind. It was not a new image, for the picture had haunted her since Deidre's shocking accusation the night Jonathon had returned to Brentwood Manor. But until now, the image had included soft words whispered, gentle caresses building to passion consuming and welcomed by both. At last Emily's fear was assuaged knowing that Jonathon's love was hers alone.

She imagined what it must have been like for him when Deidre threatened her life and that of their baby. Remembering how weak he had been, even at her last visit when they had made love, she knew he must have felt vulnerable and powerless. He had still been unable to rise from the bed for any length of time, and Emily had found it necessary to assist him even in undressing. How they had laughed and teased each other, and then how gentle and tender their lovemaking had been. Even in his weakened state, Jonathon had been a wonderful lover, and Emily felt a flush seep through her at this memory. She longed for him with all of her being, hungry to feel his arms around her again. A familiar stirring started low and spread throughout her body. She laughed at herself, looking down at her rounded midsection, and then she sobered as she wondered if perhaps he would not find her attractive now.

The stillness of the summer night wrapped the room in serenity. Yielding to the humid air, Emily had donned only a light, silk robe left open for any cooling effect. Feeling the baby kick and move within her, Emily's hands instinctively went to her belly.

She gently prodded encouraging return kicks and smiled as she felt the life of her child so enthusiastic and flourishing. Rubbing her skin with jasmine-scented oil, she closed her eyes and breathed deeply of the aroma that she loved. The reality of the situation was confusing at best. How would they heal from this? How would they go on from here? Had her rejection of Jonathon the night of his visit turned him from her and straight into Deidre's waiting arms? She had been so angry, so hurt. Unable even to recall what she had said to him, she knew that she had dismissed him—perhaps he had given up on her. It was not the first time she had said hurtful things to him. There was much forgiving to be done by both.

Hearing the soft sound of her bedroom door opening, she opened her eyes and again looked in the mirror. Jonathon's eyes reflected back at her from where he stood in the doorway, motionless and tentative. Their eyes held, and a jumble of emotions ran through her: fear, longing, relief, joy, hope and desire. His gaze held hers as he stepped into the room and closed the door quietly. Emily watched him, transfixed. He came to her and in the mirror's reflection each studied the other. Slowly, he raised his hands and placed them on her shoulders; she gasped softly as she felt his skin on hers. They were frozen in the moment. Silence enshrouded them broken only by the night sounds of crickets and the sputtering of the candles. She felt a silent tear brim then trace along her cheek, past her lips leaving a salty marker of its presence. Leaning forward, Jonathon bent and kissed her shoulder, his lips soft and warm, his breath like a feather teasing her skin. Emily trembled. He knelt beside her, and she turned, facing him. His eyes searched hers, and, taking her hands in his, he bent his head and kissed each palm.

"Emily, I am so sorry," he whispered. "I ask your forgiveness; I will do whatever it takes to win back your love." His voice was soft in the still air. When he looked up, his eyes found hers once more. Silvery tears caught the candlelight as they streamed down his face, and his eyes glistened in its glow.

Seeing him before her was so unreal for Emily, and she felt as though she were moving in a dream. Nothing felt real, and time seemed to creep. While she heard his words, she seemed unable to comprehend them, much less fashion a response, so she simply gazed at him, trancelike.

Jonathon lowered his head again, his voice barely audible.

"I know I have hurt you beyond telling, Em, but I pray it not be beyond repair."

Feeling the desperation in his voice, Emily reached below his chin and raised his face to hers. Was he really here, kneeling before her? How long had she waited for this moment? Why was she unable to respond and assure him of her love? She saw the crease between his brows, anguish evident in his eyes.

"I love you."

The simplicity of her statement was all she could manage, yet it held within it the hope of their future, the promise of their life together.

Jonathon crumpled into her arms, shaking. He buried his head against her shoulder, and his tears dampened her robe.

"My love," he breathed into her hair. Straightening, he held her face in his hands and gently kissed her. He leaned back and looked at her, his eyes shining. Brushing back her tawny hair, he let it flow across her shoulders and down her back. He took in her body enlarged with the evidence of their love, and with wonder in his eyes, he traced the curve of her belly, a soft smile playing on his face. A hearty kick surprised him and he laughed out loud looking back at her. Joy mixed with pride glowed on his face.

"Em, our baby! How he has grown!"

She laughed with him and covered his hands with hers. "Indeed he has! I waddle like a duck when I walk!" Her words tripped over the giddiness rising within.

Jonathon bent to her belly and spoke. "Good day, my fine fellow, I am your father." The baby kicked at the sound of Jonathon's voice. "Oh-ho, so you recognize me, I see. I have been away, but I shall be here when you make your appearance, my lad…" He looked at Emily as he continued. "…I give you my solemn oath." His eyes burned into hers with love and promise.

Emily reached out to caress his face and smiled softly. "We know you will be here, Jonathon."

He wrapped his arms around her and drew her close. His hand reached up and stroked her hair, and then he leaned in and kissed her. Fire burned within Emily as his lips sought hers, and she pressed herself to him, yielding to his embrace.

He kissed her as a starving man, hungrily tasting her sweetness. He lifted her from her chair and carried her to the bed laying her down gently and lying alongside her. He covered her face, her neck, her breasts with kisses, his hands searching, roaming, caressing her body. Emily threw her arms around his neck pulling him closer, wanting to climb inside his skin, to unite forever. Her hands slid across his back seeking any part of him within her reach. Hungry for each other and stirred with pent up desire and longing, they moved in the frenzied dance of lovers long parted.

Suddenly, Jonathon moved away and looked at her in alarm. Emily met his eyes, confused.

"Em, am I hurting you, or our baby?" he asked, concern etched on his face.

Emily laughed. "No, Jonathon, as long as you do not throw me in the air or toss me on the ground, I believe I will be fine—as will the child." She smiled into his eyes and drew his face to hers. She kissed him softly, and smiled reassuringly. Then she kissed him with a passion so familiar, so dear, so urgent, that he stifled a cry in his throat.

"My God, Em. My God,"

He kissed her throat, along the swell of her breast, the soft pink tip of her nipples. He traveled down to her belly and covered it with kisses, then returned and rested his head on her breasts. She stroked his hair and pressed a kiss on the top of his head.

"Emily, I need to tell you—" he began.

"Hush, Jonathon. David has already told me about what Deidre did."

"I could not…I was unable to…I did not want to…"

"I know, Jonathon."

He buried his face in her neck. "I should have been able to stop her. Damn the woman—I should have been able to hold her back!" he cursed.

Emily continued stroking his hair. Images of that encounter invaded her mind, and she fought them with all of her being. Even after David had told her how Deidre had exploited Jonathon, the question of why he reacted as he did, physically, haunted her…as it did now. Awkward and uncomfortable, David had tried to explain the physiological differences between men and women causing some embarrassing moments for the two of them. While Emily had accepted what he had said, she was still bemused. Jonathon was her first and only lover, and the workings of men, beyond her knowledge of him, remained a mystery. Awareness crept into her mind. What had happened between Jonathon and Deidre was a fact that could not be cancelled or altered. The result, Deidre's pregnancy, was a fact, too. It was not a matter of understanding what had occurred with Jonathon; it was a matter of trust. Understanding it would not change it, but not forgiving it could destroy them. What it came down to was this: did Emily trust Jonathon? Did she love him enough to overcome her lack of understanding? Could she forgive him and move past it? The last would be difficult with the evidence of his encounter with Deidre growing within the woman everyday…right under Emily's roof. Emotion was not the only requirement, love alone would not be sufficient; Emily suddenly knew that she must go beyond love to a decision, to conscious acceptance of Jonathon and the consequences of this encounter. She had to delve into herself, into her spirit and rise above doubt, above jealousy, above mistrust. Her spirit must love at her core, selfless and forgiving.

As if coming out of a trance, Emily looked up seeing Jonathon scrutinizing her.

"I love you, Jonathon. What happened is in the past." She looked away, searching for her words, and then looked back at him. "I do not understand it, but it is irrelevant that I do. What is relevant is my love for you. If you need me to forgive you, I do so, but there is no need. I understand that what occurred was in order to protect me and our baby. I am sure it was an impossible position for you to be in, and you did what you believed would keep us safe. I love you now; I love you always." She drew his head down and kissed him tenderly.

Nuzzling her neck, he rubbed her back, and then slid his hands down to her hips and thighs. She ran her hands along his arms, down his sides, across his buttocks. Her desire intensified, and Jonathon gasped when he felt her hands stroking him, urging him.

"I think it is time you made love to me, sir," she laughed softly.

"Em, will you be all right?" he asked.

Her violet eyes laughed up at him, the corners turning up enticingly. Her answer was a long kiss.

• • •

Jonathon's light kisses along the back of her neck awakened Emily. Rolling over to face him, she smiled into his eyes.

"I cannot believe you are here," she whispered.

"I am here, Love."

He brushed a wisp of hair out of her eyes, and then traced his finger along her cheekbone and pressed it against her lips. Leaning forward, he kissed her mouth and Emily pressed herself into him wrapping her arms around him. He answered her kiss with an urgency that sent fire through her blood. His hands explored her body while his lips held her captive in a kiss. Their desire rose and their lovemaking was passion answering passion as if to make up for the time they had been apart. Finally spent, they lay in a tranquil embrace, satisfied and drowsy.

"I must see to Andrew." Emily finally spoke.

"I heard about his injury. Some of my men were on guard duty in the yard and informed me of what happened here." Jonathon pulled her closer. "I should have been here to protect you."

"You were in pursuit of Captain Walters. That was where you needed to be," Emily said.

She saw his face harden at the mention of Walters's name.

"I pursued him for days, but the bastard eluded me."

Emily felt a tightness grip her stomach at the thought of that British officer still free. Looking back at Jonathon, she reached up and caressed his face.

"I love you, Em." Jonathon's soft, brown eyes searched hers. "You know that, do you not?"

"I know that." His lips against hers ignited a fire of longing, and she answered it in kind. He wrapped her in his arms and cradled her, rocking her gently.

"I fear I will keep you here the entire day, Mrs. Brentwood," he laughed.

Reluctantly, she eased from his arms. Rising, she donned the mauve silk robe that cast shadows curving along her skin, radiant in the dawn. Jonathon reached out and ran his finger along her thigh producing chills. Giggling, she enveloped herself in the robe and planted a light kiss on his forehead.

"You make it difficult to leave our bed, Jonathon."

"We will have many nights here, Love."

•  •  •

Jenny slowly came awake, stiff from half-sitting, half-lying across Andrew's bed. She eased up, stretching her muscles into compliance. Looking down at Andrew, she was relieved that his breathing was even and deep. She removed the cloth from his forehead and another wave of relief washed through her as she realized that his fever had broken. Her heart swelled with gratitude, and it was all she could do to keep from calling out in joy. She immediately soaked the strip in the basin, wrung it out and returned it to his forehead.

"Oh, Andrew, you are going to be all right," she whispered to him. Unable to stop herself, she leaned over him and kissed his forehead, each cheek, and finally, lingered on his lips. Sitting up, she brushed back a lock of his hair, and then she straightened the sheet that covered him.

"Again."

Jenny turned and looked around the room, bemused.

"Again."

She heard it another time and realized it was Andrew speaking.

"Andrew? What do you need?"

"Again." His voice was soft and raspy, and he peered at her from the corner of his eye.

"Do you need a fresh cloth? Some water?"

"No. Again. Kiss." A small smile played at his lips.

Understanding his request, Jenny blushed.

"Please. Again."

Laughing with a mixture of embarrassment, relief and a desire to comply, Jenny leaned down and brushed her lips against Andrew's. Regardless of how dry and chapped his lips felt, Jenny had never enjoyed a kiss so thoroughly. With her face still close to his, she smiled into his eyes. She saw a returning smile in his, and then they closed.

She reached for another strip of cloth, wet it, and pressed it against his lips. He nodded his thanks. She repeated this a few more times, trying to moisten his lips and allow some water to seep into his mouth. Rising, she stepped to the bell rope and pulled it. Perhaps Andrew would be able to take some water and nourishment.

In a few moments, Mr. Gates entered followed by Dulcie who carried a tray with water, tea, biscuits, ham and fruit. Jenny jumped up to greet them.

"Mr. Gates, Dulcie, Andrew's fever has broken!"

Gates rushed to the bed and examined Andrew. Jenny saw the broad grin break across his face as he felt Andrew's forehead and checked his breathing.

"You have done a fine job, Jenny," he said, smiling at her.

"Thank you, Mr. Gates. Your instructions were very effective."

Dulcie brought a glass to Mr. Gates. Taking it, he turned to Jenny.

"Would you do the honors, Jenny?"

Smiling at him, she sat beside Andrew, reached beneath him and elevated his head enough to drink. He sipped the water, and then smiled weakly at her.

"Welcome back," she whispered. His wan smile sent a surge of happiness through her.

"Broth is what he needs now, Dulcie. Can you see to it that some is prepared?" Gates asked.

"Yes, Mr. Gates. Whatever Master Andrew needs, I can do it!" Tears glistened in her eyes as she looked at each of them in turn. Before closing the door behind her, Dulcie paused and looked back at Andrew. Jenny heard soft singing follow the woman down the stairs.

Jenny pondered how little there had been to sing about at Brentwood Manor lately. With Jonathon missing, a pall had settled over the family, and with the arrival of the British, fear and anger had added to the gloom. Perhaps fortune was finally turning around for them. Jenny knew that Jonathon had arrived late the night before, which must be a tremendous relief for Emily. How difficult these months must have been for her, not knowing

Jonathon's fate. Jenny looked down at Andrew and knew what agony she would have suffered had she lost him. She whispered a prayer of thanksgiving as she replaced a cool compress on his forehead.

Hearing the door open, she turned to see Emily and Jonathon enter the room, hands clasped, eyes shining. It was clear they had enjoyed a wonderful reunion the previous night.

"Emily, Andrew's fever has broken," she said. "Good morning, Uncle Jonathon." Still elated at Andrew's improvement, her greeting was gleeful. Emily smiled at her and hurried to the bed. Rising, Jenny offered her place to Emily who sat beside her brother. She felt his forehead and cheeks and smiled up at Jenny.

"Your ministrations worked a miracle, Jenny. I thought I had lost my brother."

"Mr. Gates provided clear instructions…" Jenny studied her hands, looked back at Emily and then smiled.

Emily grinned at Jonathon. "Yes, it is amazing what Mr. Gates and a woman in love can accomplish."

Jenny felt her face flush and she cast about the room for something to focus on. Had she been so transparent? She had fallen in love with Andrew on their first meeting, but thought she had been most discreet. Obviously, love was a difficult emotion to hide: witness Emily and Jonathon whose love suffused the room.

Emily rose and embraced her, and Jenny felt the kinship that only the fear of losing one's beloved can produce.

"Thank you, Jenny. Thank you for taking such skillful care of my brother. I believe he will always be in good hands."

• • •

For a time, joy returned to Brentwood Manor. With Jonathon and David both home and Andrew recovering steadily, a lightness came over the family. Randy had seen to the transport of the

British to a jail in Williamsburg, and Mr. Gates and the crew had returned to the *Destiny* to prepare to sail for the Committees of Correspondence. Jonathon knew he had but a few days to spend with Emily, so he devoted all of his attention to her.

Captivated like a new lover, his eyes followed her, observing her every movement, entranced by her grace despite the change in her body. When she looked up and caught him watching, her eyes danced and her laughter floated across to him and settled like an airy veil that cloaked him in peace. At night when they lay together, he placed his hand on her belly feeling the urgent kicks of their child, and he was filled with wonder at the miracle of life within her—their life, created by their love.

One morning after they had walked in the garden, Emily was in need of a nap. The June nights were already warm, and he knew she had not slept well the night before. Leaving him on the veranda, she headed to their room. Jonathon sat on one of the chairs and stretched his legs out in front of him. A sense of peace filled him, and he wished he could remain here with Emily, but he knew he must sail soon. Gates was preparing the *Destiny*, loading supplies and sending out scouts to ensure a safe route to Philadelphia. Jonathon knew Thomas Jefferson was finalizing a draft to be sent to Great Britain and the new Congress would be gathering to sign it. Part of him itched to be there, in the middle of these historic events, but part of him ached to linger at Brentwood Manor and live in peace.

Restless, he rose and walked to the out buildings to inspect their stores and determine what he needed to bring with him upon his return. He walked along the paths that led to the nearest field when he heard a voice behind him.

"Jonathon."

He turned slowly.

"Deidre."

His jaw twitched.

"Will you not inquire as to how I am feeling?"

"I care not how you are feeling." Jonathon started to turn away, but she grabbed his sleeve.

"Do you not care how your child fares?" Deidre ran her hand down her belly.

Jonathon stared out at the fields. All of the nights he had held Emily and felt their baby move and kick, he had marveled at the miracle of life. He had forgotten—no, denied—that life was growing within Deidre, too. How could something so sacred result from something so base? Yet he was the father of both, one a miracle the other a consequence. He turned back to face her, squinting into the sun.

"What do you expect from me, Deidre? You have threatened my wife and child, in fact, attempted to injure—perhaps kill them, and you want me to say, 'Good day, Deidre. How are you feeling on this bright June day?' Well, that will never happen. You have shown your true nature, I wish to be nowhere near you."

"Jonathon," she said, her voice soft and cajoling. "You know I did everything for us. So that we could be together." Her eyes glinted in the sun, a smile lit her face.

"No, Deidre, there is no *us*! Can you not get it through your head that there never was any *us*?" Jonathon hissed. Heat rose within him as anger roiled in his gut. He clenched and unclenched his fists fighting the urge to strike her.

"Darling, there is *us*—three of us now. And you must keep in mind that if *she* bears a daughter, I may carry the heir of Brentwood Plantation." She smiled at him as if she had just bestowed a prize, and he gazed at her, incredulous at her boldness. It suddenly occurred to him that she actually believed all of this to be true. It was not boldness at all—it was delusion. An icy fear crept through him as he looked into her eyes. Expecting to see cold calculation there, he instead saw tenderness, innocence. She was not acting or plotting; she believed everything she was saying, and that awareness enveloped him with dread. Emily and their child were in more serious danger than he had ever imagined.

"Deidre, I think you should be examined by Dr. Anderson. I do not believe you are well."

Her face brightened and she beamed at him reminding Jonathon of just how beautiful—and desirable—she was. Though thicker through the waist, her figure still took his breath away, and her green eyes glowed emerald in the sun. When they had been lovers she was captivating and sensual, but he felt no desire for her now, just a cold pit in his stomach as he realized the fragile nature of her mind.

"Jonathon, how sweet of you; see, you do care. I will send for him today. I am sure our child is healthy for I feel well. But as you wish, Darling, I will have Dr. Anderson come. Now, shall we stroll a while? I believe walking is very good for me in my condition." She took his arm, but he wrested it away.

"No, Deidre. We are not going to stroll. We are not going to do anything together. I am allowing you to remain at Brentwood Manor only because you carry my child. You are to confine yourself to your room and areas away from the veranda and gardens. You are not to be anywhere near Emily. Do you understand?"

As he was speaking, he saw her bright smile shift to a dark, angry glare. The transformation was eerie, and he shuddered. She stepped back and glowered at him.

"So, you intend to play games? You want me to become jealous of her? You deny your love for me even though I know it to be true? Be very careful Jonathon." She pivoted on her foot and strode back to the manor. Jonathon watched her with a sense of dread.

• • •

Emily's throat ached from suppressed sobs, and tears filled her eyes. She was trying to be brave for Jonathon for she could see the sorrow in his eyes as he prepared to leave for the *Destiny*.

"Love, it is an exciting time, for we are severing ties with Great Britain to become our own country—'the united States of America.' That is the term Jefferson used in his Declaration. Em, we will be in command of our own destiny. We will be free of the shackles of unrelenting, burdensome laws of Parliament." His voice was charged with excitement; his eyes danced with elation. "I must leave you for a time, but I promise again, I will be here when our child is born."

Pulling her into his arms, he kissed the top of her head breathing in the scent of her hair. She buried her face against his chest, and the tears she had been holding back flowed freely, dampening his shirt. She held him as close as possible, and a strong kick from the baby was even felt by Jonathon. He laughed and patted her belly. Smiling up at him through her tears, she saw the pride he felt.

"Our child is wishing me safe travels," he laughed.

"Be safe, Jonathon, and hurry home to me," Emily said.

Lowering his head, he pressed his lips to hers in a fierce kiss that spoke of his passion. Emily's arms went up around his neck pulling him closer, answering in kind. Finally he released her, brushed a lock from her face and smiled into her eyes. She nodded; she must let him go.

They descended to the hall where the rest of the family awaited him. Andrew was seated by the front door, his first venture from his bed. Emily noticed how pale her brother was, but he had insisted on being there to send Jonathon off. Jonathon hugged each in turn, and then took Emily into his arms once more. Ignoring the others, he bestowed a long, lingering kiss and then released her. Her knees felt weak, and he left her breathless as he eased his embrace.

Turning he looked at each person, his gaze resting on David who nodded slightly in return glancing at Emily. She looked from one man to the other, but Jonathon hushed her with a light kiss, placed his tricorn on his head and walked out the door. Emily felt her heart drop and choked back a sob. Joanna stepped over and placed an arm around her shaking shoulders.

"Come, Em. Let us have some tea." Joanna led her to the parlor where Dulcie had set the tea service. As Joanna poured, Emily heard the sound of horses' hoof beats growing fainter. She wiped at her eyes.

"It seems as though we are apart more than together," Emily said.

Joanna took her hand and held it. Emily felt comforted in that gesture and smile appreciatively at her sister-in-law.

"Your love is strong, Emily. You and my brother have suffered so much together, and it seems to only make you stronger. I know you are a gift to him."

David entered and scanned the room, his gaze settling on Emily.

"Are you ladies well?" he asked.

Emily raised one eyebrow as she looked at her brother-in-law. His consideration did not seem to stem from her obviously distraught state, rather, it seemed somehow protective. David did not demonstrate sentimental feelings, and if anything, he was uncomfortable with them. So this sudden concern did not strike Emily as sentimental at all. She looked at Joanna, who was straightening a fold of her skirt.

"What is this about, David?" Emily asked.

David blushed and stammered. "About? Whatever do you mean, Emily? I was merely inquiring as to your well-being."

"You must admit that events have been stressful of late, Em. David, that is very sweet of you. I believe we are just fine. Will you join us for tea?" Joanna asked, her voice light.

Declining her invitation, he left the women to enjoy the morning.

Drained from the emotion of the day, Emily retired to her room to rest before dinner. The staircase seemed unusually steep as she climbed it slowly. She knew her energy was low because of Jonathon's departure, and in addition, the baby appeared to be growing bigger each day. She held the bannister as she ascended aware of her balance, sometimes uncertain. Reaching the top, she paused for a moment, and then walked toward her bedroom door. Glancing up, she saw Deidre glowering at her from the east wing.

# Chapter 13

Dawn crept into the room with a promise of a sweltering summer day. Faint sunlight teased the corner of the rug beside the bed, and before it had traveled across the rest of the rug, Andrew was awake and feeling restless. Mr. Gates had advised bed rest for at least two weeks, but Andrew had slipped out of bed several times already to sit by the window and watch the activities outside. He could not bear another day confined to his room, and decided he would rise and dress before anyone could protest.

He started at the sound of his bedroom door inching open, and rose on one elbow. His tousled hair fell over his eyes, and finding the cotton sheet, which he had kicked off during the night, pulled up it to his chest. No sense in scandalizing whoever was bringing his breakfast. The door opened wider, and in walked Jenny.

"Oh! You are awake." Her soft voice sent a tremor through Andrew.

"Awake and feeling rebellious," he said.

Her eyes were a silvery gray against her pale blue gown, and her hair was tied back loosely with a ribbon. She carried a tray to the table beside his bed avoiding any glance toward his sheet-covered body. He was fascinated by how gracefully she walked, and his eyes never left her.

"You look much improved today—stronger. What is your rebellious mind considering?" she teased.

Her single dimple showed, and Andrew felt desire stirring. He reached out to her; at first she demurred, and then she took his hand. Pulling her to the bed, he looked up at her. His heart thumped in his chest at her nearness, and the compulsion to draw her down to him, to wrap her in his arms, was unbearable.

"I owe my life to you."

He saw the blush rise in her face as she looked away.

"Mr. Gates gave excellent instructions."

"Yet you were the one who tended me, who stayed with me through the night, and who was there when I awoke."

Her blush deepened as she remembered kissing him awake.

"You must be feeling better, Andrew, but I could easily break your grip and escape." She laughed, swinging his hand back and forth.

"Jenny."

His voice was low, and his eyes held hers as he drew her down to sit beside him on the bed. He saw her eyes soften, laughter replaced by desire and he pulled her to himself. Their eyes met. Her face was inches from his. He felt the warmth of her breath against his face, saw her lips, full and dewy, and slightly parted. Reaching up, he ran his fingers through her hair, loosening the ribbon and causing a cascade of jet black tresses to fall across his chest.

"Jenny," he whispered.

He kissed her softly at first, brushing his lips across hers. Heat rose within him and his kiss intensified, his tongue sliding across her lips, and when she parted them, he felt himself tumbling into bliss. She made a soft noise in her throat and moved against him, stroking his face. His arms pulled her closer and she pressed against him answering his passion with her own. His mind reeled and he ran his hand along her side feeling the curve where her tiny waist arced out to her hip. Tracing fiery kisses along her neck, he cupped her breast and she gasped and found his mouth again. His desire raged and he felt as though his mind had abandoned him and all that was left was sensation—wonderful sensation.

Jenny pulled away. He reached for her, but she stood and stepped back. Noting the evidence of Andrew's passion by the bulge beneath the sheet, Jenny blushed and looked away. Looking back at him, she laughed and wagged her finger at him.

"You are a rebellious one today," she laughed.

Andrew's mind was still reeling from their encounter, but he smiled at her ruefully.

"Does this mean you will not be rebellious with me?"

"I must be the voice of reason, Mr. Wentworth. Remember our promise to maintain appropriate behavior—for many reasons, as I recall. First, because you are a gentleman, though your behavior this morning disproves that." She laughed and kissed him lightly on the forehead, and then quickly sidestepped his grab for her. "Second, out of respect for Uncle David and his kindness for hosting me. Third, to save Uncle David's hide should anything untoward occur and cause my father to commit fratricide!" She bestowed a smile upon him that made obeying their promise that much more difficult.

"Well, I believe the only thing to do then is to rise and greet the day," Andrew said as he began to lift the sheet.

"Oh, no! Please wait until I have removed myself from your presence!" Jenny face drained of color as she hastened to the door.

Andrew laughed and replaced the sheet.

"All right, Jenny. I will behave as a proper gentleman. But I am anxious to leave this room, and today I intend to do so."

"I will await you in the parlor, Andrew." She blew him a kiss and disappeared.

He smiled and stretched, feeling warm and happy. Instinct seemed to take over when Jenny was in his arms. Perhaps he was not schooled in the ways of love, but he did not need Deidre to instruct him in how to love Jenny, for she beckoned the passion from him without any need to think or plan. He laughed at how insecure he had felt and wondered how he could have ever considered Deidre's offer. He knew it was because he wanted to be a good lover for Jenny. Now he realized that loving each other was something they would learn together. And it would be magnificent.

• • •

Gusts blew across the deck of the *Destiny* tempering the July heat that beat down on the crew. The trip to Philadelphia had been without incident, but business with the Sons of Liberty kept Jonathon there a week longer than expected. He was anxious to return to Virginia so he could reach Brentwood Manor for the birth of his child. His child. What miracle was this? All of the years he had spent sailing and tending to the Brentwood property seemed inconsequential now, though before meeting Emily they were all that mattered to him. He had once told Emily he had two loves: the *Destiny* and his land. How fickle a man's heart turns when love enters his life. And now, when he thought he could never love more, a new life wrapped around his heart. But he must stop; he needed to concentrate on setting out to sea. For now, musings about Emily and their baby had to stay in the back of his mind for they would soon be in dangerous waters patrolled by the British.

The *Destiny* glided out of the harbor and into the open water. Men climbed the rigging adjusting the sails to best utilize the winds. Jonathon strode the deck watching his men work, offering words of encouragement or joining in a jest. They were all in high spirits as a result of the gathering in Philadelphia where the members of Congress had adopted and signed Jefferson's document, "The unanimous Declaration of the thirteen united States of America". They had broken ties with Great Britain. Jonathon felt exhilarated, too, having worked toward this moment for many years, sailing for the committees and working for the Sons of Liberty. It seemed unreal, but the reality was being illustrated in skirmishes throughout the colonies. And in battles at sea.

The wind blew them east out into the Atlantic and then south toward Virginia. Jonathon hoped the winds would continue and so speed the trip back to Yorktown. He leaned against the railing, hands clasped and looked out at the sea. He had doubled the watches knowing that the British were sailing these same waters. For now, the men carried out their tasks, and the *Destiny* sliced through the water, stately and powerful. Jonathon's hopes rose.

• • •

They had been at sea for several days, the wind steady, their progress good. Gates approached Jonathon as he was reading a chart.

"We are making good time, Captain," he said. His gray hair was tousled by the wind, his cheeks ruddy from the sun.

"Yes, Mr. Gates. The wind has been steady, and for that I am thankful."

"I know you are anxious to reach Yorktown, Captain, and then on to Brentwood Plantation. Emily's time is nearing." Gates smiled and clapped Jonathon on the back.

"Indeed it is, and I have made a solemn vow to be there for the birth."

Gates frowned slightly. "That is noble, Captain, and of course you want to be there, but it may not be in your hands to decide."

"I will do everything in my power—," his words were cut off.

"Ship, ho! British ship approaching from the north!" yelled a voice from high above them in the crow's nest. Both men looked up, shading their eyes against the afternoon sun. Men clambered to position and Jonathon shouted commands as he rolled up the chart and stuffed it into its tube. He tossed it to a passing crewman and leapt into action. The frantic movement on deck belied the actual organized activity that was occurring. Every crewman knew his station and his responsibility in the event of an attack, and each was scrambling to his post. Jonathon looked through the spy glass and saw the ship descending upon them. It was a British navy frigate, and he knew it held more guns than the *Destiny*, but the *Destiny* had the advantage of speed and agility even loaded as she was with cannon. It was possible he could outrun the British ship, but the temptation to rid them of one more vessel was too tempting.

"Come about!" Jonathon shouted.

Men adjusted the rigging, and the ship slowly changed direction. The British frigate closed in quickly and fired two of their cannon; one overshot the *Destiny* and the other slammed through the ship's rail. Jonathon gave the signal, and the *Destiny* let three cannon fire in return. One shot fell short of the frigate, but two landed on the deck. Jonathon felt his blood pumping through his body; his mind cleared, and his focus cut right to the frigate: where it lay, how it was positioned, even where the British stood on the deck. It was as if a higher sense came to life and he could see each drop of water as it sprayed against the ship. Another cannonball hit the fore topsail of the *Destiny*, and a man screamed as he dropped like a rag doll to the deck. The falling timber impaled a crewman into the gunwhale. Jonathon checked both men; they were dead.

Cannon answered cannon and the battled raged. Jonathon strode the *Destiny's* deck yelling orders, helping where needed and encouraging his men. A cannonball hit aft spilling two crewmen over the side, their screams muted by the next cannonball that hurtled across the deck. Other men were wounded by flying debris.

Jonathon knew they could hold out against the frigate, but they needed to deliver a fatal blow. He maneuvered the *Destiny* to maximize the range of his cannon. He gave the order and three cannon fired in succession; the shot from the first ripped through the main sail, the second one devastated the forecastle, and the third shot landed on the deck, striking the captain and two other crewmen.

Jonathon's voice was raw from barking out orders above the din of battle. Men scrambled to reload the cannon as quickly as possible keeping up a steady barrage. Two more cannon were fired from the *Destiny*, one hitting the deck of the frigate, the other ripping a hole in the side of the ship near the water. Suddenly fire erupted on the deck of the British ship, and sailors yelled, scrambling down from the rigging, running in panic. Jonathon watched as the fire licked the lower sails which caught and erupted into flaming banners. Timbers from the rigging fell to the deck spreading the fire quickly. No more cannon fire came from the frigate.

"Should we move in, Captain?" Gates asked.

"Wait a bit, Gates, they still could fire on us." Jonathon did not want to take the chance that some of the sailors would continue to fire even if it meant being trapped in a burning ship. The flames were spreading quickly, and with no sails, the frigate yawed into the waves. The gaping hole in the side of the ship dipped below the surface of the sea, and the ship began to take on water. There was no possibility of being fired on now, so Jonathon gave the order to approach the frigate and take prisoners. As the *Destiny* neared the frigate, the British ship gave out a low, loud moan and slanted into the waves. Men were screaming and scrambling to the higher parts of the ship, and Jonathon gave the order to lower boats into the water, but to no avail. With a shudder, the ship sank into the sea.

Smoke hung in the air burning Jonathon's lungs, but he listened as the crew of the *Destiny* raised shouts of "Huzzah" at their victory. He laughed as his men slapped each other on the back and raised their fists in triumph as the last of the frigate sank below the waves. Then they turned sober eyes to the deck where their dead lay still and the wounded moaned in agony. Gates hurried along the deck assessing wounds and ordering the injured taken to appropriate stations.

Jonathon searched the waves for any survivors and, finding none, ordered the sails to be set for full sail again. Leaning against the rail, he stared into the churning sea. While any battle got his blood pumping and thrust him into the role of commander, he always felt a sense of disquiet at the end. Perhaps it was a normal aftermath to his body's complete immersion into the instinctive mode of self-preservation, a kind of natural balancing. But he knew it was more than that; he knew it was a sadness at the loss of lives on both sides. He also knew that he was fighting for a just cause, for freedom, for liberty and for the spirit of a new nation founded on those beliefs.

• • •

Emily gasped as tightness gripped her belly. She had felt this sensation before, but never this powerfully, and it took her breath away. Joanna glanced up from her sewing and watched as Emily ran her hands across her abdomen.

"Are you all right, Emily?" she asked.

Emily nodded. Joanna put down her sewing, her eyes watching the movement of Emily's hands.

"I am fine, Joanna. I have had another of those contractions that seem to squeeze my entire middle. Oh my! And it does not help when my child then kicks like a mule!" She laughed. Although concerned about the pain she knew she would endure during childbirth, Emily felt eager about actually holding this tiny being in her arms. But she did not want the baby to arrive early; he had to give Jonathon time to return.

As if reading her mind, Joanna took her hand.

"Emily, I know that Jonathon promised he would be here for the birth…"

"And he will be, Joanna! I believe it with all of my heart."

"I believe he will be, too, Emily. If it is at all within his power to be here, but—," Joanna squeezed her hand.

"I have to believe it, Joanna. Too many times I have nearly lost him. I cannot bear to think that again. If he is alive, he will be here."

Joanna nodded. "Yes, Emily. Yes, he will be. How are you feeling right now?"

Emily smiled. "No more contractions. I believe it was just preparation."

• • •

Andrew was almost fully recovered though his shoulder was stiff and sore. He donned a light linen shirt, cotton stockings, and tan breeches before attempting to pull on his boots. Sitting on a chair, he carefully bent forward gripping one boot and gingerly tugging it on. He sucked air in through his teeth as pain shot through his shoulder. Determined, he gritted his teeth and yanked on the other boot deciding that completing the task faster would lessen the pain. Lightheaded from the exertion, he leaned his head back against the chair and closed his eyes.

After resting a few moments, he slowly stood and started for his bedroom door. Glancing out the window, he saw Jenny in the garden. Yes, he was glad to be up and about.

Stopping in the dining room, he filled a plate with leftover leg of lamb, pork pie, tomatoes and eggs, and biscuits swimming in syrup. He poured coffee into a cup and sat at the table to enjoy Dora's breakfast fare. While he ate, he pondered his plans for the coming fall. He was to return to William and Mary College to continue studying, and though he looked forward to that, he was reluctant to be away from Jenny. Her presence at Brentwood Manor had become so much a part of their routine that the thought of not seeing her everyday filled him with sadness. Each evening the family sat on the veranda enjoying the breeze. On rainy evenings, they enjoyed games of whist, and he chuckled thinking of how competitive Jenny was. Always good-natured, she enjoyed teasing him if he was losing, and she flung empty threats at him when he was the victor. He loved how her eyes lit up when the game was favoring her, how she would smile and reveal her dimple, rendering him so befuddled he was unable to concentrate. No, it would be difficult to not have Jenny in his life every day. Thoughts of her compelled him to make quick work of breakfast and hurry outside.

Andrew scanned the garden for any sign of Jenny, but he did not see her. Thinking she might be sitting down on the lawn, he traced a path through the flower beds and shrubs searching for her, but to no avail. He wandered around the grounds checking the veranda and outbuildings, and then guessing she might have decided to go riding, headed down to the stables.

Odors of hay and horses welcomed him as he entered the darkened interior. His nose tickled at the dust that floated in the air, and he heard the gentle rustle of the horses in their stalls.

"Jenny? Are you in here?" Andrew called, looking in each of the stalls. "Are you hiding on me, Jenny?" He yanked a stall door open thinking she might be lurking behind it.

"Jenny is not here, Andrew."

He turned and Deidre stood before him. Backlit by the sun through the stable door, her hair was a radiant, golden halo. She stood almost as tall as he, and her green dress was cut low, her breasts swelling above the bodice. She smiled at him through her lashes.

"Jenny is not here, but I am, Andrew."

"Good day, Deidre."

She moved close and played with the strings on his linen shirt, her hands pressing against his chest. The scent of musk rose from her hair and enveloped them. He stepped back.

"Are you afraid of me, Andrew? Are you afraid of women? Do you fear you will not please? I can help you; I can show you ways to please Jenny that will make her call your name out."

Suddenly the stable was stifling, and Andrew felt dizzy. He shook his head to clear it, and stepped away again as she advanced on him.

"I am not afraid of you, Deidre, and I do not need your schooling in the ways of love."

"So you and Jenny have already traveled that road. I see."

"Do not dare to say such things about Jenny," Andrew said.

"Oh, the knight in shining armor; how valiant of you. But Andrew, you and Jenny are young and inexperienced. Think of what I could provide to help you to please her." Deidre stepped to him and pressed her breasts against him. He tried to retreat, but his back was against the stall door.

"Deidre, I am not interested in what you have to offer."

Reaching up she pulled his face toward hers. The effect of her breasts, full and warm; the musky scent of her; and the closeness of her lips disconcerted him. Taking advantage of his distress, Deidre placed her hand on his buttocks and pulled him against her pelvis. Rubbing against him, she kissed him, her tongue prodding and licking.

"Andrew!"

Like a shot, Jenny's voice pierced the air. Andrew pulled away and pushed Deidre aside. He looked at Jenny, her face ashen.

"Jenny—no!"

She spun and ran from the stables, her sobs floating back to him. Turning, he glared at Deidre.

"You planned this. You knew she was nearby, and you intended for her to find us."

Deidre's eyes glinted in the murky light.

"Of course not, Andrew. I wanted to help you."

His eyes raked her.

"You want to help no one but yourself, Deidre. You wish to destroy anyone who finds happiness in life. You tried to destroy Emily and Jonathon, and now you are trying to destroy my happiness with Jenny."

"Jonathon? Jonathon loves me. I am to have his child." Deidre's haughty stare had melted into a look of confusion.

"Just listen to yourself, Deidre. You take pleasure in destroying the happiness of others."

"Jonathon wants me to stay at Brentwood Manor to bear a son. His heir. He loves me." Her voice became sing-song and childlike, her eyes glazed, and she stumbled out of the stables into the daylight.

Andrew's eyes followed her, a feeling of confusion enveloping him. Watching her transformation both fascinated and repulsed him. He did not understand what he had just witnessed, but he shivered in the August heat.

He needed to find Jenny and explain what she had seen. Surely she would understand once he described Deidre's strange behavior. But how could he explain something he did not understand? All he knew was that Jenny was hurt and he wanted to take that hurt away.

Returning to the manor, he took the stairs two at a time and hastened to Jenny's bedroom door. Knocking, he called out her name.

"Jenny? Jenny can I please talk to you?"

No answer. No sound at all from the other side.

He knocked louder.

"Jenny? Jenny, please let me in. I can explain."

Nothing. He tried the door. Locked. So she must be in the room.

"Jenny, please. Jenny, I love you, please let me in."

He tried for several more minutes before giving up. Turning to leave, he saw Deidre's door close.

"Damn!"

He pounded down the stairs slamming the front door as he left.

• • •

The oppressive August heat bore down on Jonathon, a drastic change from the cool sea breezes he'd been used to for the past month. His shirt clung to his back, the sweat dripping in rivulets down his neck and along his spine. Sweltering, he often brushed away drops of perspiration that dripped from his hair into his eyes and blurred his vision. Astride Neptune, he was galloping along the road at a quick pace, thankful for his swift mount. Stephen Alcott had kept Neptune groomed and exercised in anticipation of Jonathon's return, and when he had arrived at Stephen's home earlier that day, he was grateful for his friend's practicality.

Jonathon's heart beat a quick rhythm as he rode, for he knew Emily's time was near, and he was determined to keep his promise. Memories of their precious time together before his trip to Philadelphia had been the source of his strength while they were apart. Smiling to himself, he remembered her laughter at her own slower pace, all the while glowing with the joy of their child. Her scent of jasmine filled his mind, and the image of her lying in the candlelight, her skin luminous, her eyes afire with passion stirred him to nudge Neptune to a faster gait.

Jonathon usually slowed to a leisurely speed once he reached Brentwood property, but today he was a man driven by love and his solemn vow. The lush, green forest flew by unnoticed as he focused on the road ahead. Once again sweat blurred his vision and as he raised his hand to wipe his eyes, a shot passed just over Neptune's head grazing Jonathon's left arm.

"Halt!" The voice echoed in the trees.

Jonathon reined in Neptune who reared and snorted. When the horse landed, it sprang back, its path blocked by a company of riders. Jonathon was surrounded by the scarlet of British uniforms, stark against the verdant countryside.

# Chapter 14

August drenched Virginia in heat and humidity. Emily's clothing clung to her damp skin, her hair hung in heavy ringlets try as she might to tame them with combs. Movement was unbearable with the weight of her baby, but she defied the summer's torturous conditions, strolling the gardens each morning. Knowing that soon she would hold her baby—hers and Jonathon's baby—kept her spirits up and compelled her to stay active. Her back was particularly uncomfortable this morning, and she rubbed it as she walked. The baby, so active for the last few weeks, had suddenly quieted and a whisper of fear for his health niggled at the back of her mind.

She did not roam far from the manor because her need to visit the necessary seemed constant. She laughed as she remembered a desperate urgency to relieve herself that morning, and she was sure that trying to run with her lopsided figure provided an amusing sight of awkward loping and desperation. Pausing, she felt her abdomen tighten as it had been since early morning. Each time the tightness was more intense, now growing more painful than uncomfortable. She turned and started back in the direction of the manor, her heart beating faster as she realized the consequence of these sensations. Along the path she had to stop, for the cramping made her gasp, it was so sudden and so strong. Clutching her belly, she felt its hardness, solid like the brick of the manor. Rivulets of sweat formed on her forehead having nothing to do with the heat. Nearing the manor, she scanned the veranda for Joanna because she knew this was the beginning of her labor. As if on cue, Joanna appeared at the French doors leading out to the terrace and, spotting Emily, she waved gaily, and then looked closer, her smile fading and concern covering her face. She ran to her sister-in-law and took her arm, supporting her weight.

"Emily, are you well?" she asked.

"Joanna, I believe—," Emily began, interrupted by a steady flow of fluid that covered the ground and her slippers. "Oh my," she whispered and looked at Joanna. The women began to laugh, and Emily's eyes released tears of joy mixed with pain and fear. Joanna's arm went around her and supported Emily's weight.

"We must get you inside," she insisted. Emily winced as a stronger contraction wrapped around her abdomen.

"Yes," she managed to whisper.

As the women entered the manor, Joanna called out for Dulcie who appeared as they made their way up the curving staircase.

"Dulcie, it is Miss Emily's time. Send someone for Dr. Anderson and get fresh water and linens quickly," Joanna instructed. Dulcie sped to the back of the manor to get the necessary items.

Entering Emily's room, Joanna helped her to bed, removed her saturated slippers and stockings and began to remove her frock.

"He is not here, Joanna," Emily whispered against the tightness in her throat. "Jonathon promised he would be here when our child was born."

"Emily, it may not be possible for him to be here. He is in grave danger right now, and to come to Brentwood Manor would surely mean his death."

Emily closed her eyes blocking the threatening tears; the thought of her husband not at her side at such a time was unbearable. The thought of his death, insufferable. Her heart was torn between wanting Jonathon here and wanting him safe.

"I do not think I can do this alone, Joanna. I am so afraid," Emily said.

Joanna eyes were soft and compassionate. She brushed damp curls off of her sister-in-law's forehead and gently patted her shoulder.

"I know I am a poor substitute, Emily, but I will remain with you every minute," Joanna said softly.

Emily smiled her gratitude and then her face contorted as a powerful contraction went through her. She gripped Joanna's hand until the pain subsided and then released her hold. She smiled apologetically.

"I am sorry, Joanna, I did not intend to hurt you, but that pain was so severe," Emily laughed. Joanna nodded sympathetically.

Emily's labor continued throughout the morning, and she welcomed Joanna's ministrations as she wiped Emily's face and neck with wet cloths that were as cool as the summer heat would allow. Resting between contractions, Emily felt emotions that ran the gamut of excitement at the birth of her baby to despair at the absence of Jonathon. Afternoon brought suffocating temperatures and humidity, and Emily often felt faint and nauseous suffering with the heat and the pain. She vacillated between sitting, pacing and lying down, sometimes too weak to get up from the bed.

Dr. Anderson arrived in the early evening and checked Emily thoroughly, pronouncing her labor normal and reassuring them that with the exception of the August weather, everything else was suitable. The evening provided a slight breeze, but insufficient to offer effective relief of the heat and humidity. Exhaustion, intensified by the weather, threatened to overcome Emily as she strained with each contraction, almost unable to comprehend what was occurring within her body. She tried to mute the groans of agony that escaped her mouth, concerned that they would disturb the others, but Joanna held her hand and encouraged her to vocalize any discomfort that she felt. As promised, Joanna had remained beside her throughout the day, leaving the care of Will to Dulcie and her daughter. Emily's thoughts constantly were of Jonathon, wishing he could have held true to his promise to be with her, trying to understand why he could not be. All she understood in some moments was a tremendous agony accompanied by the feeling that her body was being rent in two.

"I am breaking in half! I am breaking in half!" she screamed.

Dr. Anderson examined her once again and nodded at Joanna.

Suddenly there was a commotion in the hall, and the door swung open. A British soldier clad in his brilliant scarlet uniform entered the room where Emily was writhing on the bed, overcome with pain. All motion stopped as if captured by an artist's brush. Emily looked across the room unable to comprehend the bizarre scene. Descending from the strongest contraction she had yet experienced, she blinked attempting to understand.

"Michael?" she whispered.

Michael Dennings stood in the doorway aghast, staring at the vision before him. Recovering his composure, he stepped aside. Jonathon rushed into the room toward Emily, scooping her into his arms and burying his face in her neck.

"My love, my love," he murmured over and over against her throat.

"Jonathon, oh, Jonathon, you came as you promised," she laughed and cried simultaneously. "Oh, oh, my God, my God," she then cried out. Clutching her belly, she half sat up, unable even to cry out. Dr. Anderson moved immediately to her side.

"You both had best leave," he said. Michael needed no further encouragement, and hastened out.

"I shall stay," Jonathon said.

"That is highly unusual," Dr. Anderson replied.

"I shall stay," Jonathon insisted.

Emily interrupted their brief discussion with a long, low moan. Again Dr. Anderson checked her and saw the baby's head crowning.

"The baby is coming now, Emily," he said softly, looking reassuringly into her eyes. "It is time."

Emily's eyes focused within, her entire being absorbed in the enduring human activity of participating in new life. She felt her body instinctively respond, all systems, organs, functions concentrated on this one goal: birth. Pushing, she felt the baby move lower, sundering her body, a life force beyond her control. And suddenly release, a wet, flopping sound and a hearty wail announcing the arrival of the newest Brentwood. She saw Dr. Anderson take the baby and tie the umbilical cord, attending to the remainder of the birthing process. Joanna took the infant and gently washed and swaddled the baby. Hovering like a mother hen, Jonathon beamed as befits a first-time father. He returned to Emily's side.

"Emily, Emily, we have daughter. A beautiful daughter," he smiled through his tears.

Joanna handed the baby to Emily. Feeling her tears of relief and joy spill over, Emily beheld her daughter, so petite, so perfect. She kissed her forehead and tucked a finger within the infant's tiny grip. Slowly guiding the child, she held her against her breast. The baby looked up at her, rooted, and found the nipple, latching on with a healthy sucking. Emily's eyes met Jonathon's and the depth of love she felt for him shocked her in its profoundness.

"Grace," she said. "We shall call her Grace."

• • •

British soldiers surrounded Brentwood Manor lounging in the shade of oaks or walking into the cool of the woods. At last they had captured their quarry, but many were puzzled at their captain's generosity in bringing him to his home before returning him to Norfolk. Captain Dennings was a fair and effective officer who had won the respect of his men, so they did not question his orders; they merely complied. This arrest would bring them honors, for they had been one of two contingents sent on a specific mission to capture Jonathon Brentwood. Why not enjoy his food and the comfort of his home before traveling the road again? It was with this self-assurance they relaxed attempting to exert as little energy as possible in the sweltering heat. They would billet here tonight and travel to Norfolk in the morning.

• • •

Jonathon and Michael sat in the parlor smoking celebratory cigars. Exhausted after the delivery, Emily was upstairs sleeping peacefully, Grace in the cradle beside her bed. When Jonathon had exited the bedroom, he brought Grace for Michael's inspection, and then Michael escorted him downstairs.

"She is a beautiful baby, Jonathon," Michael said, blowing smoke rings above his head.

"She is indeed." Jonathon's grin covered his face. He took a deep pull on the cigar. "Thank you, Michael. This is twice your kindness has touched my family. You did not have to allow me to return for Grace's birth."

Michael stared into the smoke that surrounded him. His youthful face had changed since Jonathon had met him in London and disrupted his marriage proposal to Emily, a proposal she had refused in order to sail to Virginia with Jonathon.

"You still love her, do you not, Michael?"

He did not answer. The men continued to smoke in silence, the only sound the ticking of the clock.

"I have to return you to Norfolk, Jonathon," Michael said.

"Yes, I know."

"It is not because…" he began.

"No, I know that, Michael. We are at war now; it is your duty. You are an honorable man," Jonathon said.

Silence enveloped them as each man reflected on his situation.

• • •

Subtle shades of dawn fell across the bed where Emily and Jonathon lay entwined in each other's arms. Stillness suffused the house, and a slight breeze stirred the curtains as Jonathon sleepily nuzzled Emily's neck eliciting a contented sigh. Both were exhausted from a night spent quieting Grace who seemed to awaken just as they were falling asleep. Emily had nursed her several times after which Jonathon would walk the floor gently bouncing her in attempt to quiet her crying. At first wary of holding such a tiny, frail being, Jonathon had barely moved while Grace was in his arms. Smiling, Emily then showed him how to prop her in his arms and support her head. He had never felt so clumsy in his life as he did the first time he held his daughter, but a smile spread across his face as he looked down at her tucked against his chest. Now she slept soundly as the two of them awakened.

Emily snuggled into Jonathon burrowing into his arms. He held her closely as he came awake realizing that these would be their last moments together. He closed his eyes and breathed the scent of her hair burying his face in it. Stroking her skin, silken and radiant in the early light of dawn, he committed every curve of her body, every inch of her face, to memory. A lump rose in his throat at the thought of never seeing his wife and daughter again, and he closed his eyes against the tears that filled them. He could not make this more difficult for Emily; he had to remain strong.

Sensing her eyes on him, Jonathon looked down and saw her gazing at him. His breath caught at her beauty, violet eyes shining with unshed tears, tawny hair spread out like a halo across the pillow. Seeing one tear escape and roll down her cheek, he brushed it away with his fingertips. He kissed her forehead and drew her near.

"I love you Em, never doubt that."

"I know, Jonathon. To my very core, I know," she whispered.

"I must leave today."

She nodded against his chest, shuddering with her sobs. He felt her tears, wet against his skin, and he fought back his own. Running his hands along her back, he kissed the top of her head, and then tilting her face to his, kissed her deeply. They clung to each another as if trying to absorb every part into themselves.

"We have been parted too often, Love," he said, stroking her hair. Determination surged through him. "I will find a way to return to you. I swear to God, I will find a way." His voice was strong; her eyes looked at him, hopeful.

"I believe you will, Jonathon."

He heard a soft rapping on the door.

"Captain Brentwood, we will ride in an hour," Michael Dennings's voice was quiet.

"Yes, Captain Dennings," Jonathon replied.

A sob escaped Emily's lips, and she buried her face in his chest.

"Oh, Jonathon, how can I let you leave?"

He held her as she cried, his own tears finally releasing to join hers. Sitting up, he cradled her in his lap and stroked her back, kissing her shoulder. His heart felt as though a knife had been plunged into it and twisted. No amount of British torture would compare with the agony he felt as he held his wife for the last time.

Slowly he slid Emily onto the bed and rose. Stepping to the cradle, he stared down at Grace who slept peacefully, and he ached at the realization that he would never know his own daughter. He placed his hand on her tiny back and she whimpered.

"Do not cry, Grace. Your father loves you." His voice felt strangled as he spoke through the tightness in his throat. Her swaddled shape shimmered through his tears, which dropped onto her blanket.

"Oh, Jonathon." Emily's strangled voice carried all the anguish he felt. She rose from the bed and stood beside him as together they gazed at Grace. How had he attained all a man could dream of only to lose it so quickly? Had he been captured before he had ever known Emily, he would have suffered, yes, but now to lose his beloved wife and daughter? This was beyond any enduring, beyond any torture.

Slowly, he began to dress pulling on his breeches and linen shirt. He drew up his stockings and donned his shoes, each movement heavy and slow, like slogging through mud. Emily watched him from the bed, silent tears running down her cheeks. He had no words of comfort for her; he had no promise he could make.

"I will return to say good-bye," he said, brushing away her tears and kissing her eyes. He turned and walked out their bedroom door.

• • •

Andrew leaned his arm against the window sill staring out at the scarlet jackets moving about on the lawn below. He felt helpless, unable to stop them from taking Jonathon to Norfolk. They had confiscated all of the firearms upon their arrival, so there were no weapons with which to fight. He slapped the frame of the window in frustration. What kind of man was he to stand here and do nothing? Riding for help was impossible as well since they had stationed men at the stables. David had traveled to Williamsburg for a gathering of the Virginia leaders to discuss their plan of action against the British now that all-out war was ahead. He was not expected back for a week or more. They were stranded.

He paced the room trying to find a solution, but nothing came. He had grown close to Jonathon, admiring him even before they left London over two years earlier. Jonathon had allowed him to work the ship alongside his crewmen, teaching him the ways of sailing with patience and good humor. And Jonathon had saved his life when he fell into the sea during a great storm, diving into the roiling waves not thinking of his own safety. Certainly Andrew had returned the favor when he aided Jonathon after escaping the British in Norfolk, probably saving his brother-in-law's life as well. And now, here Jonathon was again, captured and preparing for departure for Norfolk and a British prison. Exasperated, Andrew grabbed a pewter mug and threw it across the room, slamming it against the hearth.

He could not stay confined in his room any longer, so he left his room and headed for the dining room and breakfast.

As he entered, he saw Jonathon standing at the window looking out as he himself had just been doing upstairs. Jonathon turned upon hearing Andrew enter.

"Good morning, Drew."

"Good morning, Jonathon. How are you?" He felt foolish after he said it, for it was evident by Jonathon's haggard face that he had not slept much the night before.

"In just a few hours I have learned how a mere infant can dominate one's life," he said. His smile was rueful and Andrew knew it was not due to lack of sleep.

"Grace is beautiful," Andrew said. He stepped to the sideboard and took some sausage and biscuits. Normally his appetite resulted in a heaping breakfast platter, but this morning he was not hungry. He sat and watched Jonathon staring outside.

"Is there nothing we can do, Jonathon?"

"I am afraid I am at their mercy, Drew. Michael must return me to Norfolk for a trial, and probably a hanging." Jonathon wiped a hand across his eyes. "I will leave Emily and Grace alone." He turned to Andrew. "Promise me you will care for them, Drew. Promise me you will keep them safe." He choked back a sob and Andrew walked over and hugged him and patted him on the back.

"You know that I will, Jonathon," he said between teeth gritted against his sorrow. Releasing Jonathon, Andrew stood back, looking him in the eye. "You know that I will."

Michael Dennings entered the room and nodded to the men.

"Good morning, Jonathon. Good morning, Andrew."

Andrew was struck by how odd it was to see his lifelong friend standing before him in a British uniform. He recalled games they had played when their families gathered in a park or at someone's manor for a ball. He and Michael were two of the fastest runners and often competed with each other in races. Andrew always knew that Michael was fond of his sister Emily, and was surprised when she refused his marriage proposal. Michael was crushed by that, but having seen Emily and Jonathon together these last years, Andrew understood. Now he looked at his friend who would deliver Jonathon into the hands of a British court, with their lack of mercy, who would condemn him and hang him.

"Michael, is there not something we can do?" Andrew cried.

A look of consternation crossed Michael's face as he seemed to struggle with an inner conflict.

"Andrew, I am a soldier of King George III. I have my orders and I must act upon them." Turning, he looked at Jonathon. "I am truly sorry, Jonathon." He cast his eyes to the floor.

"Andrew, Michael must do this. There is no other way," Jonathon said.

"Damn it, Michael, surely there must be something—," Andrew swiped his hand across the table sending his platter flying into the wall, crashing in pieces to the floor.

Michael stared at the scattered bits of food and shards of china as if an answer might lie within them. He shifted his eyes to Andrew, then Jonathon. "There is nothing."

Jonathon nodded acknowledging the truth. "I must see Emily once more before we leave."

Michael nodded. "I would like to speak to Emily, if she will allow it."

The two men left together and Andrew slammed his fist on the table.

• • •

At a tapping on her door, Emily called, "Come in." She was surprised to see Michael standing behind Jonathon at the door.

"Em, Michael would like to speak with you," Jonathon said.

Pain shot through her as she looked at her friend who would deliver her husband to his death.

"No!" Her voice sounded harsh and her legs began to tremble.

"Emily, please—," Michael called over Jonathon's shoulder.

"You arrest my husband, intend to take him to prison where he will surely hang, and you want to pay a call?" The words scratched out of her throat, cracked with anger and sorrow.

Jonathon stepped aside and gestured for to Michael come into the room. "Em, just give him one minute. He needs to speak to you."

Emily felt the tears burning her eyes. How could she have more tears? Had she not cried enough to fill an ocean? Why would Jonathon allow him into their room—this man who would see him killed?

Michael stepped over and stood before her. She looked into his eyes and gasped. He was still in love with her; his eyes were soft and sorrowful and full of tenderness. She realized that he struggled with his duty as a soldier and his abhorrence at hurting her. Shifting her gaze to Jonathon, she saw him close his eyes and nod at her. He knew it, too. He wanted Michael to have a chance to ask her forgiveness. Her emotions roiled. How could she forgive him for condemning her husband to death? Yet there was no arrogance, no sense of triumph within him, only sorrow and remorse. She looked back at him.

"Please, Michael, please. Can you do nothing to save him?" She reached up and grabbed his lapels. Crushing the scarlet fabric in her hands, she pulled him toward her. "Please, Michael! There must be some way!"

"I am sorry, Emily. I ask you to forgive me." A single tear ran down his face.

"Michael. How can you do this?" She released his coat and stepped back. "How can you kill my husband?"

"I am sorry." He turned and walked to the door. Stopping next to Jonathon, he spoke. "I will gather my men. Be prepared to leave within the quarter hour." He walked out the door.

Emily ran to Jonathon.

"I cannot let you go! I will not let you go!"

Grace's cries pierced the air.

"Emily, I have no choice." He pulled her to him and crushed her against his chest. She felt his breath, ragged and heaving. "I must go, Love."

"No, Jonathon, no, no, no!"

Grace's cries cut the air, incessant and demanding.

"I love you, Em. Always remember that I loved only you." He released her and strode to the door.

"Jonathon, no!" Emily cried, collapsing on the floor. Grace's cries matched her mother's.

# Chapter 15

Jonathon felt as empty as shells he had found along the shore. Hollow. The sounds of Emily and Grace's cries echoed in his ears, blocking out any of the soldiers' conversation or sounds from the surrounding forest. Shoulders slumped, hands tied to the saddle horn, he felt drained of energy, of life itself. There was no escaping now for no one knew where he was. He would have a quick trial and a quicker hanging for not only had he assisted the Sons of Liberty, he had sunk a British frigate. That crime would be added to the charge of treason. No, there was no escape.

At least he had kept his promise to Emily and had been there for Grace's birth. Grace—so tiny and defenseless. Who would care for her now? Andrew, of course, but soon he would be making his own way in the world. David and Joanna. Thank God for his sister and her husband for they would be Emily's family and help her to raise Grace. Exhausted from lack of sleep and the emotion of leaving Emily, Jonathon felt his head nodding and he dozed intermittently.

The afternoon sun slanted through the trees as they made their way along the road. Jonathon's head shot up as he heard the approach of a rider. The soldiers reined in and circled around him, each man reaching for his musket or pistol. Through the trees they heard hoof beats coming closer, and Jonathon's spirits rose. But bursting out from the edge of the woods, another scarlet coat appeared: Captain Walters.

He reined up next to Michael and a grin spread across his face.

"Brentwood," he sneered. "I believe the numbers are on my side this time."

Jonathon felt the bile rise in his throat. His hands twitched in the ropes that bound him, the desire to attack Walters charging through his body.

Walters guided his horse over to Jonathon's. Taking his knife, he ran it along the side of Jonathon's face.

"I am going to enjoy seeing you swing," he snarled. "It is unfortunate that we are so far from Brentwood land. My intention had been to amuse your wife with your suffering. And amuse you with hers. I suspect my journey will take me back that way, however, so she can still enjoy my, ah, attentions. Think about that while you swing from the gallows."

Revulsion ripped through Jonathon's gut as he glared into the captain's leering eyes. The thought of this bastard's hands on Emily gripped him with fear and hate.

"Oh, so you see the possibilities as well, I see." Walters laughed in his face. Then he turned to Michael.

"I will take over this unit, Captain Dennings, for delivering Brentwood is a personal mission of mine." He moved as if to take the lead, but Michael guided his horse to block him.

"No need, Captain Walters. We are taking Brentwood in."

"Indeed you are not, Dennings. I am in command now, and I order you to stand down."

Michael stood his ground. "I believe we are of equal rank, Walters. I am in command of my troops."

"Is that so? Well, we may have to rectify that." In a swift movement, he drew his pistol and fired hitting Michael in the chest knocking him off of his horse. The soldiers drew their weapons, but Walters fired again above their heads.

"You are under my command now, soldiers! Put your weapons down."

Confusion showed on their faces as they looked at one another. Trained to obey, one by one they put away their weapons.

Jonathon watched in horror as Michael writhed on the ground, blood pooling on the ground beneath him. He looked at Jonathon and tried to speak. A gurgling sound came from his mouth and from his chest. Jonathon tried to inch his horse over to where Michael lay, but Walters grabbed his reins.

"Where are you going, Brentwood?" His horse stepped in front of Jonathon's blocking his view. Jonathon glared at him. Inching his horse over again, he looked beyond Walters and saw Michael's lifeless eyes staring at the sky.

•  •  •

Andrew sprinted to the stables as soon as the soldiers were out of sight. He was worried that the troops would take all of their horses, but it would have slowed them down too much to do so. And Michael would not have been so vindictive. He ran to Neptune's stall and led the horse out to saddle him. Turning, he saw Jenny standing at the door. His heart stopped and he stood stock still.

"I am going with you," she said.

As he looked at her, her mouth set in a firm line forcing the dimple to show. Her eyes flashed slate gray above her green riding outfit. She stood, feet planted, arms folded and he knew there was no arguing with her.

"We have no weapons," he said.

She pulled a knife from a sheath tucked in her waistband, and he smiled at her.

"You are amazing, Jenny." His voice was soft, and he longed to reach out and pull her into his arms. But he held his place, and she looked away.

"I have no plan." Andrew raised his arms feeling helpless. "I just know I cannot simply stay here and allow Jonathon to be taken without a fight."

Jenny nodded. "Let us discuss possibilities as we ride."

They saddled the horses and set off in the direction of the troops. They rode in silence for a while, and Andrew longed to tell

Jenny what had happened between him and Deidre in the barn. He knew this was not the time for it; they had to concentrate on freeing Jonathon. He turned his thoughts to options they had, but he never lost mindfulness of the nearness of Jenny. When the breeze shifted, it carried her scent of lilac with it, and as he scanned the woods on either side of the road, his gaze always lingered a little longer to the left where he could glimpse her profile.

"I think we can ride to Stephen Alcott's in an hour's time. We could send out some of his workers to area plantations to bring help," Andrew suggested.

Jenny nodded. "Yes, that might work, although the British will have quite a lead on us. They likely will reach Norfolk before we can catch up with them."

"At least we would have reinforcements—and weapons. We would probably arrive before Jonathon is—," He could not finish the sentence. His eyes clouded with tears and he blinked them away before Jenny could see them.

"What could we do, Andrew, just the two of us?" Jenny asked.

Andrew thought for a moment. "We have only the knife, Jenny. We would be up against the whole troop of armed soldiers." He thought for a while. "If we stole up to them at night and found Jonathon…I am sure they will have him tied up; we could free him, perhaps. But if they have guards…"

They looked at each other. They had to try something.

• • •

Emily sat on the floor of her bedroom rocking an inconsolable Grace. She had tried nursing her, but to no avail. The baby's cries continued. Emily clutched her head with one hand, pulling on her hair to anchor herself for she felt she was losing her mind. Her sides ached from sobbing, her breasts throbbed as her milk came in, and her eyes burned from crying. Grace's cries tore at her heart, and so did the thought of Jonathon in the hands of the British. She remembered the marks on his back from the cat-o'-nine-tails when he was in the cabin. They would do worse this time in payment for his escape, and then they would hang him. Her heart felt like it was being torn in two, thudding within her chest.

"Oh, God," she sobbed as Grace wailed.

Joanna came in and rushed over to Emily.

"Emily, dear, let me help you!"

Emily gratefully handed Grace to her, but the baby continued to wail. Joanna tugged the bell pull to summon Dulcie. She placed Grace in the cradle momentarily while she helped Emily into bed. Propping her on pillows, she wet a cloth, wrung it out and laid it across her forehead. Gasping, Emily tried to calm herself and breathe evenly. Joanna picked up Grace and cooed softly as she paced the room with her.

When Dulcie arrived, Joanna quickly gave her instructions. The woman left to acquire what was needed. Grace's wails lessened, but the she was still discontented.

"Emily, Grace is hungry, but you need to calm down before you will be able to nurse her."

Emily nodded, breathing deeply and trying to overcome her misery. Dulcie returned with a tray and poured chamomile tea for Emily. Still shaking, Emily took the cup which rattled against the saucer. Her despair was easing with the gentle ministrations of these two women. She sipped the tea and laid her head back on the pillow. She needed to concentrate on her baby for this moment. She looked at Joanna and nodded. Joanna eased Grace into her arms, and the baby cried and struggled at first. Emily's heart sank; she did not have the strength to bear Grace's demands, but what was she to do?

"There, there, Grace. Mama is right here with you, my love." Emily's voice was soft and low.

Grace turned her head at the sound of her voice and began rooting; she found the nipple and began to suck heartily. Emily thought her breast was being sucked right through her toes and she fought the urge to call out. Grace's tummy shuddered twice from the exertion of her crying, and then she settled down in contentment.

Emily closed her eyes and let the tears fall silently down her cheeks. She felt Joanna wipe them with a cool cloth, and she opened her eyes and smiled weakly at her sister-in-law. The waves of fear that had consumed her were waning, and she looked down at her baby who nursed happily, her tiny fist pressed against Emily's breast. Emily stroked the downy, dark hair that curled around Grace's head, damp from her crying. As if on cue, Grace looked up into her eyes and Emily felt as if she had just glimpsed eternity.

"Her eyes and hair are dark like her father's," Emily said.

"Yes, though they could lighten as she grows," Joanna answered.

"No, I believe she will look like her father." Emily's eyes again filled with tears as she thought about Jonathon. Looking at Joanna, she saw that she was crying, too.

"Joanna, what can we do?"

"Pray, Em. Pray."

• • •

Jonathon leaned his back against the tree and watched the soldiers. He noticed how their eyes met across the fire, and then slid across to look at Captain Walters, a silent exchange that seemed to indicate their dislike of the officer. While riding with them this morning, he had noticed the respect and loyalty they had for Michael, evident in their voices and mannerisms. Even while they billeted at Brentwood Manor, their posture and gestures spoke of admiration for their commander. Their commander whom Captain Walters had killed in cold blood.

Walters ambled over to Jonathon and squatted down before him.

"Hungry, Brentwood? Have some stew." He placed a pewter bowl a foot away from Jonathon, just beyond his grasp. Hands and feet still tied, Jonathon would have to crawl to reach the bowl. He stared at the officer.

"Come on, now, Brentwood, get your food. Here boy, here you go!" He whistled and gestured to the bowl as if to a dog. "Now do not be a bad boy. Come get your food. Come on!" He laughed and pulled out his pistol, pointing it at Jonathon's head. "Get your food, Brentwood, or I shall blow off your mouth so you cannot eat it."

Jonathon continued to stare at him. Perhaps dying right here with a quick bullet would be preferable to death by hanging.

Walters cocked the gun. Jonathon braced himself hoping that the shot would be clean and deadly. The other soldiers froze watching the bizarre spectacle, not breathing. Walters laughed, uncocked the gun, and replaced it in his belt. He pushed the bowl to Jonathon with the toe of his boot.

"You are a brave one, Brentwood. I give you that." He laughed and went over to a tree and relieved himself. The soldiers relaxed and eased back into their activities. One of the soldiers sitting nearby scooted over to him and gave him a spoon, lifting the bowl so Jonathon could hold it in his bound hands.

"Thank you," he murmured to the soldier. The soldier nodded, looked at Walters, and spat on the ground.

The night sounds surrounded him, and Jonathon thought they had never sounded sweeter. He heard the far off hoot of an owl, the chirping of crickets, and the rustling of underbrush as forest creatures settled in for the night. He took a deep breath and let it out slowly. He wondered what Emily was doing right then. Was she feeding Grace? Was she sleeping after such a busy night and emotional day? He longed to be with her, to hold her in his arms and assure her that everything would be all right. That he would never leave her again. He longed to hold Grace and kiss her silken hair and soft cheeks. His arms ached for Emily, to see the desire that deepened her eyes to violet. He would carry the image of her lying naked beside him, her skin luminous in the candlelight to his grave.

Walters approached him again.

"Stand up, Brentwood," he ordered.

Jonathon glared at him. Walters took out his pistol and whipped it across Jonathon's face, and then he pulled out his knife, held it in front of Jonathon's face, malevolent shadows dancing across his face in the light of the campfire. In one swift move, he lowered the knife and cut the ropes that held Jonathon's feet.

"Stand up! Now!"

Slowly, Jonathon rose to his feet. Dreading what might happen next, he distributed his weight evenly on both legs to stop his knees' trembling. He believed he would not see morning.

"Walk over there." Walters indicated a stand of trees just beyond the light of the campfire.

Jonathon turned and walked in the direction he had indicated. As he passed him, one of the soldiers stood up.

"Captain Walters, sir, we have orders to bring Captain Brentwood in alive."

Walters thrust his face into the soldier's. "Are you giving me orders, soldier?"

"No, sir. I am just relaying to you what our captain—,"

"Your captain seems to have had a serious accident, son. I am now your captain, and you will follow my orders. Do you understand, soldier?" While he shouted these words, spit from Walter's mouth spewed into the soldier's face. He stood at attention not blinking or wiping it from his face.

"I understand, sir."

Walters looked around the rest of the group, daring them to oppose him. Jonathon saw them shifting uncomfortably and looking away. He did not blame the soldiers; they were under Walters's command now; he held their lives in his hands, and that was a precarious place to be.

Walters shoved Jonathon forward, and together they walked into the dark woods. Jonathon felt the cold steel against his back. His one thought: Emily.

• • •

Clouds covered the half-moon lending little light along the road. Andrew estimated that they had traveled an hour since leaving Stephen Alcott's home. Stephen had insisted on lending them rifles and feeding them before they traveled on. Andrew had to admit that having a full stomach made it easier to think. Stephen would enlist the aid of neighbors and send one of his workers into Williamsburg to get more help. But both of them knew that it might not be in time.

He and Jenny trotted along the road taking care that their horses not stumble on rocks or tree roots. They came to a crossroads, and Andrew reined Neptune in; Jenny rode up beside him on Shadow.

"What is it, Andrew?"

"There are two ways they could have gone. One way is faster, but the other is a better road. Would Michael want speed or ease of travel?" He looked down each road searching for any evidence of his choice. With so little light, it was difficult to see any sign of their passage.

"Which way would—," Jenny stopped speaking as Andrew held up his hand, gesturing to her. They hurried their mounts into the woods on the side of the road. He was certain that he had heard hoof beats. Straining his ears, he listened to the night sounds. Nothing out of the ordinary was within earshot. Jenny cocked her head, intent on listening, too, and a lock of hair fell into her eyes. He clenched his fist at his side in an effort to not brush it aside. She looked at him, and he slowly raised his hand and gently pushed the tress back into place. Their eyes met, and Jenny's gaze turned to fear. Suddenly Andrew heard the cock of a pistol near his head.

"Do not move," a deep voice said close to his ear.

Andrew raised his hands to indicate his lack of weapon.

"Step out into the road."

They led their horses to the road, confused by the sound of a soft chuckle.

"And what do you think you are doing in these parts, Andrew?"

"Randy!"

Andrew was grateful to be mounted, for his legs had turned to rubber.

"And Jenny—you would follow this rascal to the woods at night? Are ya' mad, girl?"

"Randy, they have Jonathon!" Andrew's relief was quickly replaced with urgency.

"Aye, I know, lad. I have been tracking that scoundrel Walters since Jonathon went to Brentwood Manor. He is a slippery one, though. I thought I had lost him until he came across the other British unit and fired his gun. I followed the sound and discovered their camp. The brute killed Michael Dennings."

"What?" Andrew shouted rising up in the saddle. Randy held a finger to his lips, and Andrew eased back down. He felt as though he had been punched in the gut, and sorrow gripped him. Michael had been a good friend despite his loyalty to the king. Andrew knew that if Jonathon had any chance of humane treatment, it would have been because of Michael's intervention. Now all hope for Jonathon was lost. Despair filled him at his apprehension for Jonathon, and at the thought of losing his childhood friend.

"We must do something," he said, his voice low.

Informing Randy of their visit to Stephen Alcott's and the plans they had made, Andrew began to formulate a plan of his own. He knew the chances of reinforcements finding them, let alone arriving in time, were slim. Somehow the three of them would have to defeat the entire troop of British soldiers.

. . .

"Emily, Andrew and Jenny are gone."

Emily looked up at Joanna and noticed the furrow between her brows. Joanna sat beside her on the bed. Still reeling from the events of the morning, Emily tried to focus her muddled mind on Joanna's words—and why they seemed to upset her.

"What do you mean they are gone?" Emily took a deep breath and tried to concentrate.

"I did not say anything earlier this afternoon thinking that perhaps they had just gone for a ride together, but…well, since they have not been getting on lately, I doubted that was the case. We held supper awaiting their return, but still they have not arrived."

"When did they leave?" Emily asked, a cold fear starting to grip her.

"Immediately after Jonathon and the British," Joanna said.

Emily's mind cleared as the ramifications of Joanna's words sank in.

"Oh my God. They are going to try to rescue Jonathon," she whispered. Goose flesh broke out on her skin despite the smothering August heat. She closed her eyes and breathed a prayer, "Please, God, do not let me lose my brother as well." The trembling started at her shoulders and flowed through her body. "What shall we do, Joanna? What shall we do?"

Joanna took her hands.

"I do not believe there is anything we can do, Em."

. . .

Walters prodded Jonathon's back with his pistol. Jonathon wrestled with the ropes that bound his hands. Seeing this, Walters slammed his pistol across the back of Jonathon's head causing him to lurch forward and, unable to balance with his hands bound, fall to the ground. His head spun momentarily from the blow, and he shook his head to clear his vision. Walters grabbed him by the left arm and hauled him up to standing. The image of Michael Dennings lying on the ground, still and lifeless, came to his mind. In a few minutes it would all be over. Jonathon had been in many precarious situations before and had saved himself through cunning and strength, but he was at a loss for ideas as the stinging blow made his head reel. The forest sounds surrounded them; an owl hooted nearby, once, twice, three times. Twigs crackled beneath their feet. Jonathon's ears fixed on the sounds.

"So you will shoot me in the back, like a coward would, Walters?" he taunted.

"What does it matter, Brentwood? No one will find you out here."

"Perhaps it should matter to you, Walters. Perhaps you should experience some sense of integrity in how you kill people, though I have seen no evidence of it as yet."

Walters jammed the pistol into his back and cocked the trigger. Jonathon waited.

"Perhaps you are right, Brentwood. There is no sport in simply shooting you. It would be much more pleasurable if I were to see you suffer a bit."

"Why not release my hands and provide some sport to your game?" Jonathon said as he turned to face him.

"Oh, no, Brentwood. I am not a fool. Your hands will remain bound."

Rustling emanated from the trees behind Walters; he turned to look. Again an owl hooted, much closer this time. Jonathon cocked his head, listening.

"I told you soldiers to stay back," Walters yelled in the direction of the camp.

No one appeared. Jonathon took a step back toward a tree as Walters turned to him.

"Thinking of escaping, Brentwood?" he laughed. "You will not run far with a bullet in your leg." He raised his gun, but the rustling behind him was closer and he spun about in that direction. Keeping his pistol pointed at Jonathon, he stepped over to check the trees behind him. Nothing. Now the owl hooted in the tree just behind Jonathon and he edged toward it, his eyes never leaving Walters. Jonathon felt the hard metal of a pistol being tucked into his hands, and then saw Randy melt into the shadow of the tree. Walters returned his gaze to Jonathon who watched as an evil grin spread across the captain's face.

"I have waited a long time for this moment," he sneered.

"As have I," Jonathon said. Raising his arms in front of him, he pointed the pistol at Walters. Both fired at once, sounding as a single shot. Jonathon felt a searing pain in his thigh, and he collapsed onto his other knee. Lying a few yards in front of him, contorted like a twisted tree branch, was the body of Captain Arthur Walters. Blood oozed out of the bullet hole between his eyes.

Looking behind him, Jonathon saw Randy step out from behind the tree. He half-laughed, half gasped for breath at the sight of the six-foot-four frame of his best friend. He felt the sturdy clap of Randy's arm around his back as his friend helped him to stand. Drained, he stood on his good leg while fire surged through his wounded thigh.

"Your timing was impeccable, Randy."

"I think it was a mite late, Jonathon." Randy looked ruefully at Jonathon's leg.

Hearing the rustling again, Jonathon scanned the woods in that direction.

"Who assisted you?" he asked looking around. He felt his jaw drop when Andrew and Jenny crept out of the forest. "How the devil did you get here?" His smile struggled with the wince caused by his pain.

"How is not important, Jonathon. The why is what we must attend at present." Andrew said as hurried over to Walters and began stripping him of his coat and breeches while Jenny turned away and concentrated her attention on the forest. Tearing off his own breeches, Andrew donned the British uniform. Clapping the tricorn on his head, he grabbed the musket, bayonet and pistol Walters had carried. "Now for my charade."

He crept back into the trees heading in the direction of the camp. The others followed, Randy supporting Jonathon. Circling the campsite, Randy helped Jonathon to sit, propping him up against a tree with a clear view of the camp.

Across from them at the edge of the camp, beyond the light of the campfire, Andrew marched not speaking. The soldiers watched him, looking at one another and shrugging their shoulders. Andrew wove through the trees, and then headed back into the woods. He shot his pistol into the air, and reappeared a few yards from where he had been. The soldiers stood and gathered at the edge of the woods observing the strange behavior of their captain and murmuring to one another. Silently, Randy crept into the camp gathering weapons while Jenny stealthily moved among the horses untethering them. They returned to Jonathon helping him to walk toward the road.

Andrew slipped deeper into the woods drawing the curious group after him. Now they were chuckling at the bizarre behavior of their leader. Nudging and pointing, they started to laugh as he disappeared into the woods. Suddenly they heard hoof beats and saw their captain ride off into the night. At the same time, a shot cracked and their horses, spooked, ran in every direction, some trampling through the campsite. Racing back the soldiers scrambled in confusion searching for their weapons and trying to catch their horses. In the chaos, they did not hear the sound of two other horses galloping down the road.

• • •

Grace's whimpering brought Emily awake. She stretched and rubbed her eyes, burning with lack of sleep after a restless night. Rising, she leaned over Grace's cradle and caressed the baby's hair.

"You look like your father, Grace," Lifting the baby into her arms, she cooed at her, and as she changed her wet linen clout, she talked of Jonathon. "You will know your father, if only though my words." Tying the strings of the dry clout across Grace's stomach, Emily then slipped the wool flannel pilcher over it finishing with a dry cotton gown.

The weight of her sorrow was like a physical burden that ached in her heart and dwelled in her mind, but she had to be strong for Grace; it was Jonathon's last request. She tried to sing a lullaby as she nursed the baby, but the sad, sweet words caught in the tightness of her throat. She rocked and snuggled and kissed her baby, but for now that had to speak for her.

After feeding and dressing Grace, Emily freshened up. The room was already stifling in the morning heat, so Emily dressed in a light cotton frock, cotton stockings and soft leather slippers. She could not remain confined in her room for even with the windows opened wide, no breeze moved the lace curtains. Cradling Grace in her arms, Emily headed downstairs.

Entering the dining room, Emily realized that just being there lifted her spirits a bit. Cradling Grace in one arm, she began to spoon fruit onto her plate. The smell of Dora's cooking made her aware of how ravenous she was for she had eaten little since Grace's birth.

"Emily, let me help you," Joanna said as she entered the room.

Juggling Grace and the plate had been tricky, and Emily was happy to hear Joanna's voice. She turned and offered either to Joanna, who laughed and chose Grace.

"Of course I would choose to hold you whenever possible," she said softly to the baby.

Emily smiled at her realizing how blessed she was to have such a supportive sister-in-law. Joanna had been her companion through many trials, a voice of reason, a sympathetic ear, and a wise counselor. As Emily selected biscuits and cold meats, Joanna continued to speak softly to Grace. Setting her plate on the table, Emily poured coffee for Joanna and herself and joined her at the table.

"Are Andrew and Jenny back?" she asked.

Still gazing at Grace, Joanna replied, "No, not as of this morning."

"I worry for their safety. What can they be thinking? They cannot go up against a troop of armed British soldiers."

"Perhaps that was not their plan, Emily. Perhaps they went to seek help."

Emily thought about this. Maybe if they rode like lightning, found a group of men who were armed, mounted and ready to ride, maybe then there was hope. Her heart sank at the thought of Jenny and her brother in danger. She buttered a biscuit as she pondered the possibilities of their mission.

"How long will it take them to get to Norfolk?" Emily asked.

"I do not know. I suppose it will depend on their route and what they encounter along the way."

"Once they reach Norfolk, there is no hope for Jonathon for it is a Tory stronghold. I doubt there will be any to help him there."

Joanna looked up from the baby, tears in rivulets down her cheeks. Emily's sorrow grew as her heart reached out to embrace the sorrow of Jonathon's sister. She wondered how she would endure this agony. Her eyes fell on Grace, asleep in Joanna's arms, her eyelashes soft against her cheeks, her tiny fists balled and pressing against her cheeks.

This is how she would endure.

• • •

Dawn greeted the group with thin light that flickered through the trees. Jonathon awoke to a searing pain in his thigh; reaching down he tried to loosen the tourniquet made from the sleeve of Captain Walters's coat. Randy had efficiently tied the scarlet cloth around his upper thigh stemming the bleeding, and there was no untying it. The remainder of the jacket was a pile of charred ashes in the fire.

They had ridden for a few hours to distance themselves from the soldiers, not that they could have followed for most of the horses followed their trail leaving the British to travel on foot. The ride and loss of blood had weakened Jonathon, but he gritted his teeth against any complaints; they had saved his life. He looked across at the three of them just waking, and he smiled to himself. Who came up with such a crazy plan? Whoever it was, it worked.

Randy rolled over and looked at him.

"I see you are still alive. Good work." Rising, he strolled off into the woods to relieve himself. When he returned, he grinned at Jonathon. "I imagine you would like a short walk in the woods yourself." Jonathon smiled gratefully and took the arm that Randy offered. Stiff from lying on the ground, he grunted as he stood, leaning heavily on Randy.

When they returned, Jenny and Andrew were awake silently laying out the food Stephen Alcott had provided. Jonathon watched Jenny spreading out the food, carefully avoiding Andrew's eye. Andrew, in turn, kept glancing at her, his eyes soft, telling of his longing. Whatever had occurred between them involved pain and forgiveness; he hoped they would reconcile.

"We need to remove that bullet," Randy said. "There is no water nearby, and it would be best if we could find someone more adept than I. Do you think you can travel this morning, Jonathon?"

Jonathon nodded as Jenny handed him some ham. Biting into the meat, he realized how hungry he was. Was it just a few hours ago that he had eaten that stew? How the threat of death can disrupt the concept of time.

After eating a quick breakfast, they mounted their horses and turned in the direction of Williamsburg.

•••

Andrew watched Jenny as she rode in front of him, her slender body swaying in unison with the gait of the horse. Her hair was a black river cascading down her straight back. When she turned to view the surrounding woods, her profile was striking, high cheekbones and upturned nose enchanting. They had not spoken since leaving Brentwood Manor other than to discuss plans for Jonathon's rescue. Occasionally their eyes would meet and he watched for any indication that she was willing to listen to his explanation about Deidre. But she would not hold his gaze; instead she looked away.

He had been amazed at her clear thinking as they plotted Jonathon's escape. She had been the one to suggest distracting the soldiers rather than go in with guns blazing, and he saw the wisdom of her plan since they had no guns. How fortunate that Walters had decided to take Jonathon away from the group soon after they had arrived. Just a few minor adjustments to the original plan and it all fell together. Yes, Jenny was an amazing woman, intelligent, beautiful, and intensely angry with him. He had to find a way to convince her that he wanted no part of Deidre Manning. He frowned at the thought of that woman who had tried to destroy not only his happiness, but Emily and Jonathon's as well.

He looked back at Jonathon and was shocked at his ashen face. He was listing, and only Randy's outstretched arm supporting him kept him in the saddle. Andrew knew it was imperative to remove the bullet and bind up Jonathon's wound as soon as possible. Turning to look ahead, he scanned the road and observed that the trees were clearing up ahead; they were approaching the countryside near Williamsburg. He nudged his horse into a canter and pulled ahead of Jenny.

"I am going to ride ahead and find a place to stop and care for Jonathon," he called as he passed her.

Several miles up the road, he came to a modest farmhouse with chickens pecking at the front yard and children tending lambs in the pasture. A woman emerged from a hen house with eggs cradled in her apron.

"Good day, Mistress. My friend has been shot, and I wondered if we could stop here to tend to his wound."

The woman looked at him askance, eyeing his soiled, rumpled clothes. The children had come up to stand beside her, and she shooed them indoors. Turning back to Andrew, she set her mouth in a firm line and shook her head. At the sound of another horse, she shielded her eyes with her hand and looked down the road. Jenny rode up and reined in her horse beside Andrew. Andrew watched her take in the situation and then speak.

"Good day, Mistress. We are in sore need of water and clean cloth to tend my uncle's wound. We would be happy to pay you for any inconvenience we may cause."

The woman continued to stare from one to the other.

Andrew caught Jenny's glance before she took a deep breath and continued.

"My uncle was shot by a British soldier…"

The woman grunted, and then a smile slowly lit her face.

"You fought those lobsterbacks? Well, where is your uncle, Lass? Bring him here." Her face broke into a wide grin. Thankful that he had shed Walters's jacket, Andrew spun his horse around and sped back to Randy and Jonathon.

Galloping back, he reined in his horse when he reached them.

"There is a farm up ahead that will take Jonathon in for care. The lady of the house is obviously *not* a Tory," Andrew shouted as he rode up to them.

"Not a moment too soon, lad, for I think Jonathon is done in," Randy said.

In a short time, they reached the farmhouse and Randy slid Jonathon off his horse. Supporting him on either side, Randy and Andrew brought him into the house and into the back bedroom indicated by the woman. Laying him on the bed, they started tugging at his breeches causing Jonathon to cry out in pain, but the woman brought in a sturdy kitchen knife and efficiently cut the pant leg through exposing the ragged wound in his leg. Blood had clotted around the hole, and bits of fabric from Jonathon's breeches clung to it.

"That is a nasty one," the woman said. "I shall bring some water."

Andrew watched Jenny follow the woman out of the room. Randy grunted.

"She is a fine lass, that one."

"Yes," Andrew answered still staring after her.

"You had best hang on to her, Lad, or someone else will snatch her away." He clapped Andrew on the back. "Now let us see to this rascal." He turned to Jonathon and began to rip back the rest of his pant leg.

Jonathon's unfocused eyes stared out of a pallid face, and he mumbled. Andrew knelt beside his bed and spoke to him softly.

"We are about to remove the bullet, Jonathon. Then you can rest and heal."

Returning in a few minutes with a basin of hot water and a clean sheet, the woman motioned to Jenny to tear it into strips.

Despite the heat, the woman lit a small fire in the hearth and held the knife blade in it for a moment, then instructed Randy to place a folded strip of cloth between Jonathon's teeth. Andrew's stomach lurched as the woman thrust the knife point into Jonathon's wound and twisted it, pulling upward. Like a spray, blood and the bullet shot out of Jonathon's leg. He arched his back and cried out in pain against the cloth clenched in his mouth, and then he passed out. Still kneeling beside him, Andrew looked down to see blood spatters crimson against his white shirt. Bile rose in his throat, and he fought the urge to retch closing his eyes against the scene. He breathed deeply and bit his lip to stem the waves of nausea. Looking up, he saw Jenny's pale face staring at Jonathon's leg, the quivering black curls around her face mute witness to her trembling. Rising, he crossed over to her and placed his arm around her waist. Her body quivered as she leaned into him.

As if she performed this procedure every day, the woman simply said. "There. It is out."

Taking a folded quilt, she placed it beneath his leg to elevate it, and then carefully bathed the wound with fresh water. She applied a poultice to the wound and the scent of lavender and chamomile filled the room.

Jonathon stirred. Rinsing out another cloth, she placed it across his forehead.

"We shall see," she said. She looked at each in turn, and Andrew, for the first time, noticed how clear and alert her eyes were. Her gaze settled on him as he stood with his arm still around Jenny's waist, and a smile settled on her lips.

"This is a place of healing," she said in a soft voice. Then she looked back at Jonathon.

"He will recover, but it will take time."

"I shall return to Williamsburg to fetch a wagon so we can take him back to Brentwood Manor," Randy said.

The woman raised one eyebrow and looked at him for a moment, "He should not travel for a while," the woman warned.

"We cannot presume upon your hospitality, Madame," Randy said.

"If he is a part of Brentwood Manor, he is welcome to stay as long as needed, for I know of the patriot Jonathon Brentwood," she said.

"This is Jonathon Brentwood." Andrew felt a surge of pride as he said the words. "He is my brother-in-law."

"I am honored to have him under my roof. I am honored to have helped such a Son of Liberty." Her eyes glistened.

# Chapter 16

Stars were tossed across the black velvet sky and the moon hung on a tree branch to the east. A cooling breeze rose up as Andrew saw to the horses. Jenny watched him from the back door of the farmhouse, and a tremor fluttered in her stomach. She ached to go to him and feel his embrace once more. Despite the horror of watching Jonathon as the bullet was removed, Jenny had been aware of every move Andrew had made that afternoon, and when he came to her and held her, the trembling was not just because of Jonathon.

Barely aware of her movements, she stepped out and stood on the step captivated by Andrew's movements, smooth and sure, as he brushed down the horses. Without thinking, she approached him wanting only to be near him. He turned as she neared, surprise flickering across his face.

"Good evening, Jenny," he said, his voice soft on the night air.

"Good evening, Andrew."

They looked at each other for a moment, neither speaking. Jenny finally looked away, and Andrew resumed grooming the horse.

"The breeze is refreshing," he said as he brushed the horse's flank.

"Yes. It is a lovely evening."

Andrew kept brushing; the horse sidestepped a bit, and Andrew moved to the horse's other side. His movements were steady, but his eyes shifted from his task to his view of Jenny over the horse's back. She glanced at him, caught his eye, and returned her gaze to the heavens. Her heart pounded at his nearness, and she searched for something to say to keep her there. Picking up a brush, she ran it along the horse's neck.

"Jonathon is resting well," she said.

"I am happy to hear that," Andrew replied.

Silence.

Jenny was confused; she had always been able to handle any circumstance in which she found herself. In fact, many times she knew that she controlled the situation, but it was different with Andrew. She felt like a schoolgirl, tongue-tied and awkward. And after what she witnessed between him and Deidre, she wondered that she was speaking to him at all. If they were lovers, she wanted no part of him, and yet she was irresistibly drawn to him. What was it about Andrew that she found so irresistible? Many suitors had called on her in Boston, and they were charming and handsome and most were quite well-to-do. She knew that she could have had her pick. But Andrew charmed her with his absolutely guileless nature; he never put on airs and there was an innocence about him that tugged at her heart. Yet, the scene she had beheld was not innocent, and if he were involved with Deidre, he certainly had not been honest with her.

Lost in her musings, she had not noticed Andrew return to her side of the horse. The touch of his hand on hers brought her back to the moment. Frozen in time, his hand covered hers where she held the brush against the horse. She felt the heat of his body beside her, felt his breath against her hair. Slowly, she looked up into his face and saw his smile, soft and gentle.

"Jenny, I need to explain…"

She moved away and looked down at the brush, worrying its bristles.

"You need not explain—," she began, but he placed his finger beneath her chin and tilted her face up to his.

"I do. Please allow me this chance, Jenny."

She looked at his eyes, full of misery and hope at the same time. Nodding, she put down the brush. He took her elbow and led her to a bench beneath a sprawling oak tree. The scent of phlox floated to them on the night breeze, and the warm air embraced them. Sitting down, she felt Andrew turn to her and take her hand. The trembling that had begun as she watched him from the farmhouse door returned, and she planted her feet firmly on the ground, pulled her elbows in and clenched her teeth in an effort to stop it.

"Jenny, what you saw in the stables was not what it appeared. I was looking for you as I had hoped we might go riding. Deidre came out of nowhere—I did not know she was there." He looked away, his eyes darted about as he tried to gather his thoughts. "She had been proposing—that is—suggesting—that is offering herself to me. I am sorry to reveal such a distasteful subject," he turned to her, his eyes direct and clear, "but I must, Jenny, if you are to understand what occurred. I refused her offer, for I knew that our love was all I wanted. I did not need her assistance in order to offer my love to you. She pursued me even after I refused her several times. And then, in the stables—I did not know she was there. I turned and she pushed herself against me, kissed me, and, well, as you saw." He looked at the ground. "I suppose you could argue that I am a man and I could have easily pushed her away." He looked back at Jenny. "But it had happened so quickly, and she had just accosted me when you came in…Jenny, it was as if she knew you would find us."

Relief flooded through her. She believed him with all of her heart, for the sincerity was evident in his eyes as they burned into hers. One tear escaped and ran down her cheek.

"I believe you, Andrew."

His face came close to hers and he searched her eyes. He scanned her face, her hair, her eyes and he kissed her briefly, searching her face again. Her desire for him burned within her and a longing started deep in her belly and spread through her body. His mouth closed over hers and she arched her body against his. She could feel his heartbeat, strong and steady, against her own, his arms encircling her and pulling her into him. His hands brushed through her hair and he kissed her eyes, her cheek, her throat, returning to her lips, on fire with passion.

"Jenny," he whispered into her hair. "My Jenny."

A cough interrupted their embrace, and breaking apart, they saw Randy in the yard.

"Well, Andrew, I see you took my wise counsel," he said as he approached them.

Jenny looked at Andrew quizzically, and he gave her a small smile.

Randy continued. "Jonathon is sleeping soundly after a bit of rum. The wound does not seem to be putrid, so I think he will recover from it. I intend to leave for Williamsburg tomorrow to procure a wagon so Jonathon can return home to recuperate. It would be best for you two to return to Brentwood Manor ahead of me to inform Mrs. Brentwood that her husband has been snatched from the gallows." His voice softened. "Emily needs to know as soon as possible that Jonathon is alive."

"We shall leave tomorrow as well then, Randy," Andrew said.

"Excellent. Jonathon is in very capable hands here, and I will return for him as soon as possible. Well then, I will leave you two to continue your…ah, conversation." He winked at Andrew and turned toward the farmhouse.

Jenny looked up at him feigning indignation. "So, you discuss me with any ear that will listen?"

Andrew bowed his head and looked at their entwined hands. "Randy raised the issue, Jenny, not me. He said you were beautiful and that I should not lose you through my own reticence." Looking up at her he saw the laughter in her eyes and sighed in relief. "Oh, Jenny, I thought I was in danger of losing you again."

"No, Andrew. I am afraid you might be encumbered with me for a long time." Leaning forward she kissed him.

•••

Emily felt a tugging at the sleeve of her nightgown. Coming awake, she sat up and looked around. Deidre stood at the side of her bed.

"Come quickly, Emily. It is Jonathon." Deidre whispered speaking fast and low.

Emily rubbed her eyes and looked around. The night was still, and the moonlight streamed in through the window. She realized that it must be near midnight.

"What did you say? Why are you here, Deidre?" Trying to clear her mind, Emily felt disoriented. She felt Deidre pulling her up, tugging at her arm, and she pulled away from her.

"What do you want, Deidre?"

"It is Jonathon, Emily. Jonathon has returned, but he needs you. He has been injured, but he escaped. Come, Emily, Jonathon needs you."

"Jonathon? Jonathon is here? He is alive?" Emily felt a rush of joy as she hastened to get her robe. "How? Where is he?" She rushed for the door as Grace whimpered in her sleep. As she turned to go to the cradle, Deidre again grabbed her arm.

"The child is fine; she is asleep. Come with me." Her voice was brittle in the dark room as she led Emily to the door. "He is asking for you. Come quickly."

Emily's mind struggled to make sense of what was happening, but exhaustion still held her, and her thoughts were muddled. The one thought that called out stridently was that Jonathon was alive. She hurried along behind Deidre. When they reached the staircase, Deidre paused to allow Emily to continue down, but Emily stopped as well.

"Go on, Deidre, show me where Jonathon is," Emily nudged her to the front. Deidre looked confused for a moment, and then her eyes cleared, glinting in the light of the oil lamp she carried.

"Of course, Emily. Come this way."

Their slippers were soundless on the marble stairs as they descended. The house was still except for the ticking of the clock in the parlor. Deidre led the way to the back of the house and the door that led to the out buildings.

"Why is Jonathon out here?" Emily asked, disquiet invading her stomach. "Where are we going, Deidre?"

"He is in hiding. The British are not far behind him." Deidre's voice was low and urgent.

Emily's hope that Jonathon was alive mixed with a feeling of dread. She stopped and pulled Deidre back by her arm, and in doing so caused her robe to fall open. In the dim light, Emily saw that Deidre was growing larger with child, and her heart dropped with the reality of it. She looked at Deidre's face, a mask of deceit and hatred staring back at her, and fear overtook Emily in that instant.

"This is a cruel trick, Deidre. Jonathon is not here."

"No thanks to you," Deidre spat at her. "If he had not returned for the birth of your..." She did not finish the sentence. "The British will hang him and the fault is yours." She grabbed Emily's arm. "Now you will pay for what you have done. And when you have paid, then your daughter will."

Emily tried to pull away, but Deidre had extraordinary strength. Opening the back door, she pushed Emily out into the night. Struggling, Emily tried to release her arm from Deidre's iron grip, but to no avail. She dug her feet into the ground, but it was dry, and she simply slid along the surface raising dust. Stepping behind her, Deidre grasped her other arm and pulled it back using the belt from her robe to tie Emily's hands behind her.

"Deidre, that is enough. Untie my hands." Emily wiggled her hands trying to loosen the knot, but it only caused the corded cloth to dig into her skin causing bloody gashes.

"Help!" Emily shouted. "Someone help me! Dulcie! Jedadi—" her cries were cut off by a blow to her mouth. She staggered back from the impact. Her heart stopped when she caught Deidre's face in the lamp's glow. Her eyes shone with madness, her mouth was pulled down on either side with hatred, and she sneered at Emily.

"No one is going to hear you. No one is going to help you."

Emily opened her mouth to scream, and Deidre forced a handkerchief into it, balling it as she pushed. Emily's screams were muffled, falling mutely into the night. Deidre grabbed her arm and pushed her toward the outbuildings.

"I was going to make the staircase your death scene, but you did not cooperate. But there are always other options, Emily dear. I will simply lock you in one of these and set it on fire. No one will hear your screams."

Emily kicked at her, but Deidre dodged and laughed at her.

"You are no match for me, Emily. Hatred for you fuels my strength and the thought of you dead fans the flame. With you and your child gone and Jonathon hanged, Brentwood Plantation will be inherited by my child. I will not have Jonathon, as I should have, but I will have all that was his."

Panic gripped Emily at the thought of Grace left in Deidre's hands. What would the woman do to her? Terror paralyzed Emily, not only for her own circumstance, but even more so that her defenseless, tiny daughter would be harmed at Deidre's cruel hands. She fought wildly. She could not allow Deidre to get to Grace.

Deidre pushed Emily toward the smokehouse, and Emily felt sick. This was where Captain Walters had attempted to rape her. Her mind whirled with terrible memories as they neared the door. The handkerchief in her mouth was choking her, and she was unable to swallow so saliva ran out the side of her mouth and down her throat gagging her. Just as Deidre was about to open the door, she stopped.

"No, I think I shall select a different fate for you." Her laughter terrified Emily. Following Deidre's gaze, Emily looked across at the stables and then at the oil lamp in Deidre's hand. The light glowed upward casting evil shadows that danced and flickered across her face. She grabbed Emily by her hair and pushed her in the direction of the stables. Unable to balance, Emily fell to the ground landing on her left arm and then falling face down into the dirt. Her milk had let down, and the front of her gown was damp, the dust sticking to her like obscene handprints on her breasts. Deidre pulled her to her feet glancing down at her soiled clothes.

"Poor Grace must be very hungry. She is probably crying for her mother right now. Poor baby will never see her mother again." Gripped with fear, Emily had to do something to save her baby, but what could she do? She looked at the woman who seemed possessed, hair wild and flowing down her back, eyes glinting like ice, mouth a cruel slash across her face. She thrust her face into Emily's. "Do not worry. She will not be hungry for long." She laughed, almost a cackle, and panic seized Emily at the thought of Grace being harmed by Deidre.

Emily's arms felt as if they would pop out of her shoulders and the ache traveled down to her wrists still bleeding from her efforts to loosen the bonds. Her back throbbed from being arched back, and her breasts felt as though they would burst. Tears ran unchecked down her face, but urgency for action burned within her. Deidre pulled her along toward the stables, looking back at her and laughing at her distress.

"Are you afraid, Emily? Good. You should be. Your death will not be pretty, and it will not be quick. I promise you this—neither will your daughter's be." Emily looked at her hardened face and despair clutched her. They entered the stables and Deidre cast about for rope, not letting go of Emily. Emily twisted and fought, but was no match for Deidre's strength. It was as if some demon possessed her and gave her power. Emily turned and tried to throw Deidre off balance, but the woman regained her equilibrium and spinning back slapped Emily causing her to fall to the hay-strewn floor. Deidre then kicked her in the stomach. Emily gasped as the force jolted through her, and then could not catch her breath at all. Her vision went black except for thousands of white specks that floated before her eyes. Finally, her sight cleared and Deidre was swinging reins in front of her.

"I hate you. I have hated you since the first time I saw you in the church. You have stolen everything I have lived for, and now you will die for it." She reached for Emily who kicked out at her knees, pushing one kneecap back.

"Damn you," Deidre screeched. She clawed at Emily snaring her nightdress and dragged her across the floor. Emily cried out as splinters pierced her skin and hay and dust battered her face. Deidre forced her against the upright post of a stall and tied Emily's arms to it with the reins. She stood, limping on her injured leg.

"I have waited a long time for this moment. You are going to die now, you English Tory whore."

Deidre cupped her hands and gathered hay in a pile just beyond Emily's feet. Lifting the glass cover from the oil lamp, she tipped it spilling oil onto the hay. Picking up several pieces of straw, she lit them from the flame of the oil lamp and dropped them onto the mound she had created. The dry hay immediately ignited, and Deidre stood and laughed above it like a witch.

"Now to your daughter, Emily," she shouted, turning to run out the door.

Smoke was filling the stable, and the acrid smell filled Emily's lungs. The horses were bucking and rearing in fear, pounding their hooves against the stall doors in an attempt to escape. Emily had contorted her wrists to make them wider as Deidre tied them to the post, and so intent was she on murdering Emily, she had not noticed. Emily struggled against the reins, twisting her hands back and forth trying to undo the knot. The smoke intensified, and the flame followed a trail of hay across the floor to one of the stalls. The horse's eyes were wide with fear as it thumped the walls and neighed in terror. Emily could barely take a breath the smoke was so thick, and she could see nothing but blackish gray smoke billowing about her, and a single line of flame moving across the floor.

At last, she released her hands from the reins and stood. Groping her way, she found the bench that held the tools. Feeling along the counter, she found a knife and turned it upside down in her hands, sawing with the sharp edge against her bonds. As she worked, she ran out into the night. She heard the cries of the terrified horses, but her mind was set on one thing: saving her baby. She heard horses again, but outside the stables, and out of the corner of her eyes, she saw two riders approaching. At that moment flames burst out of the window of the stable, and horses were neighing wildly.

"Emily! Emily!"

"Andrew! Help me!" Emily shrieked. Jumping down from his horse, Andrew took in his sister's appearance from her soot covered face to her soiled nightdress and the red mark of Deidre's hand on her face. He cut through the belt that had bound her hands. "Free the horses. Deidre—she is going to kill Grace," the words ended in a gasping sob as she ran toward the manor.

Andrew and Jenny ran to the stables.

Emily ran to the back of the manor, through the door and into the main foyer. Soft candlelight from two sconces threw shadows across the marble floor she sprinted to the stairs. She took them two at a time and rushed to her bedroom door. The door was slightly ajar, and the sight inside brought her to a dead halt.

Deidre stood holding Grace, cooing into the baby's face.

"How can I kill you when you look just like your father? You are not her child at all. You are Jonathon's, and now you are mine. *She* is gone, and you will never miss her." She placed the baby against her shoulder and nuzzled her head. Emily's stomach turned over at the sight. What should she do? Perhaps Deidre would not kill Grace after all. If Emily showed herself, Deidre might revert to her crazed behavior. At present, she seemed calm, almost tender with Grace. Emily waited to see what Deidre would do.

She held the child in her arms again, looking into her face. "But you are hers, not just Jonathon's and she will continue to live through you." Her face darkened and her soft smile altered to a scowl. "No, you must die, too." She looked at the child, her eyes narrowed, her brow creased.

Emily did not breathe. As long as Deidre was holding Grace, she was in peril. *Put her down.* Emily willed the thought. *Put her down.* She watched, not daring to move yet.

Feeling a presence behind her, Emily turned and saw Jenny. She put a finger to her lips and indicated she stay where she was. Turning back she peered into the room.

Deidre held the baby out as if to drop her, and Grace began to wail. Deidre was startled back to sanity, and she looked at Grace as if seeing her for the first time, and then she looked around the room. Her eyes were confused and she appeared dazed. Still she held the child away as if not knowing quite what to do with her. Walking over to the cradle, she lay the crying baby down and turned toward the door. Now, Emily stepped out to face her. Deidre stepped back, confusion deepening on her face, then it transformed into terror.

"You are dead!" she cried out.

Emily took a step toward her.

"Are you a ghost?" she whispered. "Oh my God."

Emily took another step toward her, and Deidre crumpled to the floor. Jenny ran into the room and helped Emily lift the woman off the floor. They led her to her room, Grace's cries echoing behind them. As they walked toward the east wing and Deidre's room, Joanna's door opened and she stepped out.

"What is going on—Emily! What has happened to you?" she cried.

"Joanna, please help Jenny. I must see to Grace."

Joanna took Deidre's arm and the three continued to Deidre's room.

Emily rushed back to Grace who was filling the bedroom with her complaints. Bending over the cradle, she lifted her daughter into her arms, sat in the rocking chair, and loosened her nightgown. Grace struggled against Emily's efforts to feed her, until finally the baby rooted and began to nurse. Emily felt the powerful tugging and the milk surging through her breast. Emily sobbed as she watched her daughter's beautiful face settle into an expression of contentment.

Emily's emotions were raw, and her grief over losing Jonathon was at the surface of her mind. If she had lost Grace, too, there would have been no joy in living. Her intense love for Grace brought feelings of tenderness to the surface to mingle with her sorrow. Hearing approaching footsteps, she grabbed one of Grace's blankets to cover herself while she nursed her.

Andrew entered, and she saw the exhaustion on her brother's face, but it was mixed with something else—happiness? Her brow creased as she waited for him to speak. As he crossed the floor, the odor of smoke and burnt hay accosted her as he knelt before her.

"Jonathon is safe."

Her mind reeled as she heard the same words that Deidre had said to her just a while earlier.

"What do you mean, Andrew? Did you see him in prison?"

"He is not in prison, Emily. We rescued him from the British. He is recovering from a gunshot wound at a farm near Williamsburg. Randy will bring him home as soon as he is able."

"But surely the British will come back for him…"

"No, they were stranded with no horses or weapons. A contingent from Williamsburg has probably rounded them up by now and returned them to Yorktown." Andrew smiled at her.

"But Captain Walters vowed..." Her voice trailed off.

"Captain Walters is dead, Em. Jonathon killed him."

Emily felt numb. Too many emotions had run through her this night.

"Em, I have some sad news, too. Michael is dead. Captain Walters killed him."

Emily looked at Andrew as if he had spoken a foreign language. Then his words registered and she began to weep. The image of Michael's earnest face as he proposed to her flooded her mind. Her body shook, racked with sobs, and Andrew gently took a sleeping and content Grace and laid her in her cradle. Then he knelt beside his sister, took her in his arms, and held her while her grief and joy poured out.

"Jonathon is...alive? He is...coming home...for good?" she asked gasping between sobs.

"Yes," Andrew said.

She broke down sobbing again, drenching his soiled and sooty shirt.

# Chapter 17

It was well past two o'clock in the morning, but the group in the parlor was wide awake. A mix of joy and grief held them and infused their conversation.

Andrew looked into his brandy glass and swished the amber liquid around. "Jedadiah and some others were awakened by the horses; they were instrumental in extinguishing the fire and saving most of the animals. We had to put one down because his injuries were too severe; it was the horse in the stable nearest the start of the blaze." He glanced at Emily.

"That must be the horse that was so afraid, the one that was in the stall where Deidre tied me to the post." The acrid air wafted in through the windows reminding Emily of the danger she had been in, and she shivered despite the warm, still night. She felt the silken fabric as Joanna put a shawl around her shoulders.

"We locked Deidre in her room, so there should be no danger now," Joanna said. Emily felt her gently pat her shoulder, and she looked down at Grace's sleeping face.

"She was going to kill my baby," Emily said, her voice soft, barely able to form the words.

"Grace is safe now, Em. Deidre will remain locked in her room until we know what her fate will be. Jonathon will have to determine that when he returns," Joanna said.

Tears blurred Emily's vision as she looked at Andrew and Jenny. "Tell me again how you saved Jonathon."

Andrew laughed and beamed at Jenny. "Jenny devised a brilliant plan, and Walters played right into it."

Jenny blushed and looked down at the wine goblet in her hands. "We had little choice. It was a bit like David and Goliath, I am afraid. The three of us against a group of British soldiers. We certainly did not have numbers or might on our side, so that left only our wits."

They commenced to repeat the story of Jonathon's rescue adding details that they had forgotten in the initial hurried telling. Emily and Joanna laughed at the image of Andrew cavorting in the woods in the guise of Captain Walters. Emily began to feel her aching muscles relax, and she basked in the knowledge that Jonathon was alive and safe.

After a while, conversation faded and serenity filled the room. Exhaustion overcame Emily and she rose to excuse herself. Everyone agreed with her that it was well past time to seek their beds.

Slowly climbing the stair, Emily paused to look down the east wing hall. Lying in front of Deidre's door was a sleeping Jedadiah. She smiled and entered her bedroom. Gently laying Grace in her cradle, Emily picked up a pillow and blanket from her bed and returned to the hall. She slipped the pillow beneath Jedadiah's head and covered him with the blanket. He stirred, smiled up at her, and fell back to sleep. Returning to her room, she climbed between the sheets and surrendered to sleep.

• • •

As the others left the parlor, Andrew hung back and reached for Jenny's hand. She turned to look at him, one eyebrow raised inquiringly.

"Stay for a moment, Jenny," he whispered.

She stepped back into the room and he led her to the settee. The glow from the candles cast shadows across her face, and her hair was a mass of untethered black curls framing her face. Raising his hand, he brushed the errant locks from her face and pressed them behind her ear. She smiled at him, stabbing him through when her dimple revealed itself. He chuckled.

"You could defeat the whole British army with the power of that dimple, Jenny."

Her laugh floated to him in the soft light, her eyes twinkling with delight.

"As you could with your flattery, Mr. Wentworth," she teased.

His eyes held hers and his arm encircled her shoulders. The flicker of the candle's flame danced in her clear, gray eyes, inviting and full of desire. He bent his head to her and softly ran his lips across hers; his tongue parted them searching for her response, and Jenny yielded to his kiss, answering in kind. His head reeling from her reaction, he pressed her down against the seat and moved above her. Fueled by the tumult of emotions he had felt throughout the night, his craving for her overcame him and he wrapped her in his arms, crushing her to himself. Jenny clung to him, a small moan escaping through their kiss.

His hands ran along her sides, glorying in the curves that mapped her form. Embracing her with his left arm, his right hand slid along her waist, her hips, her thighs, and traveled up to claim her breast, so soft, so warm. She pushed against him, demanding and insistent and he accommodated her request. Their bodies moved together in rhythm, and she shifted her legs to move closer to his hips.

"Jenny, oh, Jenny," he whispered against her throat. His head dipped down to taste the swell of her breasts.

Jenny hands ruffled through his hair, along his neck and down his back as she arched against him. Her touch was like fire to him, igniting passions he had never known, and his body was raging with desire. Somewhere, deep in his mind, sense called out to him, and he propped up on his elbows. The movement only served to press his hips closer to hers and Jenny moaned with longing. He moved away, and Jenny opened her eyes and gazed at him.

"What is it, Andrew?" Her breasts moved with her breathing and he wanted nothing more than to take her right then and there.

"Jenny, I made a promise to you, and I must honor it."

"Must you honor it right this moment, Andrew?" Her eyes were wide, her half-smile subtle.

Andrew laughed as he drew away from her. "You are a temptress, and I seem to fall willingly under your spell."

"And yet, the spell is broken." Her eyes twinkled as she pouted.

"The spell you cast over me will never be broken, Jenny. I am yours eternally." He kissed her forehead. "But I shall not be the cause of your undoing. Instead, I shall control my baser emotions and resist devouring you right here."

"Such consideration! You are indeed a gentleman, though I am not sure a gentleman is what I need right now." Jenny laughed, peering at him through her lashes.

"You will undo me yet," Andrew laughed, and then his face sobered. "Truly, Jenny, I want nothing more than to carry you up to my room and make love to you all night. But I am a man of my word, and I will not break my word to you, ever. I wish we could simply lie together all night, hold each other in our sleep and awake entwined in each other's arms. But I cannot trust myself to hold back. I ache for you, Jenny."

"Andrew, this is not the night that you should make love to me all night," Jenny said.

"I know."

"But not only for the valiant reason you suggest." Her eyes were alight with mirth.

"Then what reason?"

She nodded her head toward the east window where the sky showed the pale evidence of a nearing dawn.

"If you are going to make love to me all night, I demand a full night!" Her laughter was music that danced through his mind, and he joined her in it.

"Jenny, I have never met a woman like you. You have stolen my heart. I shall escort you to your room, where I shall take leave of you and return to my own."

They rose and walked toward the staircase.

• • •

Emily sat on the veranda enjoying the September sun which was not as punishing as August's had been. She watched as Grace slept, contented, in her cradle, making tiny sucking noises in her sleep. Looking up, she laughed as Joanna played with Will on the lawn. His stubby legs carried him across the grass, arms outstretched trying to catch his mother. His giggles filled the warm air, and he squealed with delight when he finally succeeded, grabbing Joanna's skirt. She swung him up into her arms and whirled him around until his laughter echoed on the breeze.

Emily watched a butterfly flit among the asters until it landed on one, pulsing its wings. She closed her eyes and breathed in the scent of late summer, phlox and fresh air with just a hint of a drier, cooler breeze.

Her body was recovering from the physical and emotional turmoil she had endured in the past few weeks. The encounter with Deidre had sapped her strength for a number of days, and her sole focus had been on caring for Grace. How close she had come to losing her daughter at the hands of the woman who also carried Jonathon's child. Was it jealousy or madness that drove Deidre to such odious attempts on her life and Grace's? Suffering from grief and despair over Jonathon's capture and presumed death had been enough of a strain, but to add Deidre's attempt on her life was devastating. Her recuperation had been slow, but steady, and it was in this moment of clarity that she realized how wonderful she felt.

She breathed deeply and slowly opened her eyes. Dust rose up along the far end of the drive, and her heart stopped as she strained to see the riders. Shading her eyes with her hands, she slowly stood and craned her neck to see them as they rode along the tree-lined lane. She noticed Joanna stop and pick up Will, starting toward the terrace. Emily began to tremble, her legs suddenly feeble. Recognition dawned on her like the sun bursting from behind a cloud, and one rider spurred his horse to a canter, waving his tricorn.

"Jonathon." She choked his name out with a sob. "Jonathon!" She ran toward the drive, her legs barely able to hold her up. Jonathon reined in Neptune, and slowly raised his leg over the saddle and dismounted as she ran to him. She fell into his arms weeping, tears streaming down her face.

"My love," he whispered into her hair.

Emily choked back a sob as his mouth covered hers, her arms reaching up around his neck. Waves of joy shuddered through her as she strained to hold him ever closer. The trembling in her legs spread to her whole body as she understood that, at last, Jonathon was safely home with her. He kissed her face, her eyes, her throat, as she laughed and cried at the same time.

"Jonathon. Jonathon." Only that word held all she felt in her bursting heart.

"Love," he answered.

Randy stopped beside them, laughing.

"With a welcome like that, Lad, I would be leaving and coming home as often as possible." He dismounted and took Neptune's reins. Leading the horses away, he chuckled. "No wonder you were in such a blasted hurry."

Jonathon smiled into Emily's eyes, his hand caressing her cheek. He turned and looked at Brentwood Manor. "I thought I would never see my home again." Looking down at Emily he stroked her cheek again. "Even worse, I thought I would never see you again." His eyes brimmed with tears.

Emily smiled at him through hers. "Welcome home, Jonathon."

"Where is Grace?" He scanned the veranda and spotted the cradle.

"She is waiting for her father to come home," Emily said.

Arms around each other, they began to walk toward the manor, but Jonathon winced in pain and stopped.

"I am afraid I must take it slowly, Love."

Emily placed her shoulder beneath his arm to support him.

"Let me help."

Together they walked to the veranda.

•••

Laughter filled the dining room during supper. Emily could barely eat, so filled with happiness as she sat beside Jonathon. Their hands remained clasped beneath the table for most of the meal, and she felt him squeeze hers often, usually accompanied by a wink. Dora had prepared a special feast for Jonathon's return, and when she brought in the platter with the roasted leg of lamb and set it in front of him, he grinned like a child at Christmas. Next came a steaming onion pie scented with apples and nutmeg followed by carrot puffs, and spinach and eggs. By the time she served the Seed Cake, everyone laughed as they moaned and rubbed their distended stomachs.

"Dora, you are an angel from above, for this must be heavenly fare," Jonathon said.

Dora blushed and smiled.

"Thank you Master Jonathon. I am...we are...all of us...so pleased to have you home." She curtsied and quickly ran back to the kitchen house.

Andrew's eyes were glazed, and he sat staring at his plate.

"I believe that is the most I have ever eaten in one sitting."

Emily laughed. "Oh, no, my brother, I have seen you indulge in as much or perhaps more, but this certainly measures up to any previous efforts."

Everyone laughed.

They moved to the veranda to enjoy the evening, but Emily soon noticed how drawn Jonathon's face was. Exhaustion from the exertion of his trip and the strain of his injury had taken its toll. Emily rose and took his hand.

"Jonathon, I believe rest would hasten the healing of your injury."

He smiled at her, the tiredness evident in his eyes. She helped him to rise and they turned to leave.

"Now that is assuming you allow him to rest, Mrs. Brentwood," Randy laughed. The others joined in.

"Well, Mr. O'Connor, there are many ways to minister to an injured man," she tossed over her shoulder.

Surprised laughter followed behind them and she heard her brother speak.

"I believe she bested you there, Randy."

Laughter erupted again.

• • •

Soft candlelight lit their room and a breeze from the window billowed the curtains. Emily led Jonathon to the bed and helped him to ease onto it. Kneeling, she removed his boots, taking care with his injured leg. She looked up and caught him gazing at her, his brown eyes tender and warm. Smiling, she rolled down his stockings, gently pulling them off his feet. He untied his shirt and Emily helped him to lift it over his head, tossing it to the floor. He laughed.

Reaching out, he turned her around and began to loosen the stays of her dress. She felt his fingers against her skin as he worked the fasteners, and a tingle ran down her spine. When he had completed his task, the dress fell forward and he turned her around again to face him. Her light silk camisole was like gossamer in the candlelight, and the shape of her breasts showed through. He traced their contour and Emily felt shivers of desire pulse through her body. He pulled her into himself to stand between his thighs, and he buried his face in her breasts. She leaned her head atop his, brushing her hands through his hair. The sensation of his arms around her brought tears to her eyes, for at one time she thought she would never be in his embrace again.

"Love," he whispered against her skin.

He drew her down on the bed with him and stroked her back, and then ran his hand along her hips, down to her thighs.

"Your skin is silken; I thought I would never touch it again. The weeks I spent recovering, I lay there dreaming of this moment. But perhaps it is too soon..." he said.

Emily smiled. "Make love to me, Jonathon."

Oh, Em," he said burying his face in her hair.

She kissed his forehead, his eyes, his cheeks until his mouth found hers and his kiss devoured her. She felt as if she were falling into a timeless, endless whirlpool. Her body ached for his and she strained against him yearning for union. He rose above her, his eyes burning into hers, and he entered her, gently at first, and then unable to still his passion, with throbbing intensity. She felt as though she floated in the air, as if her arms were spread wide, her body spread wide to receive the heat of intimacy, the exquisite fire of passion. She was consumed by her need, her longing and she held him within her. They moved together in a mystic, ancient rhythm known to lovers since before time was counted.

Laughing and crying they held each other, neither wanting to move apart. Emily's hands roamed Jonathon's body, hungry for the feel of him, as if that need would never be fulfilled. At last, spent, Jonathon rolled onto his back and Emily curled into his embrace. A sense of peace that had evaded her for so long, settled upon her and she slipped into a serene sleep.

• • •

Emily awoke to Grace's whimpers, and she silently slid out of bed. Picking up the baby, she laughed quietly as Grace arched her back and stretched out, and then curled her legs back becoming a little squirming ball. Emily chuckled softly and nestled the baby against her, but Grace was hungry and started to fuss. Not wanting to wake Jonathon, she delayed changing her daughter opting to feed her first. She sat in the rocking chair and brought the fussy baby to her breast. Grace immediately settled down to nurse. Emily watched her, fascinated as always, and curled the baby's fingers around her own index finger. She softly hummed a lullaby to a gratified Grace.

Feeling eyes on her, she looked up to see Jonathon watching her. She smiled at him.

"I had hoped we would not wake you."

"I would not miss this moment for the world, Love."

Emily gently brushed Grace's smooth, brown hair.

"She has her father's coloring."

"I hope she has her mother's temperament," he laughed.

Rising, he went to Emily's chair and knelt beside her looking at their child. He lifted her tiny fist that rested against Emily's breast and curled her fingers around his as Emily had.

"There is much power in such a tiny hand, for it has conquered this man."

• • •

Jonathon returned from a ride in the fields just before dinner. His leg was healing well, and riding had become much more comfortable in the past weeks. David had returned from Williamsburg with news of developments in the war with Great Britain, and Jonathon knew he would be called upon to sail in the future. For now, he was relishing his time with Emily and Grace, and being home on his beloved Brentwood Plantation. As he rode up to the stable, he saw the progress being made on it since the fire. Soon it would be completely repaired. As he always did as he approached Brentwood Manor, he took in the view of it, basking in its symmetry, proud of its heritage. Though it was the only home he had ever known, he never tired of looking at it. As his gaze fell on the east wing, he saw Deidre looking out at him. Even from this distance, he could sense her longing to be with him. Their eyes met for a moment, and he looked away.

Joanna had urged him to place her somewhere far away from Brentwood Manor, but he refused. Her child—their child—must be born at Brentwood Manor, for if she bore a son, he would be the heir. Jonathon shifted in his saddle. This was a conversation he needed to have with Emily, for although it had been discussed among some of them, she was not privy to that conversation. He could not bear to reveal such difficult news to her; she had suffered so much already. But she must be told, and he must be the one to tell her.

· · ·

Andrew sought out Jenny on the veranda. His news might be distressful for her, he was not sure. Their love for each other was growing each day, and they could hardly bear to be apart. As wonderful as that was, it was also becoming more difficult for them to stay apart at night, and more than once, Andrew had lain on his bed fighting the urge to go to her room. And she had confessed the same to him. His news would change that.

Jenny looked up from her book when he approached her.

"Good day, Andrew."

"Good day, Jenny. You look beautiful."

She was dressed in a gown of rose silk trimmed with ivory lace at the bodice and elbows. Her breasts swelled above the bodice and he swallowed once to calm the stirring within. Her clear eyes were slate blue reflecting the September sky, and she smiled showing her single dimple.

"Jenny, I need to tell you something."

"What is it, Andrew? You look so serious."

"Jenny, my term at William and Mary is due to start, and I must go to Williamsburg soon."

"Oh," she said slowly. "I see. How often will you return to Brentwood Manor?"

"I will come as often as possible," he took her hands in his. "I promise you this."

She nodded. "It will be difficult not to see you every day, Andrew."

He leaned his head against their clasped hands.

"I know, Jenny. I shall die without you beside me every day."

He looked up at her and saw tears glistening in her eyes.

"Do you love me that much, Jenny?" He was surprised at her reaction, for Jenny was a very sensible young woman, but he was pleased at the evidence of her feelings for him.

"That much and more, Andrew Wentworth. I suppose there is one bright side to this," she smiled.

"What is that?"

"If we are not parted soon, we will be unable to hold true to our promise." She laughed and kissed him lightly.

He felt as though a burden had been lifted. Although it would be difficult for them to be parted, he knew their love was strong and enduring.

• • •

Emily sat by the window embroidering a frock for Grace listening to distant thunder. The humidity had promised a storm, and she was glad for it, for it might cool the air. Grace slept soundly in the cradle beside her, and Emily was amazed at how quickly her tiny body was growing as evidenced by the way she filled the cradle and her clothing. She smiled to herself, grateful for Grace's good health, for many women she knew had lost their babies at birth or soon after. She looked over at the sleeping child who breathed softly and slept peacefully.

Jonathon came into the parlor, and Emily's heart leapt up at the sight of him as it had ever since he returned. Another thing to be grateful for: her husband's life.

He sat in the chair opposite hers and glanced at the cradle.

"You know, I believe Grace has slept long enough. Perhaps I should wake her." His eyes twinkled.

"Jonathon, you had best not or Grace's mother will be very upset. That does not make for a tranquil household," she warned.

"But I believe the child misses her father."

Emily looked up to give him a stern look when a movement outside caught her eye. Deidre was walking from the manor to the necessary, and Emily gasped at the sight of her. She was large with child now. Emily had not seen her since the night Deidre tried to kill her, and the shock of seeing her so obviously with child took Emily's breath away.

Jonathon had followed her gaze, and he swore softly.

Emily looked at Jonathon, and a stab of pain went through her. She knew she had forgiven him, but she could not help her feelings when confronted with the reality of the situation. Deidre was going to have his child. She looked at Grace and then at Jonathon. Would he love that child as much? Would he long to hold that child and watch it grow and play with it? She could not breathe, and she felt tears sting her eyes.

Jonathon knelt beside her chair.

"Emily, I am so sorry," he said.

Her throat ached as she fought for control. She merely nodded.

"Emily, Deidre's child will never mean to me what Grace means to me. She is ours, born of our love." Emily looked at him, fighting the urge to ask what Deidre's was born of, but she knew. That child would be born of deceit and cunning, and how would that affect it?

"Can you not send her away, Jonathon? It hurts me so to see her. I still fear her even though she is locked in her room and only allowed out with an escort. I do not trust her."

"Emily, I cannot send her away."

"Why not, Jonathon?" A thought struck her that ripped into her heart. "Do you care for her, Jonathon? Is that why you keep her here?" She felt tears spring to her eyes and she blinked them back.

"No, Em. I do not care a whit for her. But I must consider the baby."

"Your baby," Emily said softly.

Jonathon looked out at the gardens. He did not speak for a moment.

"Yes," he said in a low voice. "My baby."

The sound of thunder rolled in the distance, and the wind picked up blowing the trees.

"Emily I must explain something to you."

"What is it, Jonathon?"

"It is the reason I allow Deidre to remain here."

"Go on."

"If Deidre bears a son...," he could not continue. He looked at the floor.

Emily was puzzled. She had not considered whether Deidre carried a boy or girl, in fact, she had never applied a sex in thinking about the child. She had always referred to the child as "it" both in conversation and in her thoughts. Thinking of it as a boy or girl humanized the child, and Emily could not bear that. Once the child was born, she could no longer deny that it was a living, breathing person—born of Jonathon and Deidre. Her thoughts had never gone beyond that.

Jonathon looked up at her and took her hands in his.

"Emily, if Deidre bears a son, he will be the heir of Brentwood Plantation."

Emily felt as if she had been slapped. She gasped and fell back against the chair, dazed. Slowly she looked at the cradle and the thought crept into her mind. *What does this mean for Grace?* She looked at Jonathon, dumbstruck. She felt as if all of her breath had left her. Again a movement outside caught her eye and she watched as Deidre made her way back to the manor.

Brentwood Manor.

• • •

Andrew looked up from his packing and saw Jenny leaning against the doorframe, arms folded, a smile playing at her lips.

"Would you like assistance with your packing, Andrew?"

She went to him and took the linen shirt that he had balled up in his hands. Laughing, she shook it out, folded it neatly and placed it in the bottom of his valise. She peered up at him through her lashes, her single dimple disclosing her mirth, and making his knees weak.

"What shall I do without you to care for me, Jen?" he asked, feeling the smile break across his face.

"I do not dare to think of it, Andrew." She leaned in and kissed him.

Andrew embraced her and pulled her to himself, answering her light kiss with the intensity of his desire and his despondency of leaving her. His mouth moved over hers hungrily as if he must savor every sensation of holding her and kissing her to store up and take with him. He felt her hands brush through his hair as she answered his passion with her own. Finally, he released her and they turned back to the packing.

"I will visit as often as possible, Jenny. For certain, I will be home for the Christmas holidays."

Her face was angelic as she smiled through the tears that glistened in her eyes and threatened to spill over. She nodded.

"I will count every day, every hour until we are together again, Andrew."

He looked into her eyes, transfixed by her beauty and his longing for her. Desire surged through him; fire began in his belly and pulsated to his limbs. He pulled her into him again, holding her close, stroking her hair.

"Jenny, it is so difficult to leave you."

She buried her face against his chest, nodding her assent.

"Andrew, are you almost—oh, excuse me," Emily said as she walked in upon the scene. "I can return in a few moments."

Andrew pulled away from Jenny.

"No, Em, that is fine. I must leave. But it is so difficult," he said, looking at Jenny.

Emily smiled. "I understand, Drew. Take a few more moments, and I will send Jonathon up to help you with your bags." She withdrew, closing the door behind her.

Andrew took Jenny into his arms again pressing his head against her hair and breathing in her lilac scent.

"I shall write to you every day, Andrew," Jenny whispered.

"And I shall write to you, Jenny."

"Well, we had best finish your packing, or Jonathon will find us just as Emily did." Jenny turned to his bed and shook her head at the mound of clothing that lay atop it.

"Were you planning to simply scoop it up and deposit it in your valise?" she laughed.

"Something of that nature," Andrew laughed.

Together, with some instruction from Jenny, they neatly folded and packed his garments.

...

Life at Brentwood Manor eased into a tranquil rhythm and one ordinary day blended into the next. The oppressive heat and humidity of summer transformed into warm days and cool evenings of the coming fall, and the garden surrendered its riot of summer blossoms for the golden and russet tones of autumn.

Congress called upon Jonathon to sail again as the war waged along the coast. His ambivalent feelings wrestled between happiness to return to the *Destiny*, and sadness to have to leave Emily and Grace. He worried, too, about Emily's safety while he was gone. Deidre had remained securely confined in the east wing of the manor, but just the same, he wanted to lie beside Emily each night to ensure her safety. Such thoughts roamed his mind as the family relaxed on the veranda one early October evening. Watching Emily as she and Joanna chatted and laughed about Will's antics in the garden that day, he was entranced by her silken skin, which glowed in the light of the setting sun. Her blue-violet eyes twinkled with merriment as she listened to Joanna relating Will's adventure. Longing stirred within him, and he knew that as much as he loved standing on the deck of his ship, nothing in life compared with being at Emily's side. As he watched her, she lifted Grace from her shoulder and laid the baby on her lap. Leaning forward, she smiled at Grace who waved her arms and kicked her legs in response. Emily's voice was soft and gentle as she cooed at the baby. Looking up, she caught Jonathon's watchful eyes and locked them with her own. Passion stirred within him, and he raised his eyebrows at her. She laughed, nodded slightly, and turned to finish her conversation with Joanna.

"Oh my, Grace needs to be changed. I believe I will get her ready for bed and then retire myself."

Standing she said goodnight to everyone and went inside. Jonathon stood, stretched and yawned and made his excuses as well. As he said goodnight, his sister smiled.

"You look exhausted, Jonathon. I hope Grace will not disturb your sleep."

"Sleep is not what concerns me." He winked at her.

# Chapter 18

Spirits were high as Brentwood Manor was transformed by the hanging of the greens. Despite the war that continued to rage, especially in the towns along the coast, Jonathon and Emily decided to hold a ball at Brentwood Manor. Swags of evergreen cascaded down the marble staircase, and candles were lit in every window casting a soft glow against the panes. Wreaths decorated each door decorated with apples, holly, feathers, pineapples and even some shells Jonathon had brought back from his recent voyage.

Jenny was especially jovial as they decorated the house. Andrew's last letter announced that he would arrive the afternoon of the ball. Her heart felt as if it would lift out of her chest and float above her, and she hummed a merry tune as she attached the last apple to the wreath for the front door. Emily had been helping her, and Jenny saw the smiles she tried to hide as they worked together. Emily had been wonderfully supportive while Andrew was away, listening to Jenny's stories about him even if she had told them before. Jenny knew that more than anyone else, Emily understood what it meant to be parted from the person you love.

"I think it is finished, Emily, what do you think?" Jenny asked backing up to look at the wreath from a distance.

"It is wonderful, Jenny. You have a gift for decorating, that is certain." Emily stood beside her examining the lush greens festooned with holly, fruits, feathers and ribbons. "It is a symbol of abundance and celebration. You have spent hours on it to make it look perfect, and it does."

Emily's compliment filled Jenny's heart and again she had the sensation of it floating away. What more could happen to make her feel so joyous? She gazed around the foyer and took in the garland along the staircase, the greens surrounding the candles and the silver ribbons tied on to the sconces, reflecting the candlelight. Everything looked beautiful. She carefully lifted the wreath keeping the leather strap free to hang it on the front door. It was so large that she had to peer through the middle of it to find her way.

"Would you help me hang it, Emily?" she asked.

Emily opened the front door, and Jenny stepped out onto the porch. Looking through the center of the wreath, she saw something blocking her way: a man's longcoat over a silk shirt with lace falling at the neck. Lowering the wreath, she looked over it and into Andrew's eyes.

"Andrew!" she shrieked, and abandoning all care, let go of the wreath to throw her arms around him. It fell to the floor of the porch between their feet as they embraced and kissed.

"Jenny, your beautiful wreath!" Emily cried trying to reach between the two in order to salvage what she could of it. Laughing, she slipped it out and lifted up. Feathers were askew and fruit dangled precariously from the greens.

"Oh, my word! Look what I have done!" Jenny laughed, not letting go of Andrew's arm. If her heart had been soaring above her moments ago, now it soared to the heavens.

The three of them returned to the foyer laughing, Jenny and Andrew holding hands.

"Do not worry, Emily. I can repair the wreath and have it hanging up before our guests arrive." Jenny said. She looked at Andrew feeling as though she had not seen him in years, yet feeling as though they had never been apart. "Everything is in place now."

• • •

Emily placed the last comb in her hair and tried to tame an errant curl that insisted on falling down the back of her neck. The combs were encrusted with sapphires that sparkled in the candlelight and matched the drop earrings Jonathon had given her. The sapphire necklace lay across her collarbone with one large sapphire dropping to nestle at the top of her décolletage. She had placed a patch on the swell of her left breast and one atop her cheekbone. Royal blue silk swirled around her legs as she slowly spun to see her reflection in the mirror. White lace cascaded at her throat and elbows matching the inset in the front of her skirt. Jonathon beheld her from his seat, his black longcoat draped across his lap, white breeches tucked into shiny, black leather boots, and white lace billowed at the neck of his white silk shirt.

"You tempt me sorely, Love," he murmured.

"Our guests will be arriving soon, Jonathon. We must constrain our baser passions." Emily twirled before him sending the scent of jasmine wafting over him. Leaning forward, she planted a kiss on his head while affording him a generous view of her breasts.

"Have mercy, Emily!"

She laughed and twirled away. It had been so long since they had entertained, and she felt giddy. Her heart beat quickly, and she caught herself giggling. *What is wrong with me? I am like a young girl.* But life had been so difficult for them this past year, and now they had so much to celebrate.

Jonathon donned his coat and held out his arm to escort Emily. Taking it, she bestowed a smile of love and gratitude, and inside, she said a prayer of thanksgiving for the wonderful man she had married. Together they headed toward the stairs. A sound caught Emily's attention, and she stopped to listen. A pounding noise came from the east wing. She saw Jonathon's face darken, and he released her hand from his arm. He turned down the hall toward Deidre's room.

"She is not going to ruin this evening."

• • •

Guests mingled in the supper room and ballroom their laughter echoing off the walls. Tables were covered with plates mounded with beef, poultry and fish alongside fruits and puddings, and on others, bowls of wassail stood next to jugs of cider and decanters of wine, rum and brandy. The clinking of glasses and toasts to good health rang throughout the rooms as couples danced jigs and the La Royale, their faces bright with Christmas cheer, both spirit and spirits. Jonathon whirled Emily around the floor, laughing with her as she tried to keep her balance. Looking across the floor, he spied Andrew and Jenny who seemed to have eyes only for each other.

"I believe your brother is hopelessly smitten," Jonathon chuckled.

Emily followed his gaze. "Indeed."

"How long will Jenny stay with us, do you suppose?" he asked.

"Longer than she originally intended, I suspect," Emily laughed.

Just then David and Joanna danced up to them and stopped.

"We were just discussing how cupid seems to have found the mark." Jonathon nodded toward Andrew and Jenny, watching as they nonchalantly stood close enough so that their arms touched.

"I believe they think no one notices," Jonathon said pulling a serious face.

Joanna laughed. "It would be difficult to be anywhere near them and not notice."

"I remember that feeling of trying to be discrete and hold back any indications of my desire." Jonathon looked into Emily's eyes.

"I think Andrew has been more successful in holding back his desire. As I recall, Jonathon, you seduced Emily fairly early on."

"Me? I seduced Emily?" His eyebrows shot up and he looked from his sister to his wife. He saw the laughter in their eyes.

"Jonathon, you are not suggesting for a moment that it was I who seduced you? You are too much a gentleman to make such an insinuation." Emily looked demurely at her hands.

"David, support me here, man!"

"Oh, no, Jonathon. It would take weeks of tender whispers and many gifts to oppose Joanna." He laughed and placed an arm around his wife.

They all laughed and Jonathon's mind was filled with the memory of Emily's body lying against the muslin sheets in the cabin, her voice low, her eyes inviting. Their first time together was etched forever in his mind.

Jonathon took Emily's hand and pulled her into the dancing couples that were passing. David and Joanna joined them.

• • •

The laughter and music swelled as dancers swirled around in step. Suddenly, at one end of the room, people began looking around and voices lowered, then little by little, conversations dropped off until finally, the music stopped. Faces turned toward the ceiling as the sound of pounding and then a loud crash disrupted the gaiety of the gathering. Jonathon stormed out of the room followed by David and Andrew. Confusion showed on the faces of the guests and an uncomfortable murmuring buzzed about the room. Emily stepped to where the musicians were stationed and held up her hands.

"Apparently there is very strenuous cleaning and repair going on upstairs." Her voice was raised so that all of the guests could hear her, but it was not enough to cover the sounds from above. "Please, it is nothing to be concerned about. Let us continue our Christmas celebration." Smiling, she motioned to the musicians who picked up their instruments and began to play, and people began to move and talk tentatively. In a moment, the noises ceased and the festive atmosphere returned to the gathering.

Joanna led Emily into the supper room and poured them each a glass of wine. Speaking softly, Emily said.

"Deidre's only desire is to see me miserable." She took a hearty sip of the wine. "Or dead."

Joanna nodded. "You are right, Emily, and we must always remember how dangerous she can be. She must be a terribly unhappy woman. As well as being mad."

Emily looked at her sister-in-law, grateful for such an advocate. "No matter how desperate things get, Joanna, you always seem able to make me smile."

• • •

Jonathon unlocked the door to Deidre's room and swung it open. She was sitting by the hearth, pounding the black, cast-iron poker onto the andiron. Her hair fell about her face in disarray looking more like spilled straw than its usual golden radiance. She turned to look at him with hollow empty eyes. Across the room, the ewer and bowl lay in shards on the rug, water dampening the roses in the pattern.

"Deidre, you must stop," Jonathon commanded as he entered the room.

David and Andrew stepped in behind him.

"Jonathon." Deidre's voice was scratchy and she reached out to him.

"Deidre, you must stop," he repeated.

Tears streamed down her face as she held her hand out to him. He ignored it. The memory of her standing naked before him in the cabin, mounting him, forcing herself on him, caused bile to rise in his throat. He would never forgive her, and he certainly would never forgive himself for what happened between them.

"Jonathon, you are entertaining, and you have not invited me. I will put on a gown, my green one, I think. Remember how we danced when I wore it to your Christmas ball before you sailed to…" Her face transformed from weeping to hateful in a second. "…before you sailed to England and brought *her* back." She spat the words. "You were mine, Jonathon. We were meant to be together, and *she* stole you from me." Vitriol spilled from her words.

She rose up on all fours like a cat, her face creased in a frown, her eyes unfocused. Jonathon saw Andrew step back. Awkwardly, Deidre stood moving her skirts so as to not step on them. Her gown billowed over her enlarged belly, and Jonathon stared at it, transfixed. This was his child. His mind rejected the thought, but he knew it was true. This was his child as much as Grace was his child. And if this child were a boy, he would be the heir. His skin crawled and he felt sick.

"I will kill her." Deidre's face was a garish mask, her mouth slack, her eyes dark. Her voice brought Jonathon back to the moment.

"You will never get near her, Deidre."

Her eyes brightened at his words to her and her demeanor changed again.

"Jonathon, bring me with you to the ball," she whimpered.

Dulcie appeared behind him with a tea tray.

"I brought you some tea, Miss Deidre. I will stay while you drink it," she said.

Walking over to the table, she placed the tray on it and poured a cup. Handing it to Deidre, she spoke softly. "This will help calm you down. Then we can talk about the ball you went to."

Deidre looked from Jonathon to Dulcie.

"Go on, Miss Deidre, drink your tea."

Deidre sipped the tea and sat on the edge of the bed.

Dulcie turned to the men and motioned them out of the room.

Jonathon looked back at Deidre who sat on the bed staring at nothing, rubbing her belly.

• • •

The men returned from upstairs, and Emily had never seen Jonathon's face so angry. He picked up a glass, poured some brandy and downed it in one gulp. Emily's throat burned just watching him. He pounded the glass on the table and looked over the crowd.

"It seems so cruel to keep her locked up," he said softly. He gripped the table. "But she is mad. She tried to—kill you and Grace," he said looking at Emily.

"What else can be done, Jonathon? She cannot be allowed to move about freely, for she will threaten Emily again," Joanna cried.

"I sometimes think that locking her up has made her madness worse, but it cannot be helped." He looked off in the distance. "I saw it in her eyes when she came to me in the cabin. I think the seeds of evil were planted when she killed her husband, Robert."

The music floated in from the next room mingled with the laughter of the guests, a stark contrast to the emotions roiling within Jonathon, fear for Emily mixed with guilt for his part in this drama. Somehow he should have been able to thwart Deidre's plan when she came to the cabin. Now the result was the child growing within her womb. His child—perhaps his son. He poured another brandy and tossed it down.

"We had best return to our guests. Thank you for resuming the festive mood, Love."

"Jonathon, what was she doing?" Emily asked.

The image of Deidre like a cat on all fours burned into his brain.

"It matters not, Love, for she is mad."

•••

January brought bitter cold and icy rain to welcome the New Year, and Brentwood Manor settled into quiet days of ordinary activities and evenings spent around the hearth playing games of whist. Jonathon and David took turns traveling to Williamsburg to stay current with the course of the war against the British, neither traveling at the same time in case Deidre caused more trouble. Emily and Joanna stayed busy caring for the children, and Jenny occupied her time writing letters to Andrew and reading. A sense of peace pervaded the house, and each family member was grateful for it.

It was a rainy evening when Jonathon arrived from his recent trip to Williamsburg. Emily sprang up to meet him as he entered but kept her distance until he had removed his hat and shaken off the raindrops that had gathered in the folds of the tricorn. Laughing, he carefully swung his heavy woolen cloak off of his shoulders spraying cold rain across the marble floor. After hanging it on a nearby hook, he opened his arms wide.

"Now, my wife, grant me a warm welcome home."

Emily ran to his arms, feeling as much love as when he first came back to her from the British. His face was cold against hers, and his hands traced icy circles across her back.

"Jonathon, come to the fire and warm yourself," she laughed. She took his hands in hers and rubbed them until they began to warm up. Arms wrapped around each other's waists, they joined the group in the parlor.

"What news, Jonathon?" David asked rising from his chair. He poured a brandy and handed it to him.

"It is good, David. It is good. General Washington and his troops were able to defeat the Hessians at Trenton. Tales of crossing the Delaware on Christmas night tell of brutal conditions, almost impossible with the ice blocking their way and a nor'easter blowing. But, by God, they did it! And on he led his men to a battle at Princeton where he surprised Cornwallis's rear guard and routed the British again. I am told the Pennsylvania militia would have followed Washington to hell and back. In less than a fortnight, he claimed two major victories."

"By God, that is happy news, Jonathon!" David clapped him on the back. The two men clinked their brandy glasses together in a toast.

"To Washington!" Jonathon beamed.

"To Washington." David downed his drink.

Emily watched her husband as he announced his news. His face shone in the firelight, and his eyes danced with elation. She knew how long he had been working for the cause of freedom, and his dedication to the cause was embedded deeply in his spirit.

• • •

Grace lay on Jonathon's lap cooing and smiling at her father. He watched his daughter with the same sense of wonder he had felt upon first seeing her. How could such a tiny being send pangs of tenderness through him? He had sailed in deadly storms at sea, had fought and killed for the cause of freedom, had suffered torture at the hands of the British, all of which should have hardened him against such an unexpected assault leveled by this tiny infant. But no, one smile from his Grace and he surrendered to her magic.

"How are you this fine day, Miss Grace?" he cooed. Oh no, he was using that strange voice again—the one only she could elicit from him. He cleared his throat and started again, this time in his usual baritone.

"How are you this fine day, Miss Grace?"

The baby laughed out loud at him, waving her tiny fists and kicking her legs.

"I see you prefer a voice more suited to your brave, manly father."

She laughed again, and his heart melted. One of her tiny booties fell off, and he gently grasped her ankle and kissed the sole of her foot. She squirmed and laughed with delight.

"Oh, my, Miss Grace, I believe I am in extreme danger when I am with you, for if you asked me for the moon, I would find a way to get it for you."

"You will spoil her terribly, I can see that already." Emily laughed as she set down the tea tray. Jonathon watched her flowing movements as she poured their tea, captured by her lissome beauty as she sat beside him.

"I am a ruined man, caught between the dual menace of two irresistible women."

Emily's eyes danced as she handed him his teacup. "A danger you have brought on by your own doing, Captain Brentwood."

Her words had a different effect than she intended, for it reminded him of other consequences of his actions. Deidre would deliver his other child any day now. Would he feel the same love for that child as he did for Grace? And what if she delivered a son? His stomach lurched at the thought and he suddenly felt drained of energy. Why had he allowed Deidre to lie with him? Why could he have not had the strength to hold her back? He would pay for the rest of his life for that one afternoon.

Looking up, he saw Emily's eyes on him. She took his cup and saucer and set it back on the tray. Taking his hand, she moved to face him.

"Jonathon, guilt will eat away at your heart for as long as you allow it, and it will harden your heart against loving those most dear to you. I know this because I suffered such guilt when I thought you had died in Norfolk. I blamed myself because I demanded that you take me back to England, and I believed that if I had not made that demand we would not have been there for the British to shoot you. I carried that guilt for a long time, even considering ending my own life because I could not go on without you." She looked at Grace. "It was because of our child that I went on; she saved my life. Whatever guilt you are feeling about the child Deidre carries, you must release it. As difficult as it is for me to acknowledge your other child, it is a fact. You are the child's father, and the mother will not be capable of caring for the baby. She—or he—will have only you."

Jonathon caressed Emily's cheek and ran his thumb along her lips.

"Emily, you are remarkable. I thank God for you every day."

He wrapped his arm around her shoulder and pulled her close to rest her head on his shoulder. Together they looked down at Grace who smiled and waved in contentment.

...

Ice covered the lawns and grounds surrounding Brentwood Manor on the late January morning with sleet falling in torrents making roads impassable and keeping the occupants of the manor at home. The family was at dinner when Dulcie burst into the dining room.

"Miss Deidre's baby is coming." She ran out toward the kitchen house to gather the necessary items.

"It will be impossible for Dr. Anderson to attend the birth," Joanna said looking around the table, her eyes resting on Emily. "I must help her, along with Dulcie."

Jonathon looked at Emily, too, his eyes full of sorrow. A surge of compassion rushed through her, and she looked at Joanna.

"I will help, too."

"No, Emily. I do not want you near that woman," Jonathon said.

"She cannot hurt me in her condition, Jonathon, and no one should bring a child into the world without help."

He stared at her, his eyes soft and tender.

Emily and Joanna left the room and headed for the staircase. Hurrying up it, Emily heard a moan coming from Deidre's room. Upon entering, she was shocked by the woman's ragged appearance. Dark circles smudged the skin beneath her eyes, and her hair was matted and snarled. Seeing Emily she sneered at her.

"Get away from me you whore!" she screamed, then doubled over as another contraction grabbed her. "Oh, my God," she cried out.

Joanna went to her bedside as Emily poured water into the basin. Casting about, she saw one of Deidre's towels flung across a chair; she picked it up and dipped it into the water. Walking over to the bed, she started to place it on Deidre's forehead, but the woman slapped her hand away with such force, Emily stumbled back.

"Stay away from me! I detest you!" Deidre's voice was hoarse with hatred, and her face was screwed up in a scowl.

"Deidre, calm down, you need to focus your strength on your baby right now," Joanna said, her voice low and soothing. She picked up the damp cloth Emily had brought over and wiped Deidre's face. Deidre looked at her and nodded.

Dulcie entered with a stack of clean linen cloths and towels followed by Jedadiah with more water and a hot tea kettle. Jedadiah averted his eyes so he would not see the scene on the bed, and then withdrew closing the door.

Emily's stomach clenched as she watched Deidre writhe in agony with each contraction. Had it been so painful? She could not remember now, for the minute she had looked at Grace, all memory of pain had left her. Trying not to anger Deidre anymore, Emily stayed away from the bed, instead, wringing out fresh cloths as needed and keeping the kettle hot in the fireplace.

The afternoon wore on, and Deidre's labor intensified. As Emily observed the women tending her, she wondered if Deidre would bear a son. She wondered if the child would even live, for many times women lost babies at birth, especially their firstborn. For a moment she allowed herself to think, perhaps even hope that might be the case, but then felt sick that she could ever entertain such a thought. She shook her head to banish it. This child was

Jonathon's and like it or not, would be in their lives forever. And if it were a boy, he could change her life forever.

As the afternoon sky darkened to dusk, Deidre entered the last stage of her labor. Joanna and Dulcie propped her up as the contractions came faster and harder, and they prepared for the delivery.

Emily dug her fingernails into her palms with anxiety. Except for her own labor, she had never witnessed one, and the incredible pain Deidre was in allowed sympathy to flow over her. She wanted to help, but her presence only increased Deidre's distress. Finally, Dulcie spoke to her.

"Miss Emily, you are either going to help raise Miss Deidre up or you are going to have to catch the child," she said.

"Oh my," Emily said and she hurried to take Dulcie's place so the woman could assist the birth.

"Noooooo!" Deidre screamed trying to push Emily away, but a strong contraction caught her and she fought to breathe.

"Time to push now, Miss Deidre," Dulcie said.

Deidre snarled, her teeth clenched and she groaned low in her throat as she leaned forward. Leaning back she rested, her eyes closed, gasping for breath.

"Again, Miss Deidre."

"Aarrgggghhhh," she howled as she leaned forward.

"Here is the head. One more push, Miss—,"

"Aarrgggghhh," she cried, and the baby emerged, a bluish, wriggling bundle that let out a lusty wail.

Emily's heart seemed to stop beating as she held her breath.

"Congratulations, Miss Deidre. You have a beautiful baby girl."

"Nooo!" Deidre screamed. "It is a boy! It must be a boy!"

"Well, I know the difference between a girl and a boy, and this is surely a girl." Dulcie chuckled as she gently washed the baby.

Deidre's eyes bored into Emily's with hatred so tangible Emily felt the hairs on the back of her neck stand up.

"Get out." Deidre snarled at her.

Emily and Joanna lowered Deidre to the pillows, and Emily walked to the door.

"This is not over." Deidre spat after her.

Closing the door behind her, Emily leaned against it and began to weep. Her knees gave way and she slid to the floor crying silently. Jonathon had another child, but at least he did not have a son.

. . .

Jonathon and David rose as Emily came into the parlor, and Jenny poured her a glass of hot mulled cider. Seeing the exhaustion on her face, Jonathon led her to the settee and awaited the news.

"Jonathon, you have another daughter," Emily said quietly.

His breath came out in a long stream. "Thank God."

He sat beside her and wrapped one arm around her shoulder, but she did not move.

"Em, are you all right?" he asked softly. He could feel her trembling and removed his longcoat to place around her shoulders. As he watched her, tears ran unchecked down her cheeks, and he brushed them away. She sat like a statue and he waited until she was ready to speak.

"Birth is a miracle, but to be there with her was like being with the devil." Emily's voice was barely a whisper. "I have never felt such hatred in my life."

Jonathon drew her close, and she laid her head on his shoulder. Jenny had brought down a quilt from her bedroom and snugged it around Emily's lap.

Jonathon's emotions churned within him. He had another daughter, but at what cost? His wife sat beside him trembling at the shock of attending the birth. He would do whatever he could to make this right, he vowed this to himself.

Emily sat up and turned to Jonathon, her lids heavy over tired eyes.

"You should go see your daughter, Jonathon."

"No, Love. I will stay with you."

. . .

Emily had been sleeping soundly for over an hour as Jonathon lay beside her. She had nestled against him, her soft breath tickling his shoulder. At last she turned to her other side, rolling away from him, her breathing even and deep. He slid out from under the covers and donned his breeches and shirt. Silently, he crept out of the room and headed to the east wing.

Unlocking the door, he stepped into Deidre's room. Dulcie sat dozing in the chair, and the cradle was tucked by the hearth. Jonathon stepped over to the cradle and looked down at the sleeping baby. Gently he lifted her into his arms noting what a good size she was, and he sat beside the fireplace gazing at her perfect face. Unwrapping the blankets, he counted her fingers and toes and removed her bonnet. Her hair was golden like her mother's, soft and wavy. He brushed his hand across it and the baby shifted and hunted for her fist.

"Her name is Victoria," Deidre said.

He stood and walked over to stand by the bed.

"Victoria for victory. My victory over *her*."

"Deidre, you will destroy yourself with that hatred."

"I want to destroy *her*. I want her to be in agony as I have been in agony since she arrived."

"Stop, Deidre."

"I will not stop, Jonathon. You were meant to be mine."

"We have gone over this before…"

The baby started to whimper, and Dulcie roused in her chair. Jonathon paced, rocking the baby in his arms to soothe her, but to no avail. Her whimpers turned to incessant cries. Dulcie took the child from Jonathon and brought her to Deidre who simply stared at the baby.

"Your baby is hungry, Miss Deidre," Dulcie said, urging her to prepare to nurse the child.

Deidre slowly raised her hand to her shift and slipped it off of her shoulder exposing one breast; Jonathon turned away.

"There was a time you enjoyed this view, Jonathon," she said in a low sultry voice.

Dulcie busied herself tidying up the cradle.

"As I told you, Deidre, that was long ago," he said as he exited the room.

• • •

As Grace slept for longer periods throughout the night, Emily began to put her in the nursery affording less distraction when she and Jonathon were together in their room. At first, she was reluctant to be so far away from her baby, but she found that she slept more soundly, and Sarah, one of the maids, slept in the nursery with Grace. If Grace woke in the night, Sarah would bring the baby to Emily to nurse her.

Emily entered the cheery room one afternoon upon hearing Grace's cries. Yellow chintz curtains framed the windows brightening the winter's fading sunlight. Mahogany wainscoting ran along the lower walls beneath the yellow ocher paint with heart stencils in pink and green that ran along the ceiling. Several samplers that Emily had stitched during her pregnancy hung above the crib, and the wall opposite the windows had a quaint forest scene painted on it. Emily felt happy whenever she was in this room because the colors were so bright, and because Grace was here.

She crossed over to the crib and looked down at Grace who wailed louder when Emily did not immediately pick her up.

"Come here, my sweet girl," Emily said as she lifted the complaining child. Though she ate well and was very healthy, Grace was petite. Emily sat in the rocking chair and loosened her gown as Grace started to settle down. She nursed while Emily sang to her softly. After a while, when she was satisfied, Grace would smile up at Emily, not letting go of her breast.

"You are a silly one, Grace," Emily said softly. Grace smiled again. "You are my precious little girl."

She tucked her finger inside Grace's balled fist and brought it to her lips kissing the baby's hand. She wondered if Deidre felt the same about her baby. Emily learned that she had named the child Victoria—an unusual name, Emily thought. The child was over a month old now, but Emily had not seen her. She stayed in Deidre's room, and the weather was too inclement for Deidre to venture outside with her. She knew that Jonathon visited with the child to ensure she was taken care of properly, and he said Deidre seemed to have become more rational since the baby's birth. Emily could not imagine anyone loving a child as much as she loved Grace, and overwhelming joy rushed through her. She nestled the baby closer. Grace giggled, and Emily could not imagine life being sweeter.

• • •

Emily lay with her head on Jonathon's shoulder as they spoke softly in the dark. He ran his hands along her arm feeling her silken skin, and he kissed the top of her head. They spoke of ordinary things, what they had done that day, Grace's newest efforts at grasping objects, and the news from Williamsburg about the progress of the war. Their conversation faded and they lay in silence for a while. Finally, Emily spoke and Jonathon could tell by her voice that what she said was different than the ordinary.

"Jonathon, I must ask you something."

"What is it, Love?"

"How do you feel when you look at…at your other child?"

Jonathon shifted his position, propping up on his elbow to look down at her. Moonlight streamed in across their bed and he saw the worry in her eyes.

"I shall not lie to you, Emily. Are you sure you want to ask this question?"

Emily looked into his eyes for a moment.

"No, I am not sure, but it is eating me from inside."

He brushed a tendril from her forehead and kissed it.

"I feel…I feel tenderness toward Victoria."

The sound of his saying her name was a knife in Emily's heart.

"Do you love her?"

Jonathon pondered her question for a moment trying to be honest with himself, knowing he owed her that much.

"I do."

They lay there in silence, and he rested his head against hers.

"Emily, I would move heaven and earth to change the course of events, but there is nothing I can do to change them now. Victoria is an infant; she does not have the sin of my actions on her. When I hold her, I feel a tenderness that I cannot deny. Do I love her as I love Grace? Not at present, but I do not spend as much time with her as I do with Grace. I am so sorry if my words bring you pain, but I cannot—I will not—lie to you."

Emily's eyes glistened with tears that ran down along the sides of her face and into her hair.

"Does she look like you as Grace does?"

"No, she has her mother's fair hair, and she is bigger than Grace was at birth. Where Grace is petite, Victoria is not. She is already close in size to Grace."

Emily thought about that. She knew that Grace was healthy and thriving, and it was not unusual for babies to vary in size. As difficult as it was to hear about Victoria, Emily could not deny her curiosity.

"Thank you for your honesty, Jonathon. I must learn to accept her—no, to come to love her as she is your child and I love you so."

Jonathon bent his head and kissed her softly. He wrapped his arms around her and dozed. Emily stared at the ceiling.

• • •

Emily was not happy that Grace and Victoria shared the nursery, but she saw the sense in it. With their expanding family, they were running out of bedrooms, and it was much easier for Sarah to tend both girls if they were in the same room. She was taken aback the first time she entered and saw both cribs, and as Grace was sleeping peacefully, she walked over to Victoria's crib.

The baby slept, one fist pressed against her lips. She made sucking sounds just as Grace did, and her face was angelic. Soft blonde curls peeked out from beneath her cap, and Emily saw what Jonathon meant about her size. She was larger than Grace had been, but her features were delicate. Emily had to admit that Victoria was a beautiful child.

• • •

Deidre was allowed to come into the nursery when Victoria was awake if Grace was not there. Jonathon would stop in to visit Victoria during these times for two reasons: one to check on Victoria and secondly to ensure Deidre behaved herself.

She seemed calmer since the birth of Victoria, and the madness seemed a distant memory to him as he watched her with their child. She was taking care of herself now, and her natural beauty had returned. Their conversations were brief, but he did not detect any of the loathing toward Emily in her voice.

"Victoria seems to be thriving," he said.

Deidre brushed the baby's hair with her hand.

"She is very content."

Jonathon watched her, and she seemed no different than any other mother nursing her child. He detected a softness in her eyes that had never been there.

"You love her very much, do you not, Deidre?"

She did not look up, but continued to gaze at the baby. "I have never known such love." She looked up at Jonathon.

"I am aware of the destruction and fear I have caused, Jonathon. I do not know what possessed me, and I hope you will find it in your heart to forgive me." Her gaze returned to Victoria.

Jonathon was silent, watching for signs of deceit. But she continued to gaze, enrapt with her baby. She looked up at him.

"I understand if you do not trust me, nor do I blame you. I can only prove my sincerity in how I live my life now. I thank you for allowing me to stay under your roof."

Jonathon shifted in his chair, uncomfortable with his ambivalent feelings: on the one hand he wanted to believe her words, on the other a feeling in his gut said "beware".

• • •

The storm woke both babies at the same time, and Sarah rose to tend them. She changed Grace first and, when she noticed that her crib linens were soaked, she brought her over and laid her in Victoria's crib while she changed that child. By the time she finished, Grace was sleeping soundly, so she left her in that crib and took a crying Victoria to Deidre.

After Victoria was fed and sleeping, Sarah took her back to the nursery and placed her in Grace's crib with its fresh linens.

Yawning, she turned down the oil lamp and returned to her bed and fell into a deep sleep. She did not realize that she had forgotten to lock Deidre's bedroom door when she left her. Nor did she hear Deidre enter the nursery and take the baby.

• • •

A clap of thunder shook the house when lightning struck a tree in the yard. Emily sat bolt upright, a sense of unease troubling her.

"Jonathon, Jonathon, wake up. Something is amiss." She shook him until he stirred.

"Wha...what is it, Love? Is the storm raising your passion?" He reached for her, but she evaded his grasp as she slipped out of bed.

"I must look in on Grace," she felt an urgency course through her. "Jonathon, please come with me."

He struggled to wake up.

"Grace is fine, Em. It was just thunder."

White light flashed in the windows as another rumble of thunder crescendoed and then rent the night with its reverberation. Emily felt her brow furrow, and she set her mouth in a firm line. Jonathon looked at her, crawled out of bed, and followed her out of the room.

Emily's heart stopped when she beheld the scene before her. Deidre stood at the nursery door and stared at them. Her eyes glinted in the candlelight, and she sneered when she saw Emily.

Dashing to the top of the staircase, Deidre gazed over the curving bannister to the marble floor below with an infant clutched to her breast. She looked back at them, eyes glazed with her madness.

"All I ever wanted was you, Jonathon; we were meant to be together." Her gaze shifted to Emily. "But *you* bewitched him despite your Loyalist sympathies. Now you will pay, Emily, for

I shall take away what you cherish most in life—your baby." She leaned over the railing and began to loosen her grip on the child.

"Deidre, wait. You know I have always cared for you. Let me hold you," Jonathon's voice was soft and tender as a lover's. "Deidre, we have lived our lives together, shared memories, and now share a child." As he spoke he cautiously inched toward the dazed woman. She eyed him suspiciously at first and moved to hang the baby over the rail, but the tenderness in his voice seemed to reach her, and she drew the baby back a bit.

"Deidre, come to me," Jonathon said, his voice low and soothing. Emily saw her waver, her eyes locked on Jonathon, and then back to Emily, who still stood frozen in place.

"You attempt to seduce me *now*, Jonathon? When I hold the life of your child—yours and *hers*—in my hands? It is far too late for you to convince me at this point. I am going to kill what you love most." She hung the infant over the rail suspended in a blanket, but in one movement, Jonathon was beside her and caught the baby before she could release her. Loathing burning in his eyes, he glared at her. Looking down at the baby, his eyes widened, and he gently tugged the bonnet off the baby's head revealing soft blonde curls.

"Do you not even know your own child?" he seethed.

Deidre stepped back as if she had been struck; losing her footing she arched backward then forward flailing to grasp the rail. Pupils dilated with madness and hatred, her wrathful eyes first registered confusion, then awareness, then fear as she groped madly for something to save her. Jonathon holding their child was the last thing she saw before she plummeted down the stairs to her death, screaming in terror and defeat. Twisted in a bizarre contortion, her body lay at the foot of the stairs, her golden hair strewn around her head like a halo. Blood trickled from her mouth and pooled beneath her broken form, a scarlet shadow against the white marble floor.

Hearing the screams, others hurried out to the hall each recoiling in horror at the scene below. Emily, trembling violently, felt Joanna's arm encircle her waist. She watched David begin a slow descent to the main floor, his eyes dazed with the horror before him. Jonathon stared at Deidre's body, hideously contorted below him. Victoria whimpered, awakened by the commotion, and Jonathon pressed his lips against her forehead whispering soft assurances, gently bouncing her in his arms.

Slowly Emily released herself from Joanna's protective embrace and went to Jonathon. Looking into his soft brown eyes, she reached up and caressed his face, then shifting her gaze to Victoria, she gently took the child from his arms. She again looked up into his eyes, and nodded slightly her unspoken love, assuring him. She looked down through her tears and placed a gentle kiss on the blonde curls.

Jonathon wrapped her in his arms, the baby between them.

"My love," he whispered. "My love."

• • •

Spring brought warm weather, sunshine and Andrew to Brentwood Manor. Emily saw Jenny's reaction before she saw her brother as he rode up the drive. Stopping halfway along the road, he dismounted and grabbed Jenny as she threw herself into his arms. She reached up and removed his hat as he kissed her soundly, and then she placed it on her head as they walked arm-in-arm back to the manor.

Emily smiled as they came up the drive, and Jonathon came up from the stables where he had been preparing to ride.

"Andrew!" Emily said as she kissed her brother's cheek.

"Good day, Em." He looked at his sister carefully. "How are you?"

"I am well, truly, I am," she reassured him.

He looked down at the two cradles on the veranda and whistled.

"You certainly have your hands full," he laughed.

"It is almost like having twins, but you can certainly tell them apart," Emily smiled.

Andrew picked up Grace who wiggled excitedly in his arms. Her dark curls danced across her head as she played with the lace at his throat.

"You have grown, young lady!" he said.

Emily picked up Victoria, who laid her head on Emily's shoulder and stared at Andrew.

Joanna joined them, bringing mugs of ale and cider and freshly baked gingerbread.

"Oh, how I have missed Dora!" Andrew exclaimed. "I must kiss her in thanksgiving for this welcome home."

"You seem to be kissing everyone for your welcome home," Jonathon teased looking at Jenny.

"You had best not kiss Dora as you did me, Andrew, for I want no competition to make me jealous." Jenny said.

David rode up from the nearest field and joined the group on the porch just as Andrew returned from the kitchen house.

Emily looked around the gathering and said a silent prayer gratitude for her life, for her family. As if reading her mind, Jonathon looked across at her and smiled, his eyes tender. He stood and raised his glass in a toast.

"To my beloved wife who has taught me what it means to love. To our family who surrounds us with support and caring. To our country, newly formed, that will allow us to pursue our dreams and live our lives in freedom."

Their voiced blended in shouts of "Here, here" and "Well said".

• • •

A spring breeze billowed the curtains in their bedroom as Jonathon and Emily lay together basking in the afterglow of their lovemaking. Jonathon curled around Emily, his arm draped over her hip and he nuzzled the back of her neck.

"Jonathon?"

"Yes, Love?"

"When did you fall in love with me?"

Jonathon pulled her toward him so they faced each other. Emily saw the twinkle in his eye, and his mouth turned up at one corner.

"It might have been the time you called me an arrogant cad, or perhaps the day I caught you scantily dressed and bathing in a nearby stream."

She lightly swatted him on his shoulder laughing as she remembered the times of which he spoke.

His face sobered and he looked into her eyes.

"Truly, Em, the first moment I beheld you descending the stairs, I was besotted. Your eyes caught mine and drew me under your spell, and I knew it was hopeless to resist."

Emily warmed at his words, and her body tingled.

"So while we were at sea, the whole time we sailed, you fought the urge to ravish me?"

Jonathon chuckled. "It was probably fortuitous that I was injured so seriously, for I do not think I could have held my desire in check living in such close quarters all that time."

"You are teasing me, Captain Brentwood."

"One thing I do not dissemble about is my love for you. I take that very seriously. Here allow me to show you."

He drew her into his arms and covered her mouth with his.

"I believe you sir," Emily whispered against his lips.

# More From This Author

## (From *Love's Destiny*)

*London, April 1774*

Emily Wentworth waged a battle between grief and anger. Today grief was winning.

She sat lost in thought, burrowed deeply into the comfort of the brown leather chair, one of two that sat before the large fireplace in the study. It was a room she visited often, one that usually brought a feeling of warmth and closeness to her father when he was away at sea. Today, however, an aching emptiness filled her as it had for the last two weeks since she had received word of her father's death. A violent winter storm had surged across the Atlantic ravaging George Wentworth's ship, the *Spirit*. The few survivors rescued by a passing merchant ship spoke of George's bravery in his futile attempts to save his men and his ship.

Emily gazed around the room that reflected her father. Well-loved books lined the shelves on the walls surrounding the enormous mahogany desk where he pored over ledgers and charts when he was home. Emily smiled as she remembered how he would set them aside when she entered the room.

"Am I bothering you, Father?" she would ask, her timid smile revealing a dimple in each cheek.

"Nothing is as important as you, Em," he would chuckle, falling willingly to her ploy.

They spent hours talking of his voyages, Emily sitting entranced with his tales of the wild animals and exotic people of Africa, of lands scorched under unending heat and sun, of women dressed in beautiful silks in Asia. She imagined she could hear the vendors hawking their wares in crowded markets, the bustle of the people, the lilt and cadence of their languages, the smell of exotic spices and the aromas of mysterious foods. He also told her stories of the colonies in America and the proud spirit that was the cornerstone of that land. Emily tried to picture the vast territory yet to be settled and the rugged Indians who lived there. She knew some were friendly and helped the British, while others were fierce and terrifying. She wondered about the men and women who would travel across the ocean to live in a land so far from their beloved England.

Emily stared at the embers dying in the hearth. The room took on a chill as the sun settled in the west. Her cheeks were wet, and she realized that she had been crying. Rising, she paced the room. She touched the smoke-stained pipes, always stationed on his desk, and ran her fingertips lightly across the books that lined the shelves. She had read many of them herself, unusual for most girls of her day. George Wentworth had insisted that reading and writing be a part of her education.

"No child of mine is going to be a simpering idiot! There is more to life for Em than embroidery and coquetry," he insisted. "She will receive an education as fine as her brother Andrew's!"

Emily smiled to herself. Father usually got his way, if not with his charm, then with his temper. But her mother, Jessica, had agreed that Emily should be well educated, as she had been herself. Many evenings at supper her parents had drawn her into conversations and asked her to share her opinions. Consequently, at social affairs when the women gathered together, she was bored with their prattle and gossip, sometimes catching her mother's amused glance as they smiled in camaraderie.

"You must not think you are better than others just because you have had the benefit of an education," Jessica would admonish when Emily mocked those "prissy know-nothings." Jessica was always pleasant to the other ladies even though, as Emily suspected, she was often bored, too.

Emily missed the late evening chats they shared after such events. Jessica had died of consumption two years earlier. The family was just recovering from the shock of her death.

"And now they are both gone," Emily whispered.

Jessica's death had brought Emily and her father even closer. Although she was only seventeen, he began to leave much of the running of the house to her, trusting her judgment. Yet, she was still his little girl.

She reached for the open letter on the desk. Her father's solicitor had given it to her after the reading of the will. She knew the words by heart, but she looked at them again as if willing them to change:*My Dearest Emily, Your reading this means that I am either dead or lost at sea. This must be a difficult time for you and Andrew. Draw on your faith in God and your love for one another to see you through. You have a quiet strength, Em. You helped me through my grief and sorrow at your mother's passing. You are so much like her, not only in looks, but also in courage, gentleness and honesty. Now you must help Andrew. You must be strong for him.Please know how much I love you both. That is why I have taken measures to see that you and Andrew are properly cared for. I have appointed my dear friend, Captain Jonathon Brentwood of Virginia, as your guardian. He is a good man, Em, and a trusted friend. He saved my life once, and that is why I am entrusting him with the dearest treasures in my life. You and Andrew have brought me more joy than you will ever know. I love you both and will be watching you from the caring arms of our God in heaven. Your loving father*

"Come and eat, darlin'." Etta Mason had come into the room. "You cannot spend all your days hidin' in here and missin' your father," she said gently. The housekeeper put her arm around Emily's shoulders and led her out of the study.

"Oh, Etta, I miss him so," Emily whispered through the lump in her throat, fighting back the tears.

"I know, darlin'," she replied.

Andrew was already at the table. He stood up when Emily entered and held her chair.

"How are you, Em?" he asked. He loved their father very much, but he was aware of the special bond his father and Emily had shared. He wished he could help her.

"Oh, Drew, when is that colonial captain supposed to arrive?" she cried, anger claiming the upper hand now.

"Now, Em, Father would not appoint an ogre to be our guardian. I am sure Captain Brentwood will be a kind man."

Emily looked at her younger brother. He was probably right. At fifteen, Andrew had more common sense than many of the older suitors who had been calling on her.

"You are right. It is just that everything is so different for us now. With no one left in either Father's or Mother's families, we have no choice but to go with this colonial to Virginia. We may have to accept his guardianship, but I do not have to like it!" Her blue-violet eyes sparked with defiance, and her soft full lips set in a firm line.

Andrew smiled to himself. At least thinking about "that colonial captain" had distracted Emily from her somber, brooding mood that had become so common of late. He loved to see her spirit revive. No one liked to tangle with Emily; she had a quick temper and a sharp tongue. Yet she was fair and had a strong sense of justice.

"Well, his letter said he would arrive as soon as his business was settled in France. He thought with fair weather and a good wind he should arrive by the end of this month. I would say another week or two," Andrew answered, watching her eyes and guessing how quickly her mind was working. "Please, Emily, give him a chance. He was Father's friend remember."

"You are right, Drew. I shall try," she smiled fondly at her brother.

· · ·

Emily viewed her reflection in the mirror. Thick dark lashes made a startling contrast to clear, blue-violet eyes. She wrinkled her delicate nose.

"I am too short," she thought. "And my hair...I must wear it up."

She pushed her long, thick, tawny-colored hair up from the nape of her neck. Golden highlights danced off it in the evening sun that streamed through the window.

A plan had formed in Emily's mind as the weeks had passed, bringing the inevitable meeting with Captain Brentwood closer. She needed no guardian—why she was seventeen years old. Andrew and she could continue to live here in London. Surely their inheritance would be an adequate income on which they could live comfortably. It was silly to even appoint a guardian for them.

Her heart lifted as she thought of her foolproof plan. That was why she must appear a mature and self-assured woman. But she wrinkled her nose once again at her reflection.

"Bah! I look like a child, and Captain Brentwood will be here any moment." She rang for Mary, her maid. She looked at her reflection pleased with the effect of her hair pulled up and back, making her feel more confident.

Mary scuttled into the room wringing her hands. She had already spent hours assisting her mistress with numerous anxious, and often reassessed, preparations for this meeting.

"Quickly, Mary, dress my hair high, and...well, sophisticated. I need to look mature...older. Oh, you know what I mean."

Mary hesitated. Etta was only the housekeeper, but she clucked over Emily and Andrew like a mother hen. If she did not approve, Mary would really get a dressing down. As gentle as Etta could be with the children, she could be equally stern with the servants.

"Come on, quickly, Mary," Emily insisted. It was time to start asserting her authority and look the part of woman of the house.

Mary did not want to tangle with Emily's temper either, so she quickly picked up the brushes and began to dress the girl's hair.

Emily surveyed the results. Her black, high-necked dress set off her creamy white skin. With her hair piled high on her head, she appeared taller, more dignified. She was sure her plan would work, and in spite of her sadness, her spirits lifted. There was a knock on the door.

"Come in," she called.

Andrew entered. "He should be here…Oh, Em, you look so different …" Andrew stared at his sister. The transformation was remarkable.

"Do I look older, Drew? Do you think our plan will work?" Her eyes sparkled for the first time in weeks.

"I hope so, Emily. But please do not set your hopes too high. What do you think Captain Brentwood will be like?" Andrew asked.

"Well, he was Father's friend, so perhaps he will be a bit like Father. Perhaps not as robust, perhaps a bit older…I do not know. I just hope he agrees to our plan. I do not see why he would not. He probably does not want to be burdened with us any more than we want to be uprooted and moved to those savage colonies." Emily was not to be dissuaded; her plan would work. "We could continue to live here…what does it matter to him where we are? I have to convince him that I am capable of running this household and Father's estate."

Captain Jonathon Brentwood stared out the window of his coach. Lamplighters were making their way along, igniting the lamps that lined the streets of London. The *clop, clop, clop* of the horse's hooves beat a rhythm against the night as he pondered his new role as guardian of his dear friend's children. It was not a role he relished. And his dealings in Europe were becoming more tenuous as friction mounted between the colonies and England. Most of his time would be spent in the colonies now as trade and prosperity were growing there. And as the rebellion grew, he had other duties to attend.

The timing of this guardianship could not have been worse. But George Wentworth had been a mentor and had become one of his closest friends. Jonathon would honor the promise he had made to him. His experience with children had been limited, and when he was exposed to them, he was bewildered by their endless energy and their proclivity to mischief. He hoped George's children were not quite as lively and imaginative as some he had spent time with. George had told him many stories of Little Em and Andrew. From his stories they sounded well-behaved and mannerly. They certainly would tie him down more than he had been used to in his 28 years of bachelorhood. He had written his sister Joanna explaining the situation. Surely she would help him watch over the children so he could continue sailing. She and her husband lived in Brentwood Manor, the family home. David was a good manager, and the plantation was thriving under him. Jonathon would soon have to take over, but he wanted to sail for a few more years. Well, he would get this situation settled soon, and then he could set sail again.

The coach came to a stop in front of the handsome London townhouse. As he stepped down from the coach, Jonathon noticed an upstairs curtain fall back in place. He took a deep breath, straightened his cravat, and went up to the door.

•••

"He is here, Andrew. You go down first. I shall be right there, but let me talk to him alone. I am so nervous; I have eaten nothing all day!" She ran to the mirror as Andrew closed the door. "Oh, dear God, please let this work," she whispered. She lifted her chin peering sideways out of her eyes. Raising one eyebrow, she nodded her head regally. She had been practicing all week. "It must work!"

As she descended the curving staircase she saw a tall figure with broad shoulders and dark hair studying the portrait of Jessica, Emily's mother. Jonathon Brentwood turned and looked up at a younger version of the portrait he had just viewed. Surprise flickered across his face, quickly replaced by a lazy, engaging smile.

"So you are Little Em," he drawled. Not quite, he thought to himself. He gazed at the beautiful tawny-haired girl whose blue-violet eyes threatened to drown him.

Emily was stunned. This was her father's friend? Soft brown eyes gazed at her with amusement. They were set in a bronzed, handsome face. He was dressed in a blue longcoat and cream-colored breeches that enhanced his tall, lean figure. His broad shoulders and brown curly hair tied back at the nape of his neck completed the picture of a strikingly attractive man. Emily's cheeks felt flushed under his close scrutiny, and a strange tingle ran through her body. She reached the bottom of the stairs and looked up into his warm, brown eyes again as she extended her hand.

"Captain Brentwood? I am pleased to meet you." Emily was annoyed at the tremble in her voice. He bent and kissed her hand, his lips brushing softly against her skin. Their eyes met as he straightened. Emily tried to steady herself, unable to make her heart stop beating so hard. She was sure he could hear it. She reminded herself of her plan, and quickly regained her composure, straightening to her full height.

"You must be exhausted after your long, hurried voyage. May I offer you some tea," she paused noting his suppressed smile, "or some brandy?" she added.

"Brandy would be fine. Thank you…uh…Miss Wentworth," he replied still fighting back the smile.

Emily led him into the parlor and rang for the maid; Etta appeared. Emily knew this would be difficult for Etta still thought of her as a child.

"Two brandies please, Etta." She raised her chin as she had practiced before the mirror. Etta started to protest, but something in Emily's eyes stopped her, and she hurried off to get the drinks.

"Please sit down, Captain Brentwood," Emily said coolly as she sat on the end of the settee. To her confusion, Jonathon sat beside her rather than in the chair she had indicated. A crooked smile played around his lips as though he attempted to hide a joke. He thought of the "Little Em" of George's stories and chuckled to himself. Nothing had prepared him for this beautiful girl who was trying so hard to be a woman.

"We have much to discuss, Miss Wentworth," he said as Etta returned with a tray carrying the decanter and two crystal glasses.

"Indeed we have, Captain," she replied.

Etta set the tray on the table in front of Emily. The housekeeper poured brandy into the glasses, and Emily was grateful for she had no idea what an appropriate amount would have been. She thought Etta rather stingy based on what was in each glass, but she took them and handed one glass to Jonathon.

"Thank you, Etta; that will be all." She turned to Jonathon, dismissing the housekeeper.

"Hmmmph!" Etta grumbled as she left the room.

Jonathon silently saluted Emily and then took a drink from his glass. Emily sipped hers and tried to choke down the spasms of coughing that threatened to overcome her. She had sampled wine before at social gatherings, but had never tasted brandy. Heat spread down her throat and she blinked the tears out of her eyes causing her to miss the fleeting smile that crossed Jonathon's face. It was a few minutes before she caught her breath enough to speak.

"Captain Brentwood, I loved my father very much and always obeyed him as he had my welfare as his concern above all else. However, with all due respect, sir, I think in this last instance he erred."

Jonathon raised an eyebrow encouraging her to continue.

"I realize you were his dearest friend, and I appreciate your generosity in this matter, but as you can see, sir, I am perfectly capable of taking care of myself and Andrew. I think Father often thought of us as much younger than we actually are and so made provisions that we obviously do not need. With the wealth Father accumulated on his voyages, Andrew and I can continue to live here quite comfortably. Eventually, I will marry, and Andrew will stay on in this house. So you see, Captain Brentwood, I appreciate your willingness to care for us, but it is unnecessary."

She took a deep breath. Would it work? She wanted to squeeze her eyes shut and cross her fingers for good luck. Instead, she maintained her composure though it took all of her strength.

Jonathon continued to look at her with that amused expression. He took another drink of his brandy and, putting down his empty glass he eyed hers and looked at her inquiringly. Emily lifted her glass to her lips and sipped again. It seared her throat and brought tears to her eyes once more. She could not speak for a moment, and when she finally took a breath, the fire returned. She cleared her throat and felt warmth infuse her. Her cheeks felt flushed and her breath came in short gasps. Finally, she spoke.

"Well, Captain Brentwood, do you not agree that this is a simple solution for all of us?" The room seemed very warm.

"Miss Wentworth, I can see that you are a very sensible, as well as capable, young woman ..."

Emily's spirits soared.

"... and you are correct when you say that your father thought of you as younger. Why, he would call you 'Little Em' and tell me of how you sat in his lap and begged for stories. Or how you would tease the cook into an extra helping of dessert, and how, on a hot summer's day, you would totter across the lawn with just your...ah, well, suffice it to say I was expecting someone much younger."

Emily was blushing furiously at his last reference to her childhood. She avoided his gaze. She had to convince this man that she was mature and responsible enough to be on her own. Goodness, the room felt warm, and it seemed to be tilting a bit. Not thinking, Emily reached for the last of her brandy. Again her throat burned as the fiery liquid made its way down. Finally, she spoke.

"Well, as you can see, Captain, Father was mistaken. I am quite capable of looking after Andrew and myself."

"Yes, I can see that. In fact, you are quite a lovely young woman." Jonathon leaned back against the settee, casually resting one arm behind Emily. He saw through her charade and could not help teasing her for she was so serious. "I imagine you have captured the hearts of all the young men in London. How many suitors have lined up at the door asking for your hand and whispered their undying love in your delicate ear, promising ever to be true?" He had leaned forward and his breath touched her hair, his eyes held hers. His voice was soft and silken as his arm encircled her shoulders. Emily sat gazing at his warm, brown eyes, captivated. The room was warm, and the firelight flickered on their faces.

Suddenly Emily caught herself and sprang from the settee, her head swimming, desperately needing some air.

"It is a beautiful evening, Captain Brentwood. Shall we step out onto the terrace?" she asked trying to steady her trembling. It did not help that the room seemed to be moving, too.

The half-moon perched on a treetop, and the stars sprinkled across the ebony sky. They walked silently out to the garden, the smoky smell of well-stoked fires filling the crisp air. Emily felt a little steadier. They sat on a bench beneath a tall oak.

"May I speak frankly, Captain?"

"By all means, Miss Wentworth," Jonathon smiled.

"I do not want to go to Virginia with you any more than you want to be burdened with me. I fully intend to stay here with my brother. Father's intentions were good, but he was wrong to do this to either of us, and I believe you see the sense in this, too." Emily folded her hands in her lap as if to end the discussion.

"Miss Wentworth, may I also speak frankly?"

"Of course," Emily nodded.

"In the carriage on the way over here, I would have given anything to be rid of this responsibility. But now, having met you, Miss Wentworth, I am not so sure I want to be relieved of my duty. I was expecting a young child. Instead, I find a beautiful young woman who has made it perfectly clear that she does not need me. Yet I find that this is just what I want—for her to need me." Emily could feel her embarrassed blush start at his words. "No, I do not think I will be remiss in my duty. In fact, I am sworn to my promise even more having met you. How can I desert this fair damsel in distress? Why, it is my opportunity to be a knight in shining armor come to rescue a fair maiden." He leaned forward taking her hand. "Is it possible, my lady, that out of many I might claim your heart?" His voice was low; his eyes sparkled. "Oh, but one kiss from your sweet, gentle lips to carry with me forever would be so kind."

Emily felt a new rush of warmth course through her that had nothing to do with the brandy. She knew he was teasing her, yet she tingled with excitement. Just the thought of his soft lips against hers, being held in his strong arms…what was she thinking? She stood quickly.

"I fear you mock me, sir, when all I desire is to settle our lives so we can each go our separate ways. Please just agree with me that this solution would be best and we shall be finished with it."

"I do not mock you, Emily," Jonathon spoke softly, "but even if I wanted to, which I do not, I could not agree to your plan."

"Why ever not?" she cried near tears.

"Because your father's will states that I hold everything in trust for you until you marry. Or, if you do not marry, until you reach age twenty-one. I am afraid you cannot be on your own until such time."

Emily's face went white. Tears welled in her eyes, and she turned quickly so he could not see them. It would not do to cry. Not here, not now. Her mind raced. She would be packed off to the colonies, and she was helpless to stop it. What could she do?

"Then I shall marry." She had not realized that she had spoken aloud. Michael Dennings had called quite frequently lately. She was sure he would propose soon. Of course, now he would have to wait until Emily was out of mourning. "That is what I shall do."

Jonathon cleared his throat. "There is one more thing. I must approve the marriage."

"You what?" she shouted. "Do you think, sir, to take my father's place? How dare you come here and tell me what I can and cannot do? Whom I may or may not marry? Who gives you the right?" She shook with rage. Her upswept hair was coming loose; tendrils tumbled and framed her face and shuddered with her anger.

"Your father, Emily."

Emily stared at him, her mouth half open.

"Father?"

"Yes, it is in his will also. Your father loved you very much, Emily. He made it very clear that I was to watch over you and Andrew. You both were so dear to him. I promised that I would take the best possible care of you. George was one of my closest friends; my promise to him means a great deal to me," he said gently.

The loneliness Emily had felt for the past month flooded over her again. Tears stung her eyes and a dull ache settled in the pit of her stomach.

"Excuse me, Captain Brentwood, I am not feeling well. Good night." She swept past him. Jonathon heard her choke back a sob as she ran back in through the terrace doors. He stood there for a moment staring after her, confused. What should he do with this woman-child?

• • •

Emily peered thoughtfully over her teacup at Michael Dennings as he spoke to her. Many of the matrons in the social circles had already paired them and awaited an impending engagement this season. Michael's sandy-colored hair matched his eyes. Emily had never noticed his eyes before, and if someone had asked her their color, she would have been at a loss to answer. She did remember, however, the soft brown eyes that had warmly perused her during Captain Brentwood's visit.

She must stop comparing them. But she knew that would be difficult, for that was all she had done since Michael had arrived for tea. Of average height, he was shorter than Captain Brentwood, and not nearly so broad in the shoulders. He wore a tan longcoat over a tan vest and matching breeches. So close were they to the color of his hair and eyes that Michael just seemed to run together, nothing distinctive, and a passing stranger would take no notice of him.

Emily had known Michael for years, and, though he was amiable enough, rack her brain as she would, she could not think of a single extraordinary thing he had ever said or done. That was Michael, ordinary and predictable, but a good, safe husband who could keep her in England. And that, thought Emily, is what I need to make him see.

"Do you not agree, Emily?" Michael repeated.

"What? I am sorry, Michael, what did you say?" Emily smiled prettily, and Michael was appeased.

"I said it is dreadful what is occurring in the colonies. Why, they are close to open rebellion!" he answered.

"And I am sailing right into it," Emily murmured.

"I do not like the thought of your traveling over there, Emily. In fact, Mother and I were discussing it just last night. She said it is not proper for a girl of your delicacy and upbringing to be thrust into a savage land. She said it is scandalous for a genteel young lady to go off across the ocean, unescorted, with some sea captain. She said it is a shame you have not been betrothed by now, and if you were not so opinionated, that is …"

Emily ignored the last remark. She had heard it whispered before. She was more educated than was usual for a young lady of her station; consequently, no man wanted a wife who might have ideas and opinions of her own—not to mention a wife who might be smarter than her husband. She attributed this gossip to jealous girls whose mothers would not allow their education to progress any further than French knots and curtsies.

"Michael, Captain Brentwood is my guardian, so I am properly escorted. Andrew will be with me also. And the colonies are not a savage land anymore. Why, there are large towns such as Boston and Philadelphia, and ships arrive from England frequently. I will not be shut off from the world in some remote and distant land."

What was she saying? This was not at all what she had planned. Why did she suddenly feel defensive about a land she had no desire to see?

"Well, as far as Captain Brentwood is concerned, Mother says he has a reputation with women. She says that having you on his ship is as good as ..."

"Captain Brentwood has been a perfect gentleman in my presence," Emily snapped. Her cheeks flushed as she recalled his silken voice in the garden and the feel of his strong, firm arm around her shoulders. Michael misread her blush for anger, which was partly true.

"Do not be angry, Emily. I just do not want to see your reputation sullied."

"It is good of you to be so concerned," she retorted.

What was wrong with her? She was ruining her opportunity to stay in England. Yet, as she studied Michael, doubt slowly spread through her. She imagined passing the years as his wife. It would be safe and comfortable, but certainly not exciting. They would live in London and have children. And Mother Dennings would visit on Sundays and expound on her pet theories. Or worse, perhaps she would live *with* them and subject them to daily sermons. And the years would run together, much as Michael's appearance.

Michael had been speaking again, and his last sentence brought Emily back with a start.

"Emily, will you do me the honor of becoming my wife?" He was on one knee in front of her.

"Am I interrupting anything?" Jonathon's clear baritone rang through the room causing Michael to jump to his feet, and startling Emily as much as Michael's proposal had.

"Captain Brentwood," Emily breathed feeling strangely relieved, "do come in."

Michael shot Emily a bemused look. Jonathon strode in and seated himself on the settee beside her. His eyes sparkled when he looked at her, and he took her hand in his own and patted it in a fatherly gesture. She slipped it away.

"Captain Brentwood, may I present Michael Dennings. Michael, this is Captain Jonathon Brentwood." Emily glanced at Michael noting his sour expression. Jonathon extended his hand, which Michael reluctantly shook. The two men sized each other up.

"Well, Captain Brentwood, when do you plan to set sail for Virginia?" Michael finally asked.

"I have some legal matters to which I must attend, and some supplies to order and load. I imagine *we* shall set sail in a fortnight," he stressed the word "we" while looking at Emily. Unable to meet the gaze of either man, she looked down at her hands folded in her lap.

Michael shifted uncomfortably wondering why Emily had invited Captain Brentwood in at such an inopportune moment.

"I imagine you are anxious to get home to see your family and…uh…dear ones." Michael emphasized the latter cynically.

Jonathon leaned back casually stretching long, lean legs out in front of him.

"Yes, I am anxious to see my sister and her husband. As for the rest of my family, they will be with me on the ship."

Michael glowered at him.

"I think not, Captain Brentwood. I have just asked Emily for her hand in marriage. She will remain in England, where she belongs." He breathed the last decisively.

"No, Michael," Emily whispered. If she had shouted it, the impact could not have been greater. Michael's head whipped sharply back to her; his mouth gaped open. Jonathon searched her eyes. "You are a dear friend, Michael," she continued, "but it would be wrong for both of us if we were to marry."

Michael rose in bewilderment. He looked from one to the other.

"You are responsible for this," he shouted at Jonathon's composed face. He turned to her, "Emily, please reconsider."

"No, Michael. I am sorry," she spoke gently.

Michael shot a baleful glare at Jonathon, then turned on his heel and left. Jonathon looked down at Emily, but she could not meet his gaze. Her head was whirling with the events of the last few minutes. Michael had offered her exactly what she wanted, a chance to remain in England, but she knew it was not right for her. The idea of sailing into an unknown life with the man seated next to her was, somehow, appealing.

"It is just as well," Jonathon teased. "I would not have approved the engagement in any event."

"You arrogant cad," Emily seethed. "How dare you assume what you can and cannot do concerning any matters in my personal life?"

"But you forget, Emily, I am your guardian. Your safety, your health, your happiness are all a precious burden that I will happily carry."

"Who do you think you are that you can presume so much? My happiness will never be dependent on you! I think it is best that you leave at once!"

"Oh, I cannot leave, Em. I am staying for supper."

"You are what? How—?"

"Andrew invited me. He, at least, has some manners." He hid a smile.

"And I do not, I suppose?" Emily rose from the settee placing a hand on each hip. Her blue eyes had darkened to violet with her anger, and a blush heightened in her cheeks. Her jaw was set, and her full soft lips clamped into a firm line.

Jonathon replied easily, "Well, he did have the courtesy to ask a new member of the family to supper. After all, if we are to spend weeks together in the close quarters of a ship, I would deem it necessary to become better acquainted. I am sure that by the end of the voyage we shall know each other *very* well," he smiled wickedly. "But things will go much more smoothly en route if we develop a closer relationship now."

"I have no intention of developing anything with you, Captain Brentwood. And as for the family, I consider all of this to be a totally unnecessary, legalistic mix-up and nothing more. If I never get to know you better, it will be fine with me. Mrs. Dennings was right; you are a rake. Why, you probably have a woman in every harbor. I should have accepted Michael's proposal. He knows how to treat a lady with decency and respect."

"And now you are without the benefit of Mother Dennings' exhortations, too. You've told me of her strong opinions and disdain for anything not of England. Oh, I can picture all of you gathered 'round the cozy hearth listening to her prattle on about the immorality of the savage colonies and their provincialism," he laughed. "No, Em. No such life for you. You have too much spirit, too much drive for what Michael Dennings and his mother could offer."

Emily was startled at how his remarks mirrored her thoughts of just minutes earlier. Could he read her mind?

"And I suppose you could offer so much more? Tell me, sir, would traipsing off to some backward land with you be so much better? Will you then find me a suitable mate who will offer me all I deserve? Hah! You will probably deny me any suitable young gentleman who is courteous and kind. You will keep me a spinster. To what end, sir? What game do you play?" She had paced across the room during her tirade, unaware of admiring eyes that followed her graceful gait.

"Aye, Em, I could offer you more than your Mr. Dennings. I could show you places of such beauty and wonder as to take your breath away. Mountains that soar up and kiss the floor of heaven. Lush forests that stretch as far as the eye can see, full of trees so big that two men with arms outstretched would be hard pressed to span the diameter and touch their fingertips end to end. Our 'backward' land, as you call it, has cities with shops to rival London's. What is more, we judge a man, not by what his ancestors were, but by what he can wrest out of life and shape into his own. A man can build his worth from nothing; he can become wealthy, influential, anything he wants, on his own merit, not someone else's. It is a rich land, Em, full of promise for people with spirit. People like you and Andrew who draw strength from an inner reserve. Come with me because you *want* to, Em. See for yourself what Virginia is like. I believe one day you will love it as I do." Jonathon's eyes were shining as he spoke passionately of his land. Emily felt sudden warmth for him. But he was asking so much.

"I cannot say that I *want* to go, Captain Brentwood, but I have no choice in any event," Emily sighed.

Jonathon saw the confusion in her eyes. She seemed to look deeply into the realm of possibilities before her, and complicating it all was the still-fresh grief for her father. He began to realize his own growing hope that she would indeed *want* to go with him. He understood her pain and the enormity of her decision, for he knew it must be her decision. He tried to lighten her mood.

"Emily, must you be so formal? Please call me Jonathon."

Andrew burst into the room. "I have been down to the wharves, Jonathon. Everything is progressing smoothly. What a beautiful ship the *Destiny* is! Mr. Gates sends word that the mizzenmast is repaired and we should sail on schedule," his eyes danced with excitement.

Jonathon grimaced. They had run into a pirate ship far north of the Barbary Coast, and the *Destiny* had sustained considerable damage. But the pirate ship had suffered her wrath and limped off the worse for wear. Jonathon would have pursued her had he not been on his way to England at the behest of George Wentworth's will. He hoped their crossing to Virginia would be without incident.

"That is good news, Andrew," he replied.

Emily noticed his concern. "Did you encounter trouble, Captain?"

"Nothing we could not handle," he grinned.

Supper was announced, and Jonathon offered his arm to Emily. She could think of no reason to refuse without appearing rude, so she tucked her hand through the crook of his arm. She felt the firm muscles of his forearm through the fabric of his sleeve. She glanced sideways at his strong profile with its aquiline nose and square jaw. He caught her glance and winked at her. She quickly looked away. Why did he disturb her so?

Discussion at the table was lively with Andrew firing a myriad of questions at Jonathon about Virginia. His excitement was apparent, and he was anxious to set sail. Jonathon answered his questions patiently, laughing at his enthusiasm.

"I wish your sister was as eager about this voyage as you are," he laughed gently, glancing at Emily. She had enjoyed listening to his tales of the colonies, but had remained silent for the most part. Now she raised her eyebrows at Jonathon.

"Captain Brentwood, I am leaving everything I know and love. Allow me my reluctance, sir."

"But, Emily, have you not been listening to Jonathon? It sounds like paradise over in Virginia. Can we set sail earlier?" Andrew's eyes shone.

"No, Andrew," Jonathon laughed, "I need time to ready my ship. And to convince your sister that she really *does* want to come."

"You have a difficult task ahead of you, Captain Brentwood," she replied. Andrew chuckled at her proper form of address.

· · ·

Emily watched in the mirror as Mary brushed out her hair. She had to admit that the evening had passed pleasantly enough in Captain Brentwood's company. He had piqued her curiosity with the tales of his homeland. And he was even more handsome, if possible, when he was caught up in stories about Virginia as his eyes sparkled and his smile showed straight, white teeth against skin bronzed by the sun and the sea.

Emily climbed between the lavender-scented sheets and closed her eyes. It had been a trying day. Michael's proposal had been her goal on rising this morning, but the day had not gone at all as she had planned. None of her plans were working out lately. It was as if someone were interfering with her destiny...*Destiny.* She slipped off to sleep.

· · ·

Jonathon had stopped off at the Golden Pheasant Inn and sat in the corner table of the common room drinking his ale. He needed time to think before returning to his ship. It had been an enjoyable evening. Andrew was an enthusiastic as well as knowledgeable boy. George Wentworth had hoped Andrew would follow in his footsteps when his education was completed. He was already well versed in the ways of sailing, and seemed to have the natural talent of his father.

Emily was an enigma. She vocalized clearly her reluctance to sail to America, yet her eyes had glowed as she listened to his stories, leaning forward, chin resting in her hand, concentrating on every word, then catching herself, sitting up primly, feigning indifference. He caught her lost in thought once and wondered if she were reconsidering Michael Denning's proposal. He thought not. Searching her eyes today he had seen only firm resolution. No, Michael Dennings was not the man for Emily Wentworth.

"'Scuse me, Captain Brentwood, can I git ya another ale?" A plump, pretty girl was smiling down at him. Millie leaned forward to take his empty tankard revealing much of her ample bosom. "Can I git ya anything else, Love?" she asked invitingly. Jonathon had been at sea a long time, and normally this invitation might not have been unwelcome. But his mind was preoccupied with his new station in life—that of a guardian.

"Not tonight, Millie," he replied. He watched the girl turn and sway her hips provocatively, no doubt in the hopes he would change his mind.

Jonathon rose and went out into the night. Settling George's estate and readying the ship for departure were enough to busy a man. But the problem of what to do with Emily taxed his mind the most.

In the mood for more Crimson Romance?
Check out *Through Gypsy Eyes*
by Killarney Sheffield
at *CrimsonRomance.com*.

# About the Author

Elizabeth Meyette is an author, poet, and blogger. Her first novel, *Love's Destiny*, took thirty years from inception to publication because her career as an English teacher left little time to concentrate on her own writing. Deciding to retire from teaching early to pursue her writing career, she found that *Love's Spirit* took about $\frac{1}{30}$ of the time that *Love's Destiny* required. Elizabeth lives in Michigan with her husband Richard and often finds inspiration for her writing as she enjoys the beauty of the Great Lakes.

Visit Elizabeth Meyette at: *www.elizabethmeyette.com.*